THE FACES OF A MAN AND A WOMAN GREW IN A HALO OF LIGHT

Louise realized *she* was the woman, and yet it was not she. And she knew the man was Owen Morgan—not as he was now, but as he had once been. At the sound of his voice speaking a strange archaic language, she passed into the woman's body as effortlessly as slipping on a garment. Her present self fled like a shadow and she was resurrected as another, as Sancha, standing face to face with Hugo, the man she loved more than life itself.

They were saying goodbye for the last time. She pleaded, revolting against fate, abjuring every sacred thing she had lived by, as if such a sacrifice would bind Hugo to her forever.

Just as the light began to fade, she heard his reply:

Sancha, I swear to you
that no matter where you may be,
no matter how long it will take,
by all that is sacred,
I will find you.

By All That Is Sacred

Laura Gilmour Bennett

AVON BOOKS ⬦ NEW YORK

Originally published in Great Britain as *A Wheel of Stars*.

AVON BOOKS
A division of
The Hearst Corporation
1350 Avenue of the Americas
New York, New York 10019

Copyright © 1991 by Laura Gilmour Bennett
Cover illustration by Walter Wick
Published by arrangement with Laura Bennett & Jean Gilmour Harvey
Library of Congress Catalog Card Number: 91-92233
ISBN: 0-380-76320-6

First Avon Books Printing: December 1991

AVON TRADEMARK REG. U.S. PAT. OFF. AND IN OTHER COUNTRIES, MARCA REGISTRADA, HECHO EN U.S.A.

Printed in the U.S.A.

RA 10 9 8 7 6 5 4 3 2 1

To D. L. M.

THE SOUL GOES ROUND

UPON A WHEEL OF STARS

AND ALL THINGS RETURN

G. K. Chesterton:
The Dagger with Wings

BY ALL THAT IS SACRED

PROLOGUE
1971

Wisdom and power radiated from his deep-set black eyes and his mouth was a thin ascetic line. Dark, gaunt and stooped, he was as alien to the local race of sturdy, ruddy-faced meridional people as a desert falcon in a rain forest. Walking up the narrow village street at dusk, he passed a woman with a baguette tucked under her arm, who looked obliquely at his dust-caked clothes and bandaged forehead.

The man let himself in through the door beneath the faded *Brocante* sign. When he had locked it behind him, he made his way to the back room by feeling a passage past the bric-à-brac and furniture. He turned on the single globe in the small cubicle that was almost filled by a desk, a chair and a safe. Through the window he had a glimpse of the star-filled sky before pulling down the blind. The sudden movement made him feel giddy. He shut his eyes and braced himself against the desk until the vertigo had passed, then bent down to open the safe. Pulling the heavy door ajar, he reached inside. As soon as his hand touched the cloth bag he felt weak with relief that it was still there, even though the thieves had taken a much greater treasure. Filled with a sense of incalculable loss, he mourned the holy book. For consolation, he drew the chalice from the bag and cradled it in his palms, the lines of his face softening in wonder as if he were looking on a newborn child. As he pressed his mouth to the cool, dry surface, a prayer sprang to his lips. He began to whisper in a lost language, repeating a fragment of ritual that had been unspoken for centuries, the words conjuring up a host of precious images that had become his reason for living.

It had taken him a lifetime to discover the central purpose of his existence. He had studied the riddle long and hard, delving to the bottom of an inner pool that in the beginning had been disturbed by so many ripples. Like a blind man whose sight had returned with agonizing slowness, he had waited for the confused images to clear, until one day illumination came and he found through his inner eye that he had the power to see places and objects from the distant past as if through a distorting prism. As time passed, the intensity of what he experienced eclipsed the reality of his present lifetime. Then, painstakingly, like an archaeologist, he had unearthed particles of memory, piecing them together with infinite patience and with a purpose.

Replacing the chalice in the bag, he shut the safe and leaned against it, his hands outstretched in supplication. Ever since he had recovered the relic he had been waiting for some sign, some spark of illumination to instruct him in what he should do. The events of the day had left him badly shaken and he was frightened that he was about to fail in his duty just at the moment when he was offered the chance to redeem his past mistakes. Glancing round the room, he decided to sleep on the desk to keep watch over the safe. It was only a question of time before the ruffians who had robbed him would discover that he possessed a further treasure of inestimable value. But if they tried to rob him of the chalice, they would first have to take his life.

A few days later the bell over the shop door rang and the man darted out of the back room in alarm, realizing he had forgotten to lock the front door. The young man with curly dark hair whom he saw browsing among the bric-à-brac had obviously ignored the sign that said the shop was *fermé* and had walked in regardless. He was about to tell the unwanted customer to leave when something stopped him. Adjusting his glasses, he peered at the stranger from a distance, unable yet to trust the violent bolt of recognition he felt as soon as he saw his profile in the light filtering through the dusty window. The man had a strong, broad back, good shoulders and a sensitive face. When he picked up a tall candlestick that came from a church, their eyes locked in intense mutual curiosity.

"*Bonsoir, monsieur,*" said the young man with a friendly nod. "I was just passing and saw the door open, so I came in." He spoke in fluent French, with an accent that seemed English.

The proprietor said nothing, but moved round the counter to get a better look at him.

"*Combien est l'encrier?*" the young man asked, picking up a china inkstand.

"Ten francs," he murmured. "But it's damaged . . ." He stared fixedly at the young man, wondering if it was really possible that he could be oblivious of the importance of their meeting. He was now satisfied beyond all doubt as to his identity. Moments later, when the Englishman had paid him for a small box, the proprietor said in a voice harsh with emotion:

"*Monsieur,* perhaps you might be interested in something of value. Something rare—even unique!"

When the young man had gone, the *brocanteur* stood at the counter of the empty shop, staring into the gloom. Tears coursed down his cheeks like rain bathing dry earth. Blinking, he saw the box the man had bought still sitting in front of him. After what had happened between them it was trivial, meaningless, but he was moved by happiness to grab it and rush to the door of the shop.

When he looked out, there was no sign of the Englishman. He had gone. Turning his head, the man stiffened in shock when he saw a teenage boy lurking not far away. The moment their eyes met the boy whirled round guiltily and started to walk towards a bicycle standing nearby, but the man was certain of his identity, even at a distance. An angry cry rasped in his throat as he saw the boy disappear up the narrow street.

1

Some time in the dark center of the night Louise Carey came back to consciousness, roused by a rocking movement that came from the bowels of the Sierra mountains to the east. The bed shook gently, then more insistently, jolting her violently awake. When her eyes flew open, she blinked at the marbled light from the swimming pool dancing on the wall as her heart thudded against her chest. Conscious of the weight of her body on the cool sheets, she lay absolutely still, unable to move as she waited for the next tremor.

"It's finally happening. This is it—the big one," she thought.

Struggling to pull herself together, she wondered what she should do. She dimly recalled that people were told to stand in door frames because they would bear the weight of the house if it were to fall down. But her body seemed incapable of movement as she lay there in the darkness until she realized the tremor had stopped and that she could have been dreaming. Through the silence she became aware of an almost imperceptible humming, which she thought at first was the drone of an airplane far, far away. As she listened, it reminded her more of crystal being lightly struck with a fingertip. It was as if a bell had been ringing before she had awakened, leaving a clear faint note lingering on the air like a summons. She looked over the bedclothes towards her dressing table, where glass bottles glinted in the shadows. Though the sound had faded, Louise felt troubled, as though by a vivid dream that refused to come back upon waking.

She lay still for a moment, half waiting for another earth tremor, but now she was sure she had only imagined it. Her forehead was damp with perspiration, the bedcovers tangled,

4

and when she turned on the lamp and saw it was two-thirty in the morning, she slipped out of bed and went to her dressing table. Passing her fingers lightly along the tops of the bottles, her hand hesitated over a ruby crystal bell. She touched the sharply cut edges and retracted her hand in shock when she felt it vibrate. Startled, she stared at the dim outline of the bell, not wanting to touch it again; but she forced herself to grip the handle. This time she felt nothing, but running her fingers round inside the rim of the bell she confirmed what she already knew: that the glass clapper had been broken soon after Ambrose and Dorothy Lethbridge had given the bell to her parents as a wedding present in London in 1944. It hadn't rung in forty-four years. And yet it had rung in her dream. The proof was the vibration she had distinctly felt when she touched it.

Starting to shiver, Louise climbed back into bed, her mind on the Lethbridges. She reached over to turn off the bedside lamp and saw her address book lying open near the telephone, reminding her that she had copied down the Lethbridges' address as an afterthought when she was clearing her father's effects from his home in Phoenix after his funeral the previous month. Throwing back the bedcovers again, she thumbed through the book. It would be ten-thirty in the morning in England. She picked up the telephone and dialed, then listened to the distant ring. When a voice answered, she said uncertainly:

"This is Louise Carey speaking from California. I'd like to speak to Dorothy Lethbridge, please!"

The following week Louise settled into the first class compartment of a train minutes before it was due to depart from Euston station in London. Arriving at Heathrow that morning, she had taken a taxi into town to inspect the collection of an up-and-coming young leatherwear designer, expecting to place an order for her autumn collection. The designer had proved to be disconcertingly elusive about closing a deal there and then, and Louise was forced to leave with no firm arrangement. Now, feeling harassed and disoriented after making a dash for the train, her confidence flagged. She was no better off than when she arrived and could find no reason for justifying the expense of this last-minute detour to England.

Closing her eyes, Louise swallowed the rising sense of panic that she had lived with for the past year. All the comforting clichés that her close friend Ellen Brady had repeated on the journey to the San Francisco airport filled her head: "You've got nothing to lose, go for it. Everything is ahead of you. Now is the time to put the past behind you and set your sights higher than ever . . ."

Unbuttoning her trenchcoat, Louise glanced at the man seated across from her, whose face was obscured by the pink pages of the *Financial Times*. As soon as she rested her brief-case on the floor, the train jolted forward, causing it to fall onto his highly polished black shoes.

"I'm terribly sorry," she exclaimed, but he didn't even bother to look up from his newspaper.

She leaned back in her seat, determined to relax for the journey to Hemel Hempstead, where Dorothy Lethbridge would meet her and take her to Little Gaddesden. When the straggling suburbs of London had disappeared, the landscape opened up to gently rolling green countryside marked by distant Norman churches, ploughed fields divided into neat parcels by hedges and copses of trees still retaining a few withered leaves. Electrical towers and sprawling factories seemed out of place in countryside that gave the illusion of having resisted the twentieth century. A film of white frost streaked the shadows where the sun had not penetrated and dramatic clouds swept the blue horizon, casting giant shafts of light on distant towns and villages. Louise gave herself up to the monotonous swaying of the train, wanting to forget for a while that her entire future rested on the challenges that would reveal themselves within the next few days. For a moment her restlessness and uncertainty vanished as she felt herself hurtling forward to a much more peaceful, sane world than the one she had left behind. She asked herself why at this particular juncture in her life she felt the compulsion to interrupt such an important business trip to pay an overnight visit to an English couple in their sixties whom she had never met. And yet, deep down, she felt she knew the answer. Now was the time when she needed anchors in her life, and the Lethbridges, who had known her parents during the war years in London, represented a solid piece of the past to which she needed to cling after her recent divorce and her father's death.

An hour later she was driving through the Hertfordshire countryside beside the rosy-cheeked Dorothy Lethbridge. The moment she had met the vivacious silver-haired woman waiting on the platform, bundled up in a red wool scarf and tam-o'-shanter, Louise knew she had been right to come.

"These country drivers," exclaimed Dorothy as she pressed down on the accelerator of her ancient Morris to pass a van on the narrow road. Her Skye terrier barked wildly from the back seat as if egging her on.

"He seems to enjoy it," Louise laughed, but she felt relieved when the old car was safely rattling down the tree-lined road again.

"Marlowe loves traveling, don't you, Marlowe?" said Dorothy. Casting a smile at Louise, she said, "Ambrose is happy as a lark at the prospect of meeting you. You're the image of your mother, but with your father's brown eyes and hair." She glanced at Louise's shining dark hair, brushed back from her arresting profile.

Dorothy's fleeting but intense scrutiny made Louise feel self-conscious for an instant, yet, as they drove along, she felt a spontaneous familiarity had already sprung up between them. Meeting Dorothy in person, Louise was surprised that she was neither as eccentric nor as bookish as she might have imagined an acclaimed writer of historical novels to be. Her down-to-earth manner, her lively expression, contradicted the image Louise had always held of Dorothy as a quiet, intellectual woman.

"By a stroke of luck I found a book of yours at the airport, *Blood on the Cross*. I started it on the plane and couldn't put it down."

Dorothy beamed with pleasure. "It's just come out in America, but just between us, I don't think it's my best. If you'd like, I'll give you one of my earlier books. They're the ones I'm most proud of."

"That would be wonderful. I've neglected reading for the past few years. I can't think of a better incentive to start again than reading books by someone I know."

"I can't quite get used to the idea that my books are on sale all over the world. To me, it seems nothing short of miraculous."

"If that stack of books at the airport is anything to go by, you must be very popular in the States."

Dorothy gave a shrug. "I don't know anything about where my books go or who reads them. My agent and publisher take care of all that. I just scribble away in my study and I'm always amazed when someone tells me they've seen my books in Hong Kong or Brazil."

Louise smiled inwardly at her modesty, at the same time wondering why such a successful woman was driving a car that seemed to be held together by bits of string. As they rounded a bend she caught sight of an impressive graystone castle looming ahead.

"That's Ashridge," Dorothy informed her. "It's built on the foundations of a thirteenth-century abbey. It's a college now."

"It looks ancient," remarked Louise, tracing the convoluted turrets against the sky, which was beginning to cloud over.

"In fact, it's Victorian Gothic. Yes, Marlowe, we're nearly home," she said to the dog, who was straining to jump over the seat.

"I can see where you get some of your inspiration, living here," observed Louise.

"Yes, I've been so lucky to live here for much of my life. You could say my career was built on inspiration," she added.

"I'd love to hear about your books and how you conceive your plots and characters."

"Would you? Every time I find myself saying this it sounds fanciful, but they seem to spring onto the page of their own accord. It's as if they're actors waiting in the wings for their cue. I have the strong feeling that they have lives of their own and that I'm simply invited to drop in for a while."

"How fascinating," said Louise, feeling a twinge of envy for the richness of Dorothy's inner life.

As they emerged from a thicket of trees, Dorothy turned the car abruptly into a drive well concealed between high hedges. They came to a halt in front of a red brick Jacobean house with leaded windows and curling chimneys, flanked by yew trees moving in the wind.

"What a beautiful house," Louise murmured, pulling her bag from the back of the car. The dog danced at Dorothy's heels as she filled her arms with shopping. Louise took a bag from the seat and followed her to the front door, noting she had left it unlocked. This more than anything, she thought, showed the contrast between their different worlds.

"It wouldn't surprise me if it snowed tonight," Dorothy remarked, leading the way into the house, "although it's practically unheard of at this time of year—even with our wretched climate. After all, it *is* nearly April."

"Yes," Louise agreed, sniffing the dry wintry air.

They entered the hall, lit by the diffused light from a small leaded window at the top of the wooden staircase, its banister set with carved acorns. The scent of beeswax was in the air and Louise looked down at the shining floor obscured by frayed oriental carpets. Thrusting her umbrella into a stand by the door, Dorothy took off her coat.

"We'll just leave the shopping here for the time being. Now I'll take you up to your room, and then we'll come down and have a cup of tea. Ambrose ought to be home any minute. He's giving an interview in Oxford today. His book isn't coming out for another three months, but the publishers are getting a head start."

"How exciting," said Louise, aware that Ambrose Lethbridge was famous in his own right.

"This is his *magnum opus;* he's been working on it for twenty years."

They climbed the creaking stairs and Louise followed Dorothy down the passage to her room.

"The bathroom's the first door on your left. I'm afraid there's only one. You're in Alice's old room—my daughter. She's married to a sheep farmer and lives in Australia now. Our son, Hugh, lives in Vancouver. He's a professor at the university."

Louise followed her into a light, airy room with a four-poster bed hung with blue-and-white chintz. Curtains in the same pattern draped the windows, which rattled in the wind. Dorothy touched a match to a pile of twigs and paper in the fireplace, creating a blaze that offered no warmth in the chilly room. Louise looked round for radiators. As if reading her mind, Dorothy said:

"The room will warm up in no time. By the time you've had your tea it will be nice and toasty. When you're ready, just come downstairs to the kitchen. It's to the right, at the foot of the stairs,'' she said over her shoulder.

"I'll be down in a minute. Is there anything I can do?''

"No, it's all under control. You and I can have a chat while I do a few last minute things. You'll have time to lie down before dinner if you feel like it.''

"What time are you expecting your guests?''

"Oh, not until about eight.'' Pausing at the threshold, she looked at Louise. "My dear, I'm so glad you came.''

"Thank you. And so am I,'' said Louise. When Dorothy had gone, she put her bag on a chest, thinking of the unexpected rapport she felt with Dorothy. Though she had gone, her warmth seemed to linger in the room. Louise unfolded a black suede suit and hung it in the wardrobe. Still thinking of Dorothy Lethbridge, she felt a stab of regret that she would have to leave in less than twenty-four hours. Sitting on the bed, she watched the fire and half listened to the wind outside. Coming to Little Gaddesden had made her realize how close to the surface her emotions were. Looking round, she reminded herself she was now in a world where she ought to trust her instincts.

When she had unpacked, Louise scanned every object in the room as if it would tell her something more about the people whose lives she had entered unexpectedly. There was a china basin and jug on a marble-topped stand, a *petit point* hearth rug, a framed sampler, silhouettes in oval frames and a tin of biscuits on the bedside table along with a water jug and glass. She turned to a bouquet of roses in a china bowl, which filled the room with a faint suggestion of the summer that had ended months ago. Louise thought she had never seen anything so magnificent. Blood-red and delicately textured, they bloomed as richly as if they were rooted in the living soil. Leaning forward, she buried her face in the mass of petals and inhaled their intoxicating fragrance.

Browsing through the books on a shelf, Louise saw several volumes by Dorothy herself. She was reminded of her own ambition years ago, before she had married, to be a doctor, a goal she had abandoned without too much soul-searching at the time. Looking at her image in the wardrobe mirror, Louise asked herself whether, if she could turn back the clock, she would have given up so easily. Long ago she had taken a turning where the road branched, choosing the gilded trappings of the good life as opposed to a more abstract fulfillment. She had even put off having children until it was probably too late. Glancing down at her manicured nails, Louise was unexpectedly confronted by doubts about what she wanted out of life. She was battling to keep her financial security, a luxurious house and a social position, but a small voice whispered "Why?" insistently at the back of her mind. Staring blankly at the bleakness beyond the window, she wondered what had prompted her to ask such a disturbing question in the first place. Now, with so many hurdles ahead of her, was not the time or the place for soul-searching. Now was the time to be strong and resolute in solving her problems.

Closing the door of her room behind her, Louise descended the stairs to the kitchen, where Dorothy was making meringues at a long scrubbed-pine table.

"There you are. Sit over there by the Aga, my dear, where it's warm. I'll be finished with these meringues in a minute. Milk and sugar?" she asked, pouring a ribbon of hot dark tea into the china cup.

Louise looked round the big old kitchen, its open shelves crowded with apothecary jars, enamel saucepans and dishes. A cauldron of stock simmered on the back of the massive coal-burning Aga, which warmed the entire room. Herbs and dried flowers hung from wires overhead and potted bulbs peeked through moss at the windowsill, beyond which she could see the trees tossing in the wind. In the corner the terrier shifted in his basket as he dreamed. He opened one eye when Louise pulled out a chair.

Dorothy said: "I've been thinking about you while you were upstairs. You've really had the most harrowing time during this past year, haven't you?" The tone of her voice underlined her genuine sympathy.

"To tell you the truth, it's been holy hell," Louise replied, feeling a strong wish to confide in Dorothy. "First Dad fell ill, then Frank left me and consequently my business began to slide."

"Your father mentioned to us what you'd been going through in his last letter."

"Did he? It's on my conscience that Dad worried so much

about me in the end. My life seemed to be falling apart and I was helpless to do anything about it. It still grieves me to think he died wondering what would become of me. He was very old-fashioned in that way and didn't think a woman could take care of herself. I guess all fathers think of their daughters as little girls.''

"Yes, they do, and yours was no exception. But you mustn't torment yourself with the idea that you added to your father's burden. In a way, it might have kept his mind off his illness."

"Yes, that's what I keep telling myself," said Louise thoughtfully. Hearing Dorothy repeat the words made her belive it for the first time.

"You're in the fashion business, aren't you? Something to do with leather?"

"Only just," Louise admitted. Meeting Dorothy's level gray eyes, she didn't feel the need to hide anything from her.

"You poor dear. Yet another problem to cope with. How did you get started in the business?"

Louise took a sip of tea. "It began as a bright idea about eight years ago. I was working at a routine job and I wanted something more challenging to do. It happened that a good friend of mine was in retailing and she helped me get started. I worked as a leather buyer for a while to get some experience before I opened my shop in Palo Alto. It's call Bella Figura."

"What a good name," Dorothy said.

"Until two years ago it was very successful. But with the divorce and the time I took off to take care of Daddy, well, to tell you the truth I'm on the verge of going under."

"You are?" replied Dorothy mildly, "Well, my dear, you certainly don't look it. You look on top of the world. Your father was so proud of you."

"I don't know what's going to happen if I don't accomplish a series of near miracles on this trip to Milan."

"Now, that's the big trade fair for fashion, isn't it?" Dorothy asked.

"Yes. And I missed it last year. It meant I had no new stock for the autumn, and I'm here for this show to try to make up for it. But what happens is that if you've missed a season, the important names in the business, which you worked so hard to get, won't sell you a thing. I might well go home empty-handed.''

She stopped speaking, feeling she had explained it all neatly and succinctly, without sounding too sorry for herself.

''My intuition tells me you won't go home empty-handed. Not at all. It wouldn't surprise me if this trip turned out to be the most successful you've ever had.'' Dorothy reached out and patted her hand affectionately. The warmth and certainty in her voice conveyed a feeling of optimism that lifted Louise's spirits.

''Were you surprised when I said I was coming?''

Dorothy gave her an enigmatic little glance as she beat a bowl of egg whites. ''Not really. I rather expected to hear from you sometime.''

It was on the tip of Louise's tongue to make excuses about her impulsive visit to Little Gaddesden. It still seemed odd that she had been awakened by an imaginary earthquake and that she had heard a bell that hadn't rung in years. And even now she couldn't understand what had prompted her to call Dorothy in the middle of the night.

''While you're here I hope you'll think of us as old friends. I was so fond of Kay and Lou, even though the miles separated us.''

''Frank and I came close to visiting you once when we were in England. Now I wish we had.''

''Tell me what happened between you. Was it something that had been going on for a long time?'' asked Dorothy as she piped a meringue onto a baking tray.

''No, just out of the blue,'' Louise confessed. ''It came as a shock when he took me to one of our favorite restaurants in San Francisco. He leaned across the table, took my hand— I thought he was going to say something romantic—but he looked deep into my eyes and said, 'Louise, we have to talk.' Then he dropped the bombshell. He said he'd fallen in love with another woman. She's a lot younger than me, has a ready-made family—two children—and now they've got another one of their own on the way.''

''That must have hurt you very deeply,'' Dorothy murmured sympathetically.

''I had a few bitter moments. Frank always said he didn't

want children. I guess he didn't know what he was looking for until he found it.''

"That's very generous of you, I must say. And now you're in the process of rebuilding your life. It's rather exciting, though, if you think about it. And you seem like such a positive person.''

"I like to think I am. I'll need every ounce of optimism I possess to put the business back into shape.''

"Only business? Isn't there anyone new in your life yet?''

"No, I'm afraid I've become a bit cynical. And very fussy.''

"Well, there's nothing wrong with that," Dorothy reflected. "Your husband wasn't involved in the business, I gather.''

"No. He was an executive in a software company in Silicon Valley, but his company transferred him to Sydney when he met Miss Australia," she said with a disparaging smile. "The thing is, high fashion is very competitive and capricious, as I was saying. If you miss an important collection in Europe, as I did, you find it hard to retrieve yourself. I won't know until I get there if I can do it, but I'm determined to try. Anyway, I don't want to bore you.''

"Bore me? On the contrary, I'm fascinated.''

Louise gave her an appreciative nod. "I suppose you squirrel it away in your memory bank to use in one of your books.''

Dorothy laughed. "I don't have to worry much about fashion, writing about the Middle Ages, thank heavens. I just describe the odd dash of ermine or a jewel-embroidered sleeve. But tell me more: is this a make or break situation for you, then?''

"Oh, very much so," said Louise, holding out her cup as Dorothy poured her more tea. "But, then, I've always thrived on adversity and I love a challenge. I'm luckier than most women. I have a reason to get up in the morning, a place to go, so why complain that it's difficult? It's really a very exciting business, to be honest, and I wouldn't trade it for anything.''

When Louise met Dorothy's serene gray eyes, she realized the older woman could see right through her. Her cheeks flushed with shame, as if she had told a lie.

"I'm not really as sure of myself as I sound.''

"Have you ever thought of doing anything else?"

"No, not really. It's my livelihood, and a very good one when it's successful. I'll find a way to scrape by. Otherwise I'd have to sell my house, which I'd never do. I decided moving on top of everything else would be just too much."

Dorothy smiled doubtfully. "Sometimes it's better to start afresh; don't you think so?"

"I don't know. I've never tried. I'm afraid I'm so entrenched in California, I could never live anywhere else." A determined note crept into her voice. "That reminds me, I brought some pictures to show you." She opened her handbag.

Dorothy dusted off her hands and took the photographs.

"That's the last one I have of Daddy, taken when I visited him in Phoenix six months before he died."

"Ah yes. Still the same smile, the same way of cocking his head at the camera. How I regret we never made it over to Arizona or that he didn't come here again. But at least we kept in touch."

"If it hadn't been for that, I wouldn't be here now. Dad was always a brilliant correspondent. Here are a few more pictures to give you an idea of my house and garden."

"What delicious luxury you live in," Dorothy remarked, glancing through the snapshots. "I can see you're an inveterate collector."

"Yes," she said unashamedly and with a note of pride, "I adore beautiful things."

"It's like paradise, isn't it?" Dorothy said, looking at the photos of the huge swimming pool set in a lush garden. "And who takes care of all this for you? It must be a full-time job."

"I'm lucky to have a very good Mexican couple. He tends the garden and she looks after the house." She added matter-of-factly: "Of course, it's awfully big for one person."

"Yes, that's just what I was thinking. You say you're planning to stay there, though?"

"Right now, hanging on to the house is my greatest incentive to get the business moving again. I suppose I've been very spoiled."

"But aren't you ever lonely?"

"No, I'm much too busy," she said, almost believing it.

Dorothy looked at her closely. "I doubt if you'll be alone for long, Louise. Just meeting you, I can see that."

Louise shook her head. "You know, Dorothy, I don't think I'll ever get married again, not after what happened."

"Rubbish. How old are you?"

"Thirty-five. I wonder if I want to be in the position where I put my life and my happiness in someone else's hands ever again."

Dorothy came round the table and put an arm around Louise's shoulders. "You may not realize it now, but an entirely new life awaits you, and when it comes you will reach out for it without hesitation."

"You say that as if you have some kind of premonition."

"Perhaps I do." Dorothy hesitated, as if she had said too much, then busied herself at the table again while Louise watched her.

Until then, she hadn't noticed Dorothy's fine, smooth hands, which seemed out of character. Her long, tapering fingers moved surely and with grace as she put the finishing touches to the tray of meringues and then cleared the table. Here in this warm kitchen smelling of sweet spices which spoke of an older and more established way of life, Louise felt a coil of tension inside her begin to unwind.

Dorothy looked at her steadily as she rinsed and dried her hands. "I didn't finish what I wanted to say. I wish you and I had more time to talk. Time is so short, so precious . . ."

Louise looked at her expectantly.

"It's just that I was thinking perhaps what you're doing at the moment isn't right for you. Don't be afraid of something new if it comes along." She turned at the sound of someone stamping his feet outside the kitchen door.

"Come on, Portia, heel," came the brusque command. The door was flung open and the towering figure of a man in a deerstalker and a green cape stood at the threshold.

"Down, Portia. Will you obey, girl," he said testily, his concentration broken by the red setter circling his legs. As the dog retreated to the basket by the Aga, where Marlowe raised his head in recognition, the man set down the box of eggs he was carrying. A smile broke across his serious, scholarly face when he saw Louise sitting there.

"And this, of course, is Louise," said Ambrose Lethbridge. "You look exactly like your mother."

"Do I?" Standing up, she wondered how to address him. "I'm so happy to meet you, Professor Lethbridge."

"Professor! That's so formal and makes me sound as old as the ages. Ambrose, just call me Ambrose," he corrected her, with mischief twinkling in his eyes. Brushing aside her hand, he clasped her to him, burying her face in his prickly wool cape. She came up for air with a laugh and kissed his cheek, as he evidently expected.

"Did you have a good flight?"

"Just fine, thank you," she replied.

Looking at Ambrose Lethbridge, Louise was instantly enchanted. He seemed to fill the room with his presence. At first glance he seemed the opposite of Dorothy, his plump, practical wife. Though he was a scholar, he possessed a vitality that was the mark of the extrovert. His nobly aging face was framed by bristling white hair and his skin had a ruddy glow that suggested the outdoors. Louise could imagine him roving the muddy fields on a crisp day, Portia at his heels. Hanging up his cape and hat, he stationed himself across the table as Dorothy poured him a cup of tea. He pulled out his pipe and struck a match. All her father's photographs had been lost in a move, but Ambrose Lethbridge perfectly fitted her image of him, including his Holmesian attire, an ancient green Harris tweed jacket with leather patches at the elbows and his regimental tie.

They passed half an hour talking about Louise's father and mother and the war years during which they cemented their friendship, and then about Louise's trip to Milan. Dorothy was wrapping a fillet of beef in pastry. From time to time Louise would catch her eye and they would exchange a smile.

Dorothy glanced at the big kitchen clock as the hand flipped to six-thirty. "Darling, have you told Louise about the guests we've invited tonight?" Ambrose asked. Turning his head toward his wife, he winked. "Just remind me who's coming. It's slipped my memory."

Dorothy was standing perfectly still, her hands folded, oblivious of what he had said. She was staring at the window pane above the kitchen sink where the beam of the outside light caught a swirl of snowflakes as they beat against the glass. Her expression was solemn, even sad, and Louise wondered what memory the sight of snow had conjured up. As Dorothy met Ambrose's eyes, an unspoken communication passed between them and Louise felt conscious of the private language shared by two people who had been close companions for so many years. Dorothy shook herself from her reverie, saying, "You know perfectly well who is coming, darling. There's Canon Ramsey and his wife, Lucy and Charles and, of course, Owen."

"Owen? I thought he was in Switzerland. I'm sure he told me that he might stay over to ski this weekend if the snow was good."

"No. In fact, he's coming straight here. I talked to him last night. Now, let me think. Canon Ramsey is a jolly fellow and Lavinia, his wife, is a brilliant portrait painter. Charles and Lucy farm not far from here. She's a bookbinder and works with the loveliest leather, which might interest you, and he plays in a jazz band and raises ornamental pheasants. They're great favorites of ours."

"Tell her about Owen," Ambrose urged, reaching for the teapot. "You'll like Owen. He's a lot younger than the rest of us and very good-looking to boot. I think you might find him interesting. And," he added cheerfully, "he's single."

Dorothy shot him a disapproving look for his lack of subtlety.

"Well, there's no crime in being single, is there?" said Ambrose defensively.

Louise laughed at this clumsy attempt at matchmaking. He didn't know her well enough to realize that her emotional needs, which she had once thought so intense, had retreated comfortably into the background. Warmth and tenderness seemed like luxuries that might have the power to heal, but also the power to wound and destroy. In spite of Dorothy's comments, Louise knew it would be a long time before she would want to do more than rebuild her business interests.

"Oh my goodness, look at the time," said Dorothy. "I'm sure Louise wants to go upstairs and lie down before dinner. They're coming at eight." She gathered up the rolling pin and knives and put them in the sink.

Louise rose to go upstairs, feeling strangely disoriented.

She had been living on adrenaline and was more tired than she had thought.

"Are you sure there's nothing I can do?"

"Nothing at all, thank you. My housekeeper, Mrs. Hawkins, will be here at any minute and she'll see to everything."

"See you for drinks in the library at eight, my dear," called Ambrose. "If you need me to come in and stoke up your fire, just give me a shout."

"A fire in the bedroom is such a treat, I'll make sure it keeps going," she called from the doorway.

Moments later Louise slid beneath the cool sheets of her bed and picked up a book of Dorothy's she had found on a shelf. She began to read *The Dark Citadel* and soon became absorbed in it . . .

The sun had just gone down behind the chain of mountains, reducing the jagged heights to black shadows against the red sky of spring. The woman stared at her six-year-old daughter across the fire she was feeding with twigs that they had gathered on the long journey, six days and nights away from the sound of church bells and the probing eyes of the Inquisitors. When the fire waned, she crumbled a heap of dried moss, making it flare again. The flames flushed her face pink and chased away the dark hollows below her eyes. She shivered and drew her rags about her, not from cold but in a kind of bleak gratitude that they were safe at last. But the distant tinkle of a goat's bell coming from the pastures below, already swallowed up by the darkness, reminded her that even now, so far from a settlement, they were not yet alone. The chilling howl of a hungry wolf on the prowl made the woman whisper an incantation and make signs in the air to protect herself and her child, who had been gazing impassively into the fire. The woman imagined she must be thinking of food, but instead the dark-eyed little girl said:

"What is a witch, Mother?"

The woman did not reply, but stared at her mutely. So often the child's curiosity, or lack of it, surprised her and somehow she had assumed that her daughter had absorbed the answer to her own question along with the milk from her breast. The age of wisdom had arrived much earlier than she might have expected.

"A witch is a wise woman who knows the oldest prayers on earth, just as shepherds know legends and troubadours spin poetry or priests chant their scriptures."

"And what is a heretic?" the child asked.

The woman unwrapped a gritty lump of goat's cheese and a hard knot of bread, dividing it between the two of them. *"You, child, are nothing yet. You are a blind mouse that has not yet opened its eyes to the world."* She clasped her daughter's cool, dusty hands for a moment before placing lumps of bread and cheese into each of them. *"When your hands are like mine, then you will be a healer, not a witch or a heretic. Close your ears to those cruel words, because they will make you doubt the gift I will pass on to you. Poor child,"* she murmured in an unaccustomed fit of sentiment. *"I have nothing else to give you. You have only a bed of leaves and the sky over your head, and I cannot promise what will come tomorrow."*

They fell to eating and did not speak again until they had satisfied themselves and drunk from the stream nearby. When they had finished, they pressed near the fire, prolonging as always the moment of going to sleep. That night neither of them felt their usual uneasiness at being among the mountains, alive with ghosts and demons. Even the elements were not their enemy on this mild spring night and they knew that nothing would harm them. When the wolf howled again, the child murmured:

"Tell me, Mother, do priests eat children?"

The woman smiled. *"What makes you ask such a thing?"*

"Because when we used to see them, they reminded me of wolves. Their mouths are always growling in speech and their eyes are yellow and hungry too."

"True, child, but, unlike wolves, they are not frightened of fire." The woman's mouth twisted in bitter irony at the memory.

As the child curled into a ball, the woman began to talk of the burning of heretics and the massacres she had witnessed.

". . . and I crawled from the pile of corpses, my hair and clothes stiff with blood. The Crusaders, sent by the Pope, ripped open women with swords and skewered the children

*like eels on a stick. And yet I was saved,'' she murmured
with wonder, as always when she spoke of it, "to heal, and
to hope . . ."*

*She began to talk of what she understood and loved best.
"My mother, and hers before her, told me to gather herbs
for fevers and madness, but only when the moon is waning.
Those herbs that cure stomach ills should be cut when the
moon is in its first quarter and not afterward, and those for
sores, in the second. Summer is the best time, and the higher
the plants grow to God, the better . . ." She crossed herself,
seeing the child was fast asleep and that a great disc of moon
had appeared from behind a cloud, as if heralding a new
season free from want and fear.*

Louise hadn't intended to fall asleep, but the mesmeric play
of the shadows from the fire on the ceiling and walls made
her eyes unbearably heavy. The book slipped from her hand
as she listened to the gentle rattling of the windows in the
wind.

When she awoke some time later from a deep, dreamless
sleep, she became aware of voices murmuring outside her window in the garden below. Her heart pounding, she threw off the
blanket and looked at the dying embers in the fireplace, beginning to remember where she was. With a start she realized all
the guests must be arriving for the party and that she had over-
slept. Fumbling for the bedside lamp, she was relieved to see
by her traveling clock that it was only seven-thirty and she had
plenty of time to be ready by eight. Then who were the men
speaking so excitedly below her window?

She went across and pressed her nose against the glass.
Staring out into the darkness she could see the snow was still
falling. She listened intently to the voices outside which were
becoming more heated, but she couldn't make out a single
word they were saying. They were not speaking English, she
realized, but something that sounded like French, which she
herself spoke tolerably well. From the almost quaint musical
quality of the voices as they argued, she decided they were
speaking in some kind of patois. She was just wondering
whether she ought to alert Dorothy about the commotion
when the voices died away, leaving the room silent.

2

Just before eight, Louise buckled the belt of her black suede suit in front of the mirror on the wardrobe door. She shook her dark shoulder-length hair and brushed the richly embroidered lapels of her jacket, then reached for the gold and diamond earrings tucked into her jewel case. Giving herself a critical once-over in the mirror, she realized she would have been happier in something much less glamorous for Dorothy's quiet dinner party. Reaching for her watch set with diamonds, she clipped it on anyway, feeling naked without it. She had always had a passion for beautiful jewelry, but lately she had found herself wondering if she should give up her expensive baubles. She had been through the argument with herself several times, and had always concluded that her business demanded she should wear the best that money could buy.

"There you go again, more negative thoughts," she muttered to herself. She tilted her chin, making a resolution that within a year she would be back on top financially and under her own steam. When that happened, she would reward herself with some wildly extravagant present in order to prove how far she'd come. Clenching her fist in a little salute at her image in the mirror, she went downstairs.

Crossing the hall, Louise entered the book-lined library, where Ambrose was putting a log on the fire. He turned expectantly at the sound of her footsteps. "Ah, Louise, I'll be with you in half a second." Pumping the bellows, he cursed under his breath as a puff of smoke curled above the mantelpiece.

Louise looked round the room, which, though shabby and furnished with no particular regard for harmony of color or style, was one of the most inviting rooms she had ever seen. The faded red velvet curtains had been drawn across the leaded windows and lamps cast pools of warm light on gateleg tables, a fine Tudor chest, frayed Persian carpets and a

22

big, well-used sofa and chairs covered with faded chintz slip-covers. It was the private retreat of two highly cultured people who had rarely bought anything new in forty years of marriage and who had ignored material luxury for intellectual pursuits. She glanced at the careless jumble of framed family photographs, the books that lined two walls from floor to ceiling and a spiral of library steps in the corner.

Ambrose, who tossed down the bellows now that the fire was blazing, had changed into a burgundy velvet smoking jacket and evening trousers that brushed the tops of his needlepoint slippers. "Aren't you punctual?" he said, kissing her cheek. "And you look ravishing. Dorothy will be down in a minute. Sherry? Gin and tonic? Dry martini?"

While he poured them a drink at the butler's tray, Louise sat on the old-fashioned sofa and watched the fire leaping to life in the grate under the stone chimney, which was blackened by years of use. She sniffed the fragrance of wood smoke mingling with the dry, evocative odor of old books. There was an underlying suggestion of dogs and polished wood, overpowered by the perfume from a bowl of roses nearby, the same rich red roses that had been placed in her room.

Ambrose presented her with a crystal glass brimming with sherry. As she touched it to her lips, he said:

"I hope none of our guests are held up by the weather. It's unusual for us to have snow at this time of year. Don't worry, though. It's expected to melt by morning."

"It suddenly hit me when I was upstairs that Little Gaddesden was here before Columbus even discovered America. I wish I were staying longer. It must have a fascinating history," Louise said.

"Well, the monastery where the college now stands was founded in the thirteenth century by an order called the *Bonshommes*, who followed the Augustinian rule until the Dissolution at the time of the Reformation. This part of the world is steeped in romance and mystery, much embroidered by time. Believe me, if you live here, you're as susceptible to it as anyone."

"Who were the *Bonshommes*? They must have been French originally?" she asked, her curiosity pricked.

"Yes, although no one knows for certain. My theory has always been that a number of them came from the remnants of a sect called the Cathars, who flourished in the Languedoc before they were extinguished by the Inquisition, because they, too, were called *Bonshommes,* which means, of course, the good men.''

"Really?'' said Louise, raising an eyebrow. "Isn't that peculiar. That's the second time I've run across the Cathars in the last few months. I gave Daddy a book of photographs about the Languedoc when he was in hospital. There was something about them in that. History isn't my strong subject,'' she confessed. "You say they came here after the Inquisition?'' He nodded. "Do French tourists sometimes come to Little Gaddesden to visit the college because of that?''

"Oh dear, no,'' he said with a laugh. "The historical relationship has never been established—it's just my theory.''

"I see,'' she mused, dismissing the voices she had heard from her mind. "My father said that you've had a house in France for years too.''

"Yes, we bought a house near the Pyrenees in the mid-Fifties and we spend part of every summer there.''

"It's a place I know nothing about. I tried to cheer Daddy up by telling him we'd take a trip there when he got well. He thumbed over that book again and again. You could say it became almost an obsession with him toward the end.''

"Well, he was of French extraction. Perhaps his family came from there.''

"I don't think so. They were from Alsace originally.'' Louise took a sip of sherry, thinking of her father's curious dying wish to have his ashes scattered somewhere in the Languedoc, a request she had failed to honor. Now, talking to Ambrose, she suddenly felt ashamed. "He said a lot of strange things before he died. He was heavily sedated so he wouldn't feel the pain.'' Tears sprang to her eyes unexpectedly.

They were interrupted by the entrance of Dorothy, who was glamorously transformed by a full-cut black velvet dress nipped at the waist. There were pearls at her throat and ears and she had brushed her gray hair, creating a silver halo round her flushed, unlined face. Ambrose kissed her affectionately and Louise sensed the physical attraction that was still very much alive between them. She blinked, realizing that she had been staring.

"Did you have a good nap?" Dorothy asked.

"I went out like a light. In fact, I'd probably still be sleeping if it hadn't been for some people chattering away outside."

Dorothy looked at her with an unruffled smile. "What a nuisance."

"I'm not sure who they were, but I got up and went to the window because I thought everybody had arrived for dinner. But then I realized they were speaking in what seemed like French patois, though I couldn't make out what they said."

Dorothy looked at Ambrose. "Oh, that would have been some friends of ours from the village who pop by from time to time. They can be terribly noisy when they get worked up about something. We're at the other end of the house, so I didn't notice," she added by way of explanation.

"Do you think there could be ghosts in Little Gaddesden?" Louise asked. She couldn't quite think why she had come up with the notion.

For a moment the room tingled with the suggestion. Louise gave a skeptical smile to let the Lethbridges know she wasn't serious.

"You don't believe in things like that, do you?" asked Dorothy.

Louise shook her head. "Of course not."

A knock at the door signaled the arrival of the first dinner guests. Ambrose and Dorothy turned to welcome two couples and introduced them to Louise. She shook hands with the canon, a small, balding man with a jolly expression, whose shirt-front was adorned with a Celtic cross. His wife, a dimpled blonde in a frilly pink dress, was nothing like Louise's image of a clergyman's wife. Charles Moore, with his red, weather-beaten face and callused hands, was more what she would expect as a farmer, and his wife was plump and shy. They all gathered round the fire, talking about the unseasonable weather.

The canon's wife said, "This wretched snow will ruin your roses, I'm afraid, Dorothy. Dorothy's roses are famous," she added to Louise. "She somehow manages to make them survive the winter, but no one knows her secret."

"It's no secret, really. They're well protected from the wind and weather in the old courtyard."

Ambrose filled Louise's glass with sherry again and she stood with her back to the fire listening to the pleasant murmur of English voices. It struck her that the mellowness within the room was caught like wine in a glass, away from the cold and darkness beyond the walls. She was aware that the knot of tension between her shoulders had vanished. The atmosphere enfolded her like gentle hands, conjuring up a sensation of permanence, peace and trust, all of which seemed to emanate from Dorothy. Content not to think any further than the present moment, she knew she wouldn't want to leave when tomorrow came.

Moments later she was puzzled to see Dorothy glancing impatiently at her watch. With one hand she toyed nervously with her pearls, resting the other on Ambrose's arm. She said to him in a worried whisper:

"What do you suppose has happened to Owen? He should be here by now."

Ambrose said benignly: "I'm sure he'll be here at any moment, darling. Perhaps we ought to call Heathrow to see if his flight was delayed."

"I don't want to sit down without him, but we'll have to if he doesn't come soon."

When Dorothy left the room looking distraught, Louise said to Ambrose:

"Is anything wrong?"

"Dorothy is fussing because Owen Morgan isn't here yet. We're both very fond of him. In fact, he's like a second son to us."

Just then Dorothy came back into the room. With a little gasp of frustration she said: "Apparently it's as clear as a bell in Geneva, so his plane must have taken off on time. I can't imagine what's keeping him."

Ambrose smiled indulgently and turned to Louise again. "Dorothy's not normally a worrier, but she's always fussed over Owen. We were his guardians when he was at school, because his parents were posted abroad." Turning to Dorothy, he said: "Don't you think we should ask Mrs. Hawkins to put the soup on the table?"

"Yes, you're probably right. No doubt Owen will arrive the moment we sit down," she said with a little laugh, as if trying to reassure herself.

"Is there anything I can help you with?" asked Louise.

"No, no, thank you, but perhaps you could tell everyone that dinner will be on the table in five minutes."

After she had made the announcement, Louise slipped upstairs.

When she had touched up her lipstick, she walked down the cold passage, stopping at the top of the stairs at the sound of a man's voice accompanied by the stamping of feet below. As she descended, Louise saw Dorothy holding open the front door to admit a stocky, dark-haired man of medium height whom she judged to be in his early forties. Opening his arms, he hugged Dorothy laughingly and then dusted the snow from the shoulders of his navy overcoat. Louise felt disquieted by the man, whose appearance had been heralded by a gust of cold air in the hall. Every detail of him registered in her mind, from the sound of his voice to the snowflakes melting on his curling black hair, which was flecked with touches of gray. She stood hesitantly at the foot of the stairs, feeling that he was the intruder, not she. His entrance had struck a discordant note and introduced a tension that hadn't been there before. She eyed him critically, thinking he had disturbed the atmosphere, wondering why she was so quick to jump to conclusions about him.

"Owen, I was so worried about you. I was becoming frantic," Dorothy confessed.

"I'm so sorry, Dorothy. The baggage was held up for some reason and then on the way here there was an accident on the motorway that caused a snarl-up. I hope I haven't ruined your dinner."

"Don't be silly. I was just worried about you."

"It's wonderful to see you. You're blooming," he said. Handing his coat to Dorothy, he looked round and saw Louise standing at the bottom of the stairs.

"Oh, Louise, come and meet Owen Morgan," Dorothy called. "Owen, this is Louise Carey. Her father and mother were old friends of ours."

Louise put out her hand. "How do you do?"

"Ah, an American," he said, raising an eyebrow. A mischievous grin played round the corners of his mouth.

"Yes, that's right," she replied evenly, wondering if she detected a note of condescension in his voice.

"Get Ambrose to fix you a quick drink and we'll go in to dinner," said Dorothy. Her gray eyes had clouded and she seemed distracted. She gave them both a quick smile, then disappeared.

Louise felt herself bristle when she saw Owen giving her a quick once-over, sizing her up from her suede pumps to her diamond earrings and her dressy suit, which she knew he must think was over the top for a country dinner party. His direct blue eyes didn't miss anything as they glided over her and she met his gaze coolly.

Louise preceded him into the library, where he obviously knew everyone from the friendly hellos being exchanged. All her muscles were jammed with the old tension that had so miraculously disappeared earlier. She found she was annoyed by Owen Morgan's laughter, his easy familiarity. He exuded the swaggering charm of a romantic Welshman who was attractive to women, and knew it. The cocky set of his broad shoulders irritated her all the more because he hadn't bothered to wear a tie.

Passing him, Louise fought off the sinking feeling in her stomach, then went to take her place in the dark red dining room glowing with candlelight. The uneasiness she felt didn't subside as she sat down, turning her attention to the canon. Dorothy was presiding at the head of the long mahogany table set with old family silver, china and cut crystal. In the center, between Georgian candelabra, deep golden roses fanned from an oriental bowl. Unfolding her napkin, Louise watched Dorothy as she ladled soup from a tureen. Studiously avoiding Owen across the table, she took a steaming bowl of pumpkin soup and passed it on as Ambrose moved round to pour the claret from a bottle resting in a silver basket. Seeing Louise look up at the crossbeams of the ceiling, lower than in the other rooms, he said:

"This room is much older than the rest of the house. The beams and the floor date back to the thirteenth century."

Louise looked down at the uneven flagstones, glossy with the passage of feet over the centuries. When she glanced up, Owen was studying her, but as their eyes met he looked away. Brushing her hair from her cheek in a self-conscious gesture, she picked up her spoon as Ambrose raised his glass.

"Before we begin, I would like to propose a toast to our

guest of honor, Louise Carey. We have known each other only a few hours, but Dorothy and I feel as if she has been part of our lives as her father was, and her mother too.''

As all eyes rested on her, Louise said, ''I wish my father was here with us tonight. It would have meant so much to him, but this is the next best thing, that I should come for both of us. I just want to say that I'm overwhelmed at your hospitality. I've never experienced anything like it.'' She broke off, feeling a sudden pang of emotion.

''Hear, hear,'' echoed the canon. ''Louise, it's a pleasure to have you among us.''

''You must come again and stay longer,'' said Dorothy, passing the bread.

''Why don't you come to Languedoc this summer? You could stay as long as you like. At least there we can guarantee better weather,'' Ambrose added.

Louise smiled, wondering if Ambrose had any idea what it meant to rebuild a business that had all but failed.

''I'm afraid there won't be any holidays for me for the time being.''

''Oh, what a shame,'' said Ambrose. ''Well, next year, then.''

''Believe me, there's nothing I'd love more. The thing is, the summer is when I receive all my stock deliveries. But don't let me talk about it. I don't want to even think about business until Monday.''

''What business are you in?'' asked Owen.

''I have a retail shop in the Bay Area, selling European designer leatherwear for women.''

''Bay Area? Where exactly is that?''

''That's what we call the area surrounding San Francisco: the Bay Area. Actually, I'm in Palo Alto, or at least my shop is, but I live in a place called Atherton.''

She had the disturbing impression that he didn't find what she said entirely credible, and she knew her reply sounded cool. She chewed a crust of bread, which crumbled drily in her mouth, then sipped her wine. Determined not to let Owen Morgan better her, she continued: ''Right now, I'm on my way to Milan and then Paris for my biggest buying trip of the year.'' She fixed her gaze on him to emphasize her point.

''That sounds very exciting.''

"Not really. It's hellishly demanding and I'll be very glad when it's all over." Hearing herself speak, she thought she sounded waspish, almost rude, so she punctuated her remark with a little laugh.

Owen leaned back in his chair. "Hellish? If you don't enjoy it, then why do you do it?"

"I'm afraid I have to make my living, Mr. Morgan."

"Ambrose, could you send the wine round?" asked Dorothy, bemused by the veiled disagreement between Owen and Louise. "The two of you seem to have a lot in common," she remarked. "Neither of you manages to take holidays."

With a chiding look at Owen, she added, "You've been promising to come to Puivaillon for years. I've given up on you."

Lucy said to Louise, "If you do have the time, you really should go and stay with Dorothy and Ambrose in France. Charles and I were there on our way to Portugal last year at Easter. We intended to stay only the night, but wound up staying a week. It's so beautiful, so remote. Paradise, really. Ambrose, I'll never forget how on Easter Sunday we had lunch under your cherry tree, drinking rosé the same color as the blossoms."

Ambrose dabbed his lips with a napkin and sighed. "I hate to tell you, but we had a letter from Maurice Roussel not long ago. He told us the cherry tree was brought down in a storm."

"He was so kind. He planted another one right away to replace it," added Dorothy. The rubicund Mrs. Hawkins waited at her elbow to collect the soup plates, which were being passed down the table.

"Charles, we've laid in a stock of rosé for the day it blooms," said Ambrose, bearing the Beef Wellington on a platter.

Charles laughed heartily. "Fine, fine. Lucy and I will be there to drink our share."

"June and July are supposed to be the best months," Lucy mused.

"It sounds to me as though any time is the best time," the canon remarked. "You were wise to go that far south. They say the Dordogne is absolutely ruined."

As Ambrose sliced the beef, Louise thought about what

she would be doing in the summer: toiling away in the back room of Bella Figura, prizing open boxes and hoping the contents looked as good as they had on the catwalks of Europe. She guessed by Owen's silence and the expression on his face that he had summed her up with the same rapidity as she had him. She knew she had given the impression that she was hard-nosed and brittle.

"Ambrose, some day I'll definitely be making a trip to the south of France," she said, meeting Owen's eyes. "I've been wanting to go there for years."

"I wouldn't put it off if I were you," Owen commented.

"You're a fine one to talk," Dorothy interjected.

Ambrose laughed and so did Louise. Owen gave them a sheepish smile and passed a dish of vegetables. Louise watched him, noticing things about him she had been too perturbed to see before. His wrists were flecked with black hair beneath his cuffs and he wore no rings on his strong hands. He was indifferently, but not badly, dressed. There was a stubbornness about his chin that was contradicted by a ready smile, which changed the entire expression of his face. When he smiled, his fine blue eyes lit up, losing the questioning depths that Louise found so disarming. She sensed he was continually weighing up the value of what people said and that he was impatient with banalities. She liked him better now than moments ago, but her first judgement stuck. She supposed he was true to type, a typical Celt with strong appetites, whose vibrant nature was underscored with a deep melancholy. She had little difficulty in imagining him bursting into a fit of violent temper and saying things he regretted afterward. Helping herself to the broccoli with hollandaise sauce, Louise heard Dorothy say:

". . . and if you should decide to go to France at Easter, you could stay in the house. All you have to do is collect the keys from Maurice Roussel."

"Did my father know Maurice Roussel?" Louise asked. "I heard you say you knew him since the war."

"Yes, we all met that awful night when they bombed the Café de Paris in London and so many people were killed. Maurice took us back to the Free French Club off the Mall. It was before your father met Kay. She'd just been posted to

England with the Army,'' she added, for everyone else's benefit.

"He's quite a character," said Charles. "Speaks quite good English. He's a famous herbalist, isn't he?"

"Yes, that's right, but he's a medical doctor too. He's semi-retired now, but his waiting room is often full of patients, who come from miles around. There's a great book in him, if ever he'd set himself to write it. He's been collecting material for years."

While Ambrose was slicing second helpings of beef and the canon entertained them all with a funny story about a controversial bishop, Louise noticed Owen had fallen silent and was looking at the wine in his glass.

Dorothy said: "You're very quiet tonight, Owen. Did everything go well in Switzerland?"

He looked up with a start. "Yes, fine. I was only there for a couple of days to see some new molding machinery in Zurich, then I drove to Geneva. If I seem a bit quiet, excuse me. Geneva has the reputation of being dull, but I discovered that that is a myth." He flashed a mischievous grin that made Dorothy laugh. She said to Louise:

"Owen has a factory in Swindon, in Wiltshire."

Louise raised an eyebrow, thinking to herself that he didn't look at all the type to be involved in industry. Detecting signs of a hangover in his face, she guessed that he hadn't spent his nights in Switzerland alone, which didn't surprise her. He seemed the kind of man who would have a messy and complicated love life.

"Mr. Morgan, what sort of business did you say you were in?"

"Please, call me Owen. There's no need to be so formal," he said with a nod. "Think of me tomorrow as you wing your way to Italy. You may very well be dining off one of my products. When you raise your chicken chasseur to your lips, the fork probably came from my factory and so did the tray."

"In other words, plastics."

"That's right. A simple product, but very profitable."

"Owen started with nothing—from a phone booth in Earls Court. It's a great success story," said Dorothy, beaming proudly.

"In that case, to plastics," replied Louise, raising her glass.

"And to leather," Owen retorted, and they shared a smile.

"Don't let him fool you, Louise," said Ambrose. "He's quite a chameleon, a man of many parts."

"By the way, what news on your song?" asked Dorothy.

"It looks as though EMI want to bring out a new recording of it."

"I am pleased," she exclaimed, clapping her hands. "But, then, I knew it would happen. It's such a good song—one of the best I ever heard, even though I don't pretend to understand pop music." When Louise looked inquisitive, Dorothy added: "Owen has been a famous musician in his time."

"What's the name of the song?" she asked.

"It's called 'Moody Lady.' I doubt if you've ever heard of it. Anyway, it was released years ago," he said with a shrug.

"You wrote 'Moody Lady'?" asked Louise, wide-eyed.

"Do you remember it?" It was now his turn to be amazed.

"Do I remember it? Oh yes," she exclaimed, putting down her fork. "I must have danced to it a thousand times in my high school years."

"It's nice to know my life hasn't been lived in vain," he replied with a wry smile.

"But what happened? Why did you quit music when you had that kind of success?" She stared at him incredulously, suddenly seeing him in a different light.

"There's nothing more pathetic than an aging pop musician, is there—unless it's an aging plastics manufacturer."

She couldn't quite bring herself to smile at his self-deprecating remark. Suddenly she was full of curiosity. She wanted to ask him what had happened, but it wasn't the right moment.

Ambrose remarked: "I wonder how many people end up becoming what they envisage when they are young. I, for example, always wanted to be an actor."

"That doesn't surprise me at all," said the canon, wiping his lips with his napkin. "You would have made a splendid Hamlet."

"What about you, Canon? Got any smoldering secret ambitions?" Owen asked.

"Well, you might laugh, but to tell the truth I always wanted to have a go at designing ladies' hats. It's a good thing I didn't, because they don't wear them much any more," he added with a chuckle.

"So you took up a much steadier occupation," said Owen irreverently, making the canon chortle.

"What about you, Dorothy?" asked Louise.

"Believe it or not, absolutely nothing at all. I was always accused of having no ambition."

When Charles asserted that he had never wanted to be anything but a farmer and his wife confessed to an early passion for archaeology, Dorothy said: "And what about you, Louise?"

"It sounds ridiculous now, but the only thing I ever wanted to be was a doctor. I must have been inspired by an old *Doctor Kildare* show or something."

"A doctor?" Dorothy repeated. "Really?"

"Yes, it's surprisingly out of character for me, I suppose."

"Not at all. On the contrary."

"Well, it's too late now."

"But you're a young woman. It's early days yet," Ambrose protested.

She laughed at the thought. "That's very flattering. But believe me, Ambrose, if there's one thing I'll never be, it's a doctor. Seven years in medical school, the internship. No," she shook her head. "I'm afraid it's too late."

"Ah, perhaps. But you must never lose interest in the things you love. I, for example, never miss a season of Shakespeare at Stratford," Ambrose said.

"Don't be ridiculous, darling. Are you suggesting Louise attend an operating theatre in a gauze mask as an observer?" Dorothy interjected, making everyone laugh, Louise most of all. When she looked at Owen, he said:

"You haven't told us what happened, why you didn't become a doctor."

"A very lame excuse. I decided to get married and live happily ever after." She flushed with embarrassment, thinking how shallow it must have sounded and how dull.

Heads turned toward the doorway as Mrs. Hawkins came into the dining room bearing a tray of meringues and fruit in a cut glass bowl, which she placed in front of Dorothy.

"I'll put the coffee in the library, Mrs. Lethbridge. Everything is in order in the kitchen."

"Thank you, Mrs. Hawkins," said Dorothy. "And good night."

As they ate their pudding. Louise tried to remember the words of "Moody Lady," a haunting romantic ballad that went against the trend toward hard rock music that had been popular then. For her, the song had been a litany for some potent daydreams. Between the lines there might be a clue to the enigmatic character of Owen Morgan, plastics king and rock musician, who had become an unreadable paradox.

Louise came back to the present when Ambrose said to her: "My theory has always been that if we don't accomplish what we want in this life, then we will achieve it in the next."

"You mean the afterlife?" Aware of the canon, she refrained from saying point-blank that she considered herself an atheist.

"No, not Heaven and Hell. I mean something like reincarnation, if you will."

"Do you mean you believe in that sort of thing?" Louise asked.

"You seem surprised," said Ambrose with an amused smile. "Why is that?"

"I guess I was born a heathen. I was christened a Catholic, but I stopped going to church about the time I put away my dolls. It didn't make any sense at all to me. It still doesn't, I'm afraid." She smiled apologetically at the canon, who didn't seem to be offended.

Ambrose continued: "The idea of reincarnation makes perfect sense if you think about it, and explains a great deal of the mystery of life. I find it hard to believe that just because these old carcasses wear out, our souls disintegrate."

"You're assuming there is a soul," Owen interjected.

Ambrose gave him a tolerant smile. "Perhaps. Just as you're assuming there isn't. Our bodies are but a vessel, after all. It pleases me to think that we have more than a handful of years on this blessed earth. Once these weary old bones wear out, we're off on another adventure. That is, after all, what life is. Each time we get a little closer to the truth."

"It's a nice thought," Louise said politely, thinking this

quaint notion was as much in character for Ambrose to think like this as it was for him to wear a deerstalker hat.

"But you don't think you could entertain the idea?" he asked with a twinkle in his eye.

"Not really. I believe we have one chance and life is what you make of it, here and now."

"Personally, I'm a dualist," announced the ruddy-faced Charles.

Louise wasn't sure what he meant, but she noticed this sudden talk of religion had touched a nerve in all of them.

"What about you, Canon? What do you have to say about this? Or is that a foolish question?" Owen asked.

The canon laughed indulgently. "I prefer not to attack the question on theological grounds. Aside from that, I've given the matter a lot of thought and have come to the conclusion that the universe never wastes anything. It recycles everything and so it must be with human existence. I can't accept that a human being is reduced to nothing but a heap of carbon and water after all the time on this planet."

"You haven't declared yourself yet," Louise said to Owen.

"I agree with you. This is it and, as far as I'm concerned, it's all we can ask. I just want to be sure that I've packed everything in and done it all while I can, so I don't feel I've missed out."

Ambrose shook his head, regarding Owen and Louise with a pitying expression. "The two of you are still young, relatively speaking. Things look different when you're my age."

Owen said: "Getting back to reincarnation, Ambrose, you must admit it's odd. Nobody's ever claimed to have been a slave or a peasant in a previous lifetime. They all declare they were Catherine the Great or Napoleon."

"Good point," agreed Louise, exchanging a glance with Ambrose, who didn't seem put out that her philosophy of life differed radically from his own.

He waved his hand. "Oh, I'm not talking about the lunatic fringe. I didn't suggest for a moment that we remember it. We'd never get on with our present selves if that were true, although perhaps a very few of us can recall our former lives. But I should think the true cases are never ones you read in the newspapers. No—people who experience something so remarkable would probably keep it entirely to themselves to avoid ridicule.''

He shot a benign glance toward Dorothy at the other end of the table, but she was watching Owen and Louise, who had shared a conspiratorial look while he was speaking.

''You haven't said a word, Dorothy,'' said the canon's wife.

''I'm throwing in my lot with the believers, I'm afraid, leaving the two youngsters on their own.''

''Youngsters—listen to her,'' laughed Owen. ''Maybe when we're older and wiser we'll mend our ways and come round to their way of thinking. What do you say, Louise?'' asked Owen.

She smiled and shrugged. ''I wouldn't bet on it.''

The party broke up soon after midnight and as they all stood in the hall putting on their coats, Louise was abruptly reminded that tomorrow she would be spending the night in the grandly impersonal atmosphere of the Hotel Excelsior in Milan. She embraced Lucy, Charles, the canon and his wife, feeling as if they were old friends.

''Perhaps we'll meet again. In France—who knows?'' said Charles gruffly, kissing her on both cheeks.

''Yes, why not? You never know,'' she found herself replying. The idea had planted itself at the back of her mind, where she knew it would soon languish.

When it came to her turn to say goodbye to Owen, they shook hands formally.

''Goodbye,'' he said, relinquishing her hand. ''And do try to have a little fun on your trip to Milan and Paris.''

''Thank you. I'm sure I will.'' Though he was teasing her, the cozy rapport they had finally achieved at dinner seemed to have vanished again in the cold entrance hall.

''It's stopped snowing,'' Ambrose announced. Turning on the carriage light, he peered into the walled garden, now lightly blanketed with snow.

''I was almost hoping I'd be snowed in,'' Louise spoke her thoughts aloud.

''Maybe it will happen during the night,'' Dorothy replied, slipping her arm affectionately through Louise's.

Bundled up in their coats, the canon and his wife with Charles and Lucy picked their way down the icy path, closely followed by Owen. Dorothy called after him:

"Owen, if you're on your way back into town tomorrow, why not join us for a spot of lunch at the Bridgewater Arms before Ambrose drives Louise to Heathrow?"

"Thanks very much, but I'm afraid I can't make it. I've got a lot of paperwork to do," he called. His eyes rested on Louise, who was silhouetted in the doorway. "But it just occurs to me that I could stop by and take Louise to the airport. I'm going back to London anyway and I'd be happy to give her a lift."

"I've already made inquiries about a taxi," she said half-heartedly. At the sight of Owen against the white backdrop of the illuminated garden, she knew she wanted to see him one more time.

"Nonsense, we wouldn't hear of it, my dear," Dorothy exclaimed. "But we're delighted to take her ourselves, of course." She looked at Louise to see if she agreed.

"It would be very kind of you, if you're sure it's no trouble," she said to Owen.

They arranged the time and Owen left with a wave and a smile. At Dorothy's side, Louise watched him disappear through the garden gate and into the night.

"Well," said Dorothy with a contented sigh, "I have just a bit of clearing up to do and then we can all go to bed."

Even though it was well after midnight, her vitality had not flagged. A sudden radiance made her look astonishingly young to Louise.

Cold air had swept into the house as the guests had all vanished. She felt a sad finality as Dorothy shut the door and turned off the porch light, casting the snow-covered garden into darkness and bringing the evening to an end. Louise knew that when she crawled into bed she would probably lie awake a long time, reflecting on all she had heard and seen in the hours since she had come to Little Gaddesden. When she offered to help clear up, Dorothy smiled and shook her head. Ambrose came into the hall followed by the dogs, and she said: "I'll just put the silver away and then we'll sit in front of the fire and have a nightcap. Why don't you take a stroll down the road with Ambrose and the dogs—that is, if you're not too tired."

"I'd love a walk," said Louise. "Just let me run upstairs and fetch my coat."

Moments later the two of them were walking through the clear cold night on the road skirting the wood toward the end of the village, with the dogs at their heels. They could see the moonlit turrets and spires of the college shimmering through the thicket of bare trees.

"It looks like something out of a fairy tale," Louise whispered, her breath curling icily in the air. She scanned the blurred image of the castle sketched delicately against the wintry sky. Ambrose was whistling a quiet tune as he marched beside her, calling now and then to his dogs, who rummaged in the undergrowth. She searched for something to say that might express what the evening had meant to her, reflecting that though it was only a small island in the chaos of her life, her visit to Little Gaddesden had had a healing effect, freeing her of anxiety for just a little while. Now she could go back to building her future.

Sensing what she was feeling, Ambrose said: "I hope this little break has been a pleasant diversion for you. We've certainly enjoyed it."

"So have I, more than I can say. I hope you'll come and visit me in Atherton. I have a big house with a swimming pool. I'd love you to stay as long as you like."

"That would be delightful. Dorothy and I always wanted to visit San Francisco. We should spread our wings more, travel to far-flung places before it's too late." The tone of his voice suggested their coming to America was as improbable as her joining them in France. "We've become much too set in our ways over the years."

"Well, I suppose you have everything anyone could possibly want in life, right here in Little Gaddesden, and in France . . ."

"You seem to like this place," said Ambrose.

"Yes, I do. Very much."

When they passed the Elizabethan manor house, its spiraling chimneys visible above a high wall, Ambrose remarked: "They say there's a secret underground passage between the manor and the monastery that stood on this site in the thirteenth century."

As they returned the way they had come, he began to talk about the monks who had once inhabited the ground on which they were now walking.

"I'm almost certain the monastery was the center of Gnostic heresy and that many Cathars fleeing the Inquisition in Languedoc eventually wound up here."

"The Cathars again . . ." Louise murmured.

Ambrose paused and looked thoughtfully at her. "I was thinking about what you told me earlier about your father and the book you gave him. It's really quite extraordinary. I am glad it gave him such pleasure before he died."

"What happened to the Cathars?"

"March 16, 1244. That was a dark day for civilization. The freedom of the individual was dealt a blow from which it has never quite recovered, even now."

"1244?" Louise asked.

"The date of the fall of Montségur, when two hundred free souls were martyred at the stake by the Roman Church for their beliefs."

She sensed from his reply that the event was very real to him. "Is that anywhere near your summer house?"

"Yes, by chance it is. Cathar country," he said, delivering the words with a sonorous ring.

"I thought so. A moment ago you mentioned the Gnostic heresy. What does that mean exactly?"

"Gnosis is a direct experience of God, a personal manifestation of belief not based on faith. You can imagine what a dangerous idea that was at the time. It dispensed with the clergy as interlocutors between God and man. These people were the true Christians, in my opinion."

They paused at a tall stone cross set above an ancient water trough and read its inscription, visible in the light reflected from the Lethbridge garden:

" 'He that thirsteth after me shall not perish, but shall have eternal life.' " Ambrose added in a cheerful voice: "Don't you think the goodness of the monks still lingers here?"

Louise couldn't resist saying with a mischievous laugh: "Maybe some of them have been reincarnated on the spot."

"Yes, perhaps some of them have," Ambrose replied with a thoughtful smile.

3

When he left the party, Owen drove the last few miles to his cottage down a narrow country lane bordered by high hedges. He braked hard when a badger ambled across the road. As he saw it disappear safely beyond the range of the sharp headlights of his BMW, he was reminded of the old adage that when a badger crossed your path, which was rare, it meant good luck. He smiled ironically to himself at the suggestion, wishing it were true. No lucky charm could neutralize the trick that fate had played on him that week, he thought darkly. Not even the successful outcome of negotiations over the machinery he was buying could dissolve the bitter aftertaste of the shock he had had in Geneva. As his headlights picked out the stanchions marking the entrance to his cottage, he gunned the motor and changed gears. Coming to a halt on the graveled drive in front of the small graystone house, he got out of the car and stood for a moment taking a deep gulp of the cold air, listening to the distant hoot of an owl. The snow was already starting to melt.

He entered the cold house, half wishing he wasn't on his own tonight of all nights. Throwing his bag down in the hall, the first thing he did was to pick up the telephone and dial a number in London. When he got a recorded message of a breathy woman's voice and rock music playing in the background, he slammed the phone down irritably before the message had finished. Turning on the lights, he looked round the beamed sitting room of the cottage, which he hadn't visited for nearly a month.

The stale odor of an uninhabited house surrounded him and he impatiently flicked on the central heating to chase away the dank cold. If it hadn't been for the Lethbridges' dinner party, he wouldn't have come to the country this weekend after what he had discovered in Geneva, and now he regretted his impetuous offer to take the Lethbridges'

American house guest to the airport the following day. He didn't know what had possessed him, when all he wanted was to get back to London. His gnawing restlessness filled him with a desire to mix with people in a loud noisy bar or his club in Covent Garden. Glancing at his watch, he was almost tempted to call the Lethbridges and say he had to return to London immediately, but he told himself it was too late for that and that he had drunk too much. With a sigh of irritation, he poured himself a neat whisky, switched on the stereo and lit the fire already laid in the grate. Watching the smoke billow from the damp paper and wood shavings that refused to ignite, he slumped in a chair to think, his mind consumed with what had happened the previous day. Instead, he found his mind turning to Louise Carey. His angry mood had made him surly at dinner and he felt a twinge of guilt that he had been so sarcastic once or twice, without provocation. Ordinarily he would have gone out of his way to be charming. He had liked her looks, even though slight dark women didn't usually appeal to him. From the way she was dressed, he summed her up as a rich cosmopolitan career type. He saw that she was independent, stylish and outspoken, qualities he liked more than he would admit. But later he detected a gentleness, a shyness, that surprised him. He thought of the look of curiosity she flashed in his direction now and then. Although he was in no mood to acknowledge it, he had noticed a number of things about her, from her soft dark eyes to her small elegant hands, which gestured expressively when she talked. It surprised him that he had carried away such a strong image of her face in the candlelight, her pale skin and dark hair set off by the black embroidered suede that gave her an almost regal look. She thought she was tough, but he could see that she was on the defensive. That was explained by what Dorothy had told him: her husband had left her and her father had died, all within a few months of each other. Beneath her obvious determination to keep herself together, he sensed that she was still vulnerable. Laughing at his own sentimentality, he dismissed Louise from his mind, telling himself she was probably far tougher than he was when it came down to it.

Leaning back in his chair, Owen left the present and his mind filled with a single shining image. Closing his eyes, he could see a chalice of beaten gold, a pure and satisfying shape that suggested a stream of liquid metal arrested in mid air. The memory of it had shone like a beacon in his mind for nearly seventeen years. He turned the image over in his mind, conjuring up the smooth cool touch of its surface as he admired its simplicity, its purity of design. How often he had wondered where it had come from, imagining the craftsman who had made it so lovingly, as he pondered on its history through the ages. It was without doubt the most remarkable thing he had ever owned. He had never lusted so passionately after any material possession before or since, and his heart still contracted with grief when he thought how he had come to lose it.

In his mind he retraced the chain of events on the day it disappeared. Hatred filled him, ending in a hardened vow of vengeance. There was now no doubt in his mind that he had been betrayed by Rex Monckton, a man he had thought was his friend. At this moment the lines were being drawn for battle, even though Rex wasn't aware of it. He had always been so smooth, so confident, so sure of himself, but if thoughts could travel, no doubt Rex was suffering an uncomfortable moment at his elegant home in Belgravia. Emptying his glass, Owen got up and dialed Mandy's number again, slamming down the receiver when he heard her inane message once more. He poured himself another whisky and tried to revive the fire. He knew he wouldn't sleep that night. Lapsing into a reflective mood, his mind returned to the summer of 1971, when it all began.

It was a sultry day at the end of August when he and Mandy drove out of St. Tropez in the white Triumph, part of the spoils that were left after he had squandered most of his royalties from "Moody Lady." She was sitting next to him in a white miniskirt and a tight T-shirt she had bought for a fortune at the last moment just to spite him. He glanced at her hair blowing wildly in the wind, her face obscured by big white-framed sunglasses. He could tell by the set of her mouth that she was still angry. In all the time they had been married they had never had such a violent argument as the night before, following a farewell party in the nightclub where his band, White Heat, had been playing a gig for the entire month

of August. Mandy had had far too much to drink and so had
he. When they went up to their room above the club, the
floor strewn with clothes and every surface crowded with her
makeup and accessories, she had screamed at him and thrown
a bottle of perfume, shattering the mirror, for which he had
had to pay that morning before checking out. It pained Owen
that they were facing the long trip home to England with so
many recriminations smoldering between them. But, knowing how stubborn Mandy could be, he decided to swallow
his pride.

"You still mad?" he ventured, changing into low gear as
they took a steep bend. He reached out and rested his hand
on her knee. In spite of everything, he still thought she was
one of the prettiest girls he had ever seen, with her streaming
blonde hair, her lean, tanned body, her cornflower blue eyes,
which gave his heart a jolt whenever she looked at him.

"I still don't see why," she said petulantly.

"It's only one night, or two at the most. And then we'll
head for Paris."

She gave a peal of bitter laughter. "We take these big
detours to the middle of nowhere and then we can't afford to
drive down to Marbella—even for a few days. That's all I'm
asking."

"We've been through all that. We agreed to compromise
by going to Paris." His voice was sharper than he intended,
but as he glanced at her beside him, he was tormented by
the memory of a titled Englishman whom she had met on the
quay while he was sleeping off the effects of playing in the
smoky club until four in the morning. He knew she hadn't
been to bed with him, but he had seen them dancing close
all evening and heard afterward that the Englishman had
begged Mandy to run away with him—to Marbella. When
the atmosphere was better, Owen thought he would let her
know how glad he was that her head hadn't been turned by
the moneyed playboys who were always after her. He reasoned that her discontent was only natural. After all, she
could have had her pick of any number of men and she had
married him when he was a penniless musician.

After his first big hit with "Moody Lady" two years before, they both assumed other hits would follow and that they
were on their way to fame and fortune. The first thing they

did was to buy the Triumph and move out of two rented rooms in Earls Court to a fashionable little mews house in South Kensington, which Owen bought for cash. They had acquired a taste for high living right away and began to move with a fast crowd of pop musicians, entrepreneurs and designers who frequented flashy clubs and expensive restaurants, where Owen took his turn picking up the tab. Whenever the spirit moved them, they took off for weekends in the south of France or the Caribbean. During the last year and a half, however, his income from royalties had dried up. With a shock he realized they had gone through a small fortune and that there was far too little coming in to support the kind of life they were living. That summer he had had to face the truth: the band was going nowhere. Gigs like the one at St. Tropez in a second-rate club were all they could get at the moment, and they had nothing at all lined up for the autumn in London. Sometime soon Owen knew he was going to have to find the courage to tell Mandy that he and the other members of the band had been talking about breaking up and that they were back to where they started, with nothing in the bank.

"Look at the Med behind us," he said cheerfully. "Isn't that a spectacular sight?"

When she turned to look with indifference at the sweep of the russet hills falling toward the turquoise water, he could tell by the look on her face that everything would be all right. Reaching out, he began to stroke the back of her neck.

"You bastard," she said with a laugh, arching her back with pleasure at his touch.

He sighed. She was complicated, she was difficult, but she moved him in a way no other woman ever had.

" 'Lady of my heart, just lie close to me,' " he sang under his breath, quoting the lyrics of the composition he had written just for her. He had never been able to climb the heights with any other song, and privately he called himself a one-hit wonder. Ashamed of his feeble superstition, he had made no attempt to explain the impulse that had brought him on this detour to Languedoc. He had thought about it all summer, knowing how close they would be to the region, and now it was irresistible to him to pay a visit, if only fleetingly, to the land of his first muse, the land of the troubadours.

Their poetry was like a breath of life, which he had discovered at Oxford before he dropped out to become a full-time musician. He harbored a ridiculous notion, which he could express to no one, that in Languedoc he might rediscover the source of the inspiration that had eluded him since "Moody Lady." It was like the pilgrimage of a sick man who sought a healing miracle. He wished he could share his cringing fear, his weakness, with Mandy, but in her appealing child-like way she expected him to be strong and confident, and he had no intention of letting her down. Remembering what he had put her through since their marriage, he feared that if he exposed his lack of direction he might lose her entirely. It was almost better to argue with her than to try to make her understand what was going on inside his head.

As they reached the motorway, leaving the ochre landscape shadowed with umbrella pines, Owen tried to concentrate on the present. When he considered it calmly and reasonably, he realized how lucky he was. Here they were, the two of them, with everything that mattered still intact. Though they didn't have a lot of money at the moment, they had each other, and all of France lay between them and the realities they would have to face when they returned to England. That was enough for him, he thought, pressing down on the accelerator. Mandy, tired from the night before, slept most of the way, her face obscured by a straw hat attached to a scarf secured under her chin. Every now and then Owen glanced toward her, pleased she was sleeping so peacefully. He was happy to be alone with his thoughts as they crossed the empty landscape of low, dark hills shorn by the wind west of Béziers, a sprawling modern town whose ancient medieval center he would have liked to visit. The deeper he traveled into this mysterious country, the more it intrigued him. The slanting sun shone down on crumbling ruins on distant hilltops and carved rich, deep shadows round clumps of trees that had stoutly resisted the wind. He fantasized how a crusader, a troubadour or knight might have felt when returning to such a land, where his lady awaited him. The rolling country opened up to vineyards and distant villages as he played with a tune in his head, trying to graft it to a favorite poem he had written at Oxford.

He left the main road before Carcassonne and took one of

the lesser roads to the south. He didn't wake Mandy, telling himself she needed the sleep; but he knew he had the selfish urge to follow his own impulse without compromise. He wanted to nurture the illusion that he was as free as a troubadour and could wander where he pleased.

When he stopped the car at a village to pick up sandwiches and buy something to drink, Mandy woke up. The undulating green country where they found themselves was like a gentle surf that heralded the Pyrenees, towering like great blue breakers in the distance, their jagged peaks sheathed in snow. Looking at the map, he decided to drive on until they found a village where they wanted to spend the night. The rugged country, under the dry spell of summer's end, changed remarkably with every mile. He looked at the signposts, feeling his instinct would tell him when to stop. Aware that Mandy might become bad-tempered at any moment, he forged on, not knowing quite what he was looking for.

On impulse he took a sharp turn onto a narrow, badly paved road leading to a village on a distant hill, which looked as if it commanded a beautiful view of a valley. At the sight of the crumbling fortress dominating its ramparts, Owen felt a quickening curiosity.

As they approached, Mandy said doubtfully, "Are we going to stop here for the night? There won't be any hotel in a village as small as this."

"You never know, there might be," he replied mildly. Instinct told him that this was just the sort of place where he wanted to stop, in the heart of troubadour country. He had an irresistible craving to walk on the distant ramparts, now golden in the late sun, and contemplate life.

The first thing they saw when they drove beneath the arch of the fortified village was an enchanting hotel built into the wall, with faded blue shutters and geraniums in pots soaking up the late afternoon sun. An old man perched on a metal chair and wearing a Basque beret looked up from his Pernod as they came to a halt in front of the Hôtel des Troubadours.

"See, I told you, I just had a feeling we'd find something like this." Taking his camera from under the seat, he aimed it at her.

"Okay, I admit it. You were right and I was wrong," she

said with a sweet smile, tossing her head coquettishly as Owen snapped the shutter repeatedly.

"Dorothy and Ambrose Lethbridge have a summer house in this region somewhere," he said. He had hardly seen them since he married Mandy, mainly because she felt uncomfortable in their company. Seeing the roll of film was nearly finished, Owen took shots of the ramparts and the square at different angles.

They entered the rose-tiled hall of the hotel and presented themselves at the reception desk as a stout, dark little woman bustled in, wiping her hands on an apron.

"Est-ce-que vous avez une chambre avec salle de bain pour la nuit, madame?"

"Oui, monsieur," she said cheerfully. *"J'ai une très belle chambre au premier étage, avec une vue splendide qui donne sur les remparts."*

"D'accord," said Owen, feeling a strange elation. When she told him how much it was, he smiled at Mandy, thinking of St. Tropez's inflated prices.

The *patronne* asked: *"Vous dînez à l'hôtel, monsieur, 'dame?"*

"Oui, certainement," he responded, his appetite aroused by the smell of garlic and onions simmering somewhere beyond the doors of the dining room.

They climbed the narrow wooden staircase behind the *patronne,* who led them to their room. Flinging open the windows and shutters of the spotlessly clean, simple room with a big wooden bed and crudely carved *armoire,* she said proudly, *"Voilà!"*

Owen went to the window and stared at the hills rising in tiers of purple and mauve beneath the dome of blue sky broken by pink clouds drifting across the horizon, enchanted by what he saw.

"Let's take a walk," he suggested the minute the *patronne* had left the room.

"Not me," said Mandy with a yawn. "You go ahead. I'm dying for a hot bath."

Relieved she didn't want to come with him, he kissed her cheek. "See you later."

Bounding down the stairs, he stopped when he saw the *patronne* at the desk.

"How old is the village, *madame?*"

"Oh, *monsieur,* parts of it, including the ramparts, are very old. Twelfth century, eleventh even," she replied congenially.

He left the hotel and climbed the weathered stone steps to the ramparts, where he turned toward the ruined keep. He felt like a lone eagle in its eyrie as he looked out at the palette of pure violet that stretched toward the great barrier of the Pyrenees, that cast a deep channel of shadow onto the lowlands. He drank thirstily of the pure air rising from the sunwarmed walls, which smelled of herbs and ancient stone. As he listened to the cries of swifts and the distant ring of a church bell across the valley, Owen steeped himself in the atmosphere that had accumulated layer upon layer over the centuries. The names of poets came back to him: Peire Rogier, Arnaut Daniel, Guilhem de Cabestaing. He wondered if they had stood at that same spot as they composed their love poems. For a fleeting moment the view from the village seemed more familiar to him than any place he had known. He envied the people who lived there, who worked the land and practiced trades that rooted them to the same changeless spot as their ancestors. He hated to leave, but before turning away he vowed he would keep the beauty of that day intact and he made a promise to himself that he would come again some day when he didn't have to hurry.

He left the ramparts and wandered back to the hotel along a narrow cobbled street dotted with a few shops among the houses. Seeing a faded *Brocante* sign above a shop whose windows were cloudy with dust, he opened the door. Mandy loved bric-à-brac and some small thing would please her. As the bell rang, he entered the dimly lit shop crammed with dusty, broken objects. Seeing no one, he decided to browse. He picked up a candlestick that had obviously come from a church. He noticed other religious articles among the bric-à-brac, including some dark pictures of saints and martyrs. There were rustling bird cages, glass paperweights and open drawers spilling over with dingy lace and old gloves. Hearing the shuffling of feet, Owen turned to see a small, bent man with wispy dark hair, who was staring fixedly at him with dark eyes set under shaggy brows. The intensity of his stare gave Owen a start and he wondered for a moment if he was suspected of trying to steal something.

"Bonsoir, monsieur," he said with a friendly nod. "I was just passing and I saw the door open, so I came in."

Still the man said nothing, but shuffled round the counter as if to get a better look at him. Feeling the man's eyes on his back, Owen continued to look round, aware that people in isolated villages could be very suspicious of strangers.

"Combien est l'encrier?" he asked, picking up a pretty china inkstand he thought would please Mandy.

"Ten francs. But it's damaged," the proprietor added, as if to discourage him.

"Ah, so it is," said Owen. "But that doesn't matter. It's only a chip." When the man regarded him mutely, he smiled and shrugged. "I'll just look round. I might find something else."

He began to browse again, determined not to be driven away by the man's scrutiny. He didn't seem particularly interested in selling anything and he was still staring at Owen intently. Owen could feel the back of his neck prickle as if his hair was standing on end. Straightening his shoulders, he wheeled round and looked the old man squarely in the eyes as he picked up a painted box, the first thing to hand. As nonchalantly as he could, he strolled to the counter. "How much is this?"

"Oh, that. That's just a piece of rubbish. Five francs, if you wish."

Putting the money on the counter, Owen met the man's unflinching gaze, suddenly aware that a crosscurrent of mutual curiosity was moving between them. He noticed the man's hand shake as he picked up the money and stuffed it in his pocket. He saw that his frayed navy coat was spotted and worn, and that there was something very old fashioned about his yellowed, stiff collar. He had a hawk-like nose, a sallow, lined face and a thin but sensitive mouth, and he wore small, thick glasses. It was the face of an ascetic, a refugee from a monastery or the survivor of a holocaust. His small fierce eyes seemed much younger than the man himself and they shone torch-like from the shadowy depths of his face. Owen realized with a shock that the man couldn't be more than fifty, that he was the victim of premature aging that could only have been caused by some unspeakable tragedy. He wished he had the courage to begin a conversation, but his French was inadequate to the task and the man's peculiar manner didn't invite questions. He was taken by surprise when the man said in a harsh voice, with an accent not of the region:

"*Monsieur,* perhaps you might be interested in something of value. Something rare—even unique." Without giving Owen a chance to speak, he motioned to him to step behind the counter. The tone of his voice implied that he was about to divulge some sort of secret or mystery. This intrigued Owen, but he had the presence of mind to wonder whether he was being conned. When he moved behind the counter, the man darted to the front door of the shop and locked it. Owen felt his heart pound and his mouth go dry. He wondered for a second if the man was a maniac, but followed him to an office behind the shop, which contained a table, a chair and a safe. Owen was somewhat reassured to see a calico cat curled up on a velvet cushion in the corner.

He watched with interest as the man retrieved a key that he wore suspended round his waist and opened the ancient safe, his breath coming in anxious gasps. As he withdrew a dirty linen bag and began to unknot the string, Owen noticed the man had strong, beautiful hands that could have belonged to a musician, hands not unlike his own, powerful but sensitive. He was staring at these hands when the man carefully drew forth a golden chalice, which glimmered in the twilight. A twisted smile of pride lit up his somber face.

"What is this? Where did you get it?" Owen murmured. He stared at the chalice. The man said nothing for a moment, but held the cup before his eyes as if trying to tempt him, and in those seconds Owen knew he was lost. Whatever it might cost, he knew he must have this exquisite cup, the design of which was of an austere magnificence rivaling anything he had ever seen. When he reached out to touch it, almost doubting it was real, the man moved it from his reach as though he wanted to guard its purity.

"It is very, very old. Of antiquity. And it is priceless," he breathed, telling Owen what he already guessed.

"How much?" he asked bluntly, before the man could see

in his eyes his lust to possess this treasure. It occurred to him that the chalice could be stolen.

"It's pure gold," said the man. His voice was anxious.

"Perhaps. There's no way of proving that now. How much?" By now his mind was racing ahead. He was fighting with his conscience, and common sense dictated he should not buy the chalice no matter what the price.

When the man blurted out a figure Owen could only stare at him. It was many times less than he expected. Less than the money he planned to spend in Paris. It was nothing.

"D'accord," he heard himself whisper.

The man nodded and hastily wrapped the cup back into the cloth bag, registering no surprise at all. Owen felt his head pounding with apprehension as he pulled out his wallet, but the moment he felt the weight of the chalice in his hand he experienced a quickening pleasure unlike anything he had ever known. An almost childish feeling of delight traveled down his spine and to the back of his knees. He noticed that the man had taken the wad of notes from him without counting them. He merely stuffed them into his pocket as if he were suddenly in a desperate hurry. Returning to the safe, he paused, then dipped his hand into another bag, which Owen could hear was filled with coins. He counted out five small pieces of money cast in some sort of silver alloy, stamped with a head and a crest that meant nothing to Owen.

"How much?" Owen asked. Communication between them had been reduced to the minimum.

"Take them all for fifty francs."

Owen was about to smile in gratitude, but the man's solemnity prevented him. He seemed to be giving him the coins as a bonus, but something stopped Owen. To take them for so little seemed like theft. "No, I don't want them." His voice was cool, defensive.

Seeing Owen staring curiously at the blurred heads stamped on the coins, the man said simply: *"Raimon septième."*

Owen nodded as if he understood, but the name was unknown to him. Now he sensed that all this peculiar little man wanted was for him to leave the shop. He followed him to the door and as soon as he had stepped across the threshold, he heard it slam behind him and the key turn in the lock. He saw the blind come down, with *Fermé* scrawled across it.

Realizing he had left the box he had bought for Mandy in the shop, Owen raised his hand to knock when his attention was caught by the sight of a teenage boy lurking in the shadows near a parked bicycle. Thrusting his hands into his pockets, the boy hung his head and moved away the moment Owen saw him. He looked shifty and unsure of himself, and something about his behavior told Owen he was up to no good. It crossed his mind that he ought to return to the shop to warn the antique dealer that a suspicious-looking person was loitering nearby, but he reminded himself where he was. This was an uncorrupted little corner of the French countryside, not some rough part of London. He told himself the boy was probably the man's own son and was waiting for his father to close the shop.

By now Owen couldn't bring himself to disturb the man again and he walked down the narrow street muttering the proverb about never looking a gift horse in the mouth, still unable to believe his good fortune. He now wished he had taken the coins, but it was too late. But the words *Raimon septième* stuck in his mind.

Still, when he reached the village square, as a few late rays of sun chased the cool shadows, he was glad the transaction was over. Not allowing himself to think too deeply about what he had done, he went to the car parked nearby and opened the trunk. Taking out a suitcase he stuffed the chalice in at the bottom, wondering how he was going to break the news to Mandy that he had just spent most of the money he had set aside for their trip to Paris. He was uncomfortably aware that he could offer no logical explanation for what he had done and braced himself for the delicate task of telling her that the detour to Paris would now be out of the question. Somehow he would make it up to her, even though she was bound to be furious at first. He would have to make a lot of promises he hoped he could keep, and he could only pray that she would understand the strong impulse that had governed him. He felt a kind of elation welling up inside, which counteracted his apprehension. He wasn't the impulsive type as a rule. He wasn't a collector, either, nor was he a bargain hunter. It was more subtle than that, Owen thought, entering the hotel, thinking of his friend the art dealer, Rex Monckton. How often had he heard him voluptuously describe a thing of beauty that had aroused his lust for possession, like a lover speaking of the object of his desire.

Feeling cold and tired, Owen came back to the present, and saw that the fire had died in the grate. He got up from his chair to try Mandy again. Hearing her sleepy voice on the line, he glanced at his watch and realized he had been lost in thought for nearly half an hour.

"Mandy? It's Owen. I've been trying to get hold of you all night." He had a depressing image of her lying in bed, half dressed and with her makeup still on, having come home from a party so stoned she could hardly speak. He guessed she had been out with the pack of pop musicians' ex-wives who were her friends, aging chicks of the swinging Sixties who found refuge in each other's company.

"Can't you call back in the morning, Owen? It's the middle of the night," she replied, her slurred voice full of irritation.

"Listen, I've got to see you tomorrow. Have supper with me when I get back to London, will you? I'll come by about seven."

After a pause she said: "Call me tomorrow. I don't know if I can make it."

The wariness in her voice told him she was afraid he wanted to talk about money.

"If you're busy, please cancel it. I need to see you."

In the bedroom of the house in Little Gaddesden, Ambrose was pulling on his pajamas. The curtains had been drawn across the bay window, where Dorothy sat at her dressing table in a blue dressing gown. After patting on some night cream, she picked up a silver-backed brush and began brushing her hair thoughtfully.

"I think it went very well tonight, don't you, my dearest?" said Ambrose, arranging the eiderdown on the double bed. From the corner of his eye he watched her reflection in the mirror, wondering if she would want to talk before they turned in for the night. The expression on her face told him she was looking into the far distance and had become oblivious of her surroundings, but he went on talking as if nothing had happened.

"Dinner was a triumph. My compliments. The meringues were light as clouds and the meat was remarkably tender. It is worth driving all the way to Mr. Litton in Berkhamsted, you're quite right." When she murmured in reply, he went on:

"Louise seemed to enjoy herself, didn't she? I wondered about the wisdom of throwing her in with a lot of strangers at first, but she seemed to take to us all like a duck to water. I hope she sleeps well tonight since she's got a hectic week ahead. What a lot of stamina she seems to have. An exciting business, but how difficult it must be for her. The poor girl is on her own in the world now."

Laying down the brush, Dorothy said quietly:

"I think she's far more disturbed in her mind than she let us know. If only she had more time here, to unwind, to unburden herself. If only . . ." she said, her voice breaking off into a whisper.

"You'd better come to bed, my love," said Ambrose gently. Propped up against the pillows, he tactfully searched for the right words to tap the images he sensed were swirling in Dorothy's mind. He hadn't seen her so disturbed for years and neither of them would be able to sleep that night until she had unburdened herself. Her quick gestures told him he must exercise patience and even feign indifference to what was going on. From the habit of years he knew how best to perform the role of confidant, helping to channel his wife's remarkable powers. He knew how the visions churned in her mind at a frantic rate until they slowed down of their own accord. Only then could she begin to make sense of them.

"I didn't think Owen was himself tonight," he ventured. "I've never seen him so distracted. Do you suppose his business is going badly?"

"No, no, I don't think it's that." She shook her head. "I'll call him during the week and ask."

"Ah, I see." He relaxed a little, wondering if he had been imagining things and that Dorothy was merely preoccupied with Owen.

"I hope Mandy's not on drugs again. She's very lucky that he's stood by her all these years. I do admire him. He never complains." Hearing Dorothy sigh as she stood before the bookcase, he said: "Come to bed, dearest. Your cocoa is getting cold."

"Yes, dear, I know," she said gently. She went to the bookshelf and withdrew her first published novel, *The Dark Citadel,* which Ambrose recognized from a distance by the blood-red cover imprinted with the Cathar emblem of a dove. Slipping into bed, she put on her reading glasses, then met his eyes with a tender look of apology for trying his patience. "May I read to you for a moment?"

"I wish you would." Opening the book, Dorothy said wistfully: "You know what's triggered it all off, don't you? It was when Owen arrived this evening." When she glanced at Ambrose, her eyes filled with tears and he reached out and gave her hand a squeeze of encouragement.

"Did it start with a headache?"

"Yes, it was just the same as usual, only this time it happened quite suddenly, moments before Owen came to the door. As I was in the kitchen I saw a band of purple and blue spread upward for just a second, then the doorbell rang. I went to answer it feeling quite apprehensive."

"You certainly didn't show it."

"Then, mercifully, no one noticed. It went away as quickly, as violently as it came, the moment Owen swept through the door and Louise came downstairs."

It was on the tip of Ambrose's tongue to ask what it all meant, but Dorothy's thoughts were already far away. Her glasses resting on her nose, she began to read from her novel in a low voice full of feeling. She slipped automatically into character as she recited a passage from the story of Hugo de Franjal and Sancha Domerq, two star-crossed lovers whose history reach back seven and a half centuries. Ambrose listened spellbound, even though he knew it by heart. But he knew that it was history, not fiction.

His wife's remarkable powers had always fascinated him, but months, years could pass when their lives were uninterrupted by her voyages in time. As always, he suppressed a spasm of primeval fear that he compared to the brute emotions of a prehistoric man confronted with the awesome and mysterious power of something he did not understand, such as an eclipse or an earthquake. Listening to Dorothy, he became a helpless bystander who could only wonder whether the events that had unfolded over the last thirty years were part of a greater design that they had yet to discover.

When Dorothy stopped reading a while later, the book slipped from her hand. Ambrose saw she was asleep, her chin propped forward. Gently removing her glasses and the book, he set them on the nightstand, then tucked the eiderdown around her. By her breathing, Ambrose knew that Dorothy was sleeping the dense, dark sleep of mental exhaustion brought about by the gift of far memory.

Turning out the light, he himself lay awake for some time, half listening to the wind that had risen again. He found his thoughts traveling back to the strange beginnings of Dorothy's career in the early Fifties.

They had met during the war and had married after VE Day, having their two children almost right away. During their first holiday abroad, in 1953, they drove down to the south of France, leaving the children with Dorothy's parents. It was their first holiday alone and they were both full of high spirits at being back in the country they loved, where they intended to visit sites of historic interest to both of them, as well as to have a reunion with Maurice Roussel, who had been urging them to come to Languedoc. One of their stops was Montségur, an ancient eyrie of ruined stone atop a precipice in the Pyrenees, where Christian dissenters known as Cathars were martyred by the Roman Church in 1244.

When they returned to England, Dorothy began to suffer the same dizziness, headaches and nightmares she had experienced after a bout of diphtheria when she was twelve. The doctor could find nothing physically wrong with her and when she was referred to a psychiatrist, she had confessed that since girlhood she had suffered from the distressing illusion that she had lived in another life, a bizarre secret she had confided to no one, including Ambrose. The psychiatrist reassured her she wasn't insane, but he couldn't explain the phenomenon, nor could he assure her that it would soon pass. Gathering her courage, she confided in Ambrose. He would never forget the sunny autumn afternoon when she told him about it as they had tea under a tree weighed down with apples. She was hemming a skirt and spoke in a matter-of-fact voice, looking up every now and then. In compelling detail she recounted her former existence as a noblewoman in the Languedoc caught up in the Cathar heresy during the middle of the thirteenth century. Mother of a family and wife of a landed squire, her domain had become a refuge for Cathar believers who were fleeing persecution by the Roman Church. Dorothy had recounted to him vivid memories of her favorite son, Hugo, who had fallen in love with a young woman she had taken under her protection. When Ambrose heard the story of Hugo and Sancha, he was inspired to suggest that Dorothy translate her strange revelations into a novel as a form of therapy. Neither of them could have foreseen that the story of her own past life would mark the beginnings of her successful career as a historical novelist. *The Dark Citadel* was immediately accepted for publication and when it appeared, Dorothy Lethbridge was hailed by the critics and the public as a master of the genre.

During the last thirty years she had published over twenty novels and mysteries, vividly bringing to life an obscure period of history. All these years they had kept the source of her inspiration a secret, even from their children, thinking that Dorothy's inexplicable experience had ended there. But during the intervening years people came into her orbit whom she recognized from her former life. The first time it had happened was with Owen Morgan, when he was a boy of fourteen. Dorothy had met him at the house of a friend, and Ambrose would never forget the look of shocked recognition on her face when he walked through the door. Afterwards she confessed that she recognized Owen as Hugo de Franjal, who had been her son seven and a half centuries ago.

When Louise woke in the middle of the night, it took her a moment to realize that the whispers that had roused her from sleep were really only the wind. Stretching her legs, she found the cool reaches of the bed beyond the hot water bottle that Dorothy had placed between the sheets before she went to bed. Through half-closed eyes she saw the last dying embers in the fireplace. She listened for the voices again, but they didn't return. As she tried to sleep, the faces of the guests at dinner danced in her head and snatches of the conversation came back to her. Her mind spun, then cleared, casting up the image of Owen Morgan across the table as he raised his glass to her. Her heart pounded dully as she tossed to and fro, trying to get him out of her mind, but his image stayed in her head.

She remembered the moment he entered the door, his coat and dark hair dusted with snow. Now that she was alone in the dead of night, she admitted to herself how disturbing that first impression was. A fleeting moment of recognition had passed between them, which she interpreted as a compulsion to get to know one another. The feeling was as strong as it was unexpected, yet it had happened so fast, like a flash of light seen from a corner of the eye.

Just as she was drifting back to sleep the lyrics of "Moody Lady" came back to her. She whispered them to herself, like a lullaby:

> *As we lie intertwined*
> *Time takes flight*
> *The fusing of our stars*
> *Creates the morning light.*
>
> *Flying with the wind*
> *We'll never know*
> *The seasons of the earth*
> *That make the changes flow.*
>
> *Don't cry for all you've lost*
> *Then paint a memory*
> *Lady of my heart*
> *Just lie close to me.*

4

A small brown bird fluttered nervously in the bare branches, its drab wings outlined against the white winter sky. Straddling the branch of a tree only inches away was a twelve-year-old girl dressed in rags. Her cold hands were shaking from hunger as they wielded a snare of woven hemp tied to two small stones. Her eyes glazed with concentration, she stared at the bird, which moved on to another branch. The girl screwed up her pinched little face and squinted at her quarry, already tasting the scrawny carcass once she had cooked it over a fire. Her stomach tight with hunger, she lost concentration for a moment and blinked. At the movement of her eyelashes the bird took flight. She gasped and tears sprang to her eyes as she watched the bird disappear, swooping upwards beyond the rocky hills and out of sight. She scanned the bleak horizon for a moment, unable to believe that she had failed again. The whole morning, she had sat in the tree, her legs and feet numb with cold, as she waited to snare an unsuspecting bird. Her narrow shoulders aching from fatigue, she slipped from the tree onto the jagged rocks below, disregarding the pain.

For a moment she scanned the wintry hills that rose to the Pyrenees, enveloped in boiling clouds. The first snows that had fallen in the night, lightly blanketing the stony ground, presaged an early winter, which would send hares deep into their lairs and the squirrels into the trees where she couldn't find them. That morning when she had awakened in the shepherd's hut nearby, she knew by the harsh white light filtering through the cracks in the stone that winter had already come. Now she picked up her walking stick and made her way down the rocky slope toward the hut. The clouds parted for a moment and she was blinded by a glimpse of the majestic white peaks against a field of blue. She stared at the awesome sight until the clouds had shrouded it once again.

As she descended the hill, her ears were alert to the smallest sound. There was the whisper of a distant rock slide, but all else was quiet. She paused at a mound of stones. Before her mother had died, Sancha had promised that she would follow a pilgrim or a merchant across the high meadows of the mountains and into Aragon or Catalonia, where she would be safe. Her eyes burning in a feverish face, her mother had spoken through parched black lips, entreating her daughter to leave her to die alone; but Sancha had refused. When her mother died, the girl had dragged her body from the hut and covered it with these stones. Still she couldn't bear to leave her. She kept telling herself she would depart the following

day, and the next, when the shepherds began to take their
flocks to the pastures lower in the valley.

And now it was too late. She was too frightened to return
to where she had come from, and the frozen passes of the
mountains barred her escape in the other direction. Her only
hope of survival would be to steal bread at the nearest village,
several miles down the valley. So far she had resisted the
temptation, frightened by the specter of being flayed alive or
drawn and quartered. They would gouge out her eyes and cut
off her hands if she were caught. But the memory of roasted
meat or a piece of freshly baked loaf tormented her, urging
her to steal before she lost her strength. As each morning
passed, she knew she had died a little more.

Coming to the low hut made of stones, she sank into a
lifeless heap at the entrance, her senses dimmed like a candle
sputtering to its end. Turning her back to the cold wind, she
coiled herself into a ball, muttering a prayer to the Madonna.
The world went black for a moment and when she came to
her senses, she saw a bird fly toward the tree. She brushed
her hair from her eyes and took the snare from her belt, ready
to try again.

She had just risen to her feet when the distant clatter of
hooves and the echo of voices paralyzed her with terror. She
stood motionless, listening to the approach of horsemen coming down the mountain path, calculating that if she ran across
the open ground now she would be seen. It seemed far less
risky to crouch at the back of the hut, hoping the travelers
would pass by without stopping. She waited as the sounds of
jangling bridles and neighing horses grew nearer, punctuated
by men's deep voices cursing the snow and ice that had made
the path so treacherous. She saw three men on horseback,
followed by six heavily laden mules tied together, approaching the hut. The man at the fore was obviously the leader and
probably a noble, from his appearance. Large and imposing,
he wore a fur-lined cloak and brocade hat. His shining leather
boots rested in silver stirrups, which glinted from a distance,
a symbol of wealth, but his jet black beard and bushy eyebrows struck terror in her. She saw him wince in pain and
clutch his leg as his horse stumbled and she wondered then
if the men were brigands who were smuggling stolen goods.
Hearing them speak Provençal, not Catalan, the girl knew

they were from Languedoc. She was preparing to bolt when she heard one say:

"What about resting here, near this shepherd's hut, seigneur?"

"No, we will go on," came the reply.

"But, sire, you must rest your leg. That wound is festering and you have a fever."

"No," he bellowed. "Carry on, and let's not stop in this bleak, windy place. It's another two days' journey to Quillan yet."

Flattening herself against the wall, the girl thought about what would happen to her if she were discovered. Her own mother had survived the great massacre of Béziers when she was ten years old, watching in terror as Crusaders from the north raped women and girls, then ripped them open with swords. Thirty thousand mutilated bodies bled into the gutters of the city that day and her mother nearly died of starvation and thirst before she escaped. From her mother, the girl had inherited the gift of healing the sick, using the same ancient arts as the Cathar heretics, themselves renowned healers who used not only prayers, but medicine too. The Church had branded all of them as devils. Despised, but sought after in secret, the healer and her daughter led a displaced, meager existence. The girl had been fathered by an abbot who, after raping her mother, had absolved himself of sin by branding her as a witch. He would have turned her over to the Inquisition had she not fled Perpignan. Closing her eyes the girl saw blood: the same fate, or worse, awaited her if she were caught by the men now dismounting from their horses.

"There must be someone living here, probably a shepherd," said one of the men, peering into the hut. "And the fire is still not cold."

"Where is he? Where are his sheep? All the shepherds have left for lower pastures. No, this is some kind of fugitives' den. Perhaps Cathars are hiding here."

One gave a laugh. "Perhaps a couple of Cathar women."

Realizing the men intended to stay, she sprinted as fast as she could up the slope.

"Who goes there? Stop, come back," one of them cried

when she darted away from the hut. "It must be a boy gone to warn the other thieves who are hiding out there."

"Catch him, catch him before he can tell anyone we're here," ordered the leader.

As the girl struggled up the hill pursued by the men, the sound of their heavy breathing and thundering boots bore down on her and she knew she was too weak to go much further. The wind was driven out of her as they knocked her to the ground.

"He must be half dead," said one of the men. "He hasn't the strength to struggle much. Where are the rest of you? Don't try to lie, you filthy little bugger. We know they're hiding somewhere . . ." They carried her down the hill and dumped her by the hut.

She spat angrily at the brawny man who held her in his grip. He had a filthy, bristling beard and he leered at her, exposing a row of rotten teeth. Flailing her arms against his leather jerkin, she tried to wriggle free.

"He's as wild as a stoat," the bearded one growled, jerking her painfully. "Hey, just one moment," he muttered, narrowing his eyes. Thrusting his hands inside her bodice he pulled it down, exposing her thin body to the groin. She regarded him with leaden eyes, awaiting the worst, while the other two men looked on.

"What have we here? Not male at all, but a girl," he called over his shoulder. "And I'll warrant she's a virgin, as she's not more than twelve by the size of those ripe little apples on her chest. A bit of fat and she'd be juicy for plucking. Still, can't be too choosy in the mountains." He and his companion guffawed loudly, but not their leader, whom she could no longer see.

The girl stood, head bowed, eyes closed, trembling with fear and cold as she waited for the two brutes to violate her body. She flinched with shock as something heavy and indescribably soft brushed her bare skin. Startled, she opened her eyes to wine-colored darkness as the bearded noble enfolded her in his fur-lined cloak.

"Leave this child alone. What are you anyway, savages? A few days in the mountains and you turn into animals. N go and make the fire, Boniface," he said, limping

"And you, Pons, give this child some bread. Can't you see she's starving?"

At his commands the men slunk away to obey. A flush of anger brought color back to his cheeks as he leaned against the hut. He was regarding her with black eyes full of bewildering compassion. She had never been the object of pity before, or of kindness. His high-bridged nose and prominent cheekbones gave him the look of a Spanish prince. He radiated a wisdom and goodness she had never encountered in anyone, making her wish she could trust him.

"Now, what's your name, child? Tell me how you came to be here. Are you lost?" When she didn't reply, he said gently:

"Never mind. You must eat first, little one. Pons, what's keeping you?" he called impatiently, taking a few steps that made him gasp in pain. The girl's attention was fastened on the servant who was hurrying toward them, an enormous loaf of bread under his arm. With his knife he sliced off a chunk and handed it to her.

She grabbed it, the cloak falling from her shoulders. Not caring that she was naked, she crushed the bread to her nose and smelled it, reveling in the yeasty aroma. She tore greedily into the gray, soft dough and stuffed a piece almost too large to swallow into her mouth. It was the most delicious thing she had ever tasted and tears rolled down her cheeks as she chewed, coughing as she swallowed.

"Now don't eat too quickly or too much," warned the man, who was resting his leg on a saddlebag as the servant knelt to remove his boot. "Boniface, bring her some water or she'll die of choking."

When the servant came with a cup, Sancha pulled away, clutching her bread in case he took it back.

Boniface gave her a derisory glance. "And how about a word of thanks, you little beast, instead of a scowl. You should be grateful to the man who has been kind to you. He is Baruch de Castronovo, the rich Jewish merchant from ⟨...⟩ s known for his generosity and wealth from ⟨...⟩astile to Toulouse." But the girl had hardly ⟨...⟩ile flattery. Stuffing wads of bread into her ⟨...⟩ly stared at him.

⟨...⟩e's deaf and dumb," he said with a shrug. He

offered his arm for his master to lean on, leading him to the fire he had just built.

Her mouth stuffed full, the girl called after him:

"My name is Sancha—Sancha Domerq."

She watched the man identified as Baruch de Castronovo turn white with pain as the two servants eased him on to a blanket and began to unlace his leggings, which had stuck to a hideous, suppurating wound in his thigh that could have come only from a sword or dagger.

Looking up from her bread, Sancha suddenly felt compassion for the man who had taken pity on her, but only for a moment. Seeing that everyone had forgotten her, she grabbed the big wheel of bread and bolted. One of the men darted after her, but she was too quick this time and had made her way up the hill and down a gully before he could follow. She turned and saw him give up the chase as he cursed her ingratitude, his voice echoing through the hills. Near the rim of the gorge, where she knew a cave that would provide refuge, Sancha paused, her chest heaving, and smiled in satisfaction at the caravan, now at a safe distance below. The sun had broken through for a moment, illuminating melting drops of snow on a shimmering spider's web. Feeling the warmth of the sun and the comforting swell of bread inside her empty stomach, Sancha chafed with indecision when she remembered the suffering man who had been so kind to her. The impulse to heal, to help, was too powerful to resist. It conquered her ferocious determination to eat, to breathe, to live. Setting down the stolen loaf, she began to gather spiders' webs. She crushed the silver ball in her palm with lichen she scraped from the rock with a stick. Feeling unsure of herself, she returned the way she had come. When they saw her approaching the hut, the men looked up sharply. One leapt to his feet ready to run after her, but Baruch ordered him to stay where he was.

Warily, Sancha approached the men huddled round the fire. The servants glowered at her, but not Baruch.

"I think I can help you, sir," she offered in a small clear voice. "I could try to heal your wound."

"So the cat has a tongue after all," sneered Boniface. "She's a witch, the daughter of a devil."

"So that's it—she's a healer. That's why she's in hiding where no one but devils and goblins live."

"She could be a Cathar. I wouldn't let one of them touch me. The priest told me they use demons' blood on wounds instead of praying to God as Christians should."

The servant called Pons laughed crudely. "Rubbish. She'd as soon bite your hand off as heal you. I counsel you to be careful of her, master," he muttered.

She silenced them with a look.

"You say you can heal me, child, but with what?" asked Baruch.

She returned the trust in his dark, solemn eyes with the glimmer of a smile. Asking for water, she ground the lichen between two rocks and made it into a paste in the palm of her hand. Delicately she touched his leggings, which had been split to accommodate his swollen thigh. Only a narrowing of Baruch's eyes told her he felt pain when she prized loose the leather, which was stiff with pus and blood. She felt no repulsion at the swollen blue flesh around the dark, oozing crater. She applied the lichen paste to the wound, then, when she was satisfied, she sealed it with the cobwebs. Calling for a piece of clean linen, she adroitly bound the poultice to the leg to make sure it would not move, just as she had seen her mother do. Before she finished, she let her hand hover over the wound for a moment, then murmured a little incantation. Rising to her feet, she said:

"There, it's done. It will be well within a week and will cease to cause you pain very soon, perhaps by nightfall."

The two rough, bearded men were staring at her with a changed expression, as awe battled with suspicion. She regarded them indifferently, no longer afraid. Sancha knew that in the eyes of the world her mother's gifts had set her apart, but this was the first time she had ever dared to practice them on her own. The man called Boniface murmured sheepishly:

"Perhaps you could tend to an infected blister I have on my foot, if you wouldn't mind. And I suffer from worms and terrible wind . . ."

Without replying, Sancha kneeled to examine his extended foot. Propped up on his saddlebags, Baruch regarded the wild, ragged creature who was tending each of them in turn.

"How did you come to practice the healing arts, little one?"

"I learnt from my mother, who was taught by her mother before her."

"And where is this wise woman?"

Sancha hesitated. Her mother had told her never to trust a stranger, who might be glad to gain favor with the Inquisition by accusing her of witchcraft. She weighed up the risks, feeling intuitively that Baruch was a good man.

"My mother is over there, seigneur, where I buried her. She died three days ago." Sancha pointed to the mound of stones. "I was going to cross the mountains, but it's too late now."

"In that case," said Baruch, "you will have to come back to Quillan with me." He disregarded the worried grimaces of the men at this announcement.

"But, sire, you don't know who she is. She's bound to bring trouble on your house, and on us," growled Pons. His protest was echoed by the other man.

"Silence," thundered Baruch. "It's none of your affair. Go tighten up the loads on the mules and get ready to move."

When they had gone, he muttered: "They live in fear and superstition, the poor fools. They are not paid to think, but are here to defend my goods from brigands, which they did not do too well, as you can see, because I am wounded. However, I feel better already, thanks to what you have done. *'Mens sana in corpore suno'*—that's what the sages say: a sound mind in a sound body."

Sancha didn't reply, but was staring at her bare feet. Her arms locked across her chest, she had become a cringing frightened child again. Baruch reached out and rested his hand on her head.

"You have nothing to fear, believe me, little one. You are under the protection of Baruch de Castronovo. We have no daughter living, my wife and I, only two grown sons. We will care for you. Don't look so glum," he chided.

"Yes, seigneur," she muttered, afraid to meet the eyes of this towering figure of goodness. Looking toward the caravan, she wasn't at all sure she wanted to leave.

"Now come," he called toward his retainers. "We must make haste while there's still daylight. I tell you, I feel much better already.'' He struggled to his feet and she watched him stagger toward the caravan, barking orders as he went.

When they were ready to depart and Baruch had been helped onto his horse, he ordered Sancha to be hoisted on the back of his richly carved saddle, which was hung with braid and tassels. Then he draped her in the folds of his cloak to keep her warm. As the caravan moved forward, Sancha stared back at the mound of stones receding into the blue distance. Only when she could see it no more did she turn forward. Rounding a bend in the path, she caught a sweeping glimpse of the Languedoc below, showered with light from the sun that penetrated the fast-moving clouds. The fertile land she had thought she would never see again rose in layers of purple, russets and dull autumn greens, in warm contrast to the wintry hills behind them. From this height and distance it was impossible to believe that for thirty years war, famine and religious persecution had corroded the sunlit valleys.

At sunset two days later they penetrated the hills surrounding Quillan by a road the Romans had built, which cut through the muddy fields. Laborers and tenant farmers were trudging back to the safety of the walled city for the night, their bodies bent against the cold wind sweeping down from the Pyrenees. Deep troughs of shadow cast a pall over the valley, bleaching the color from the flat, sodden pastureland that stretched to the distance. Peasants towing carts and driving oxen gave way to the caravan, and stared with lean, hungry faces after the Jewish merchant and his train of heavily laden mules. Glancing timidly down at the people they passed, Sancha could feel what it was like to trudge through the mud in slippery clogs lined with straw. She peeked from Baruch's cloak, uncomfortably aware that she was accustomed to being below, her feet on the earth, rather than mounted like a fine lady. Her ears, used to the silence of the mountains, throbbed with the sound of voices, the grinding of cartwheels and the lowing of animals that filled the air.

At dusk the animals clattered through the city gates, which would soon be closed. Baruch led the caravan down a narrow cobbled street, where the sound of so many hooves caused the townspeople to rush to their windows and look down from their balconies. When Baruch called lustily to somebody looking down from above, Sancha was heartened by the vitality in his manner. He muttered under his breath and reined in his horse sharply to restrain it from bolting. As they passed courtyards and doorways, Sancha craned her neck, wondering what Baruch's house would be like. The horses' hooves clattered down the narrow cobbled passage, which opened into a large square swarming with vendors still selling their wares by the wavering light of oil lamps. Sancha embraced the feast of sights, sounds and smells. Having lived for so long in the pure air of the mountains, she had forgotten the reek peculiar to civilization. Beyond the pervasive stench of human excrement and rotting garbage, the putrid unwashed bodies, she could distinguish the aroma of bread, beer and meat roasting over the smoking fires. Pons had dismounted and was leading the caravan through the crowd, who turned to gape as he cried out for them to make way.

"Look, look," Baruch called over his shoulder. "Have you ever seen such a thing, child?"

He pointed to a troupe of *jongleurs* with a dancing bear surrounded by a crowd. Peeking out from the cloak, she gaped at the huge beast towering above his trainer. Oblivious of horses, dogs and people, it was pirouetting daintily to the beat of a tambourine. At the sight of his peaked cap and embroidered vest Sancha felt a strange gurgling sound escape from her throat, the sound of her own laughter. She had only the dimmest memory of that joyous feeling, like something round and great trying to escape her chest. Once she started to laugh, she couldn't stop. She laughed until her stomach hurt and she almost fell from the saddle.

She felt Baruch shake with laughter himself at her wild amusement, which made her laugh all the more.

"If you like that dancing bear so much, then my sons, Mayr and Jusef, will take you to the fair," he declared.

Gasping to catch her breath, Sancha strained to catch a last glimpse of the bear as the caravan entered a narrow street lined with prosperous-looking houses, their courtyards and windows glowing with yellow light. Now that it was nearly night, shadows leapt from every wall, reflected by torches and fires, a grotesque world of strange shapes so alien to the black night of the mountains.

For the last few yards the animals had to be restrained from bolting into the courtyard of Baruch's house. The caravan passed through the gate accompanied by whinnying from the horses and shouts from the men. A dark-haired young man on the timbered balcony clambered down the steps and another appeared from the stables.

"Mother, Mother, it's Father—he's come home!"

Into the milling confusion of horses, mules and shouting men came a small, plain-faced woman in a simple gown and bonnet. She had the bearing of a lady, but Sancha noticed that she wore no jewels. Reaching out to clasp the bridle of Baruch's horse, she looked up at him with dark eyes full of gratitude. She didn't seem to notice Sancha, whose pale face was peeking from the folds of his cloak.

"Praise to God that you're home, seigneur. We've been expecting you daily." Her lips moved in prayer.

"We were delayed two days out of Aragon, when a band of brigands attacked the caravan in the night. But don't worry, they stole very little. Only one mule that was loaded with wool, not with spices, silk or silver trinkets."

"You're wounded," cried Zarah.

"Yes, but it's nothing, nothing at all," scoffed Baruch. "Mayr, Jusef—come and help your father dismount."

Sancha hung her head when they saw her hiding in the folds of their father's cloak. The intense curiosity of the two handsome young men, who resembled their father, was more than she could bear, and she shrank deeper into Baruch's cloak, covering her grimy face until only her black eyes shone from the folds.

Zarah's feet were already on the stairs that led to the house above. "I'll make preparations at once. We must send for a physician. Quickly, Mayr. Go find Jacob. Tell him your father has come home and that he's wounded."

"Not now. Perhaps in the morning," protested Baruch. As Sancha dismounted with the help of Mayr and Jusef, Baruch smiled at their astonishment. "If I'm not better in the morning, we'll send for Jacob, but not now. Mayr, Jusef—help me up the stairs and then help the men unload the goods into the store. There's some precious blue glass from Spain and I can't wait until tomorrow to see if it's unbroken. We had it packed in wool," he said to Zarah, who still didn't see Sancha hiding behind him.

"And what are you waiting for, woman?" he said, pretending to be angry. But Sancha could see he enjoyed his wife's concern. After the freedom of the mountains, she was already beginning to feel hemmed in by the closed courtyard bursting with people and animals, but an order, a harmony prevailed that calmed her skittishness. The remembrance of hunger and cold dissolved a fleeting desire to escape to the hills. Baruch had come to life and was giving orders to everyone. Zarah was standing meekly by, his cloak over her arm. They were arguing about calling a doctor, he heatedly and Zarah quiet but firm.

"We will call for no physician. Do as I say. And anyway," Baruch added, leaning on his sons as he limped toward the stairs, "the truth is, a physician has already attended me."

"In the mountains? How can that be?"

"This is she. This is my physician." Baruch moved aside to reveal Sancha. "My wound, which I thought would prove mortal, has begun to close, thanks to this little waif."

As he told the story, Baruch's eyes softened. "The truth is, Zarah, that I couldn't leave the child there to die of cold and hunger or be devoured by animals or devils, and I thought she might have a home with us."

Not replying, Zarah approached Sancha and reached for her frail shoulders. There was a long moment of suspense as Zarah tilted her chin back and looked down into her eyes, searching the depths. Sancha looked up steadily at this solemn Jewess who was regarding her so intently. She waited while her judgment hung in the balance.

Finally Zarah spoke in a kind voice. "You don't show it, but you must be as frightened as a wild hare caught in a trap. And there's no flesh on you at all. You're like a half-dead bird."

"It was a miracle she was there to help me, so far from anywhere," Baruch reminded her.

Sancha's eyes were meek with resignation, but she held herself proudly, not wishing to beg. After an agonizing moment, Zarah sighed and said:

"Come, child, you're hungry and tired." She touched Sancha's matted, lice-ridden hair without flinching. She took command of Sancha's existence, in those few words ridding it of bleak uncertainty.

5

In the grillroom of the Hôtel Meurice, Louise smiled at Sabine Harcourt sitting opposite her. Honey-blonde and tanned, she cut a bold figure in an acid-green suit with a plum patterned scarf and heavy gold jewelry.

"You look simply stunning. Is that Versace?" Louise asked. She cringed inwardly at the flattery in her own voice.

"Mmm. Like it?"

"It's fabulous. I could have sold that a hundred times over." She took a sip of wine, feeling her stomach contract at the lie that came so easily to her tongue. Louise felt impatience with Sabine's preening little gestures as she searched her bag for her cigarettes, reminding herself that although Sabine Harcourt was hopelessly vain, she was also one of the shrewdest women in fashion and the only person Louise felt she could talk to frankly.

"Don't you usually stay at the Georges V?" asked Sabine as the waiter handed her a menu.

"Yes, but I thought I'd be better here for a change," Louise replied, not bothering to mention that she had made her plans too late to book into the Georges V.

"I agree, it's a much quieter atmosphere."

There was a disapproving edge to her voice and Louise knew Sabine was thinking that she must be cutting corners, even though the Meurice was ruinously expensive. Listening to her chatter, Louise was torn between confiding in Sabine and keeping up a good front. When the waiter had taken their order, Louise made up her mind, wondering how to warm up to the subject.

It was Sabine who broke the ice.

"You really need to talk, don't you? The minute I saw you yesterday at St. Laurent I knew you were in trouble. So let's have a nice long lunch, a bottle of wine and you can tell me everything."

"I don't know where to start," Louise said, taking a deep breath. Briefly and unemotionally, she told Sabine about the divorce and her father's death.

Sabine looked at her sympathetically. "The timing couldn't have been more unfortunate, Louise, and I pity you. Vanni is so temperamental, but, of course, the press adores him. I would never order from him myself, except for a few eye-catching things for my main window, because I know what he's like. If it had been anybody else, the others might have been more understanding, but he's been saying terrible things about you. I won't try to hide it."

"Are they all saying I'm washed up, that my credit is no good any more?"

"No, no, I wouldn't go that far," she replied, but her voice lacked conviction.

"I've been turned down by at least five major designers in Milan, and now here. I'm getting desperate. If I don't fill my order books for the coming year, it's going to be a disaster. Sabine, I've been coming here for nearly ten years. How can houses that have been selling to Bella Figura for such a long time—how can they suddenly turn their backs on me? I know I'm not a Neiman Marcus, but I'm a very loyal customer. I'm desperate, Sabine. Everything that matters to me, my whole life, is riding on this trip. I came to get a good collection together and here I am a week later with practically nothing to show for it." She stopped, feeling perilously close to tears. With so much at stake, she couldn't afford an emotional outburst.

Sabine gave an indifferent shrug. "It's a very tough business, Louise. You know that. Look at me—I've nearly lost everything more than once. The stakes are high, but you have to gamble. What else do you expect? You lost an entire season—it's a gap you may never fill . . ."

Her quizzical glance suggested that she doubted whether Louise was strong enough to withstand the consequences of this setback.

Thinking over what Sabine had just said, Louise suddenly sensed that there was no sympathy in her manner, only curiosity as to whether she would fall flat on her face.

With a pitying smile, Sabine said: "It's a game of bluff. Just remember that and you'll be all right. I saw you yesterday at Montana. Your face was tense, your manner nervous. After all those rumors that went round, maybe you are not giving the right impression. It take a lot to restore confidence when you've let people down."

It was on the tip of Louise's tongue to say that she hadn't let anyone down, that they had let her down, but it wouldn't have made any difference. All Louise wanted to do was pay the bill and escape the company of Sabine Harcourt. As soon as she decently could, she asked for the bill to be put on her account, saying she had an appointment. They kissed goodbye, promising to see each other in the autumn for the next collections, or if not, the following March.

At three o'clock the following afternoon Louise was waiting anxiously for the telephone to ring in her room at the Meurice. She had drawn the heavy curtains against the gray spring light and the soft glow of table lamps lit the romantically pretty room, decorated in the style of the eighteenth century with gilt chairs and painted furniture. Picking up a copy of *Paris Match,* she thumbed through it impatiently without reading a word or seeing the pictures. Throwing it on the table, she picked up her Filofax, becoming more anxious by the minute. She had several calls to make, but she didn't dare occupy the line until she had heard from Farah Fanahzi, a young Persian designer in exile, who had told her the day before that she might be able to supply Bella Figura with her new collection. Weak with tension, Louise tried not to think of the competition, knowing she wasn't the only buyer courting Farah Fanahzi. If Farah didn't come through in ten minutes, Louise knew that she had failed and that she would have to go into liquidation when she returned home.

When the telephone rang, she leapt up to answer it. Her heart pounded when she heard the silkily accented voice of Farah Fanahzi on the end of the line.

"Hello, Louise. It's Farah here."

"Oh, hello, Farah," she replied, with no trace of anxiety. Her stomach was turning over like a tumble dryer. "I'm so glad I was here for your call. I'm just on my way out for a meeting," she lied.

"That's lucky, then."

Louise was forced to wait when she heard the click of a cigarette lighter down the line.

"Louise, I'm sorry, but Neiman Marcus hasn't come back to me yet."

Louise's heart sank at the prospect of delay, but she injected her voice with studied indifference. "I understand perfectly, Farah. It's not your fault." Her knees went weak with relief that she was still in the running.

"The thing is, my instincts tell me that you and I are going to be doing business. You know, I'm fed up with these big stores that keep you on a string. I'd much rather be with smaller, exclusive stores like Bella Figura, where I get personal treatment, somebody I can trust. But you understand my position."

Louise closed her eyes in despair. "Of course, Farah. I understand. I'll just have to be patient, won't I?"

She hoped her voice contained the right mixture of enthusiasm and indifference. A knot tightened between her shoulders as she wondered if Farah knew that she had been turned down by five major designers in Milan and now in Paris. The reason was always the same: she'd missed a season and all the big names had other customers waiting in the wings for their collections. Now into the tenth day of her trip, she was trying to inject vitality and enthusiasm into her voice, but she was numb inside. They were both playing a game: Farah pretending she didn't want to be swallowed up by the world's most prestigious department store, and Louise pretending it didn't matter to her one way or the other whether she marketed Farah's exquisite clothes. She had no choice but to wait.

"So you'll still be at the Meurice on Monday, then?"

"Probably," she said, sickened by the expense of keeping on her room for the weekend. "I may go to the country. I've been invited to stay with some friends who have a château on the Loire," she remarked, inventing the sort of explanation that would impress the designer.

"Oh, lucky you. I'm going to be cooped up in my atelier the whole time. I'll think of you amusing yourself in the country. Do have a wonderful time. We'll be in touch on Monday, then. And, Louise—I just know somehow that it's going to work out between us."

When Louise had hung up, Farah's parting words stayed in her mind, filling her with excitement and relief. Within seconds she had formed a completely new plan in her mind to save Bella Figura. After this season she would get out of the big names and concentrate on unknowns. And when she got back to the States she would shift her buying to American designers. It was so obvious that she laughed excitedly, venting all the frustration of the last disastrous ten days. The solution to saving the business was under her nose all the time, but she had been too self-absorbed to see it. Feeling everything was going to be all right after all, she smiled to herself and jotted a few notes into her Filofax. Nothing had turned out at all as she expected, but she had come up trumps none the less. She stood up and paced the room, her arms folded, feeling she couldn't wait to get back home and implement her plans.

It was Friday afternoon and Monday suddenly seemed a long way off. Looking round the luxurious suite, she knew she didn't want to spend a weekend in Paris by herself. The hotel room that was costing her a fortune seemed to close in on her, and she scooped up her trenchcoat, bag and umbrella, intending to meander through Paris until she was exhausted. She wanted to prowl anonymously through narrow little streets, distancing herself as far as possible from glamour and the bright lights of the boulevards.

Leaving the hotel, she avoided the Place Vendôme. As she hurried past the boutiques of the Faubourg St. Honoré, her eyes turned away from the glittering windows spilling with sumptuous goods. She concentrated instead on the shining wet streets under her feet, the people passing by. After walking steadily for an hour, she reached the Place des Vosges, which she hadn't visited in years.

She walked through the deep arcade, half listening to the clamor of children playing in the square, thinking to herself that the sound of children's games was the same the world over. She was just wondering where to turn when her ears picked up the strains of a simple melody played on an instrument she had never heard before. Drawn to the sweet sounds, she made her way through a circle of people gathered on a pavement near a café, where she saw a young man with tousled hair, dressed in a pullover and jeans, turning the crank of a small street-organ, which produced a hauntingly lovely melody in a minor key. Tall and handsome in an angular sort of way, he was no more than twenty, but he seemed to belong to a bygone era, as did his street-organ, which was painted with pierrots, clouds and shepherdesses. He began to sing a plaintive lament in what Louise took to be Old French, which she found difficult to follow. He was singing about the pain and loss of unrequited love. "Gilding the heart with the nobility of suffering" was a phrase he repeated that stuck in her mind. The pure, ancient lament crossed the divine between then and now, wounding her with its simplicity. She was pierced by a sudden vision of the unchanging nature of the human heart and the brevity of life.

When the song ended, the young man smiled and bowed. Louise applauded with the other spectators and when he passed his hat, he acknowledged her with a nod.

"Ma musique vous a plu?" he inquired.

Reaching in her bag for some coins, she realized her face was wet with tears. Wiping them away in confusion, she made no move to go as the crowd melted away, but watched the musician packing up his yellowed music cards and wondered why his little song had unleashed such a torrent of feeling inside her. She hummed the tune under her breath, wanting to remember it. It was as though the song had seeped through the cracks of a door that barred her memory, altering her perspective for a moment, as if a calendar had flipped forward, leaving no account of the days in between. While the musician had been singing, she realized, she had been far, far away.

When the crowd had gone, Louise was still standing there. "It pleases me that the song moved you," he said, carefully pleating the cardboard music sheets punched with holes. He didn't seem surprised at her reaction.

"Could you tell me where that song comes from?"

"It's a very old melody, so old that nobody knows its origins. The words are composed in the ancient language spoken by the troubadours."

She suddenly realized that the words of the street musician's ancient song probably had the same lilting cadence as the language spoken by the voices belonging to the unseen persons outside her window in Little Gaddesden, though she couldn't be sure. She saw that the musician seemed to be waiting for her to speak, but she couldn't bring herself to say she had heard this same ancient French in England only a week ago.

"Do you know of the troubadours and their poetry?" asked the musician.

"No, I don't; but if the poems are like your song, then they have a rare beauty," she murmured.

"The troubadours bequeathed to the world the gift of romantic love. Their early songs and poems are the first blossoms of the fruit we now enjoy without realizing the debt we owe them."

"And you pay them tribute by keeping their songs alive." She noticed the stickers on the organ's case: from Moscow to Barcelona. "And you live the same wandering existence, I see."

He laughed. "True. The kings and their courts are gone, but on a good day I make ends meet. I'm on my way to the Camargue in a few days' times."

"To meet gypsies and ride wild horses?" she said nostalgically.

"If I'm lucky. You're American, aren't you?" When she nodded, he said: "You speak French very well."

"Thank you," she said, seeing with regret that he was ready to leave. She noticed his long sensitive hands. He had a way of moving unhurriedly, of looking directly at her that was not entirely modern, as if he were truly observing her, and his soft-spoken courtesy seemed to belong to another age. He had packed up his music and poured the money from his beret into a handkerchief, which he stuffed into his pocket. Pausing to nod politely, he turned to go on his way.

"Au revoir et bonne chance," she said.

"As my song pleased you so much, perhaps you would like to read the poetry of the troubadours. There's a bookstore just on the other side of the square, where you might find something of interest."

"Merci," she said, watching him stroll slowly down the arcade.

As Louise passed the children playing in the square, a shaft of late sun cut through the gray, blinding her for a moment. Holding her hand to her eyes, she was filled with an intangible yearning. Just for an instant she knew her life for what it was: a hungry and desperate pursuit.

Unnerved by this sudden self-awareness, she did as the musician had suggested and went to the bookstore tucked into an ancient brick wall. She came out with a book of troubadour lyrics and their modern French translation. Seeing a café at the end of the arcade, she walked toward it. She decided she wouldn't return to the hotel just yet.

The sight of someone eating *frites* at a nearby table as she sat down reminded Louise that she was very hungry. She had only toyed with her lunch, her appetite destroyed by anxiety. As the waiter handed her a menu, it struck her as ironic that in one of the best hotels in Paris the food had tasted like straw, but now her mouth was watering at the prospect of a simple plate of chips, which she ordered. She was about to ask for a glass of red wine, when she saw champagne on the menu.

"Half a bottle of Moët," she said to the waiter. For a moment she flipped through the book she had bought, then sat back and looked through the window at the passers-by and the *habitués* of the café, Parisians, whose gesturing hands and shrugging shoulders conveyed a great earnestness about everything. Though her feet ached, she felt an exhilarating sense of freedom, which had crept up on her unawares. Thinking it over, she reflected that in the last two hours her own problems seemed to have shrunk into insignificance. The waiter popped the cork of her champagne and, as he poured it, she watched the bubbles leap to the top of the glass, shattering against the surface. That morning she had awakened with a feeling of dread in the pit of her stomach, which had intensified throughout the day, culminating in the telephone call from Farah Fanahzi. As she went over their conversation in her mind, an insidious idea wormed itself into her consciousness. Louise blinked as the truth exploded inside her. She didn't want to handle Farah Fanahzi's collection. She didn't want to buy anybody's clothes, from Montana to Versace. She didn't want to rebuild Bella Figura again, to battle her way to the top. She wanted out of the whole business. What had once seemed exhilarating, stimulating, rewarding and full of infinite variety now seemed ruthlessly competitive, narcissistic, greed-ridden. Every brilliant moment of creative inspiration on the catwalk was now canceled out by the petty jealousy and egotism that soured every triumph for her.

Once she had admitted the truth, she was consumed with indescribable relief. She seemed to be watching herself from a distance, like a child releasing a balloon into the sky just to see where the wind would take it. Bella Figura shrank on the horizon, becoming smaller and smaller until it disappeared. Letting go would be so easy, she thought; it wouldn't be a crime, a sin, to cut free.

Waiting to pay her bill, Louise found herself looking at a garish ceramic vase stamped with a picture of a medieval walled city nestling among the bottles behind the cash register. It looked familiar, and as she leaned forward to decipher the name scrawled on the base, the cashier who took her money saw her staring at it.

"C'est joli, n'est ce pas? I was there several summers ago. *C'est la ville de Carcassonne."*

Louise nodded, trying to remember where she had seen the image of the city. It came to her after a moment that the book her father had been so taken with had contained pictures of Carcassonne.

The light was fading when she left the café. She stood for a moment, wondering which way to go. After the warm smoky café, the bracing air was like a slap in the face. Her head cleared as she walked, but the urge to change her life was just as strong as it had been half an hour ago. Intrigued, she let herself be guided by her sudden change of heart, wondering if her fighting instincts would reassert themselves when her euphoria and the champagne had worn off. She walked back to the hotel, a new plan forming in her head; not a plan that would shape her life or give her a new direction, but simply a plan that would take up the slack of the empty weekend stretching ahead.

An hour later Louise had packed her suitcases, checked them with the hotel porter and, carrying only a small bag, taken a taxi to Orly Airport to catch the last flight from Paris to Perpignan.

6

It was a blustery spring day in Geneva. The flower-beds bordering the lake and its jetting fountain rose in a wave of color against the choppy blue water ringed by the snow-capped Alps. Owen Morgan, briefcase in hand, walked down the Quai de Mont Blanc past expensive shops and fine hotels. He had flown in from London that morning, intending to return the same evening when his business was completed at the Hôtel des Burques, which he could see ahead of him. Entering the lobby, he glanced at the people sitting in groups at tables as they sipped their morning coffee, remembering that a week ago he had been sitting there himself with Monsieur Brunet of Plastica Industria SA, discussing the purchase of machinery for his factory in Swindon. By chance he had arrived early and had gone to browse in Sotheby's auction rooms in the hotel to kill time. But today he had flown to Geneva on a much more compelling errand.

Entering the auction rooms, he paused at the reception desk to get his bearings. One sweep of the room told him that last week's display of German antique furniture had been replaced by oriental carpets and sculpture. Owen was taken aback when he approached the cabinet that had contained a display of Roman seals and early Christian reliquaries. The exhibit he had come to see was gone and in its place was a collection of antique Spanish and German pistols. Moving swiftly among the collectors who had come to browse, catalogue in hand, he could see no sign of the collection belonging to Baron Felix Hauptmann. For an anxious moment he wondered if he might have been dreaming; then it occurred to him that he had made a mistake about the date of the auction. His mouth went dry at the thought that he might have missed it. Striding to the reception desk, he waited impatiently for the smartly dressed young woman behind the counter to help him.

"Excuse me, *mademoiselle,* what happened to the collection of early medieval artifacts you had on display over there last week? The case where you now have a collection of guns."

She turned her head in the direction he was pointing. "The display has been changed, I'm afraid."

"Yes, but the items in that case were not due to be auctioned until the end of May. I've got the catalogue." Opening his briefcase, he took it out. "You see? The twenty-seventh of May."

"I really couldn't tell you what has happened, but I'll inquire," she said. With a toss of her head, she went to the office behind the desk while Owen waited anxiously. When she appeared again, he was drumming his fingers irritably on the desk.

"I'm afraid that the lot you are referring to has been withdrawn from sale."

"Withdrawn?" he repeated in disbelief. His stomach began to churn. "I'd like to know why."

There was anxiety in his voice, as if something that belonged to him had inexplicably disappeared.

"I'm afraid that's all I can tell you."

Though Owen knew he was being unreasonable, the cold gleam in the receptionist's eye and her clipped, precise English annoyed him. His Celtic blood rose as he fixed her with a determined stare.

"Do you mean that the whole collection, everything, has been withdrawn, just like that, without any explanation?"

"Yes, I'm afraid so."

"Could you give me an address or phone number where I could contact the owner?" he couldn't resist saying, although he already knew the answer.

"I'm afraid I'm not allowed to divulge that kind of information, *monsieur.* There is no more I can tell you." Her eyes flickered, then went dead as she dismissed him.

"I don't know why the whole thing is so damn hush-hush. When I was here last week, they wouldn't give me the owner's name, so I was obliged to make inquiries in London," he said mischievously, noting she didn't seem to believe him.

"It is entirely up to the vendor to withdraw a lot from

auction if he chooses to do so. And as for the seller's name, I don't know how you know . . ."

He shrugged. "I don't know why it's such a big secret." He stopped short of saying how easy it had been to discover his name. All it had taken was a phone call to a dealer he knew in London, who had an entrée to all the auction houses.

"If it isn't too much trouble, maybe you could find out if a new date has been set for the auction. You could do that, couldn't you?" Leaning forward, he looked into her eyes, turning on all his power to charm. Seeing her thaw slightly, he added: "I'm sorry I was so brusque just now, but this auction is very important to me and I've come all the way from London this morning just to see the items I wanted to bid for."

The intimate tone of his voice, his troubled expression evoked the receptionist's sympathy. Looking over her shoulder to see if anyone was listening, she murmured: "It's a bit strange. Just like that, overnight, the collection was withdrawn. I don't think anybody here knows the reason, so I'm afraid you're just wasting your time."

Owen thought for a moment. "What happened to everything? Are the objects still on the premises?"

"I think it was all picked up yesterday, but don't tell anyone I told you. I'm very sorry you had to come all the way from London for nothing. Believe me, this is most unusual."

"It certainly is," he said absently, looking round the room as the implications sank in.

"I wish I could help you. Maybe there's something else coming up you'd be interested in. What exactly was it?"

"Oh—I collect ancient seals. There were several there I was particularly interested in . . ." His mouth was dry with sudden apprehension as he thought of the chalice.

"Why don't I take your name and address? We'll be having an auction of coins and seals some time this summer."

"No, no, thank you very much. The one I had in mind was one of a kind." There was a note of defeat in his voice. He was berating himself for being so careless, for assuming that from now on things would be easy.

"Anyway, thanks for your help, *mademoiselle*." He jotted down his home address on his business card. "If by any chance the Baron's collection should come up for sale unexpectedly, I would appreciate it if you'd contact me.''

"Of course, *monsieur,*" she said demurely, now completely on his side.

Putting his pen in his pocket, he gave her a roguish smile. "By the way, *mademoiselle,* do you know that when you're angry, your eyes change color? They go a dark, unfathomable blue.''

He strolled away, leaving her staring after him in mute astonishment. Going back to the lobby, Owen dug his hand in his pocket for change and walked toward the telephone booth. He was so engrossed that he didn't notice a man lower *The Times* as he passed. Expensively dressed and with a smooth, unlined face, he watched Owen until he disappeared in the direction of the telephones. Taking a monogrammed handkerchief out of his pocket, he carefully cleaned his dark glasses. Unhurriedly, he slipped them on again, then withdrew a notepad from his breast pocket and jotted down a few lines. Noting by his platinum watch that it was nearly noon, he began to think of fresh asparagus and hollandaise sauce, with a cold lobster to follow, accompanied by a bottle of Chablis. He walked to the front desk and said to the concierge: "Are there any messages for me? Mr. Monckton, room 408.''

Half an hour later Owen was driving along the shore of Lake Geneva toward the town of Rolle in a Mercedes taxi. The water beyond the trees had deepened to slate gray and the angry sky threatened rain. Owen had been pleasantly surprised to discover the address of Baron Felix Hauptmann listed in the telephone directory, knowing that without such a stroke of luck, it could have meant staying on an extra day in Geneva. When he telephoned, there had been no reply, leaving him no choice but to drive there. He had put off several important meetings that Friday in order to pursue the quest, which had taken a dramatic new turn. Owen wondered what could have induced the Baron to withdraw the chalice from sale so suddenly. Whatever his reasons were, Owen suspected it wouldn't be easy to see him. Until the detective he had hired in London came back with his report, he was aware that he had little to go on. All the way to Rolle he was haunted by the memory of the chalice, placed so artlessly on dark blue velvet in a display cabinet in the floodlit auction hall. He caressed its pure symmetry in his mind, wondering if he would ever see it again. The tantalizing image had robbed him of sleep, ruined his appetite and his concentration. Throughout the week he had suffered an anxiety, an uneasiness that he wouldn't admit to himself, and now his instincts had proved right. He had foolishly fed on dreams of possessing the chalice again, or righting a past wrong, canceling a grievance he had never been able to forget. Instead, the chalice had reappeared after nearly seventeen years, only to disappear again within the space of a week.

He looked out of the rain-spattered window at the villas bordering the lake. Settling back for the drive, he sank into thought. Every detail of the day he lost the chalice was engraved on his mind.

He and Mandy had been back in London for over a month. One night he had come back late from a rehearsal feeling tired and despondent. As he shivered in the cold wind sweeping down the cobbled mews, the warmth of France seemed very far away. The imminent disintegration of the band preoccupied him as he approached the little yellow brick mews house with a bay window, but the moment he saw the bedroom light burning upstairs he began to feel a dread he couldn't shake off. Turning the key in the door, he hoped Mandy was asleep. Lately his departure in the morning had been marred by quarrels, usually about money. When he came home at night, they picked up where they had left off. The tension between them had even dulled his appetite for sex. On the rare occasions when they made love, it was bitter, brief and unsatisfying, in cold contrast to the passionate tenderness they had once felt for each other.

He entered the small sitting room, dominated by a piano in the bay window covered with his compositions and sheet music, and noticed with surprise that it looked tidier than usual. The Indian cushions had been plumped up, the ashtrays emptied and the magazines neatly stacked rather than strewn round the room at random. There was even a bouquet of red anemones on the table.

"Mandy?" he called up the stairs. "Are you home?"

"Hi. I'll be right down," came her voice, which seemed unusually cheerful.

Hooking his parka behind the door, he turned at the sound of her footsteps. She took him unawares when she threw her arms around his neck and kissed him.

"What's all this about?" he asked laughingly, taken aback by her warm welcome. He pressed his nose into her fragrant blonde hair and slipped his hands around her waist, exposed by a tight little sweater she was wearing over bell-bottom jeans. "I thought you'd be in bed by now."

"Can't a wife wait up for her husband when he comes home from work?"

He suppressed the sarcastic reply that sprang to his lips, ashamed of his cynicism. Her nipples hardened the moment his fingers touched them, arousing him immediately. She gently wriggled away, kissing him on the cheek.

"I've got some supper for us."

"Supper?" he exclaimed in surprise. Usually he ate whatever he could find when he came home, for she hardly ever ate with him anymore. He followed her into the kitchen, where the table was prettily set for two with candles and more flowers.

"This looks great," he murmured, pressing her to him as she opened cartons of Chinese takeout ready to be put in the oven. It wasn't her birthday or his, or their anniversary. He was puzzled, amazed by this complete change of atmosphere, but he didn't want to think too deeply, just to enjoy it. All the animosity had magically evaporated between them and he didn't want to know the reason. Admiring her rounded bottom through her tight jeans, Owen was already looking forward to getting into bed after dinner.

"Want to open the wine?" she asked, handing him a bottle and a corkscrew.

"This is turning into a real celebration," he said with a grin, which she returned with an inviting little smile that made his heart stop.

"Owen," she began hesitatingly, "I've got something to tell you . . ."

Her words struck immediate fear in him. She must be about to announce that she was having a baby and this was her way of preparing him for it. He steeled himself inwardly for what would be catastrophic news.

"Listen, sweetheart," he said, opening the wine. "Let me just run upstairs first. I'm bursting."

She shot him a hesitant look. "Sure. This will take a minute to heat up. Owen—don't worry. It's good news, really good news."

Kissing her cheek, he said: "Can't wait," then bounded up the stairs, two at a time. When he came out of the bathroom, he was so distracted by the prospect of what Mandy was about to tell him that he passed the spare bedroom, which he had made into his study, without a glance. Lately he had got into the habit of looking in to see his chalice resting on a bow-fronted chest of drawers. It gave him enormous satisfaction to see it gleaming in the shaft of light from the hallway. He came down the stairs, tension already mounting in his head as he wondered how they were going to afford a baby. In a few seconds he came to the unavoidable conclusion that he was going to have to give up music and get a job. Walking into the kitchen, he wiped the worry from his face and took the glass of wine she offered him.

"Hope you're hungry, because there's enough for an army."

"I've ravenous," he replied, noting that an awkwardness had sprung up between them.

"To us," said Mandy, clinking her glass against his.

Leaning against the cupboard, he waited for her to speak.

"OK, how should I start . . . ?" she began with a giggle. "Guess who dropped in this afternoon."

"I don't know. Who?"

"Rex Monckton."

"Rex? What did he want?"

"What do you mean, want? He didn't want anything. He was just passing by and he dropped in to see how we were, that's all," she said, a defensive edge creeping into her voice.

"I didn't mean anything by it. It's just that it seems to me he never comes by unless he wants something."

"That's a terrible thing to say about one of your best friends. I wish you wouldn't be so cynical," she said, flipping her fingers through her hair.

"OK, OK, I didn't mean it. How's the junk business going?" he said, thinking she had strayed off the subject.

"That's very unfair. It's not a junk shop, it's an antique shop," she answered with a frown.

Owen rolled his eyes impatiently. "All right, antique shop. So what did he have to say?"

"Rex has very good taste and he's very knowledgeable about lots of things. For instance, I showed him your precious chalice."

"You showed him the chalice?" Suddenly Owen was alert. "What did he say about it?"

"Well, as a matter of fact, he thinks it's worth a lot more than you paid for it. He said it might even be made of real gold. But he warned me not to get my hopes up because he said it could be a seventeenth-century gilt German wine goblet or something like that. Even so, that would be worth quite a bit."

"Rubbish. The inscription on the bottom isn't in German. As soon as I have time I'm going to take it to the V and A."

"Don't get annoyed. I told you he said it's probably valuable. Aren't you pleased?"

He snorted. "So what? I didn't buy it to sell it. We've been through all that, Mandy."

They looked at each other defensively.

"That's a ridiculous attitude, Owen. And it's not fair to me. You know we're desperate for money and not to have something worth a lot of money valued by experts is stupid."

"Valued? What do you mean by that?" His heart seemed to stop.

"He offered to show it to a friend of his who he said is one of the leading authorities on things like that. Don't get upset. He's doing it as a favor. It won't cost anything."

"You mean he took it out of the house?" Owen felt a wave of shock pass through him.

"Of course he took it. How do you expect him to value it if he didn't take it?" she retorted, her voice rising a note. "For God's sake, he'll bring it back tomorrow." She opened the oven and jabbed a fork into a spring roll.

Bolting to his feet, he brought his fist down on the table. As the salt cellar shattered on the floor, Mandy whirled round to face him, but he had already left the kitchen and was racing upstairs to the study, where he fumbled for the light switch. When the light came on, he stared at the empty space as a sickening sense of loss overcame him, followed by a terrible premonition that the chalice was gone forever. He clutched his hands to his head in anguished confusion, wondering why it mattered so much, frightened at the violence coursing through him. Slamming the door, he went angrily downstairs.

Mandy was waiting for him, her hands on her hips, her mouth a grim line, hardening her kittenish face.

"How dare you let Rex Monckton take that chalice without asking me?" he muttered, blind with his incalculable loss. Hatred for Mandy boiled up inside him, destroying his reason for a second. He closed his eyes and clenched his fists to keep himself from slapping her; then his trapped emotion erupted, bringing him close to tears.

"I'll never forgive you for this, never."

His remark struck a spark to dry tinder.

"You? You'll never forgive me? For trying to keep everything together? That's bloody funny, it really is. Unlike you. Owen Morgan, I'm a realist. I don't go round with my head in the clouds trying to dream up a lot of crappy music no one wants to record. I'm sick of being poor, of skimping to make ends meet. I felt guilty tonight because I bought a bottle of wine and some Chinese food. I don't even have a decent winter coat, and you're complaining because I let Rex do you a favor. God, Owen, I don't know what's happened to you, to us. You think more of that stupid thing that ruined our holiday than you do of me. It gives me the creeps how you're always sneaking upstairs and looking at it. Well, drop the subject, will you? Just drop it. You can tell him to bring it round in the morning." She burst into tears, then buried her head in her arms and began to sob.

Owen hung his head, unable to give her an answer. He couldn't explain, nor did he expect her to understand. Until that moment he hadn't comprehended that his attachment to the chalice could blind him to the fact that it was, after all, only a piece of metal. If it didn't sound so bizarre, he could almost believe it exercised some sort of power over him. The need first to possess the chalice, then to protect it, had been rooted instantly, at first glance, and over the past weeks he had gained an abiding sense of joy from merely looking at it. He had fantasized that this mysteriously beautiful object had probably belonged to a king in a time when men still thought the Earth was flat, when they considered the progress of their souls instead of their bank accounts. It would have been placed opposite a throne, on a banqueting table, and filled with the dark purple wine of antiquity. He felt himself privileged to own such a splendid treasure, which was like a tangible historical truth enriching his life. And now he was convinced it was gone and he would never get it back again. He hardly heard Mandy's sobs as his own grief filled him.

Driving along in the car toward Rolle, Owen recollected the day after Rex had taken the cup for valuation. He had telephoned early in the morning, distraught and full of apology to tell Owen what he was strangely unsurprised to hear. Rex explained that when he left Mandy the previous day, he had slipped the chalice into his pocket and had taken a bus to the Lansdowne Club in Mayfair, intending to take it for valuation at the gallery in Albermarle Street after lunch. At his club he had run into friends. They went off to the Colony Club and eventually ended up at a party south of the river. It wasn't until he got back to his flat in Notting Hill at three in the morning, Rex said, that he realized the chalice was gone. Owen had received the news in deadly silence, with a sense of numbing inevitability.

"My dear fellow, I'm just sick about it," Rex said in his New England drawl. "I couldn't sleep a wink and I was too cowardly to come over and face you in person. If you can find it in your heart to forgive me, I'll try to make it up to you, even if it takes me years. What I mean to say is, I want to compensate you for what it might have been worth. I feel morally obligated, so don't protest . . ."

Owen had cut the conversation short. Muttering a few words of forgiveness he didn't mean, he had coldly resisted Rex's groveling apology. He could never forgive him or Mandy for what they had done. In his heart he knew the incident meant the final break in his relationship with Mandy and that he never wanted to see Rex again.

When the silvery gray village of Rolle came into view, the taxi turned off the lakeside road and drove up a hill lined with grand houses protected by high walls. When the taxi stopped at a grilled gate reinforced with steel for privacy, Owen saw they had finally arrived at Villa La Rochette. He got out and rang the intercom as the car drove away, hoping against hope someone would answer. After the second ring he realized it had been pointless to drive all the way from Geneva when he had been unable to reach the Baron by phone.

Standing back from the wall, he had an intriguing and frustrating glimpse of the steep slate roof of the stone mansion behind towering cedar trees. He was wondering whether to go into the village to make inquiries when he heard a car coming down the road. Seeing a black Mercedes stop at the entrance to another villa, he sprinted toward it just as a uniformed chauffeur was opening the gate. A middle-aged Swiss matron in a fur coat looked up at him in surprise from the back seat of the car.

"Excusez-moi, madame," he began, out of breath.

"Yes, may I help you?"

"I'm trying to get in touch with the owner of Villa La Rochette, Baron Hauptmann. I've been phoning him from London for a week, but there's been no reply."

"Are you a friend? A relative?"

"I need to see him urgently on a matter of business."

"Then you must not know. The Baron died quite unexpectedly almost a week ago. Sunday, I believe. Though he was very old and not well, we were all very shocked."

Owen's face fell. "I see. Did he have a wife, children? Is anybody living in the château?"

"His wife died years ago and he had no children. He led a very secluded life these last years."

"Dead?" Owen repeated. "Dead," he said again. "Shit," he added under his breath, forgetting the woman in the car.

Coldly, she said: "You will excuse me, *monsieur.*"

The car rolled through the gates before he could ask her who the Baron's heirs were and where he might contact them. Turning back the way he had come, he walked down the quiet residential street, all of whose gates were closed against him.

Later, hurrying through Geneva Airport to catch the flight back to London, he glanced at the departure board. There was a flight leaving for Toulouse in half an hour. Pulling his ticket from his pocket, he headed for the Air France desk to change his booking.

7

Sancha impatiently pulled out a row of clumsy stitches she had just embroidered on a square of linen. She glanced over at Zarah, bent over her sewing, her face partly concealed by her bonnet. It was a sunny day in early summer and the two women were sitting on the wooden gallery overlooking the courtyard, where geese and chickens pecked about the cobbles, intent on finding a few tasty morsels to eat. The sound of Baruch's voice came from the storeroom below as he talked to Jusef and Mayr about his forthcoming journey to Spain. Their conversation reminded Sancha of her own housebound existence at Zarah's side. The sweet song of a thrush in a cage suspended from a beam made her wonder if it still harbored memories of living wild and free, as she did. Her hands stopped moving as she imagined the greening pastures of the Pyrenees, where brooks rushed cold and clear with the melting snows.

Sancha jerked her needle through the linen again, trying to form the tiny stitches as Zarah had taught her. Knowing she would never have the skill to embellish sleeves as delicately as Zarah was doing now, with tiny flowers and bees caught in a criss-cross of gold stitching, she cried out when she pricked her finger.

"Patience, child," said Zarah reprovingly. "You're holding the needle too tightly. You hold it like this, delicately between your three fingers. Otherwise you can't control it." Taking her square of linen, she showed Sancha again.

"It always defeats me in the end," she said resignedly. She had never cared much for the domestic tasks she had learned from Zarah during the last three years, but Sancha endured her own agonized impatience rather than upset her benefactors. In the time she had lived with Baruch and his family the order of a Jewish home had come as a revelation to her when she compared it with her distant memories of Christian dwellings. Judaic law ruled every aspect of their lives, shaping existence with a dignified etiquette found only in the houses of nobles. Sancha had become Zarah's pupil, sharing in all the domestic ritual, including the preparation of food, which required two separate sets of utensils kept in different rooms. Observing the honor bestowed upon Zarah by her husband and sons, Sancha acquired a deep respect for the way of life that was now hers. As she worked, she remembered the proverbs she had learnt: "Not money, but character is the best dowry of a wife . . . Who is rich? He whose wife's actions are comely. Who is happy? He whose wife is modest and gentle."

As she looked up at the blue dome of sky over the courtyard, Sancha's thoughts flew over the rooftops of the town and back to the mountains. A faraway look came to her eyes as she longed for the old life with all the fibres of her being, just as she had longed for it every spring since she had come here. She had filled out and was now a woman. Her hair was dark and lustrous, her face round and flushed with health, but part of her would always be untamed. She still moved with the quiet self-possession of a wild animal who had made an uneasy pact with domesticity. That part of her wished she was running now in the mountains, wading knee-deep through lush grass tufted with wild flowers. In her mind she lay in the shade by a stream, listening to the running water, letting the movements of clouds take the place of thoughts. Sancha blinked, realizing her needle had been motionless. Her sudden restlessness was quelled by hunger, now it was nearly midday. It was Friday and their meal at noon would be no more than a crust of bread in order to whet their appetites for the Sabbath feast.

Zarah looked approvingly at Sancha, who was now bent diligently over her sewing again. She was prettily dressed in a blue linen shift worn beneath a brown overdress with a tight bodice that molded her high, firm breasts. She wore the sleeves of multicolored linen Zarah had worked in a diamond pattern of scarlet, yellow and indigo. Every morning Zarah brushed and plaited Sancha's hair, which fell to her waist. Sancha wore no wimple or headcover, only a maiden's chaplet, which rested on her head above her dark eyebrows, as sleek and shiny as marten tails.

In the strife that divided the Christian world there was no place for healers, whose cures were decried by priests as coming from the devil. It was decided soon after she arrived that Sancha should absolve her mind of everything she knew of healing. In order to protect her from accusations of witchcraft and heresy, to the world Sancha was the destitute daughter of a distant relative whom Baruch had brought back from Spain.

Hearing footsteps below, Zarah glanced down at the courtyard. "Is that Beatrice? She should have come back from the market long before now. Where can that girl be? I'll soon run out of red twine if she doesn't hurry back."

Sancha peered over the balcony. It was market day and they were anxious for the Christian servant girl to return with the village gossip. The occasions when Sancha could gain permission to leave the house were very rare, though she longed to explore the streets of Quillan. Zarah upheld the custom of the faith: a woman's place was at home.

Seeing a movement from the corner of her eye, Sancha turned her head and saw Pons staring up at her, a crooked smile spreading across his long donkey face. The sight of his stained beard and frowsy hair, his big red hands dangling at his sides sickened her. She avoided the man who had torn the rags from her body the day Baruch rescued her, and she thought to herself he was even more repulsive now than the day she first set eyes on him. She didn't want to interpret the look on his face as he leered at her, lips parted. Her instinct told her he resented the fact that she was now treated as a daughter of the house.

"Mayr," Zarah called, catching sight of her son's dark head as he left the storeroom with his brother. "Look out at the gates and see if you can see Beatrice wagging her tongue with the housemaid next door."

He did as she asked, then came back, hands on his hips as he gazed up at the two of them. "She's nowhere to be seen, Mother."

Zarah rose, clutching her embroidery. "I want to finish what I'm doing before midday. If your father doesn't need you, will you go to the market for me, there's a good son."

She turned to Sancha, interpreting the look of longing that crossed her face.

"Your curiosity unsettles you, Sancha, but you are much safer at home. There is danger lurking outside these walls, especially these days."

"But what could harm me, Mother?" she asked impatiently, her eyes down so that Zarah couldn't see her defiant expression. Though they talked openly of the violence of the Inquisition in the household, it often seemed far removed, especially on a fine spring day. Sancha's curiosity about life had reasserted itself, surfacing through her bloody memories of the past. She had never spoken of her life before Baruch found her, even to Zarah, who seemed to sense that the past was better buried. The fever she had contracted soon after her arrival had blurred her memory, locking out of reach the horrors she had lived through. When Zarah had nursed her back to health, Sancha's mind was like a clean wax tablet awaiting the first impression. She began life again, this time as a Jewess, adopted daughter of the house of Castronovo. It was Zarah who undertook her education in Judaic law and custom, as Baruch, accompanied by Mayr and Jusef, traveled frequently to trade and arrange loans for the nobles of Languedoc, impoverished by thirty years of war.

"Don't look so unhappy, child. You and I have work to do. We are expecting a guest from Perpignan for supper and I hope he arrives before the Sabbath lamp is lit," she said.

Sancha wasn't listening. Resting her elbows on the edge of the balcony, she was looking down enviously at Mayr, who was locking the store so he could go to the market. Seeing the look on Sancha's face, Zarah chuckled.

"If you could see yourself. You look like a bear cub peeking out of a basket. All right," she announced, "if you promise to stay with Mayr and if you wear your cloak and cover your hair, you may go, but you must come straight back and not lose yourself in the crowd."

Sancha let out a squeal of delight, stuffing her embroidery into her sewing pouch. "Mayr, Mayr!" she cried over the balcony, "I'm coming with you."

"Hush, or I'll change my mind. Mind you do what I say and be careful. In spite of the heat, remember to keep your head covered."

Sancha ran into the house and took her cloak from a chest by the door. The garment was much too heavy for a warm day and bore a yellow circle, the mark of a Jew. She darted down the stairs and into the courtyard, where Mayr was waiting for her.

Looking into the dark doorway of the store, Sancha wondered if any fugitives were hiding there. Over the years she had seen a number of the Goodmen, Cathars, to whom Baruch gave refuge for a night. Some of them were women and they always traveled in pairs. Sancha had seen Baruch order his sons to take them food from the table, but they were never mentioned in conversation, nor was the danger of reprisals from the Inquisition if it were ever discovered that they harbored heretics. Sancha suspected that Zarah's anxious moods were something to do with the Goodmen. She had heard her tell Baruch that what he was doing was foolhardy.

As she passed through the portals of the gate, Sancha looked at the slim, dark youth walking beside her, distinguishable from a Christian by the yellow patch on his sleeve. At home by the fire or sitting at the table, he was like a brother to her, but walking in the street for the first time at his side she felt proud to be with him. As they walked down the narrow, cobbled street lined with houses, some of wood, some of stone, she threw her shoulders back and held her head high, making sure to glance every now and then at her feet to avoid stepping into the reeking sewage in the gutters. A sow and her piglets were competing with a pack of mangy dogs for garbage that had just been dumped from the window above. Sancha trailed behind Mayr for a moment, peering curiously into the open courtyards and unshuttered windows of the houses they passed.

"Come on, come on," called Mayr good-naturedly. "What could you find that's so interesting there?"

"Nothing. I'm coming." She was contrasting the filth and stench of the quarter with the order of the household in which she lived. Even the courtyard was swept and laid with clean straw when it was wet, and garbage was never left to rot and pollute the air they breathed.

Mayr was laughing at the way she was greedily lapping up every detail of the neighborhood, making her feel like a giddy child.

"I'm glad I'm not a woman," he said with a sigh. Approaching the end of the street that opened into the square, they could already hear the din of the market. "I wouldn't like to stay at home all day. A woman's life is just about intolerable, I think. A man can please himself, at least according to the Law."

Piqued at his arrogance, she said: "The proverbs say a man's happiness is his wife's creation."

Mayr shook with laughter. "Oh, Sancha, you're a wonder. You always manage to knock me down from my little pinnacle."

"It's because I care for you, brother. Your bag of conceit won't go down well with your bride, whoever she might be."

"I think we shall see very soon. I'm very nearly eighteen, so it will be arranged this year."

"I wonder if it's true that marriages are made in heaven."

"I suspect they're made by fathers and mothers looking for a sound alliance and a dowry." They were coming to the end of the narrow street, and Mayr brushed her hand affectionately.

"I'd rather think they're made in heaven, if you don't mind," she insisted.

"Sancha, you must know a thousand proverbs. If you were a man, you'd be a scholar. You read the Talmud and you do arithmetic faster than Jusef. My father said he soon won't have any more to teach you. I shouldn't tell you, though, or you'll become vain—now it's my turn to tease you."

They had reached the market square, which was swarming with people. Mayr threaded his way through the crowd, Sancha following. They were sucked into the mêlée that emitted the powerful stench of excrement, unwashed bodies and rotting cabbage. The nasal whine of vendors selling their wares carried over the cacophony of chickens, geese and goats driven by shepherds wearing hides. They jostled shoulder to shoulder with broad-faced peasants and artisans in rough woolen tunics, their bare legs, hands and faces red from exposure. At the tightly packed stalls hawkers sold peacocks, thrushes and hares, nightingales in cages and baskets, and wares of every description. There were bales of the finest wool, which Mayr told her were from England, linen from the north and Germany, spices from the Levant. She stopped to stare longingly at a bolt of shimmering green cloth splashed in deep relief with a rich fern pattern she had never seen before.

"Mayr, what is it? It's the loveliest thing in creation."

"It's known as silk and it's said to be the costliest material in the world. It comes from Venice. One day, when you're a fine lady, you can have a train five feet long of such stuff dragging after you."

She laughed and shook her head. Such lavishness was against Jewish sumptuary law, but at that moment she would have given her soul to own a piece of it.

Reluctantly, Sancha tore herself away from the cloth stall and followed Mayr deeper into the covered market to look for twine, feasting on the sight of spices heaped in pyramids on trays, unguents and attar of roses in pretty bottles, fish swimming in pots. Her ears rang with the hoarse cries of merchants touting the merits of their wares. Her pleasure faded when, through the moving wheels of a cart, she saw a pack of beggars being beaten by a bailiff wielding a thick staff. Their faces had been savagely mutilated and stumps of what had been arms thrust through their ragged sleeves, making Sancha at first take them for lepers. Some had no eyes, others no lips or noses. As they scuttled away she saw their rags were stitched with crude yellow crosses.

When she stared after them in horror, Mayr pulled her sharply by the hand. "Don't stop. Don't look that way. They're heretics. They wear the mark of their shame." His eyes darted round uneasily.

Nausea rose in Sancha's throat. The word heretic descended on her like a shroud from the deepest well of her unconscious. It was what they had called her mother. Such mutilation, worse than death, was inflicted by the Inquisition.

"I'd rather be burned at the stake than be so cruelly marked," she murmured, rebellion firing her heart.

"Hush," Mayr remonstrated. "That has nothing to do with us. We are Jews, and you are the daughter of my father's cousin in Spain, if anyone should ask."

She watched while he purchased the twine Zarah had asked for, waiting for the vendor to wind it round a smooth stick. When he had paid for it, she said sweetly: "Do we have to go back just yet? I can hear music. Maybe there are dancing bears.''

Mayr's serious expression melted into laughter. Sancha's love of dancing bears was well known to all of them, and to humor her he said:

''Bears don't play tambourines and drums. It's probably a troupe of *jongleurs* or even troubadours. We'll go and have a look, but only for a minute, mind you. Knowing my sister as I do, I guess she must be hungry by now,'' he said with a mischievous smile.

She nodded, eyeing a pile of figs nearby. The smell of meat roasting on a spit wafted over to them, making her forget the musicians and beggars. As they skirted the pillars of the marketplace she noticed a shriveled old woman surreptitiously handing out small packets wound with straw, each of a different color. Her customers were mostly women, who paid her in small coins, then hurried away. The old woman tucked the money into her bodice, looking furtively round each time. Anguish quickened within Sancha when she realized the old woman was a healer. She watched her curiously from a distance until an undercurrent of whispers rippled through the crowd. At the approach of a pair of fat, tonsured Dominicans, the healer scuttled away, but the monks were too deeply absorbed in conversation to notice her. Schooled to avoid the accusing sweep of their penetrating gaze, Sancha pulled her hood close to her face. She followed Mayr in the direction of the music, which stopped before they reached it. The crowd became more dense, pulling them along with it as it surged toward a platform. Suddenly a mood of excitement filled the air and they were jostled and pushed as people moved toward the center of the square. Sancha looked round for Mayr, who had disappeared. Taking a chance to see better, she moved above the crowd on steps set into the ramparts and pushed her way up. Soldiers had dragged a man, who wore nothing but a strip of dirty cloth covering his loins, onto a platform. There they had splayed him to two wooden drums. Two bearded executioners, their hairy chests bared, began to winch the rack tighter and tighter. Every sinew on the man's tortured body protruded in agony as the drums creaked, and a bloodcurdling howl rose from deep inside him, vibrating through the air. Riveted by horror, Sancha dug her hands into the cold stone. The louder the victim's screams, the greater the excitement of the crowd around her.

"Justice be done! Death to brigands," bellowed a man on the stairs. As the cries rang out Sancha shrank away, feeling contaminated by a nameless obscenity. A dizzying sense of shame came over her as she scanned the churning mass of onlookers, searching for the face of just one person who was repelled by what he saw; but she could find no one.

"Crush the brigand's bones! Death to all heretics too, by fire!" screeched a toothless woman standing below her, a cry that was echoed by those around her. The mention of heretics made Sancha go cold, and when she saw the woman looking curiously at her, she stared back insolently until she suddenly sensed she might be in danger. Like a snarling pack of hungry wolves, the crowd could turn on her, the daughter of a witch, who was parading as a Jewess. Not even Baruch could protect her here. Trying to force her way down the stairs packed with spectators, Sancha made a promise to Jehovah that once she was safe within the walls of Baruch and Zarah's home she would never leave.

"Let me pass. Let me by," she said, injecting an imperious note into her voice. Her mother had always taught her that when confronting peril, one measure of courage was worth a hundred of meekness. She encountered no resistance until she was halfway down; then her cloak was torn from her shoulders by a cheering spectator. Bareheaded, she gathered it round herself again as best she could. Stumbling to gain her footing, she found herself face to face with a man who had been watching her progress down the steps. She was immobilized by the disturbing power of his clear eyes, which seemed to have witnessed the misery of the world, and was unable to move further until she had drunk in the beauty of his face. A mutual sympathy passed between them. Here was the dissenter like herself for whom she had been looking moments earlier, a man different from the rest. He had the face of a carved stone angel. His cropped, sun-bleached hair curled against a forehead that was furrowed with hardship, and the grim set of his jaw and lips fringed by a golden beard suggested a kind of sorrowful outrage. It was then she noticed he was wearing a white cloak emblazoned with the red cross of the Templars. Her dim realization of what it stood for gave Sancha a shock. Passing him, their cloaks brushed, but she did not look up.

Her eyes cast down, Sancha was unaware that the Templar saw her face was stained with tears and her lip, which she had bitten, was red with blood. He was moved to utter some word to the girl, but he held his tongue, admiring in silence the beauty of a young woman whose purity of heart was written on her face. His holy vows dictated he must watch in silence as she passed, to look through her as if she were made of stone. Catching sight of the yellow wheel embroidered on her cloak, he felt confusion at the discovery that she was a Jewess. A yearning for the life of this world stirred within him as he admired the girl's coiled and shining hair, her bodice tight across her breasts, thoughts he suppressed with shame. Her stricken face, transfigured by pity, reminded him of a statue of the Holy Madonna he had seen in Lombardy years ago, a profane comparison he could not avoid. It had been years since he had noticed a woman who was as fair. He was strongly tempted to follow the Jewess, to give her some sign of his admiration, but, watching her go, he resigned himself to the fact that their worlds could never meet.

At dusk Sancha entered the dining hall, where the table had been laid for dinner with special care for the Sabbath. She brushed from the white linen cloth a few petals that had fallen from the bouquet of flowers, then stood back to admire the beauty of the blue glazed plates from Spain and the serving spoons of beaten silver. Tonight the family and their guest, a Jewish merchant from Perpignan, would share the best food the house could offer and wine from Baruch's vineyards in the Corbières, the same rich hue as the peonies clustered in a vase. Tapestries depicting scenes from the Old Testament adorned the room, and the wooden floor was highly polished. Beatrice was kindling the fire on the hearth, her duty on the Sabbath, when Jewish law forbade Zarah to touch it. It was she who had prepared the food, which was proscribed to Zarah, a custom Sancha also observed. Zarah entered the room in her best black shift and brown tunic, her sleeves tied on with embroidered ribbons, her starched headdress finer than usual. Smiling at Sancha, she signaled her to take her place. When Baruch, his sons and the merchant had entered the room, she walked to the window, which was open to the violet summer sky. Catching sight of the first star, she lit the seven-armed lamp hanging from a beam, and light flooded the room. Then she cupped her hands to her eyes to draw in the light and turn with a smile of rejoicing on her face, to take her place at the table. Covering the knives with a cloth, Baruch spread his hands over the bread as he said the blessing. As soon as he had finished, Zarah signaled for Beatrice to enter, bearing a ewer filled with water, a towel over her arm.

Sancha gave Mayr a look that showed she was grateful he had kept silent about what had happened in the market. Watching Beatrice as she offered the bowl of tepid water to the merchant to wash his hands, she thought of the man who had been tortured to death that morning. As if reading her mind, Jusef murmured:

"The Sabbath is a time for rejoicing, sister. I haven't seen you smile since we entered the courtyard."

Sancha responded with a bright smile, but her heart still felt heavy. As conversation broke out round the table, she forgot everything but the food being set before them. Her mouth watered as Zarah supervised the serving of roast capon and perch basted with garlic and rosemary. She even forgot the Templar, whose image had filled her thoughts all afternoon, as she glanced hungrily at the succulent dishes specially prepared to honor the merchant. She helped herself to the coarse bread as Jusef filled her goblet with wine and water. Restraining the impulse to heap her plate with food, something she had never entirely conquered, she took small portions of each dish and began to eat delicately, cutting off small pieces with a little silver knife and popping them into her mouth. When Beatrice had retired, the women and young men ate in silence as Baruch and the merchant began to converse.

"I am heartened to hear your vineyard is prospering. And no wonder. Your wine is excellent, even better than last year. I can sell as many barrels to export to Majorca as you will offer me."

"I can promise you as many as you want, within reason," Baruch said expansively. "My overseer says we can expect the grapes to be plentiful and good this year."

"I wonder that you don't consider leaving Quillan and coming to Perpignan or Narbonne, where you wouldn't feel outnumbered among Christians. Or even to your estate in the country."

"We are all happy enough here. But I confess I have often thought of the idea lately. And Perpignan wouldn't be so far to come on the return journey from Spain, it's true."

Mayr's frown told Sancha what he was thinking. His life, his amusements were in the town and he had never been fond of the country, as had his elder brother, who oversaw the country estate and the trading interests Baruch maintained in Perpignan.

"Our right to property in the Languedoc could change if the Pope continues to play on King Louis's conscience."

Baruch smiled ironically. "The royal tax we pay forces us to seek a much higher return on our investments than property. Land doesn't secure us in times of trouble, as does gold in a bag. Jews have known that for millennia. We have survived much in these last years, owing to the enlightenment of the lords of Languedoc, yet let us pray that now we are governed by France the worst is over and that we will be as prosperous as ever." He spoke optimistically, but his eyes clouded beneath his shaggy brows, suggesting he saw an uncertain future.

"Would you like some more capon, Yssac Salamon?" interrupted Zarah.

Sancha saw a frown cross Zarah's face as she offered the dish. The Sabbath dinner was one occasion when the talk should not be distressing. Sancha exchanged a smile with Mayr when the merchant didn't take the hint.

"The worst is not over, not while there is still a Cathar living." There was silence for a moment, as if Yssac Salamon had guessed at the heretics hidden away in the storeroom. "The northern nobles are waiting their chance to devour the last and richest estates of the Cathar lords of Languedoc, and the Dominicans, I hear, are working themselves up into a new frenzy. They say the Pope himself is afraid of them."

"I pity the Cathars with all my heart, be they peasants or lords," said Baruch. "They have suffered the same fate as

the Jews, only worse, at the hands of men who call themselves Christians.''

"They're a strange lot, but I don't know that I pity them.
They have repudiated the Old Testament and they have their
own version of the New Testament. They are like an animal
with no head. Think—if it hadn't been for them, the wrath
of France and Rome might never have been aroused. But
when they have exterminated the heretics, I fear they will turn
on us.''

While he was speaking, Sancha and the two boys avoided
each other's glance as they all thought of the fugitives who
had passed through the house that year on their way to
Montségur, where Cathars sought refuge in increasing num-
bers. It was dangerous to speak of the Cathars Baruch harbored, even to a trusted friend.

Baruch reflected. "The vanquished may yet cleanse the
land of the French, and perhaps Raimon of Toulouse will find
the courage to fight his overlords.'' Filling the merchant's
goblet, he said: "I feel as safe as any Jew can hope to feel.
I am an important lender to Catholics and heretics alike. Had
we been living in Carcassonne or Toulouse, I wouldn't feel
secure, but we are safer here. And consider this: if the Dominicans began to torture and burn Jews as they do Christians, trade would suffer. The brothers' tables would cease to
groan with delicacies and their coffers would shrink. A small
number of Jews who have obstructed them have perished, I
admit, but we must not let that fill us with terror. Until Innocent became pope, Jews and Christians were friends. It
was he who forced the badge on us.''

"Perhaps, but I advise you not to be a lender to the Dominicans should they ask you, or even the Roman Church.
These weeks I have been traveling the breadth of the land I
have sensed renewed fears everywhere," said the merchant
with a weary shake of his head. "The persecution of heretics
and unbelievers is now in the second generation. The French
king and the Roman Church covet this rich land. In their
frenzy they have even begun to exhume the dead and scatter
their bones.''

Baruch looked shocked. "Is this true?''

"Yes, in Albi. I heard the rumor only last week.''

Sancha, Jusef and Mayr were all listening intently as they

ate. A note of uneasiness had invaded the comfortable room, glowing with light from the Sabbath lamp.

"These past years I have seen brother turn against brother, children against their parents before the Inquisitor, and it has only just begun. The Roman Church and France will crush the Cathars as an excuse, then plunder the Languedoc and all its riches. No one will be safe, even you, my dear friend. We may yet see the time when I cannot sit at ease at your table and be among you, talking freely," he said with a courteous nod to Zarah.

"Perhaps we should all carry the Gospel of St. John and travel south to Montségur, where the Cathars are gathering in their stronghold. We would be much safer there, with the holy men," said Baruch in jest, to lighten the conversation.

"Is there going to be a war?" asked Sancha when there was a lull.

Baruch smiled. "A young girl shouldn't worry about war. It's always with us, like the moon and the stars; don't you agree with me, Yssac Salamon."

Sancha hesitated, exchanging a glance with Mayr. "I saw a man today in the market in a white cloak sewn with a red cross. A Templar, I believe. I remember that they are holy warriors, so it made me wonder . . ." Feeling all eyes on her, she blushed with embarrassment, but all afternoon she had been consumed with curiosity to know more about the Templar she had seen.

"That is true, my child. They defend Jerusalem against the Saracens," said Baruch as Beatrice entered with a tray of fruit dipped in honey.

"Oh yes, I recall the one you speak of," said Mayr.

Sancha pressed his foot under the table to remind him not to mention that they had been separated.

"I—I mean we, we saw him looking at falcons, I remember," Mayr continued awkwardly, suppressing a smile as he caught Sancha's eye.

Sancha was now bitterly sorry she had run home alone from the market. When she passed the Templar, some sixth sense told her his eyes had followed her as she disappeared into the crowd.

"The Templar's face made me think he was a foreigner." She was eaten with curiosity to know more about him.

"Such people are strange to you because you leave the house so seldom," teased Mayr.

The subject moved to the wealth of the Templars in the region, their fortified castles and churches, their minting of coins in Perpignan, their dispensation from Rome for usury.

"When they join the Order, they give all they possess to God," said Jusef.

"And what does God do with money? He has no need of it," Sancha remarked flippantly. Then she blushed to the roots of her hair, thinking she had committed blasphemy; but, to her surprise, laughter echoed round the table.

"A wise child, our Sancha," said Baruch with a smile.

"Other orders of the Church cast their eyes enviously on the wealth of the Templars," said the merchant.

"The Church of Rome trembles at their might," commented Mayr.

"Is it true they continue to defy Rome and will not sanction the persecution of the heretics?" asked Jusef.

The merchant said: "That is because so many landed nobles hereabouts who are either Cathar or of Cathar sympathies have sent sons to join the Templars. To kill a Cathar would be to kill their own brothers. Think of Lord Bertrand de Blanchfort, the most illustrious example."

Sancha listened intently, the image of the Templar imprinted on her mind like a saint in a stained glass window. As Baruch and the merchant conversed about trade, she said to Mayr:

"Do you suppose the Templar we saw was a noble from the region, then? Something about his expression made me think so."

"My little sister, if you traveled on the road as we do, you would see them coming to and fro with messages from their castles, command posts and churches. They even have a fleet that comes to Perpignan and Narbonne."

"They're businessmen and bankers, just like the rest of us," Jusef interjected with a note of contempt.

"And what do they believe in?" she asked Mayr, who seemed so well informed.

"They are Christians, of course, who swear to the same vows as other orders, except that they bear arms."

"Then are they chaste?" she was emboldened to ask,

knowing the answer already. When Mayr told her they were, she felt a strange fluttering in her stomach. This revelation drew her even more to the stranger.

The men began to speculate as to whether they performed strange secret ceremonies similar to those reputedly practiced by the Cathars.

"Is the legend true that they possess the cup the Christians call the Holy Grail, my lord?" said Jusef to his father in a hushed voice. "It's rumored that they have hidden it in the commandery at Béziers."

"That's some kind of wild fable, Jusef," said Zarah. "You know there is no such thing as the Holy Grail."

As the meal came to an end Beatrice entered again with the ewer so that everyone could wash their hands. A platter of highly prized morsels of loaf sugar was set before them and Baruch replenished the goblets with wine, a signal that the songs, games and riddles could begin. It was Sancha who struck the first note of the Sabbath song:

> This is the sanctified Rest Day;
> Happy is the man who observes it,
> Thinks of it over the wine cup,
> Feeling no pain in his heart strings,
> Though even his purse strings are empty,
> Joyous, and if he must borrow,
> God will repay the good lender,
> Meat, wine and fish in profusion—
> See that no delight is deficient.

8

When Louise opened her eyes to a starkly modern hotel room, her first waking thought was that she was in a hospital, an illusion dispelled by the knock at the door and the voice of the chambermaid announcing breakfast.

Moments later she ran her fingers through her hair and

poured a cup of coffee, then unfolded a copy of *Dépêche du Midi*. The bold headlines about the latest football match brought reality home to her. Topping the cup of thick dark coffee with foaming milk, she remembered how she had got there, starting from the Place des Vosges. She knew one thing for certain: she had rediscovered the adventurous, impulsive side of her character, which she assumed had been laid to rest along with first youth.

Later, searching her face in the mirror, it seemed that she and the woman who stared back at her were strangers. She had heard stories about women losing their reason in the wake of divorce or bereavement, but looking herself in the eye she felt a curious detachment. Whatever the outcome, whatever the reason, she was there for the weekend, during which time she promised herself she wouldn't think about business.

Driving out of Perpignan in the car she had rented at the airport, she faced the unknown with the sense that some pleasant discovery was awaiting her. She sped confidently down the little-traveled road penetrating into the flat plain of Roussillon, latticed with gnarled black vineyards and strangely devoid of houses and villages. The Pyrenees were still shrouded in morning cloud, but every now and then she caught a glimpse of the white peaks against a wash of blue.

As the morning cleared, she drove on through rocky hills scrolled with rosemary and thyme. Along the banks of the river she could make out the first buds of willows announcing the spring, which always came early to the south of France. She was tempted to take detours when hilltop villages beckoned in the distance, but she pressed on, wanting to penetrate into the heart of what Ambrose referred to as Cathar country. Studying the maps she had bought, she decided to head for the village of Puivaillon, where she remembered the Lethbridges had their summer house. Driving as fast or as slowly as her mood took her, all she knew was that it was somewhere ahead and that she had plenty of time to reach her destination before nightfall.

Steering the Renault became a pleasant monotony and as she looked at the passing countryside she was reminded of her father and how much it would have meant to him to be at her side. But now she was here, she couldn't dispel the feeling that her journey had nothing whatsoever to do with her lingering guilt at not scattering his ashes in this alien place. Why then, she asked herself, had she come? Normandy or the Loire were much more accessible. But words and questions faded from her mind and she gave herself up to purely visual pleasure. The austere and brooding beauty of the landscape was animated by shafts of early morning sun. The names of Corbières, Roussillon, Ariège rang in her head, imprinting magic. The country was far wilder and more empty than the photographs in the book suggested. The trick of light shaping a distant pinnacle drew her, beckoned her, as she scanned the folds of the hills, searching for ruins of Crusader castles and Romanesque churches that were the guardians of old, old secrets. Louise invariably visited strange places loaded down with guidebooks brimming with dates and names to pave the way, but here she was armed only with her curiosity, which grew with every mile. She took her time, stopping whenever she felt the impulse.

At noon she stopped at a charming fortified village for lunch in a tiny café overlooking the square. Spreading her map on the table, she saw that she could easily be in Puivaillon before dusk. She recalled Dorothy mentioning a hotel where they had put up visitors when their own house was overflowing. But the further she penetrated into the country, the fewer hotels and restaurants she had seen, confirming that she was beyond the tourist circuit.

As evening closed in, Louise congratulated herself for coming so far so fast and, after a look at the map, decided to cross the barrier of hills between her and the Pyrenees, which she wanted to see at dusk. With a sense of mounting anticipation, she drove up the lonely mountain road through the lengthening shadows. Coming round a bend, she gasped at the view spread out before her. She pulled over and drank in the sight of the magnificent chain of peaks set against the deepening blue sky, their mantle of snow a blaze of apricot. At a distance the awesome barrier between Spain and France seemed like a great city at the top of the world, with sweeping stairs of stone, towers and steeples jutting up on the horizon. Her face glowing in the reflected light, Louise stared southward, reluctant to turn her back on the fading splendor. She breathed deeply, inhaling the sweet loamy fragrance of the earth quickening to life after being dormant all winter.

In the quiet she could hear a brook rushing through the depths of the valley below. Now she knew what she had come for: for this rare moment of incomparable beauty, which implanted in her a sense of passionate attachment to this wildly beautiful land. It moved her to think how long it had been there, that it would be there forever, whether or not she ever saw it again. Her own existence seemed to shrink into insignificance when she thought of the centuries of history played out on the ground on which she stood. Turning reluctantly, she got back in the car to continue her journey.

It began to get dark much more quickly than she expected when she returned to the valley. Seeing a signpost that indicated "Hôtel du Commerce," she remembered it was the one Dorothy had mentioned, and coming over a hill she saw the village perched on the crest of a wide valley enclosed by craggy hills below the silhouette of a ruined castle.

The shops and houses were shuttered as she drove down the main street, lined with budding chestnut trees and illuminated by dim street lamps. There was a café where men in blue overalls and berets were huddled over aperitifs, and eventually she found the hotel. When she entered, the neat little *patronne* welcomed her with a smile, her dark eyes anxious as to why a foreign woman should arrive alone and unannounced in this isolated region. Louise was amused when she said brightly, *"Vous dînez à l'hôtel ce soir, madame?"* aware that the nearest restaurant was probably miles away.

Louise came down to the small, comfortable dining room just after eight, having fallen into a doze on her bed with a book on her chest. The amiable *patronne* led her to a table by the fireplace, where logs were crackling in the grate. The delicious fragrance of French cooking wafted in from the kitchen, making her violently hungry all of a sudden. Taking the menu, she glanced at the only other guests, who looked like two traveling businessmen. She was wondering whether to chose cassoulet or *confit de canard* when the voice of an Englishman speaking French made her look up. Louise frowned to herself. She had been thoroughly enjoying her anonymity, and being the only foreigner within earshot, and she didn't particularly welcome the intrusion. Looking cautiously over the menu, she blinked in disbelief when she saw Owen Morgan enter the dining room. Too shocked to speak, she stared at him for a moment as if he were an apparition. When he saw her sitting there, he looked at her blankly, mistrusting his own senses, as if he thought he had stumbled across her double. They stared at one another across the room for several seconds.

"What are you doing here?" Louise exclaimed. She pushed back her chair with a horrible scraping sound. When Owen walked up to her table, the absurdity of the situation made her want to giggle. All she could do was gape at him as he stared down at her, hands in his pockets. It struck her that the odds against their meeting like this were staggering. He stood there bashfully, she thought, an incredulous grin on his face.

"My God! Louise Carey! It is Louise, isn't it? I haven't made a mistake?"

Nodding, she emitted a comic little gasp that made her blush with embarrassment.

"I can't believe it's you. I just can't. It's uncanny." He bent to kiss her cheek. "But why are you here?"

When the shock of seeing Louise had worn off, Owen's first thought was that if she had taken the trouble to come to this remote spot, perhaps she wouldn't be glad to see him, no matter how remarkable the coincidence. But her obvious delight at their meeting disarmed him, prompting him to say with wicked irony:

"Mind if I join you? I've been pursuing you ever since I dropped you at Heathrow, because you left your comb on the front seat of my car."

At this she gave a peal of laughter. As he pulled out a chair, she thought how attractive he was. When he had taken her to the airport, she had been struck by his growing preoccupation and had sensed he was finding their small talk a strain. When they had said goodbye, he hadn't kissed her cheek, but merely shaken her hand. And yet she could think of no one she would rather meet by surprise in this forgotten corner of the world.

"Listen, before we get into how this happened, I think it calls for a celebration. *Madame, la carte des vins, s'il vois plaît,*" he called to the *patronne*, who hurried over to the table bearing the wine list.

"Did you see the look on her face? She must wonder what's going on," Louise murmured, amused.

"Let's not disappoint her," he replied with a grin. When he had ordered the best champagne in the house, Owen folded his arms and fixed her with his dark blue eyes, which were dancing with interest.

"Now, tell me, of all the places in all the world, what on earth are you doing here, anyway? I thought you were supposed to be on your way back to the States by now."

She considered a plausible explanation, deciding it was morbid and unnecessary to make excuses about her father's ashes.

"Well, that's what I'd hoped, but I had to stay over. I didn't want to stay in Paris until Monday, when I have to tie up some business, so I thought I'd see something of France. When I remembered the Lethbridges saying how lovely it was here, I flew to Perpignan and rented a car, as it was the closest place on the map." How could she explain the chain of circumstances that had led her there? And how could she say that only hours ago she felt she had come to the end of a long search while she gazed at the Pyrenees?

"And what about you?"

While Louise talked, Owen was wondering how to explain his own arrival without going into a long-winded explanation. He had flown impulsively from Geneva to Toulouse, then driven to Puivaillon with a sense of mounting urgency about the chalice. But all of that left his mind as he looked at Louise. He was suddenly tired of the chase that had absorbed his every waking moment for the last week. Now he was here, he wanted to put it away for an evening.

"When I left London this morning, I had no idea I'd be staying here tonight, believe me. Where should I begin? The trouble is, it's my life story," he reflected as the *patronne* ceremoniously brought the champagne to the table.

When they had touched glasses, Louise said, "OK, now start at the beginning. Neither of us is going anywhere tonight."

"All right, but don't say I didn't warn you . . ."

Owen reminisced about his first visit to this part of France with Mandy, and how he came to buy a gold chalice in a village not far from Puivaillon.

"What made you come to this particular spot in the first place, all those years ago? Was it the Lethbridges?"

"No, strangely enough, it was nothing to do with them. It may seem surprising that I've never visited them here. They've been asking me to come for years, but I work damn hard and have two holidays a year: one I spend in Spain or the Caribbean, the other skiing, and when I was married, Mandy didn't enjoy Dorothy and Ambrose's company. I first came here for an entirely different reason. So many years after the fact it sounds absurdly romantic, but when I was at Oxford and began to write music I was inspired by the troubadours."

"Really? The troubadours? How fascinating," she said, thinking of the book she had bought the day before.

"Yes. Later, when I was composing, I drew inspiration from their poems, their ballads, the whole mystique that surrounded them. Somehow in my brain their revolutionary, romantic interpretation of life and love transposed itself into a modern idiom. I used it very successfully until my creative impulse dried up. Looking back, I realize it was a bit daft to think that in a day I would discover the magic source of my muse, but you have to remember I was desperate at that point. I would have tried anything to put my work back on track."

"I understand. Like pilgrims going to Lourdes, which isn't far from here. From what you say, it didn't have the desired effect."

"If anything, to the contrary. Mandy was furious because I'd promised to take her to Paris, but I squandered most of the money we had on the chalice. She couldn't understand why I bought it and I had no real explanation. It was an irresistible, inexplicable compulsion, which is still a mystery to me. Anyway, six months later my marriage had broken up and I gave up music. I realized I was finished, that I had said everything I had to say. My music burnt out and then my marriage." He stopped short of telling her that his loss of the chalice had finally destroyed any hope of salvaging it.

"The obvious question is: did you come back here for inspiration again?"

He shook his head, looking amused at the suggestion. "I outgrew all that. This time I came here for a specific reason. It all started the day before I met you at the Lethbridges. I happened to walk into Sotheby's in Geneva, where I was amazed to see the chalice I had bought in that village sitting in a glass case.''

"You saw it? But how did it get there?"

"That's something I'm still not sure about."

"How can you be sure it's the same chalice? It was such a long time ago; maybe you're mistaken."

"No, it's the same one all right. There's an inscription on the bottom in a language I couldn't read at the time, which I have reason to believe is Aramàic. With great difficulty I persuaded them to take it out of the case so I could look at it, and when I did, I had no doubt. This time I copied it down as best I could. At any rate, since then I haven't been able to get it out of my mind. You see, somebody I thought was a friend duped me out of it not long after I acquired it. When I found out today in Geneva that the chalice had been withdrawn from the auction, slipped from my grasp again, I had the sudden impulse to fly down here."

"I gather you were hoping to bid for it at the auction."

"I was seriously thinking about it. I'd have to sell my cottage in the country to buy it. The estimate is very high."

"Do you want it that badly?" she asked, shocked at the suggestion. For a moment she wondered if he was in his right mind, and yet the wildly romantic notion stirred her imagination.

"You could hire a private detective," she interjected. "Try to find the owner privately. Do a deal."

He smiled. "I already have. On the Monday after I saw you. I also learnt today that the owner is dead, so now I need to find out who his heirs are. Then I just thought I'd go back to the village where I bought the chalice in the hope of finding the man who sold it to me. Maybe he could tell me more about it or help me get it back. I don't know. I started thinking on the way down: why haven't I come back before now? You're the only person I've confided in. It was on my mind the night I met you. Hearing myself describe the whole bizarre story to you, I realize it must all sound a bit mad."

Taking a sip of champagne, Louise leaned back and looked thoughtfully at Owen. "Not at all. I think the whole thing sounds absolutely fascinating. You've simply got to find the man who sold you that chalice, for your own peace of mind. You must," she said emphatically.

"Don't worry, I'm a tenacious bastard," he said with a disparaging laugh. "And if I don't get to the bottom of this, it will always haunt me."

Louise cradled her chin in her hand and sighed. "What a wonderful story— a former troubadour in search of his holy grail." She remembered the street musician in Paris. "Believe me, I know exactly what it means to be obsessed with something—I mean, other than work." She knew she had given Owen a false impression about herself when they had met before and now she wanted to dispel it.

"When I met you at the Lethbridges I got the impression you were a no-nonsense American career lady, very sure of what you wanted."

"Not any more," she said with a shake of her head. "The way things went, I've been forced to rethink the whole thing, perhaps change direction."

He looked surprised. "I'm sorry to hear that. I guess that means your trip wasn't what you'd hoped."

"No, it wasn't. But the strange thing is, I don't really care. Whatever used to be driving me has run out of steam. I want something more out of life, oh, so much more . . ." She broke off. "We were talking about this obsession of yours. It makes me think, when something like that takes over, you haven't got any choice but to go along."

She thought of the ruby glass bell ringing in the night, of Little Gaddesden, the organ-grinder in Paris, the vase in the café, the book she had given her father, all of which littered the trail to the spot where she was sitting at that moment.

"Are we talking about me now or about you?" he said as he refilled her glass with champagne.

"Oh no, I'm here because I wanted to get out of Paris." The look of skepticism on his face told Louise she wasn't a very good liar, but warmed by the pleasant dining room, the champagne and the fact that no one in the world knew where she was, it seemed she could confide her most intimate thoughts to Owen Morgan. They were interrupted when the *patronne* brought their food.

"*Voilà, monsieur, 'dame,*" she said, presenting them with a steaming dish of cassoulet.

Breaking a piece of bread, Owen studied her shiny dark hair, which fell toward her delicate chin, her downcast eyes and feathery dark brows, her small, pretty mouth and straight nose. She seemed much younger than he remembered her on the night they met in Little Gaddesden. Seeing her in this unfamiliar setting, he wondered if he were wrong about her. She wasn't a powerhouse of energy and determination cutting a swathe through the couture houses of Europe, not the dynamic, expensively dressed woman he had met at dinner a week ago. Here in the atmosphere of this modest restaurant, wearing a sweater and slacks, she was infinitely more desirable. Her manner was relaxed, her intelligent eyes were less judgemental, in contrast to the almost brittle manner she had projected a week ago. The hesitant catch in her voice, the way she looked up at him, confirmed what he had already known: that an attraction had sprung up between them the moment he entered the room.

"I was wondering," he began, pretending to study the wine list. "If you're not doing anything tomorrow, maybe you'd like to drive over to the village where I bought the chalice. It's not far from here. We could find Dorothy and Ambrose's house on the way there."

"Are you sure you remember where this village is after all this time?"

He laughed. "No, but we could have a good time trying." He vividly described the town as he remembered it, how he had stood on the ramparts at sunset, filled with a sense of history.

"You make it sound like an illuminated manuscript," she murmured.

His face went serious. "Will you come?" The idea of going there alone no longer held any appeal for him. "We could make a day of it, have lunch. That is, if you don't mind leaving early in the morning."

There was a pause as they looked at each other. "I'd love to. I can be ready as early as you like." Picking up her fork, she realized she had lost her appetite.

"I don't want you to think I'm going over the top, or that I've had too much champagne, but it's meant so much to me to talk about all this to someone."

The way he was looking at her made her feel confused and

suddenly shy. She changed the subject, drawing him out more on medieval history.

She sat back and listened as Owen talked of the medieval world, when falling stars were explained as bright sparks struck out by the wind disturbing the ether. A learned man knew the ten arts, the ten ranks of the angels, all of biblical history by heart and the history of Greece and Rome. To him, religion was one part dogma, three parts legend, and pure reason was unknown. He believed that the Earth was a globe suspended at the center of the universe, an egg floating in liquid; he believed in mermaids and griffins, in demons and in the power of gems. A scholar spoke Latin and knew the principles of music, arithmetic and geometry, even astronomy, but nothing of science. He knew about medicine, but deplored surgery, which was performed by barbers. Owen explained that this man of the world knew how to please and flatter his superiors, how to tolerate bores and fools, though he esteemed the wise and was always praying to God to save him on the Day of Judgement.

They lingered over their Armagnac until the fire had died and the *patronne* was setting the tables for the morning's breakfast. Finally, Louise said reluctantly: "I guess it's time to say goodnight."

"I suppose so," Owen agreed.

They went upstairs, lingering for a moment in front of her room in the harshly lit, narrow corridor. There was an awkward pause as Louise rattled her key in the lock.

"Well, goodnight. It's been wonderful. Much more fun than being alone."

"Yes, wasn't it?" he muttered. "Till tomorrow, then. I'm looking forward to it."

Not quite knowing how to break off, Louise put out her hand and he shook it. She watched him walk to his room a few doors away. Unlocking the door, he called:

"If you need anything, don't hesitate."

"Thanks," she replied with a smile.

"I'll see you downstairs for breakfast, say about nine?"

"Fine."

When Louise had closed the door, she leaned against it, still unable to get over the coincidence of meeting Owen in Puivaillon.

"Maybe I did leave my comb in his car," she whispered to herself with a rueful smile, thinking that was as good an explanation as any.

Slipping into bed, she reached for a copy of one of Dorothy's books, which she had given her, knowing she was too keyed up to sleep. For a long time she stared at the printed page, but when she started to read she couldn't stop. She was enthralled by Dorothy's powerfully evocative passages about life in the thirteenth century, which unfolded against the very country through which Louise had traveled that morning. The historical drama Dorothy brought to life was surprisingly fresh and immediate, although it had happened 750 years ago. Louise whispered the old and beautiful names of the characters—Sancha Domerq, Alazaïs de Franjal, Baruch and Zarah de Castronovo—who seemed like real people. Dorothy's lyrical passages evoked a distant time when men and women were ruled by exalted spiritual passions, now all but extinct, that contrasted brutally with their harsh carnal existence. As she read *The Dark Citadel*, obscure images came to life. Looking round the spare hotel room, she could easily deny the forces of magic and mystery, of destiny that determined people's lives so long ago, but she mused that the world was a poorer place without them.

When she put down the book, Louise wished there was someone lying next to her so she could talk about Dorothy's little masterpiece. Her thoughts leapt to Owen, whose nearness was like a fire burning bright and warm in the next room. Louise felt as if she were standing at the threshold of that room, but she didn't know how to step across. When she turned out the light, she curled her body round the pillow for comfort and nestled her cheek against the rough linen.

After Owen had switched off his reading light, he lay awake for a long time, retracing the events of the day and how he had come to Puivaillon under a cloud of urgency, expecting to dine alone. Stumbling on Louise so unexpectedly had diffused his obsession with the chalice, and talking to her about it, especially as she didn't think he was crazy, had somehow cleared his mind and made him all the more sure he was right to pursue the mystery until it was solved. He had stopped short of confiding to her how full of hatred he was for Rex

Monckton. He was ashamed to admit to anyone the smoldering grudge he bore against the man who had betrayed him, particularly as he had so little proof.

Now, as he thought of Louise, the memory of Rex Monckton overshadowed what could have been an exciting, if brief, encounter. Turning restlessly in the dark, Owen suppressed a dull ache of desire as he thought of her. He was divided within himself, like a man swimming in the shallows who senses dangerous depths beyond, which he knows he should avoid. Had things been different, he might have made a pass at her over dinner, he thought, and the two of them would be lying in bed together instead of in separate rooms. She had beguiled him from the moment he saw her sitting there, completely dispelling his ambivalent impression of her at the Lethbridges'. He was very glad they would be going together back to the village where he had bought the chalice all those years ago.

Punching the pillow, Owen stirred restlessly as sleep tried to overtake him. The strange coincidence of meeting Louise Carey was an omen. Tomorrow they would be travelers together, going back in time.

9

The following morning, after coffee and croissants, Louise and Owen went to his car and spread out a map while they conferred over which route to take.

"If we follow the road to Limoux, then branch onto this road here, we should arrive at this point here, where the road intersects."

She nodded, aware of his shoulder pressing against hers as he leaned close.

"On the way we can drive by Dorothy and Ambrose's cottage. It's not far from here."

As they turned down a dirt lane several miles from the

village, the sun was trying to penetrate the clouds that veiled the mountains surrounding the valley.

"It should be about half a mile down this road, if I'm right," Owen said.

Louise eagerly scanned the rolling green hills ahead, which seemed completely empty. Only the sight of a low roof of sun-bleached tiles marked the Lethbridge cottage, set against a bank of blue-gray clouds heavy with rain. They drove down the rough dirt road toward the farmhouse, which was in typical Pyrenean style, with a low, quartered roof in a jigsaw of rose-colored tiles. The exterior was a rough surface of small stones and bricks, exposed where the elements had worn away the stucco. The house was sunk in a sea of grass, its silvery shutters peeking through a cloud of trees, their leaves just beginning to open, casting a tracery of shadows on the old stone.

"Look, the cherry tree they were talking about at dinner— the one Maurice Roussel planted—is already in bloom," Louise exclaimed. "We must take a picture and send it to Dorothy and Ambrose."

Owen stopped the car and they got out. Louise took out her camera and snapped a picture of the tree, dusted with a few pale blossoms. When Owen came round the house, she called:

"Stand in front of the door and I'll take your picture."

She snapped him framed in the green doorway in full sun, a smile on his face.

"Won't Dorothy and Ambrose be surprised when I send them a print of this," she exclaimed.

"They certainly will." He was about to suggest that they kept their chance meeting a secret, but he knew it would sound strange. Looking at Louise from a distance, her hair shining in the sun, he didn't ever want to share that moment with anyone, but couldn't say so. It struck him how rarely life was invaded by such simple, direct emotions as he was feeling now.

They walked around the house, trying to peer through the closed shutters.

"It must be lovely inside," commented Louise, savoring the delicious silence that surrounded the Lethbridge retreat.

She looked up at the tiled eaves, thinking how much she would love to come and stay there in the summer.

She felt an almost physical tug as they drove away, knowing she would always remember the house dreaming in a shaft of sun against the bruised blue sky of spring and the enormous sense of peace she had felt there.

"I'm just amazed you've never come to see Dorothy and Ambrose," she said.

"Now I've seen it, I can't imagine why myself. You know, you could probably still pick up a house like that for next to nothing," he mused. He looked at her and they laughed.

"You're thinking what I'm thinking, aren't you?" she said.

"Yes, I am. I love this part of the world."

"So do I. The minute I arrived I felt I belonged here. It's a shame it's so far from California."

"It wouldn't be the same if it wasn't."

"True," she admitted. "Oh well, dream on."

"I suppose there's no chance you'd ever take Dorothy and Ambrose up on their invitation? You're obviously much too busy. Like me, you can't spare the time," said Owen matter-of-factly.

"Yes, you're right," she said. She folded her arms and sat back to enjoy the scenery, feeling disturbed that by tomorrow they would have gone their separate ways. These two unexpected days in Languedoc would fly by and in a short time they would seem unreal. Louise became aware that her arms were clenched against her chest. Thinking of the carefree time she had spent yesterday, she wondered why she couldn't capture that same feeling now. She began to distrust the beauty of the Languedoc, which had moved her so easily, feeling instead a kind of animal caution. Two near-strangers traveling in a car seemed lost in the great brooding landscape where men had made so little impact over the centuries, where great châteaux and massive fortresses had been reduced to sun-bleached ruins.

"There it is," Owen cried, his eyes trained on the distance. "It's unfortunate the sun isn't shining the way it was the last time I was here," he added as they drove up a hill toward the gray forbidding ramparts of a small village. His voice already suggested that he expected disappointment.

Louise could see that his anticipation, sharpened to a feverish pitch, might collapse under its own weight. He seemed to have placed all his hopes on this impulsive visit to a spot he hadn't seen in so many years, forgetting that people and places change. She wondered whether he had fallen prey to the glamour of the past.

When they passed under the arch through the ramparts, he said, trying to sound optimistic: "At least the Hôtel des Troubadours is still here. The shutters are even the same color, but why are they closed?"

He slowed down in front of the shuttered hotel.

"Wouldn't you know, *fermeture annuelle,*" he said dully. "Well, what could I expect?"

He searched the façade. There were no window boxes overflowing with geraniums, no old man in a beret reading a newspaper and drinking an aperitif, no bustling *patronne* to welcome them. He parked the car and got out slowly, staring at the square, not bathed in golden sun as he remembered it, but bleached of all color. An old woman with a loaf of bread under her arm walked across the cobbles, her clogs echoing in the dark well of shadow created by the church and the surrounding houses.

Louise stood quietly by, waiting for Owen to get his bearings. He stared at the hotel as if unable to accept the changes he found.

"Are you sure this is the right village? There are so many of them," she began. "Maybe they all look alike."

"This is all right. The Hôtel des Troubadours. And the ramparts—you walk that way to reach them. What a disappointment. Funny how time plays tricks on you, isn't it?" he said with a wry shake of the head. "I feel like Rip Van Winkle."

For a moment she felt truly sorry for him. He had invested the past with an aura that could never survive the years and she could imagine how it must have hurt. The last time he stood on this spot he had been a musician, in his twenties, it was the height of summer, and he had been with a woman he loved. Louise didn't say the obvious, that he would have been much better off to keep the memory intact. It seemed to her that this search for the origins of the chalice had destroyed something far more precious. As they stood there in silence, she sensed the village closing in on Owen while he came to terms with his disillusionment.

He shrugged. "What the hell does it matter, anyway? We didn't come here to sightsee. Let's go find the mysterious swarthy stranger who sold me that damned cup," he said, taking her by the elbow.

She followed him up the narrow street, still wet from an early morning shower. The town had a curiously shuttered atmosphere, and although they could smell soup simmering somewhere and heard a radio, the only person they saw was a woman presiding over a *boulangerie* that sold only baguettes and wheels of peasant bread. Like the rest of the village, it seemed lifeless.

"There it is," Owen murmured, quickening his step as he sighted the sign above the *brocante* shop, which was now almost unreadable, it was so faded.

"That's a relief," said Louise, catching up with him.

He bounded ahead of her and rattled the knob of the door. It was locked.

"Can you see anything?" she asked anxiously, peering over his shoulder as he rubbed the dusty window to see inside.

"Yes, it's empty. There's no one there. The place is derelict; it hasn't been used for years. Damn!" he cursed, pounding his fist on the door.

"I am sorry. It looks as if you've come all this way for nothing."

"I'm a bloody fool, that's what I am," he said, frowning in self-disgust. "What made me think I could come back after all this time, just when it suited me? I must have been mad."

"But it's not the end of the road. Somebody will know what's happened to him," she said encouragingly.

"After all this time? It's been nearly seventeen years."

"Let's try the bakery, anyway. That woman could well know what's become of the man. Maybe his lease ran out. Obviously there wasn't enough passing trade to support his business. It could be lots of things. He might even have moved to a better location, perhaps in a town nearby."

"Or he could have died. That's probably what happened."

They walked down to the dark interior of the bakery.

"Bonjour, madame," Owen began, addressing the woman wrapped in a white apron and standing behind the counter. "I wonder if you could tell me what happened to the *brocanteur* who used to have a shop up the hill years ago. Has he moved away?"

"Le brocanteur?" She looked at him uncomprehendingly for a moment, then her eyes narrowed in suspicion. "Why do you want to know, *monsieur?"*

"It's on a matter of business, concerning something I bought from him a long time ago."

She didn't reply for a moment, mulling over his request, her small black eyes gliding over himself and Louise.

"I don't remember any such person."

"Are you from this village?"

She nodded. "But it's too long ago. I have no recollection."

Owen looked skeptically at Louise. "She's being stubborn," he said under his breath. "Well then, do you know anyone who could help me trace this man? It's most urgent that I find him, *madame."*

"You could ask *Monsieur le maire,* but the *mairie* is closed on Sundays and he is certainly fishing. I cannot help you."

"But you must know something," persisted Owen. "If you have lived here all your life, perhaps you could remember, if you thought back." He added in English to Louise: "I'm not leaving this bakery until she remembers. You can see she knows. She's just being obstinate." He flashed the woman a smile.

Seeing the firm set of her mouth, Louise said: *"Madame,* please think. If you know something, it would be very helpful to us. It's very urgent we find the *brocanteur . . ."*

Just then the plastic fly curtain parted behind the woman, revealing a burly man in his undershirt, his chest and shoulders dead white in contrast to his weathered face and hands.

"Qu'est-ce-qu'il y a, Blanche?" he demanded, giving Owen a menacing look.

In a clipped voice his wife told him what they wanted. He shrugged indifferently.

"Please, *monsieur,"* Louise began before Owen could say anything. "We've come such a long way, from America and

England, just to see him. It's nothing bad, but to his interest, what we have to say."

Her sweet, imploring urgency softened the man's gruff manner. "It's been a long time. When did you say you saw him last?"

"The summer of 1971, at the end of August," said Owen.

The man shrugged and scratched his head. "That was the summer he disappeared. *Souviens-tu, Blanche?* It was after Odile got married . . ."

"Disappeared?" Owen murmured.

"One night, it must have been at the beginning of September. He loaded a truck with all his things in the dead of night, then left the village. That's the last anyone saw of him. No one thought much about it because he was a queer sort of fellow. Some people thought he was an Algerian or a Jew. He called himself Durand, but the police said that was an assumed name."

"Police? Was he under suspicion for something?"

"Nobody knows. There were rumors that his goods were stolen." Warmed by Owen's rapt interest, he added: "Some people thought he could even have been handling Nazi contraband, hidden after the war. Perhaps, who knows?" His black eyes glinted at the thought.

"That couldn't be true," said Owen, shaking his head.

"And how do you know that?" asked the man indignantly.

"You could tell by his face that he wasn't a thief, *monsieur,*" Owen replied emphatically. For a moment he was thrown off balance by the wild allegations he had never considered. "But tell me, when did he come to this village in the first place?"

"*Voyons*—it was about fifteen years after the war. I don't know. He stayed for years and nobody paid him much attention. We all thought he was just some sort of recluse who scraped a living by cheating peasants out of their heirlooms. But after he left, there were rumors. Didn't you read about Oradour? Everyone believes that all the villagers there were murdered by the Nazis because they stole the Nazis' gold, but no one has found it yet. So don't say it's not possible . . ."

"That's ridiculous," Owen said to Louise. "Thank you for your help, *monsieur,*" he added, nodding to the man and his wife.

"That's all I can tell you. He packed up one night in September 1971—*voilà*, pouff, disappeared, just like that!" When Owen didn't respond, he said coldly: *"Au revoir, monsieur, 'dame."* He disappeared behind the curtain again.

When they were outside, Owen said: "I'll be damned. He left just after he sold me the chalice. I don't know what to make of it." He stared up the street in the direction of the *brocante* sign.

"What do you want to do now? Should we try to find the mayor?"

"Sure, why not?" he said, and they walked back to the square. "But I suspect that in a town like this, what the baker doesn't know isn't worth knowing."

Moments later they were back where they had started, in front of the Hôtel des Troubadours.

"Another dead end," said Owen. "But I don't suppose the mayor would have told us anything, even if he had known. If I spent a week or two here, I might uncover something—I could even try the police, but I have to be back in London next week. Unfortunately, hunting down the chalice is only a sideline. I've got a business to run too."

When they were back in the car, Louise said: "I wonder about that Nazi stuff. Do you think it could be true?"

"Not a bit of it. Of course, I wouldn't want to believe it, let's be honest. But if he was dealing in contraband, why the hell would he sell me an ancient chalice of pure gold for sixty pounds?"

"You may never know the answer to that question."

"Isn't it funny? For years the whole thing has been bothering me and the truth is, even if I'd come back right away, I still wouldn't have been able to find out any more than I know now. Gone, disappeared without a trace," he murmured to himself in dismay.

"Maybe you should put the whole thing behind you, forget about it," she suggested.

"Forget it? You don't know me. I'm just getting started." Trying to shrug off his disappointment, he said: "We have the whole day ahead of us. Is there anything you'd particularly like to do?"

Louise thought for a minute. Now the search for the antique dealer was behind them, she felt they could enjoy themselves. Feeling on the threshold of a fresh adventure, she said:

"You seem to know this part of the world much better than I do. If you lead, I'll follow."

"We could drive west, have lunch somewhere and go to Montségur. That's something I've always wanted to do."

"What a good idea. Dorothy wrote about Montségur in her book *The Dark Citadel*. I was just getting into it when I fell asleep last night."

As they drove out of the village Owen said: "I used to devour Dorothy's novels when I was a kid. I was completely enthralled with them at the time. There's no doubt that both she and Ambrose influenced my decision to read medieval history at Oxford. But now when I want to relax I read John Le Carré or a good biography."

"Here we are, right in the heart of Cathar country, as Ambrose calls it."

She settled back into the passenger seat and listened, fascinated, as Owen began to talk about the Cathars.

"Why didn't I learn about this in school?"

"It's such an obscure period."

"Ambrose seems to think it changed the course of history."

"In a sense, it's true. They preached a doctrine of extreme purity, maintaining that man was inherently evil since he was imperfect and that he was the creation of the Devil, not God. That's what's known as Dualism: its essence is that evil exists, so God isn't all-powerful. Therefore he couldn't have created the world, but exists as the spirit of goodness, beauty, real enough but intangible. According to the Dualists, there are two gods, one of good, one of evil. The piety of the Cathars, the Goodmen, as they were called, strove to emulate that of Christ and made the priesthood of the Roman Church look remarkably sinful. They denied the validity of the sacraments and the principles of repentance and forgiveness. They were Gnostics, believing in the direct manifestation of divine truth from God to man. You can imagine why the Church was so keen to wipe them out."

By the time they were driving through the hilly country round Montségur after lunch, they were both anxious for their first glimpse of it. In a fold of hills Louise sighted the steep, jutting rock, its summit crowned by a ruined citadel of pale stone silhouetted against the low, scudding clouds that presaged rain. As they drove up the empty road, Louise had the disquieting illusion that if she looked round, the black ribbon of asphalt would disappear behind them. The groundless fears of childhood, that feeling of dread that could be induced by a shape, a shadow or light, which she had conquered years ago, crept up on her unawares. She peered ahead as Owen talked of the last days of the siege of the castle.

"You seem to know so much about it."

"It's Ambrose who got me interested in it when I was at school."

"And yet you've never been here." Louise opened the window to let in some air. The winding road had made her feel dizzy. "Think what it must have been like for the people imprisoned up there during the siege."

Owen parked the car at the base of a slope where the path began.

"It looks as if we're the only visitors—we can have it all to ourselves."

Louise got out of the car and buttoned up her parka against the stinging wind. The sound of cowbells reached her ears and she had an impression of deep tranquillity. The high summit where the fortress stood was set in a circle of lush green hills cradled by snow-capped mountains jutting through the clouds. They climbed the path that led toward a monument at the base of the hill, a cross mounted in stone.

"Look . . ." Louise pointed to a bouquet of snowdrops, laurel and wild flowers laid at the foot of the cross. "They've been picked since the sun rose. Someone's remembered after all those centuries." She looked round the empty landscape.

They stood in silence for a moment, listening to the wind that rasped against the surrounding shrubbery.

"You'd think the suffering that happened here would hang on the air, even after all this time. But it's a peaceful place, a holy place, isn't it?" When he smiled wryly at her, she added: "Yes, I know what I said the night I met you, that I didn't believe in anything. But there are times such as this when I don't feel quite so confident."

He didn't reply for a moment, but stared toward the west, where a break in the clouds revealed an infinite chain of snow-locked mountains breaking against the blue. "You know, bleak as it is, I find it beautiful and serene. That's where they must have constructed the palisade. It would have been a huge pyre to burn two hundred people."

"Let's walk down there, shall we?"

"Sure," he said, turning up his collar.

"How long do you suppose it takes to walk to the citadel?" Looking over her shoulder, Louise saw that thick black clouds had already descended on the summit.

"I don't know. Do you want to go up?"

"I'm not sure," she admitted. "I'm suddenly very curious, but it looks quite steep and the boots I'm wearing are hopeless."

She walked ahead of him into a stretch of wet grass. Her boots sank into the sodden earth as she circled the clearing.

"*Champ de Crémants*—field of the burned ones," Owen's voice followed Louise.

The real significance of the green square of earth suddenly hit her as she peered up at the ghostly image of the citadel fighting with the clouds. Suddenly overcome by a deep inconsolable grief, she buried her face in her hands.

Surprised to see her crying. Owen walked to her side and gathered her protectively in his arms. Yet as she cried against him, he felt bewildered and utterly useless. A trap-door seemed to have opened up and they were suspended over a chasm of inexplicable emotion. They clung to each other, waiting for the force that oppressed them to pass. In the sky, dark clouds waged war with the light, deepening the colors of the landscape. A sense of utter futility, alien to his nature, gripped Owen, making him wish for a moment that he could leave this life. An accumulated heartache welled up inside him that was so black and so bitter he couldn't understand where it had come from. The meaninglessness of existence, his own and that of everyone else, struck him cruelly. But he was guided by a premonition that as long as he held on to Louise there was something left. He held on tightly to the body of a woman he hardly knew, a body that seemed to have a comforting familiarity. As she clung to him for protection, he felt her weaknesses and strengths warring within her. In one compressed moment, he and Louise Carey seemed to know everything that could ever matter about each other. They were no longer strangers.

When her tears had subsided, it had begun to rain. He knew she was as uncomprehending as himself, and equally moved.

"Come on, let's go," he said gently.

"We can't go yet. I want to climb the hill to the citadel." She looked at Owen, set against the black backdrop of the mountain.

"Louise, we don't want to go up there, neither of us, not now." His voice was resolute, as if he had the right to protect her from danger and unhappiness. Thinking how absurd he must sound, he added, "We'll come some other day, when the sun is out, when the weather is better and it isn't so muddy."

To his surprise, she nodded in agreement and turned her back to the citadel. "When do you suppose that will be?" she murmured, drying her eyes.

They walked back to the car, not speaking. He opened the door and when she was seated, he tucked his jacket round her.

"You'll catch pneumonia."

"And what about you?" He closed the door. She listened to the rain drumming on the roof of the car as she unclenched her cold hands.

They drove in silence for several miles, the memory of what had happened hanging between them. Owen had been staring intently at the road, hardly seeing it in front of him.

"Do you want to talk about what you felt back there?" he asked.

"I don't know what to say. Once when I was at Hadrian's Villa outside Rome, I thought I could almost hear chariot wheels coming up the approach. It was like that back there— but it wasn't voices I heard. I was enveloped in an overpowering feeling that I don't think I could articulate—at least not right away. I want to think about it."

He reached out and squeezed her hand reassuringly. "You know, the power of suggestion is an extraordinary thing," he began. "It happens all over the world at the scene of great violence or grief. Battlefields, for example. It's as if time couldn't disperse all the spiritual energy that's been trapped.

If Ambrose and Dorothy could only hear me now," he added, trying to laugh.

Louise smiled, feeling the life flow back into her at the touch of his hand.

As Owen brooded about what had happened, he felt his perspective return with each mile they traveled from the site of the Cathar martyrdom. Louise's lingering grief moved him and, in the quiet cadence he would use with a child, he talked about the Gnostics, the mystic enlightenment that had threatened the power of Church and State. She committed to memory their touching belief that the world was a tarnished reflection of the realm of light, where God dwelt, and that it had been created by the Prince of Darkness, a fallen angel. She looked out of the rain-spattered window, thinking of Cathar Dualism, preached seven and a half centuries before their time, when women as well as men were priests and true Christians spurned the idea of sin, guilt and tithes, even penance that needed ecclesiastical hierarchy to impose it. The message had long outlived the martyrs who died for it.

It was dusk when they arrived back at the hotel at Puivaillon.

"I feel as if we've been away a long time," Louise commented as she got out of the car. She glanced down the long empty street, where the street lamps had already been lit and the houses were shuttered against the oncoming night.

Owen looked at the welcoming lights of the inn. "What a day. We laid one legend to rest and resurrected another."

As they walked toward the hotel, Louise didn't want to relinquish their sudden intimacy.

"Do you know, as we were driving through the village, I made myself a promise that I'd climb that hill some day."

"When that happens, I'd like to be there too. But for now I'd like to buy you a drink. Come on."

"It's my turn," she said, attracted by the sight of the fire burning in the grate beyond the glass doors of the hotel dining room.

"*Bonsoir, monsieur, 'dame,*" said the *patronne*, glancing up as they entered the foyer.

They became suddenly conscious of their bedraggled appearance. Owen caught Louise's eye and smiled. "We look as if we've been caught in a squall."

"We have," she replied.

Owen was waiting for her in the dining room when she came down for dinner. She had showered and washed her hair, and changed into gray flannel slacks and a sweater. When he saw her, he rose and pulled out her chair. She noticed he moved forward to kiss her, then drew away as if he had thought better of it. He poured her a glass of rosé, the strong wine of the Minerve that tasted of earth and herbs. As she sipped it, they regarded each other.

Arms folded, she stared at her glass for a moment, wondering what to say. "Up in my room, I found myself turning this afternoon over and over in my mind to make sense of it. I know it'll probably be doing the same thing years from now. Like you and your chalice, I suspect I won't know anything more in a decade than I knew a moment ago."

Owen's face was grave and his eyes were pensive. His answer was to reach across the table and lace his fingers through hers.

His touch aroused a wave of raw feeling inside her, reasserting the magnetic pull she had felt at Montségur. The common thread that had bound them then hadn't gone, but tied them together as surely as if they had survived a terrible ordeal themselves. She rejected the notion that they were falling in love or that they were victims of a sudden physical attraction. She felt none of the classic symptoms of an affair in bloom. She didn't feel romantic or flirtatious. Nor did she feel that ripening sense of anticipation that spelled pure desire. What moved between them was so solid, so real, it could have withstood the harsh light of a bus station or a night on a cold mountain. She felt cleansed, whole, as if the mismatched edges of her ragged life had been realigned and now presented a smooth surface to the world.

"What does it all mean?" she asked, not expecting him to know the answer.

Owen was about to say that he didn't feel he could walk away and put that day behind him when the *patronne* came to their table. As Louise ordered, he felt a cold fear in the pit of his stomach that clashed with his unbearable desire to spend their few remaining hours making love to her.

When they had chosen their food, Louise looked at him, wide-eyed, pale and serious.

"There's one thing I didn't tell you about my reasons for coming here last night. It seemed unimportant and, in a way, I was ashamed of it, but now I feel I've got to tell you . . ." When she told him how she had failed to scatter her father's ashes in a place he had never been, but had discovered in a book, he said sympathetically:

"I can imagine how guilty you feel, but it's perfectly understandable. People make promises when someone is dying that they realize afterward they can't keep."

"I feel better for telling you, that's all."

"If that's all you have on your conscience in this world, you're lucky. Now we're making our confessions, I haven't told you the whole story either," he said with a shrug. "I was, I still am, on a course of vengeance against the man who took that chalice from me."

He filled in the gaps about Rex Monckton, wishing he had mentioned it in the first place. "I'm beginning to realize that I'll have to turn every stone I can to get him. I thought by finding the *brocanteur* who sold me the chalice that he could identify it and prove it once belonged to me. Once I've got him as a witness that I bought the chalice, I could start to prove that Monckton cheated me. Coming here has strengthened my determination. I'll have the satisfaction of exposing Monckton for what he is: a cheap conman. If there's one thing I hate, it's hypocrisy. That, and being cheated by someone I trust."

There was a pause while they weighed each other up.

"Well," said Louise, "now we've got that out of the way. But we're still pursued by old ghosts."

"It doesn't seem to matter right now."

"It might in the morning."

When the *patronne* set their dinner before them, Louise began to eat what she had ordered without tasting it. Setting down her fork, she looked at Owen and he at her. Every inhibiting impulse died away as they tried to interpret what the other was thinking. As if dictated by a silent command, Louise pulled away from the table, unable to bear the charade for another moment. The anguished look on her face told him she didn't intend to come back, and he followed her. As Louise's feet touched the stairs, she felt a weightlessness at the sound of Owen's footsteps behind her. She was acutely conscious of his shadow moving up the wall as they climbed. When they reached the landing she clicked into neutral, driven by the image of their two bodies as one. As she opened the door of her room, Owen's hands guided her and she felt herself falling into a welcoming well of darkness.

Louise looked at his face, thrown into relief by amber light streaming through the thin curtains. She brought his hands beneath her sweater and placed them on her breasts. He touched her and emitted a whisper of delight.

"Louise . . . Louise," he murmured, feeling the warmth of her.

She felt an inexplicable joy as she stroked the contours of his temples, the lines of his brow, the shape of his lips, which she felt she knew already. When they were naked, they drew together, their shoulders, breasts and thighs like welded touchpoints that closed the aching breach of loneliness between them like lights across a dark valley. Owen's eyes glistened in the shadows, adoring her before he touched her. In a slow, tender movement he explored the supple curve of her spine, which bent to his hands like wheat to the scythe as she clutched his shoulders, feeling him push urgently against her. She ached to know his maleness in her hands, but shyness overcame her, as if she didn't have the right. She was twenty again, a virgin, delighting in the body of the first man who had ever loved her. Every fiber of her belonged to him.

Sitting on the bed, he brought her closer, crushing his mouth to the curve of her abdomen. Kissing his head as he held her, Louise breathed in the smell of him as she felt the living warmth of his body burn into her. The pounding of his heart pierced her chest as he drew her down to him on the narrow bed, where they fell weightlessly in a tunnel of blind yearning. When he entered her, Louise was torn through with a spasm of desire more shattering than she had ever known. Owen seemed to rage within her, nurturing the tenderest feelings at the heart of this strange, sudden passion. He whispered beautiful secret things as he loved her, which she couldn't explain and tried to cling to. Each word, each stroke of their bodies moving in unison, was driven by deep, true meaning that could never be understood or exhausted.

Afterwards, they lay side by side, replete with the emotion that still throbbed between them. Louise lay with her head on his shoulder, which was wet with her tears, trying to understand the sensations still eddying inside her. Her eyelids were unbearably heavy and after a moment she stopped fighting and slipped into a doze. The last thing she remembered was Owen pulling the covers round her.

Owen heard by her breathing that Louise had fallen asleep. Wide awake himself, he stared at the rich amber light glazing the cold, austere room, making it beautiful in the dimness. He heard the seconds pass like drops of water on stone, feeling that he was at peace as never before.

When Louise descended from her room to the hotel lobby, she saw through the lace curtains in the dining room that Owen was already there, his elbows on the table as he drank his coffee. She was dressed for the meeting that she had to attend as soon as she arrived in Paris, in a hounds-tooth check suit and black turtleneck. Setting down her bag by the reception desk, she saw a black overnight bag she guessed belonged to him. She paused for a moment to gather the courage to face him, but her stomach sank with apprehension as she opened the door. Meeting his eyes as he caught sight of her seemed one of the most difficult moments she had ever faced.

"Good morning," she said casually, sliding into the chair across from him. She was relieved when the *patronne* came immediately to the table to take her order. *"Café au lait, s'il vous plaît,"* she murmured, wondering what to say to a man who had tilted her life on its axis and whom she doubted she would ever see again.

Folding her hands, she looked at him directly. Owen's blue eyes were calm but unreadable. She knew in that telling moment that she had been hoping for so much more. But when she had awakened that morning, Louise knew they had no choice but to mistrust their confused emotions. When he left her room at dawn, she had pretended to be sleeping. Now she waited for him to speak, her mouth dry as she raised the coffee cup to her lips.

"This is very hard for both of us. In an hour we'll be traveling in opposite directions to our separate lives on separate continents. There's nothing we can do about it. I just want you to know how happy I am that you were here with me these last two days."

The troubled depths of his eyes contradicted his calm, reassuring voice, but she sensed he had already put the last two days behind him. She wanted always to remember the way his crisp dark hair was brushed back over his ears and temples, the lines that scored the sides of his mouth, his eyes that changed like the weather. What she would remember most of all were his hands, their gentleness as they touched her and yet their strength.

As Louise looked silently at him, Owen felt a powerful surge of attachment that all his practical resolutions couldn't kill. He admired the pure beauty of her face, which didn't belong to any age or epoch. He committed her to memory—her small nose, shiny dark brows above eyes full of gentle wisdom. When he remembered what it was like to kiss the delicate mouth, his resolution to make their parting as painless as possible dissolved for a moment.

As she poured herself a second cup of coffee, Louise said: "I've been going over and over it before I came down this morning, but it really distils itself down to the fact that I'm not sorry for a moment of what happened between us. I'll never forget you."

Her unspoken regret that their meeting was over flickered across the void that had sprung up between them. The sight of Owen filled Louise with a living warmth she knew would leave a painful emptiness inside her when they had separated.

Owen said: "I can't begin to explain this extraordinary thing that has happened to us. Why two souls should meet and fuse, then break apart is a cosmic riddle—no, not a riddle, an enigma."

She stopped short of speculating why they were allowing what had brought them together to tear them apart. Not wanting him to think she was weak and sentimental, she shrugged and said: "Two ships passing in the night. They signal and they keep on moving because, after all, they're going in different directions."

When they had paid the bill, they went to their separate rented cars parked side by side in front of the hotel. She opened the trunk of her car and Owen put in her bag.

Opening the car door, she said: "Good luck on your quest, Owen. I sincerely hope you find what you're looking for."

Smiling at him for the last time, she resisted the need to fill the silence with banalities.

"The same to you, Louise," he replied. He touched the curve of her cheek, then turned away.

That afternoon when her plane was airborne, it made a great arc to the south before heading for Paris. Louise looked down at the tightly packed clouds that hid the Pyrenees, wishing she could see them one last time, but the clouds refused to part.

10

In the cool gloom of the dining room Sancha folded a table-cloth, her attention drawn to a pyramid of ripe pears resting on a platter near the half-open window, which framed a rect-angle of hot, blue sky. Wiping the perspiration from her fore-head, she took off her apron and snapped it at the flies buzzing round the pears, the first of the season. At lunch Zarah had frowned at her greediness when she had asked for two. She took one from the platter and polished it on her sleeve. Just as her teeth met the smooth yellow skin, she thought of the fugitives hiding in the storeroom. She had heard Mayr whis-per to Zarah that they would slip from the house at dawn and make their way out of the city. Replacing the pear, Sancha thought how often she had been warned not to have anything to do with the Cathars. She knew Zarah had been persuaded to take them in, against her better judgement, in Baruch's absence. She wondered who they were and where they were going, and what interesting news they could tell her of the outside world. Seizing two of the juiciest pears, Sancha slipped them under her apron and went down to the court-yard.

In the heat of the day even the chickens and geese were quiet. The air was heavy with the smell of decaying ordure in the town. Hearing the distant clatter of horses' hooves somewhere beyond the gate, Sancha thought of the parched hills around the city that were sleeping in the afternoon heat. For a moment she dreamed of lying in the dry, scented grass beneath an olive tree, lulled to sleep by the cicadas as she looked up at the sky through the silver leaves.

Satisfied that no one had seen her, she unlocked the door with the key she had taken from its hiding place and entered the storeroom. The dusty smells of hay and horses hit her nose as she crept past the stables, her wooden clogs on the cobbles echoing through the dark passage. She reached the door where the fugitives must be and carefully pushed it open. In the dimness she saw two women in dark cloaks, their heads bowed in prayer. Hearing Sancha, they looked up in alarm.

She gave them a conspiratorial smile. "Don't be afraid—I'm a friend. I thought some fruit might refresh you." To show her sincerity, she pulled the pears from her apron. "Please take them, they're delicious."

She could see by their tapering fingers and high-bridged noses that they were noblewomen, though their hair and ragged cloaks were caked in dust. She was filled with humility when she saw that their mouths were like cracks in parched earth and their feet as worn and hardened as the hooves of animals. The sun and wind had bleached them of life and color, yet their dark eyes had the same brilliance as the Sabbath lamp when it burned in a dark room.

Sancha suddenly became conscious that she had been staring. Dropping her eyes, she offered them the pears, instinctively genuflecting as she extended her hands. She was moved by these frail holy women, whose tortured bodies were like once-proud towers gone to ruin.

"Thank you for your kindness," said one, in the melodious voice of a lady.

"No one knows I'm here. I came to wish you well," said Sancha. She longed to say more, to ask the women where they had come from and where they were going, but their aura of spiritual dignity silenced her curiosity.

"God be with you and grant you a safe journey to your destination," she said lamely, making her exit.

Closing the door behind her, Sancha felt her way down the corridor. She gasped with shock as she collided with the solid bulk of a man barring the exit. Baruch's servant Pons was leering down at her.

"What are you doing here?" she demanded, feeling his rank breath on her face. Nausea rose in her at the stench of him.

"Might I ask the same, milady?" he retorted. "This room is always locked and no one is allowed to enter except the master and his sons, yet I saw it open."

"It is none of your affair," she said, trying to pass him, but he sidestepped, blocking her way. "I am here on an errand for my mother. Now leave."

He laughed quietly, and she froze when his rawboned hand reached for her hair.

"How dare you touch me!"

He moved away, but her relief was short-lived. He slid past her to the room where the two women were hiding and, pushing the door open, he gave a low, insinuating chuckle as he looked inside.

"Cathars," he said, spitting out the word. "Two of them."

"Shut that door now and get out," Sancha ordered. Terror for herself had shifted to the women. "If you don't do as I say, you will be whipped," she said imperiously, daring him to defy her. Only the pulse beating in her throat gave her away. "Did you hear what I said? Shut that door now and remove yourself from this storeroom or I'll see you are punished," she ordered.

Then he gave a chilling laugh, as a giant might laugh at a child. When he pulled the door closed, they were left in the dark corridor lit only by light coming through cracks in the wood. She tried to dart past him, but Pons was too quick for her. He lunged, grabbing her by the wrist as she flew by. As he pinned her to the wall, she gagged at the stench coming from his body.

"You always hated me, even when you were nothing but a bag of bones the master brought home like a starving cat. Now you think you're a fine lady. You look down on me."

She tried to squirm loose, but he tightened his grip, grasping her hair with one hand and twisting it until tears came to her eyes. He thrust his other hand inside her bodice and fumbled for her breasts. Squeezing her nipples painfully, he began to grunt with lust.

He pulled her down the corridor by her hair and shoved her roughly into a stall up against a bale of hides, knocking the wind out of her. Raising her head, she saw he had torn away the front of his leather jerkin to reveal what looked like a purple club jutting between his legs. Then he fell on her, pushing up her dress. She felt his hand span her belly as he prized open her legs, aiming himself like a cannon at the tenderest part of her.

As he bore down on her, Sancha was suddenly imbued with the gift she had forgotten she possessed, filling her with strength. The source of her power seemed to spring from the very earth itself, burning the soles of her feet and shooting upward. In one spasm her body went rigid. Her arms shot out and her fingers splayed like stars. She spewed out a hiss, darting her tongue at him like a viper, while her eyes glowered in warning.

Pons staggered back as if felled by lightning. Grunting in panic, he stumbled, trying with both hands to protect his genitals from her curse. Lust had vanished from his coarse features, to be replaced by mortal terror that she would destroy his manhood.

"I'm bewitched," he howled. Clutching his limp penis, he doubled over and crawled toward the door.

Sancha's trance was shattered by a crashing sound at the doorway. As her vision cleared, she saw Mayr's dark head appear at the threshold, his face contorted with rage.

"Bastard! Brute!" he bellowed. Every sinew of his body was taut with fury. Sancha hardly recognized the mild, gentle Mayr, who had turned into a warrior before her eyes.

"Coward! Swine!" he cried, and grabbing a spur that hung from a post he lashed out at Pons, who squealed in pain as blood gushed from his cheek.

"I'll kill you, I'll kill you," shrieked Mayr, striking him again and again. Like a man driving a beast, Mayr forced him from the stall. Sancha listened as Mayr, bellowing in fury, pursued Pons down the corridor, cursing him as he pleaded for mercy.

When Mayr appeared again at the doorway, his chest heaving from exertion, he found Sancha huddled in a corner, her arms across her chest as she shivered violently.

"Sancha, are you all right? My sweet sister, he didn't . . . ?"
He broke off with a sob, putting his arm around her.

She shook her head, because it didn't matter. Her mind
leapt to the Cathars hiding in the storeroom. She began to
sob, wishing she could turn back time to half an hour ago.

"It was my fault; I should never have come here," she
cried, clinging to Mayr. The broken words tumbled from her.

"Thank God I came in time," said Mayr. His eyes were
full of such righteousness it made her weep. He held her until
she had stopped crying, then sank down on a pile of hay to
think. As he met Sancha's red-rimmed eyes, his face was
grave.

"I drove him through the gate and from the house," he
said. "I'm sure my father would have done the same. He
might have killed Pons because he is even stronger than I am.
Thank God it was I who found you. How did it happen,
Sancha?"

Her head hanging in shame, she told him how, in a moment of boredom, she had taken pears to the fugitives.

"Sancha, did Pons see the Cathars?" Mayr asked anxiously.

When she nodded, he buried his face in his hands for a
long moment. When he raised his eyes, they were full of
doom.

In the middle of the night the baying of a dog woke Sancha
in the inky blackness of the chamber under the eaves where
she slept. Unraveling herself from her shift and the bedclothes, she saw the moonlight piercing the holes in the shutters, making her yearn to fling them open and fill her lungs
with the cool night air. But Zarah had admonished her never
to open the shutters at night for any reason whatever, for fear
of thieves, demons or poisonous vapors.

Clinging to drowsiness, she fought the repugnant memory
of Pons. A fearful uneasiness had invaded the house since
that violent day. As the dog wailed again, she wondered if it
could be some kind of omen presaging the fall of the house
of Castronovo.

On Baruch's arrival a few days after Pons had disappeared,
Sancha had hung her head in shame as she waited with the
others in the courtyard to greet him. When he shouted im-

patiently for Pons to come and help with the load, Zarah stilled his gesturing hands and whispered what had happened. Sancha was convulsed with remorse when she interpreted the shock on his tired face. She met his eyes full of weary resignation, wounded unbearably by her betrayal of the kind man who had treated her as his daughter. Throwing herself at his feet, she began to sob, tortured rather than comforted by the touch of his hand as he spoke unforgettable words:

"You must never regret an act of kindness or charity, no matter what the consequences."

Fearing Pons might revenge himself against them with accusations of witchcraft and heresy, Baruch had come to a swift decision that as soon as possible they should all leave the city, heading for Perpignan and then perhaps Spain, or even beyond, should it prove impossible to return to Quillan. Their only comfort was in the fact that they had heard nothing of Pons, indicating that perhaps he was frightened of bringing down accusations on his own head if he went to the authorities.

The following day Baruch planned to leave Quillan with Mayr and Jusef on the pretext of delivering goods to a neighboring town, but the mules would be loaded with as many trade goods and as much gold as they could carry. Zarah and Sancha would follow, leaving the city gates on the following morning ostensibly to gather herbs and berries. To avoid suspicion, they would take nothing with them but bread and wine for the journey. Zarah had already sewn money and jewels into the clothes they would wear.

Sancha fell back on to her bed and sank into a shallow dream in which she was pursued by a faceless, nameless terror. When it subsided, she traveled to a familiar land, where green pastures blazed against the unbroken line of the Pyrenees jutting against the enameled sky. She was still out of breath after her escape from the narrow streets of the town and was running free toward a city of stones, where she could hear the rush of water flung from a high precipice into a narrow chasm. Her heart pounding, she began to run toward it, aching to feel the splash of cold water on her skin. The moving blue water was just within reach when her eyes flew open with a start. Blinded by the flame of a candle, she gasped, realizing the sound of rushing water in her dream was the rasp of straw as a hand shook the pallet on which she slept.

"Sancha, Sancha, wake up, child."

Zarah's urgent whispers brought her fully awake.

"Get up quickly, get out of bed. There's no time to lose."

"Are we going now, so soon?" she murmured sleepily.

"No, it's too late. It's the Inquisition—they've come for us."

Beneath her urgent whisper Sancha sensed a sob that longed to break. She had no time to be frightened. Zarah tugged her from bed to the narrow passage above the stairwell. From somewhere deep inside the house below, Sancha could hear men bellowing and doors being battered open. Before she could protest, Zarah had lifted a carpet and prized apart two planks that concealed a storage place Sancha had never known was there.

"Help me, Sancha," Zarah whispered as she struggled to lift the sack of coins wedged beneath the floorboards. When they had dragged the money out, Zarah said: "Now climb in and don't make a sound. If no one comes for you, stay here until all is quiet. Then leave the house; go at daybreak with your head well covered, wearing your plain shift and a kerchief, like a peasant." She pulled the shawl from her shoulders and stuffed it in Sancha's hands. "Take a scythe and join the harvesters. Keep walking west or north. Make your way to Mirepoix, to Limoux, anywhere, but don't come back here. God grant we will find each other again."

Sancha resisted as Zarah forced her into the narrow compartment. When she began to lay the planks over her head, terror seized the girl and she pounded on them with her fists.

"No—don't bury me alive," she cried.

When Zarah lifted the planks, Sancha quietened, but she started to cry when she saw Zarah's anguished face illuminated by the light of the taper she carried.

"Please, child, I beg you to be still." Hearing Baruch's voice below, she looked fearfully over her shoulder.

"The man's a liar, I tell you. My son caught him stealing from us. You take the word of this ruffian, this lout, against a man of property, a citizen . . ."

"And a Jew . . ." came the accusation, ringing through the house.

"Please," Zarah whispered urgently for the last time. Her parting gesture was to touch Sancha's forehead tenderly. As an afterthought, she pressed a few coins that she had taken from the sack into the girl's hand.

"On pain of death, conceal yourself as I told you."

The floorboards came down on Sancha's face, extinguishing the air and light. As she lay there in the stifling darkness, her own life seemed to ebb away. Numbly, she heard the heavy thud of a carpet being flung across the floorboards, muffling the sound of Zarah's footsteps. She lay there as if imitating death in the hidden compartment narrow as a coffin. Suffocated by dust and heat, she crushed the coins in her palms until they hurt, to prove she was still alive. This was what it was like to die, she thought, to be buried underground, never to see the light of day again.

For the next hours she lay immobile. The house shook as if it were being torn down around her as the soldiers sent by the Inquisitors ripped out its contents like entrails torn from a fowl. When she heard footsteps pounding overhead, followed by the sound of the carpet being lifted, she waited to be discovered, but the footsteps died away.

She heard no familiar voices, only the loot-crazed shouts of soldiers. Sobbing quietly, she swallowed her tears. Her last thought before she lost consciousness was that death was nothing to be afraid of.

When she next opened her eyes, Sancha had lost all sense of time. Thinking she heard a cock crow, she cautiously lifted the boards above her head. Crawling up onto the floor, the first thing she saw through the open window of her room was the fiery dawn that foretold another hot August day. As she got to her feet, the coins dropped from her hands, echoing through the house as they rolled down the stairs. She wandered through the empty house in a daze, hardly recognizing the doorless rooms, the chests tipped up and emptied, the broken furniture. She cut her feet on shattered crockery in the dining room, where the tapestries depicting Old Testament scenes had been slashed to ribbons. In a few short hours the soldiers had reduced the comfortable home of the Jew Baruch de Castronovo to ruin, stripping it of every dear and familiar thing. She looked round at the scene of destruction, haunted by the ghosts of cruelty, bigotry and greed.

Sancha left the house as streaks of the rising sun split the dark sky above the courtyard. She had tied a few belongings and some food into a bundle and covered her head with a kerchief as Zarah had told her. As an afterthought, she picked up a hoe lying near the shed. Shivering, although it was warm, she took her first tentative steps down the narrow street toward the gates of the city.

It was late afternoon over two months later when Sancha dared to approach Quillan again. She was sunburnt, wind-blown and caked with dust from traveling, and her feet were wrapped in rags. The trees on the hills that surrounded the city had already begun to shed their leaves. She stood motionless, her eyes sweeping down the jagged line of pink tiled roofs along the silvery stream that ran through the town. Then she descended through the scrub toward the main road, feeling sick with apprehension, but not afraid.

The sun had left the valley when she arrived within sight of the city gates. She sat down at the side of the road traveled by carts, animals and peasants returning from a day in the fields, resting against the bundle that contained her few possessions and the medicines she had made to keep herself during the coming winter.

The money Zarah had given her had now all been spent or stolen. On her way, she had met two Cathar priests *en route* to Montségur, who were full of kindness and good advice. They had raised her hopes that Baruch and Zarah and their sons, being Jews, might have been allowed to return home after forfeiting their possessions to the Church. She rose to her feet, thinking she might see the gates of home before nightfall. Walking toward the city, she shied away from the farmers and tradesmen, who might question her. She thought of the day Baruch first bore her there on horseback, wrapped under his cloak. During the last few weeks she had slept under the stars again, hardening herself to the elements. The wind had combed her hair, the rain had cleansed her face; birds had awakened her and owls had lulled her to sleep. She had quenched her thirst in cold mountain streams and fed off berries and herbs like a deer, a life that had honed her body to be lithe, quick and strong. She had sharpened her senses on danger and slaked her hunger for wild beauty, and she had rediscovered the movements of the sun and stars.

She found herself smiling at the prospect of the astonishment on the faces of the family when they saw her enter the courtyard like a prodigal daughter. She forgot her blistered feet, her hunger and thirst, as she followed a stream of peasants behind the wagons full of grapes harvested from the vineyards. Obliquely she searched every face, but recognized no one. As she approached the city gates, Sancha looked closely at a plump dark woman ahead of her, who seemed familiar. She felt a surge of delirious happiness when she realized it was Beatrice, Zarah's servant. Sprinting forward, she hurried to catch up with her. When she came closer, she could see the woman was no longer dressed as the servant of a prosperous household, but in the ragged clothes of a peasant, her face and hands weathered and dirty. When she heard Sancha call her name, she turned with a startled look on her moon face.

"What are you doing here?" There was no joy in her voice, only wariness. "Don't speak my name or talk to me. It's dangerous," she hissed. Turning her back, she walked on.

Sancha ran after her. "What's the matter with you? Why are you behaving in such a way?" she cried, on the brink of tears.

When Beatrice saw Sancha couldn't be shaken off so easily, she whispered harshly, "All right, if you must, walk near me, but stay a few paces away so I can't be seen with you."

"But aren't you on your way home now? I'll come with you; surely you understand that."

"Home?" She let out a startled laugh. "There is no home. The master's fine house is now the home of priests. Don't enter the city. Leave at once. It's rumored that Baruch is dead, but no one knows what happened to Zarah and her sons. As for you, if you enter the gates, you will be taken for a witch. Now go. I have taken pity on you because you were always kind to me, but if anyone should ever find out, I will suffer."

Sancha watched Beatrice disappear down the road, the questions she was burning to ask dying inside her. A mantle of grief fell on her bent shoulders and she stumbled off the road, her vision blinded by tears.

* * *

A freezing wind buffeted the market square at Mirepoix, rattling the coarse gray wool stretched on poles, where vendors huddled round smoking braziers to keep warm. Even the sewage in the gutters had frozen, Sancha noted, as she spread her wares with hands numb with cold. She had come to the market at daybreak from outside the city gates, where she slept with lepers, branded heretics and other outcasts. An old woman allowed her to peddle her herbs at the edge of her stall in exchange for a portion of her remedy for chest congestion. Sancha turned a deaf ear to her racking cough as the woman bound piles of kindling wood for sale, alternately mumbling to herself and spitting on the cobbles whitened by frost. When Sancha inched closer to the small fire at her feet, a withered, bony hand lashed out and boxed her on the ear. She flashed a look of hatred at the old woman, whose sun-blackened face was buried in a shawl.

At the sound of bells and bleating goats and the cries of shepherds Sancha looked down the lane, thinking how shepherds were prone to all the plagues of nature due to their harsh life in the hills. A pair of stout hairy legs covered in scars and calluses planted themselves before her eyes and she looked up to see a young shepherd wrapped in skins, with a grizzled beard and staring green eyes.

"Your fame is traveling, little healer," he muttered. "A shepherd on the hills told me you sell a powerful ointment for wounds." When he pulled off his boot to expose his blackened foot, she sensed he wanted some words of magic to accompany the medicine, but in the crowded market she had never dared whisper the incantations her mother had taught her. She had already heard pious whispers that morning that all healing was a crime against God and the Church, and knew she would soon have to move on. She reached in her bag for some of the ointment she had made from herbs, spiders' webs and lichen, the most powerful healing agents she knew.

"How are your sheep? Are they well? You could rub some of this on their ears," she said, making the shepherd laugh.

"I wouldn't waste your magic remedies. Not at such expense."

"It's cheap enough if your animal fetches a better price at market," she retorted.

"What does your husband say to such a clever wife who advises him?" He looked at her keenly.

"I have none and don't want one either." Observing the bushy bearded shepherd, who smelled as rank as his sheep, she didn't return his flirtatious smile. The recollection that she had once been plump, rich and pretty gave her a sudden dignity.

"No husband to protect you? Such a pretty girl as you?"

She shot him a look of reproach, thinking he resembled one of his flock. She was already weary of his presence and was dreaming of hot soup and a piece of bread.

When the shepherd had gone and hunger and cold bit deep once again, Sancha began to take stock. She would never marry, but for deeper reasons than she had told the shepherd. She had no family, no fortune, no home, and the only husband she could ever hope for would be a rootless wanderer like herself. Then, unbidden, the image of the Templar came to her mind from deep in her memory, where it had been living, growing all these months. His golden countenance had blistered her innocence forever.

"You were stupid to refuse a healthy young shepherd, my girl." The old crone was scowling at her as she stuffed twigs in bunches with her knotted hands.

"Mind your own business," Sancha snapped. Rebelliousness coursed through her at this brutal, coarse old woman with a streaming nose and a mouth like a black hole, who abused her continually.

Screwing up her face, the old woman said suspiciously: "Who are you, anyway, and where do you come from?"

Sancha leapt to her feet and began gathering her belongings, propelled by pride and a nameless misery.

"I asked you a question: who are you and where do you come from, with your fine airs?" It was a screeching accusation.

A pulse of fear beat inside Sancha as she hoisted her bundle over her shoulder and hurried down the lane, pursued by the woman's gibbering. She was so preoccupied, she nearly collided with two Dominicans, whose faces were buried deep in the hoods of their black cloaks. She turned her head as they passed, pretending she had lost something. The sight of their shadowy faces as they paraded through the market in warm woolen robes, their hands snugly tucked in their sleeves, filled her with loathing. Surrounded by an aura of invincibility, they surveyed the crowd arrogantly, their sharp eyes missing nothing.

She stood on a corner, turning her back against the raw wind, not knowing where to go. Feeling a tug at her sleeve, she saw a little boy with a red nose looking curiously up at her.

"Are you the person they call a healer?"

"I might be. Why?" she asked suspiciously.

"My mother asked me to find you. She said you might have something to heal my sister."

Sancha followed the boy to the far side of the market, near the *abreuvoir,* where mules and sheep were crowding to drink. The air was pierced by their bleating and neighing and the sharp commands of the herdsmen. Huddled against the wall she saw an ashen-faced woman clutching what appeared to be a bundle of rags, which Sancha realized was a child. When she saw her, the woman cried:

"Can you help me? Oh, please, please, help me, please. She's nearly dead of fever. I believe some devil has possessed her . . ."

Sancha looked down at the red, swollen face of the little girl, whose rattling breath escaped through cracked lips. She touched her burning forehead, knowing she was marked for death.

"I don't know why she's still alive. She's been like this for days."

"I'm sorry, I can do nothing. It's too late."

"You can try—to give her something, anything. I'm poor, but I'll give you all I can."

"It's not the money. You must pray for her," Sancha mumbled, turning to go.

"It's not prayers that will help, but magic. They say that you . . ."

"Who says, and what do they say?" Sancha asked sharply, looking around to see if anyone had heard them.

"For pity's sake," the woman pleaded, tears running down her cheeks. "If you have the gift, use it to help those in need.

I'll try anything. I am dry of prayers. I have prayed and prayed . . ."

Her desperation aroused Sancha's pity. Observing her more closely, Sancha decided she wasn't a peasant. As their eyes met, something told her that this woman, too, was dispossessed, like herself, and owned nothing but the rags she stood in. For a moment the horrors they had lived through flickered between them, forging a bond.

"My husband was stripped of his lands and branded a heretic; then he was put to torture and burned at the stake. I am an outcast like you—now, please, will you help me?"

Sancha's cheeks burned in shame. "Yes, of course, but it's dangerous here. I saw two priests just now."

"There's no time to lose."

Sancha untied her bundle and found the one thing in her possession that could be of any use: feverfew, which worked mysteriously in some cases and not in others. She mixed it with water, not from the *abreuvoir* but from a goatskin flask of spring water she carried with her, which her mother had told her had great powers. Together she and the woman managed to prize open the child's mouth and pour in some of the mixture. Cold and hunger would kill her, Sancha knew, if the fever didn't. In the presence of the sorrowing woman, her life blown away by misery, she forgot to grieve for herself. She spoke the words that, according to the Church, branded her as an instrument of the Devil, strange words that sprang from her unconscious memory. In a thin whisper she sang the ancient incantation that warded off the most destructive demons that induced deadly fevers. Lightly touching the baby's head, she felt the heat quivering beneath her hands, then leap up her arm, lodging in her shoulder like a pain. A moment later Sancha opened her eyes, realizing she had been in a trance. Her fingers had gone rigid and hovered over the baby's face. She saw some shepherds looking at her and realized they must have witnessed the ritual, which made her anxious to disappear.

"That's all I can do," she said, picking up her bundle. When she saw the woman fumbling in her clothes for money, she said: "No, I never take money for children. You owe me nothing."

"You must take this—for my sake. It's all I have of value to give." She pressed a small silver dove into her palm.

"What is it?"

"Someday you will know."

"Are you a fortune teller, some kind of prophet?"

"Perhaps. You must wear the dove next to your heart."

Sancha slipped the dove into the money pocket she had sewn inside her garments between her breasts, then melted into the crowd. A while later she was chewing on a crust of bread as she turned over the silver dove in her hand when the little boy came running up to her again.

"My mother asked me to look for you," he cried. "She wants you to come because my sister is well."

Sancha put out her hand to silence him, but he was so excited she decided she had better follow him through the crowd. When they found his mother, she whispered:

"It's like a miracle. All of a sudden she opened her eyes. Her face was bathed in sweat and when she cried, I gave her my breast and she took it. I had to see you once more so you could know what you have done. It's a miracle," she repeated, kissing her child, who was sucking lustily at her breast.

The boy, who had been staring at them intently, burst out: "A miracle. My sister is cured by a miracle." Laughing and dancing, he ran through the crowd.

"God be with you," murmured Sancha, anxious to go. People were already turning their heads at the sight of the delirious little boy, chanting about miracles at the top of his lungs. Sancha suddenly felt herself at the center of a circle of suspicious faces that barred her escape. A ripple went through the crowd, like the lowing of animals. Her heart pounded in fear as the noise moved like a dangerous groundswell to the far corners of the market, enclosing her in an invisible cage.

"She's a saint!" cried a woman, falling on her knees before Sancha. Her hands raised in supplication, she grabbed the hem of her dress.

"This is no saint. Such a cure could only be the work of the Devil interfering with God's will," came the sneering judgement of a man. His words whistled through the air like arrows, drawing the lines of battle. Now she felt fear and hatred writhing all round her like serpents.

"I did nothing wrong." Sancha's tremulous voice was swallowed by the din, as the crowd's muttering increased.

"*Sorcière,*" came an accusing hiss, causing squeals of alarm.

One man, braver than the others, sprang forward with a stick and hit her painfully on the shoulder, making her cry out.

"Even a witch can feel pain," he retorted, raising a few nervous titters. He laughed defiantly at Sancha.

The stupid look of swaggering pride on his face made her angry. She searched the crowd, but no one could meet her eyes.

"Won't any of you speak for me? You have seen me here these last weeks, going about my business selling herbs. What have I done to any of you?" There was no answer.

"Make way, make way for the friars, make way!" came the excited call.

Sancha saw the crowd part to allow the two Dominicans she had seen earlier by the market stall to come forward. Their appearance caused a great wave of excitement.

"What has happened here?" demanded one, fixing Sancha with a cold stare. He threw back his hood, revealing his tonsured head and a full jowled face set with small, shrewd eyes. At the sight of him Sancha's mind began to spin. Bile rose in her throat at the memory of what her own tormented mother had suffered at the hands of the clergy, forcing her to retch. A gasp went through the crowd and the Dominicans hurriedly pulled forth their crosses and held them up protectively against the witch.

"Speak, speak and reveal yourself," demanded the friar. "In the name of the Father, the Son and the Holy Ghost I command you to submit to his power."

He reeled off a long string of incantations, calling up all the saints to assist him. Sancha stared at his crucifix, which, for her, summoned up all the monstrous tortures the Inquisition reserved for witches: they were forced to swallow boiling oil and the soles of their feet were set on fire. She shut her eyes. Perhaps, if she had the power to heal a child, she could make her accusers disappear.

"Open your eyes, harlot of Satan," someone jeered.

When she did, the first person her eyes fell on was a woman of high rank, a lady who didn't belong there. For a moment Sancha thought she was dreaming of the Virgin Mary. The woman was wearing a simple gown, elegant in its plainness, and a dark blue cloak. Her translucent face was encircled by a wimple that covered her hair, making it difficult to tell how old she was. Her beauty lay in the stillness of her deep-set, pale gray eyes, her aquiline nose and straight eyebrows. She spoke in a rich, rather high voice that had the power to make the crowd fall silent.

"Friar, allow me to speak."

"Yes, my good lady," said the Dominican, raising his eyebrows querulously.

"I don't know how the events of this last hour have occurred, but there is a serious error here. This girl is no witch, but the daughter of a sergeant-at-arms who has lately been in service with my husband."

"And who might he be?" asked the other friar, his eyes full of resentment at the intrusion.

"Berenger, Comte de Franjal."

There were murmurs at the mention of one of the greatest lords of the Comté de Foix. The Lady Alazaïs de Franjal was known throughout the *comté* for her charitable works and had recently endowed a convent in her name at Fanjeaux. Daughter of a duke, her reputation as a devout Catholic was unimpeachable. The friar smiled ingratiatingly, but he was reluctant to let his captive go so easily.

"In fact, it's strange, but I came here today thinking I might find her to give her news of her father. If you let her come with me now, I will take her in charge." Handing her reticule to her lady-in-waiting, she extended her hands to Sancha. "My child, how pleased I am to see you again after these months."

The Dominican regarded her narrowly. "What you say might be so, but I must fulfill my duty and report this to the Inquisition. She had performed acts here that can only be the work of the Devil, and she must give an account of herself to the proper authorities."

"Do you take the word of a small, starving boy over

mine?'' There was mockery in her voice. ''I have been told it was he who is the cause of all this confusion.''

When the friar looked doubtfully toward the crowd, they began arguing amongst themselves. As the friar turned to restore order, Sancha had the presence of mind to whisper her name to the lady.

''Friar, if this child were possessed by miraculous powers, then she would not be in rags. So I ask you without further delay to let her accompany me back to Puivaillon. My confessor and I will watch her carefully and will send for you immediately if there is any sign of possession.''

The Dominican shrugged, glancing at the crowd, which had begun to fall away. As the bell marking midday rang out, he was reminded of the meal awaiting him in the priory.

''Come with me,'' he said curtly.

The lady-in-waiting following, they all went off together in the direction of the church. Opening the heavy wooden door, the friar admitted them to an office where a scribe was writing on a parchment.

''Because of your reputation, lady, I entrust this girl to you. But I warn you, if you fail in your duty and protect heretics or witches, your mortal soul will be in danger.''

Jotting something in the register, he suddenly seemed bored with the whole matter.

Moments later Sancha, Alazaïs and the lady-in-waiting were hurrying through the gates of the city. Expecting to be dismissed, Sancha was surprised when the lady indicated that she should accompany them to an encampment of men and horses gathered round a blazing fire visible in the distance. The men, whom Sancha took to be the lady's retainers, all stood at her approach. Alazaïs motioned for Sancha to come near the fire, where a fur had been laid, upon which rested a carved chair inlaid with ivory.

Sancha sat at the lady's feet while her maid brought hot spiced wine and slabs of bread filled with roast meat for them to eat. The wine was too hot to drink, but she bolted the food. The lady was talking to her companions and seemed oblivious to Sancha as she curled up on the soft rug, her shoulder against the chair, already dreading the moment when she would have to leave this safe resting place. The heat of the fire made her drowsy as she heard them talk of a place called Puivaillon, of which she had never heard. From the conversation, she realized she was in the company of important nobles. As far as she could gather, their purpose in coming to Mirepoix had been to ask for news of Alazaïs's only living son, from whom she had been separated for a long time. Sancha heard that she had two other sons, who had been killed in battle, and a daughter, who had taken vows in a convent.

When her companions had dispersed, Alazaïs turned her attention to Sancha.

"Tell me where you come from, of your past and how you came to be here. The way you speak suggests you are not of the town."

"Before I tell you that, my lady, I must thank you with all my heart for what you have done for me. I know that death or torture would have awaited me at the hands of the Inquisition . . ." Feeling herself about to cry, she stopped, unable to continue. She would have liked to know why she had been rescued, but a deep inexplicable tiredness had taken hold of her. She found herself repeating the same words Baruch had once said of her, wondering if she cursed everything she touched. "I hope you have no cause to regret your act of charity."

"Child, you intrigue me. I noticed first your carriage and manner today in the square, and your beauty beneath the rags, which contradict your state in life. And now, seeing your intelligence and hearing your speech, I know you are not at all what you seem. You are poor and alone. And you are a healer," she added. There was respect in her voice, not condemnation. She added in a low tone so that no one else could hear: "You are not a Cathar, are you?"

The mention of the heretics made Sancha pause, but Alazaïs's frank gray eyes told her she had nothing to fear.

"No." She shook her head.

"But you are a healer, are you not?"

"I can't deny it."

"Tell me how all this came about."

Sancha related the story of her life, leaving nothing out, including the final episode of her escape to the mountains when Baruch had been seized and tried for harboring Cathars. When she had finished, Alazaïs thoughtfully knitted her long fingers together, hands so unlike Sancha's own, which were black with grime. Sancha did not take her eyes off those fine hands, which seemed made for prayer. The two of them had been left alone by the others, who were going about the business of preparing food and loading goods bought in the market.

Finally Alazaïs shook her head. "And you, you are the adopted child of Baruch de Castronovo of Quillan?"

"You speak as if you know my father," whispered Sancha, stunned.

Alazaïs's eyes filled with pity. "Then you don't know?"

"When I tried to return, a servant in our house warned me not to come back and said Baruch was dead, but I hoped it was not true."

Taking Sancha's hands, Alazaïs held them tightly in her own, which were as dry as parchment. "Have courage to bear the truth. Baruch is dead. Please don't ask me how I know this and tell no one you heard it from me."

"And his wife, Zarah, my mother? And what of his sons, Mayr and Jusef?" All the grief she had repressed these last months gushed to the surface.

Alazaïs shook her head. "I would not dare to raise your hopes. They were all imprisoned and must have perished with him."

Sancha felt herself start to shake, even though she had given up hope a long time ago. Alazaïs squeezed her hand and left her to cry in silence huddled against the chair. Moments later, her eyes fixed drowsily on the fire that wavered with each gust of cold wind, her mourning for Baruch, Zarah, Mayr and Jusef was overpowered by her need for oblivion. Her tired limbs slackened involuntarily and she gave in to the sensation of being replete, safe and warm, which brought on an exhausted, dreamless slumber. When she opened her eyes, the wimpled figure of Lady Alazaïs, lit by a smile, came into focus. Sancha stirred abruptly, seeing that the men were packing the mules and horses and all that remained of the encampment was a smoldering fire and the fur rug on which she had slept.

"Are you going now?" she asked, rising to her feet. A mist had enclosed the colorless landscape, shrouding the low foothills of the Pyrenees that ringed the valley. Looking back at the forbidding walls of the city, she picked up her bundle.

A young page stood by, holding the chased silver bridle of a piebald horse caparisoned in gray and yellow, ready to help his lady mount. The lady-in-waiting, mounted on a black mare, rode by their side leading a gray pony, whose breath curled in the air as it snorted. Seeing it was time to part, Sancha curtsied. "God go with you," she murmured, crushing the hem of the lady's gown to her lips as she whispered a blessing.

She was startled to hear a cascade of pure laughter above her head. Glancing up, she saw Alazaïs, whose serious expression had changed to an amusement that bewildered her.

"My poor sweet child," she said, shaking her head. "I thought it was plain to you. You can't return to the village now after what has happened. As you have nowhere else to go, it is my wish that you accompany us to Puivaillon."

Sancha raised her head, wondering if Alazaïs could possibly mean what she said.

"It is a small enough tribute to pay to a Jew who sacrificed his life to save true Christians. God sent you to me to try to right an injustice by whatever small means I can. Mount this pony and travel beside me. Can you ride a horse?"

She shook her head.

"Then you will learn."

The page lifted her into the saddle. As she took the reins in her hands, Sancha felt the force of destiny strike her like the wind at her back. From the height of a horse she regarded the cruel wintry landscape, which had taken on an austere beauty. As night gathered to the west in a pink reflection, she trained her eyes on the Lady Alazaïs ahead, whose silhouette seemed to be guiding her toward a land of light.

Three days later, as the winter sun burned low on the horizon, the travelers came over the crest of a hill. Coming up behind Alazaïs on her pony, Sancha had her first glimpse of Puivaillon set on a distant hilltop, overlooking a lake that cast up a rolling mist, giving it a dreamlike and magical aura. Its sheer size and magnificence brought her heart to her throat. The jutting tower pierced with sculptured windows dominated the vast ramparts, which could have contained a village. There was an intriguing contrast of austerity and delicacy in this great stone edifice that commanded the snow-covered valley ringed by craggy mountains. At Alazaïs's request, Sancha brought her pony alongside hers. Her face was washed in coral light from the blazing sky, which seemed to be welcoming the chatelaine home. She smiled reassuringly at Sancha, seeing by the look of awe on her face that she was overcome by her first sight of her domain. Then she loosened the reins, letting her restive horse have its head.

Sancha watched her canter down the hill, her headdress and cape flying in the wind behind her. The sight of the chatelaine abandoning her usual dignity set a train of joy in her wake. In a moment, her ladies-in-waiting dug their heels into their horses and followed in pursuit. Trotting behind, Sancha trained her sights on the jutting tower of Puivaillon, wondering what world lay beyond its walls.

11

Parking his car in Berkeley Square, Owen pulled his trench-coat from the back seat as he glanced at the menacing gray sky through the leafy canopy of trees overhead. As he walked through the square, his thoughts circled round the implication of the meeting he had had that morning with the private detective agency in Red Lion Square. Passersby unfurled their umbrellas against the drizzle, but Owen walked on, not heeding the rain while he thought of the report prepared by Eurotec Limited.

When he had read the name of Betsy Lowell, a host of memories had come back to him from his Oxford days. He still retained a mental picture of Rex's aunt as he had described her: the small, steely matriarch of one of the richest families in America. Owen could see Rex, glass of wine in hand, smoking a Sobranie as he rested a frayed tweed elbow on the mantelpiece of his rooms at Balliol. Owen had been deeply impressed by him in those days; not just his social ease and his aura of precocious sophistication, but the agility of his mind, which flipped effortlessly from one esoteric subject to another, made Owen feel woefully green and uneducated by comparison.

One cold winter night, when the moon was shining on the quadrangle, their talk had strayed to alchemy and the Cabbalists, subjects dear to Rex. He had never spoken much about his past, hinting only that he came from a wealthy and influential American family with English connections. From the remarks he had dropped over the two years they had been friends, Owen had concluded he was the bastard son of a rich American and an English diplomat's wife, and that he had been shunted from one private school to another to off-load their social embarrassment. But that morning all Owen's preconceived ideas about Rex had been overturned.

Owen was shocked to discover that everything Rex had told him about himself was a blatant fabrication, his portrait of his background a skillful blend of truth and lies. The report revealed that he was born the son of a cabinetmaker in Providence, Rhode Island, and that his entire destiny was altered one summer when his father did some work for the wealthy Lowell family on their estate in Newport. There were no Anglo-American upper class parents, and he wasn't a bastard but the child of a respectable middle-class American family.

An extremely bright and precocious child, his potential was recognized by the philanthropic matriarch of the clan, Betsy Lowell, who sponsored Rex's education from the age of ten. She was not, it turned out, his aunt, but his benefactress. Rex, who possessed a talent for social advancement as well as intelligence and a highly developed aesthetic sense, did not disappoint Mrs. Lowell. When he graduated from high school with honors, she rewarded him by sending him to study art history at Harvard, then on to Oxford, where he had befriended Owen and declared his ambition to dominate the international art and antiques market. He predicted that his personal wealth and collection of paintings and sculpture would rival the Medici.

Long before the incident of the chalice, their paths had diverged widely. Looking back, Owen had recognized a decadent streak in Rex, even then. His anger over the chalice, even when Rex had sent him a much needed thousand pounds after the "accident," was tinged with resentment that Rex's generous inheritance from Mrs. Lowell had smoothly paved the way to the brilliant future he had always anticipated.

That morning in the office of the private investigator Owen had discovered that Betsy Lowell had indeed died during Rex's last year at Oxford and that she had made no provision in her will for her protégé other than to bequeath him a garden statue of Pan, whose stated value was $500. He had also learnt that, a year later, Rex's cabinetmaker father, then retired, had died leaving no property, canceling any chance for Rex to inherit money from that source.

And yet, in the spring of 1972, Rex Monckton moved his business from two shabby rooms in the Portobello Road to sumptuous premises in the heart of Mayfair. The opening had been celebrated by a widely publicized grand party. The investigator had been able to uncover evidence that Rex had financed his lavish new establishment with hard cash, the origin of which was unexplained. Owen remembered receiving an invitation to the opening party just after separating from Mandy, but he had tossed it in the wastepaper basket without thinking twice. By then he was in the throes of building a business himself and had resolutely put the whole affair with Rex out of his mind. But now he swept over the past with a strong searchlight, gathering the clues that seemed to fit.

Arriving in Mount Street, he stopped to look at Rex's establishment, which could hardly be called a shop. The gilded name of Monckton was chiseled deep into a frieze of dark green marble supported by obsidian columns set into the plate glass windows, which were discreetly geared with the most sophisticated security system. Two richly carved wooden doors that might have come from a doge's palace created an imposing entrance. Owen stood for a moment looking at the current pride of Rex's collection in the window: the radiant white marble torso of a Greek boy, bathed in a sphere of light. Plucked from some sun-drenched temple, it now stood in lonely splendor against a backdrop of black velvet. In the companion window on a gilt easel rested a dark, brooding landscape that could have been by Poussin. It depicted nymphs bathing in a pool lost in twilight, while a satyr observed them from the dark foliage as he strummed his lyre.

Owen stood for a moment, peering into the gallery, its inner reaches obscured by the dazzling spotlights. He couldn't help thinking how far Rex had come from the days when he was a callow young man with only his illusions of grandeur to sustain him. Along with wealth, he had achieved social prominence and unimpeachable respectability. The investigator's report revealed that he was the author of several important books on antiquities, that he was a trustee of the Victoria and Albert Museum and a director of Sotheby's, and that he traveled the world in search of choice pieces to offer his clientele, who included pop stars and crowned heads.

Owen turned the highly polished brass knob of the door. Entering the gallery, he pretended to be scrutinizing the statue in the window as he took in the hushed atmosphere. A handsome, thin young man in a designer pin-stripe suite acknowledged Owen from the corner where he was talking in low tones to an American couple who were admiring a Flemish triptych. Pretending to browse, Owen's eyes wandered over Rex's matchless collection of treasures, which included Sèvres porcelain, ormolu clocks and Spanish coffers. Gilt church candlesticks towered near granite obelisks, alabaster urns, bronze horses and Graeco-Roman vases that had been painstakingly reconstructed. The pictures on the green baize walls, in ornate gilt frames, were mostly of classical subjects with epic themes. There was nothing subtle, poignant or moving about any of the priceless objects on display in Owen's opinion. The overpowering grandeur of the collection seemed to empty the room of air, creating a curiously dead atmosphere like that in tomb that had been closed for years. The lifeless splendor around him oppressed Owen. Unwilling to wait any longer, his voice broke aggressively across the hushed stillness of the room.

"Could you tell Rex Monckton I'm here to see him. My name is Owen Morgan."

At the sound of his voice, the three other people turned to stare.

"Excuse me," said the assistant to his clients, crossing the Aubusson carpet with a bemused smile. Brushing back his shock of chestnut hair, he said: "May I help you, sir?"

"Just tell Mr. Monckton that Owen Morgan is here to see him. I'm a personal friend, not a customer."

The young man's eyes slid over Owen, sizing him up.

"I'm afraid Mr. Monckton is out."

"I see," said Owen. "When is he coming back?"

The young man hesitated for a moment. "If you will wait, I will check with his secretary."

He disappeared through a door concealed in the paneling, then returned in a few seconds.

"Mr. Morgan, Mr. Monckton's secretary has authorized me to tell you that he is not available at this moment."

The way his eyes shifted sideways told Owen he was lying, and he looked toward the concealed door, sensing that Rex was hovering somewhere beyond it. His eyes darted round the ceiling, past the blinding spotlights to the security camera, which was aimed in his direction.

"What a shame," Owen said, shaking his head. "As I said, I'm an old friend and happened to be passing, so I just dropped in to say hello. I'm off myself on a trip to the States this week," he added, spinning a yarn. "Tell him I came by. I'll catch him another time."

"Yes, Mr. Morgan, I'll tell him you called," the assistant said politely.

Owen walked down Mount Street without a backward glance, feeling the stare of Rex's round blue eyes like a gun trained on his back. His failure to show himself proved to Owen that he was wary, perhaps even afraid. For a moment the humid spring day vibrated with excitement spiked with danger at the prospect of his revenge.

Dorothy Lethbridge paused in the middle of the grand, high-ceilinged reception room of the Institute of Directors and looked at the distinguished guests gathered to celebrate the publication of Ambrose's book. She cast a proud glance at the three-volume set, so beautifully presented in boxes printed with a detail from the Bayeux Tapestry. Before the party Ambrose had autographed several dozen, which rested on a table shadowed by cardboard mock-ups of a medieval jousting scene, a reminder that the publisher regarded Ambrose's book as a major literary and commercial event. In the beautifully proportioned Nash room overlooking the Mall Gardens English academe, the intelligentsia and the press were drinking champagne. Catching the ringing praise of a well-known

journalist as she walked by, tears of pride came to her eyes,
which she blinked to suppress. She paused for a moment to
take it all in, thinking of all the launches for every one of her
books that Ambrose had attended, quietly giving her his support in his own inimitable way. Now, at last, it was his turn
to gather laurels while she stood quietly at the sidelines looking on, feeling as if she would burst with pride. Her sense of
vicarious achievement made her beam every time she caught
sight of Ambrose, surrounded by admirers. Even their children had flown in with their spouses at the last moment as a
surprise. Seeing her daughter nearby, Dorothy was glad she
had allowed herself to be persuaded to go to Harrods the day
before to buy the frothy dress in violet blue, which had cost
far more than she would ever have dreamed of spending.

"For heaven's sake, Mother, it's not as if you can't afford
it," Alice had scolded when she had hesitated. That morning
she had even gone to have her hair arranged in a swept-up
style and pinned with glittering combs, making her feel absurdly like a fairy godmother. All her efforts had been rewarded when she came down that evening to meet Ambrose
in the lobby of the "In and Out" Club, where they always
stayed when they came to London.

She helped herself to a second glass of champagne as the
waiter drifted by, feeling unaccountably seductive. Telling
herself she had been standing on the sidelines long enough,
Dorothy crossed the room. She nodded hello to people whose
names she knew she ought to remember, and stopped for a
moment to exchange a few words with one of Ambrose's old
colleagues. As she passed a table set with an enormous spray
of summer flowers, she proudly regarded the pile of sets of
Ambrose's life's work. Peering over a cluster of well-wishers,
Ambrose spotted her and they exchanged a long, meaningful
look, full of affection. After all these years, she felt a quickening sense of closeness to him, a rush of physical well-
being, as she realized just how handsome he still was and
how ardent.

She couldn't help noticing the contrast between his gathering and the receptions given by her publishers to launch her
new books. Coming to pay their respects to the author of *The
Life and Times of the Middle Ages* was everyone of importance with a connection to medieval history. When it had

been her turn, she reflected, the crowd invited to celebrate the launch of a bestselling historical thriller was altogether different and included actors from her television series, a sprinkling of pop stars, popular journalists and television presenters. She always felt slightly awkward at her own parties. For one night every couple of years, when a new book was launched, she shed the image of a countrywoman in wellingtons and tweeds to be fêted as a celebrity by people whose names she could never remember. She found the attention slightly embarrassing and was very glad when all the fuss came to an end and she could retire to her study in Little Gaddesden to create yet another mystery featuring Sister Ermengarde. But here, basking in Ambrose's reflected glory, she was blissfully happy. She sighed with pleasure at the sight of so many influential people having such a wonderful time. She cocked her ear to the admiring words echoing all round her, collecting them as mementoes of the occasion to tell Ambrose later: "It's a *tour de force*," "so erudite, yet so entertaining," "reads like the most exciting sort of novel," "illuminates a lost period of history."

In midstream she turned and saw Owen standing at the threshold of the room. The sight of him pained her deeply, completely reversing her buoyant mood. His normal slightly sardonic smile had been replaced by a haggard expression she could never remember having seen on his face in all the years she had known him. Glancing at her watch, Dorothy saw he was late; she had been so wrapped up in the reception that she hadn't even noticed that he hadn't arrived. She wondered what could have happened to him between the afternoon when she had last seen him at Little Gaddesden coming to pick up Louise and this moment. Those few seconds, as she watched him unawares, she guessed that something was gnawing fiercely at him, some sort of turmoil that he was deliberately keeping to himself. She thought for a moment that it might be a woman, but she knew instinctively that it was nothing so simple. Her own triumphant mood was eclipsed by his misery as she watched him search the room for people he knew. Stationing herself where he could easily see her, she returned his smile, which did not quite dispel his preoccupied expression.

"Dorothy—what a glamour girl!" he exclaimed, kissing her

cheek. "I didn't even recognize you. This is a very impressive party," he said, looking round. "I expected to find a few dons and librarians drinking warm gin and tonic."

Dorothy laughed, but in her mind the crowd melted in a swirl of color and sound as her hand reached automatically for his. In a quiet voice she said. "Owen, what is it? You must tell me. It's written all over you."

He sighed, hanging his head. "Is it that obvious?"

"The minute I saw you I knew something was terribly wrong."

He looked at her doubtfully. "This isn't the time or place to go into my problems. It's Ambrose's big night. I don't want to spoil it."

"Owen, for heaven's sake—you know I won't sleep tonight until you tell me what's on your mind. Please," she pleaded.

"Well, if you really want to know," he said with a sigh. "Let me just get a drink and pay my respects to Ambrose."

She hovered nervously, waiting for him to come back. When he came through the crowd again, a bemused grin on his face, she led him to the window where two chairs were tucked out of sight.

"Come and sit down," she said gently but firmly.

He leaned forward, one hand braced on a knee. Even in the filtered spring light every hollow and line of his face stood out, making him look years older. Her mind leapt suddenly to the dreadful conclusion that he was seriously, perhaps incurably, ill. She had no idea what he was about to say.

"Do you remember the chalice I bought in France not far from Puivaillon, just before Mandy and I split up?"

"Why, of course I do. It was that antique dealer friend of yours, the American, who took it off in his overcoat and promptly lost it. How careless of him. I remember you didn't want to have anything to do with him, and quite right . . ."

"Well, the chalice has turned up."

"What? But how? And where?" she exclaimed.

He told her about Geneva. When she looked at him dumbfounded, he said, "That's right, the so-called silver-gilt wine goblet from seventeenth-century Bavaria is, in fact, pure gold, dating from the first century A.D., and very nearly priceless."

"Why, the man's a mountebank, a swine. I remember so

well when he paid you for it. You were relieved to have the capital to put into your business, but I felt that in your heart it wasn't the money that mattered. So,'' she shook her head, "after all this time it has turned up.'' A little tremor of dread crawled down her spine.

When he told her about Betsy Lowell's will, she said: "Do you mean to say he didn't inherit a fortune after all? I remember borrowing the idea for one of my books. Then where did he get his money?''

Owen told her about his second trip to Geneva, about the death of Baron Hauptmann, adding that he was now almost certain the Baron had bought the chalice from Rex.

"You must be quite sick about it all.'' She was on the verge of saying it was only money when she stopped herself. She knew in her heart that it meant much more to Owen than that. "What steps have you taken?''

"I took a quick trip to France after my last visit to Geneva. I went to the village near Puivaillon to find the man who sold it to me, but there was no trace of him.'' He avoided any mention of his meeting with Louise Carey, who had been preying on his conscience. He could hardly tell Dorothy they had met by chance, that he had seduced a vulnerable divor-cée, daughter of her dear old friend, and had not as much as dropped her a postcard or rung her since.

"The question is, what to do next. If you're bound and determined to prove that the chalice belonged to you and Rex stole it, what about photographs? Don't you have any?''

"I hadn't thought of that,'' he said half-heartedly. "It might be an idea. Now I think of it, we did take some pictures.''

He thought of the clutter and chaos in which Mandy lived, wardrobes stuffed with clothes she would never wear again, the empty perfume bottles, the drawers full of tights with runs and dried-up cosmetics, the medicine cupboard filled with expired prescriptions. His eyes lit up: she never threw anything away. Somewhere in the tiny mews house choked with junk he was sure there was a photograph of the chalice that he had taken the morning after he bought it, when she had finally calmed down. But where to begin to look and how could he get Mandy to do it?

Dorothy was talking excitedly about forensic photography.

". . . and if you have a negative, apparently they can blow up even the tiniest picture, or even if it doesn't show up at all, it's quite extraordinary the things that are done these days. I keep my hand in on these things, wondering what the competition is doing," she added, raising an eyebrow.

Owen laughed at the excitement on her face. He could see that Dorothy was on the edge of a mystery. But the smile on his face quickly dissolved and he said: "It's no good."

"I assure you, Owen, forensic photography is worth looking into . . ."

"No, that's not it. Monckton paid that thousand pounds to me in a check. He thought of everything. You read every day about cases like this. All he has to do is produce his bank records and say he bought it from me."

"All right, but what about Mandy? She knows the truth."

"Who is going to believe Mandy, Dorothy? Tell me honestly. I tried to talk to her about this recently and she was very tight-lipped about it still. She's still very bitter."

As they looked at each other they were both thinking of Mandy's ravaged face, her history of drink and drug addiction.

"But at least it's worth a try: finding the photograph and asking Mandy to vouch for you. At the moment it's all you've got to go on, Owen. And what about Rex? Have you thought about boldly confronting him and brazening it out?"

He laughed ironically. "He knows I'm on to him and he's proved to be all but invisible. He surrounds himself with a bunch of flunkeys who protect him. But I'll get to him. I'm watching, waiting for my moment."

At this remark Dorothy felt a wave of deep disturbance and realized that events ripening in Owen's life were not as simple as they seemed. Her concern for him turned to real fear as she felt wheels that had been still for so many years start to move again. For a long time the pendulum had disappeared from sight and now, she realized, it was about to swing back with redoubled force, toward the hour, the day, the second, when the inevitable would occur. Now, with so little to go on, what could she say, what could she do if her premonitions were confirmed? With an effort, she brought her attention back to the present moment. Realizing she was neglecting her duties, she stood reluctantly and so did Owen.

"Oh, by the way," Dorothy said, "I had such a charming letter from Louise Carey a few days ago."

Owen gave a start, and a flush of embarrassment brought the color back to his face. His encounter with Louise was something so bizarre, so extraordinary that it would seem strange he hadn't mentioned it. He said, feigning complete innocence:

"I haven't had a chance to tell you what happened when I was in France. She and I met in Puivaillon by the most amazing coincidence, in that little hotel—what's it called . . . ?"

"Do you mean the Hôtel du Commerce?" Dorothy asked in astonishment.

"Sorry I haven't phoned you," he muttered apologetically, "I've had so much on my mind. Naturally we had dinner together, and even spent the next day driving round. We passed not far from your house on the way to that village where I bought the chalice. You can imagine how astounded I was to find her sitting there when I arrived. Evidently she wanted to get away from Paris just for a day or two before she tied up her business. I guess all the talk of your house in France that night gave her the idea. Even so, I was dumbfounded to see her like that. The odds must be ten million to one. I was there to see if I could dig up anything more about the man who sold me the chalice . . ."

She leaned back and looked at him, giving no clue to what she was thinking. "I don't know why you think it's so extraordinary." She was smiling to herself at the one bright spot in all the gathering darkness.

Owen looked skeptical and said with a disparaging laugh: "Dearest Dorothy, things like that might happen in the world of fiction, or even to you, but it's the first time it's ever happened to me."

Memories of Louise came back to him suddenly, a hundred fleeting sensations crashing through his closed mind like the shattering of glass. He saw her lowered eyelids, the sweet, peaceful look on her face in the dim light of a hotel room as she fell asleep, the feeling of his hands on the small of her back as he pressed his nose to her soft hair. A reluctance he didn't understand had kept him from phoning her.

"It wouldn't surprise me a bit if we see her again soon." When Owen didn't reply, Dorothy added: "She could walk through the door at any minute. I sent her an invitation for the party tonight, thinking she might be just mad enough to hop on a plane and come . . .''

Owen turned to the door, where he half expected to see her arriving in breathless haste, an expectant look on her face.

But Dorothy was saying: "She said how much she would have loved to come, in the note she sent with some lovely roses.''

The next morning Dorothy left the club before noon and walked up to Curzon Street. She had put away all the trappings of glamour from the evening before and was once again the countrywoman in sensible brogues and a mackintosh. With a neat turn of her wrist, she unfurled her umbrella against the drizzle. Normally she loved the walk through Mayfair, which still seemed steeped in an early Victorian atmosphere. On the rare occasions she was there, Dorothy found herself conjuring up an entire world peopled by women in crinolines and ringlets and men in top hats alighting from carriages in the narrow, pretty streets. Today, however, her eyes had a troubled cast and her mouth a determined set. She walked down Curzon Street past the row of fine Georgian houses, their window boxes overflowing with pansies and tulips. Her mind in a turmoil, she continued resolutely toward Mount Street, where she knew she would find Rex Monckton's gallery. When she saw the green marble front with his name chiseled in gold, hope against hope rose within Dorothy that she was wrong about his real identity. Hesitating for a moment while she gathered her courage, she was taken aback by the sight of three gold pentacles engraved in the stone that embellished his name.

"It could be just a coincidence,'' she muttered to reassure herself.

Entering the gallery, she metamorphosed from a shrewd observer to a self-effacing country lady in London for the day. Looking very unsure of herself, she cast a hesitant smile toward the slick-looking young assistant who was crossing the shop. She blinked, pretending to be dazzled by the magnificence of Roman busts, giant urns and allegorical paintings that seemed like windows into antiquity. There was some-

thing compelling about the paintings, mostly of classical subjects: insipid shepherds, leering satyrs and crumbling ruins.
They lent an undercurrent of idle enchantment that put her
on her guard. Her heart went cold at the stifling ostentation
of the objects on display, which revealed the inner essence
of Rex Monckton. From what she saw, she knew he was a
force to be reckoned with. Affecting a painful shyness controlled by good breeding, she said:

"Good morning."

"Good morning. May I be of any assistance?"

"I think you might," she began brightly. "I happened to
be at a party last night and I was talking to some people who
suggested I call in this morning to see Mr. Monckton. You
see, I recently inherited some rather grand pieces from a
great-aunt of mine. They're altogether unsuitable for the small
cottage my husband and I live in," she said with a girlish
laugh. "I was at a loss to know what to do with them. You
know, Tudor chairs, a tapestry, that sort of thing." She
glanced round the gallery.

The assistant nodded, inclining his head with interest.

"If you wouldn't mind waiting for a moment, I'm sure Mr.
Monckton would be pleased to see you himself."

She watched him disappear through the door concealed in
the paneling and pretended to browse, waiting anxiously for
him to return.

Moments later she looked up with a start as Rex Monckton
entered the room noiselessly, shadowed by a silver-gray Weimaraner. Her mouth opened in surprise when she saw him.
She had somehow envisaged a tall, lanky American, not this
man of medium height who seemed both ageless and strangely
sexless. He had a high-domed forehead framed with flat curling hair and he was smiling at her like a devilish cherub. She
saw he had the healthy glow of a man who spent his days not
in the darkness of galleries and auction rooms, but in the
open air. In a few seconds she had recorded every detail
about him with an expert eye, noting his round blue eyes,
which deeply disturbed her. He seemed an Englishman to his
fingertips, from his Savile Row suit to his Lobb shoes. His
youthful appearance made her wonder what magic or wick-
edness he had used as a charm against time. Glancing at his
dog, she saw it regarding her with the same pale blue eyes

as its master, a pink tongue lolling from its mouth. When she reached out to pat it, her hand trembled.

"What a fine animal," she remarked. "You don't see many Weimaraners in England."

"Thank you. He comes from champion stock. I have a friend who breeds them. How do you do. I'm Rex Monckton."

"How do you do," she said, a smile curling on her lips. She couldn't bring herself to extend her hand to him. The thought of contact made her flesh creep and she covered her alarm by adopting a flustered air, avoiding his eyes, which had an odd, fixed stare. "I'm Dorothy Simpson," she said, using her maiden name. "I do hope I'm not wasting your valuable time, but as I was saying to the young man, my aunt left a few things I hoped might be of interest to you . . ." She heard her own voice echoing in the room. She wanted nothing more than to flee the gallery to escape Rex Monckton's inquisitive stare. Feeling like a rabbit run to ground, she reeled off the yarn she had rehearsed. It was then that she noticed the odd ring he wore on his left hand. It looked as though it were made of iron and was set with a cornelian engraved with the same pentacle that was on the shop-front. It took all her powers of concentration to resist the powerful force that emanated from Rex Monckton and she knew she had been foolish to confront him so impulsively. She had identified him at first glance and wondered, as they sized one another up, if he too had recognized her.

They chatted for a moment, she giving the impression she was indecisive and cautious, Rex smoothly trying to draw her out. Dorothy felt her face go red with alarm and she was suddenly afraid she might faint. Rex was talking languidly, as if he hadn't noticed her behavior, but as his eyes scanned her face it seemed he was sifting through his memory, trying to place her.

When she had said a hurried goodbye, adding that she would be in touch, she fled from the shop, his card in her hand, and rushed gratefully down the street, feeling Rex's eyes following her. She could only hope he had dismissed her as a typical country eccentric who might or might not contact him again.

The sound of traffic, the sight of ordinary people passing

by, was a deep relief, but they couldn't dispel the cold shudder down her back as she repeated the name: Rex Monckton. Turning it over in her mind, it became Rex Mundi, King of the World, Prince of Darkness. On a bustling London street it would be easy to dismiss this as pure fantasy were it not for the fact that Dorothy had felt that familiar bolt of recognition when Rex walked into the gallery. The last time she had seen him was in 1244 at Montségur. Then she had known him as Gaucelm, a mercenary who defended the citadel. She walked unsteadily, seeing him before her eyes in a torchlit chamber.

Normally Dorothy would have found the walk from Mount Street to St. James's Square a refreshing little stroll that gave her the chance to zigzag her way down Bond Street and Albemarle Street, but when Rex's gallery was behind her, she waved down the first taxi she saw. Alighting in front of the London Library, she didn't even bother to ask for change from the driver as she charged up the steps and through the swing doors.

Catching sight of a young librarian behind the counter, she said in a breathless voice:

"Where would the subject of magic be located?"

"Under science, madam," he replied. When she looked puzzled, he added: "Occult science."

Nodding her thanks, Dorothy made her way down the hall and through the doors to the library, where the odor of old books struck her nostrils. Her footsteps resounded on the metal grid as she penetrated deeply down the dimly lit corridors of bookshelves that rose from floor to ceiling. When she had found occult sciences, she turned on the light overhead. Reaching for the first book she saw, she opened it at the first page, whispering aloud as she read:

" 'The driving force behind black magic is the hunger for power. . . . The magician sets out to conquer the universe. To succeed, he must make himself master of everything in it—evil as well as good, cruelty as well as mercy, pain as well as pleasure.' "

An hour later she left the library, her head swimming with terminology with which she had been only vaguely familiar before she went in. She knew that the most feared of all books of magic was the *grimoire* of Honorius, which stated that when calling the devil, the supplicant must draw a magic circle to protect himself. It said that the devil has a thousand names, that black magic can be black even unto obscenity and that the magician's symbol was the pentacle, a five-pointed star enclosed in a circle, symbolizing man in the universe.

Heading back toward the club, she knew it was no coincidence that Rex Monckton had adopted the pentacle as his logo and wore the magician's iron ring stamped with the same symbol. One person in ten thousand might recognize it, but even then they wouldn't know him for what he was. She was walking down Piccadilly as the clouds cleared, showering the streets with light that could not reach the dark corner of the world where the spirit of Gaucelm still lurked after so many centuries.

12

Tethering his horse out of the sharp wind that swept the stony hills, Hugo folded his arms beneath his cloak as he surveyed the contours of the familiar country that marked the journey home. In the valley below he could see that winter storms had ravaged the fullness of the soil, stripped the trees bare and driven animals, birds and people to shelter. Weather-beaten and battle-hardened, he considered himself immune to the hardships of winter, yet he was touched by a vivid recollection of the view from the same ridge in spring, when the roadside was carpeted with buttercups and cornflowers and the olive trees and spreading pines cast a welcome shade. In those days he had been on a much more gentle errand.

The wintry landscape warmed under the influence of memory, bringing back the song of nightingales, the sight of wheat sprouting under a sky that was more blue, more intense than he had seen during his travels to the Holy Land. He had journeyed constantly from one Templar commandery to the other during the last year on the business of the order, feeling all but indifferent to the rich and varied land where he had been born and where he had wandered when young, before his love of poetry and music had been supplanted by a love of Christ. Yet now, within two days' journey from home, he felt himself in the grip of an unexpected nostalgia. Sentiments he thought were dead in him came to life, making him feel like a young poet rather than a stoic holy warrior. He remembered the smoothness of a lute in his hands and he could feel the surge of excitement that filled him as he faced a journey to an unknown destination, composing songs about love as he went. Then, knowing he was one of a dying breed had sharpened his powers of observation as he followed in the footsteps of his heroes, the first troubadours, who had lived a century before him. Looking back, Hugo could not believe he had ever lived like the young man he saw in his mind's eye watering his horse at the stream below, who had traveled east and never returned home until now.

Now he was neither a troubadour nor a holy warrior, he reminded himself, but an ordinary man whose loyalties were still strongly Christian, but poised between Rome and the Cathar heresy that had lived uneasily alongside it for several generations, producing families like his own that were divided in faith but united in their determination to rule their own destiny. Now that he considered himself a free man, he was bound for home at last.

He scanned the folds of the hills, brushed by low, racing clouds, looking for some sign of his companions, who were supposed to rendezvous with him that night for the remainder of the journey.

Hugo was dressed as a knight, in chain mail, a leather jerkin and a thick cloak, which fell to the tops of the boots he wore laced up to his knees, and a sword was strapped to his side. Untying his saddlebag, he removed his Templar's distinctive white cape emblazoned with a red cross and buried it under some stones where no one would ever find it. Hugo de Franjal the Templar was dead and resurrected in his place was the second son of Berenger de Franjal, who had come back to defend his country against the Roman Church and the King of France.

Mounting his horse, he traveled by a cold, rushing river to

the ruins of an old castle sheltered by cypresses and pines, where he had arranged to meet his companions. As he dismounted, he realized he was not alone. A herd of goats was grazing in the bushes, disturbing the wind-swept silence with their bleating and the tinkling of their bells. From behind the ruined walls of the castle curled the smoke of a camp fire.

Hugo walked toward it, feeling vexed that the privacy of this remote place had been disturbed. When he saw a bearded old goatherd wrapped in skins leaning close to the fire, he told himself that he was probably deaf from wind and cold, and even half blind from staring at the sun, and would cause no trouble.

"My greetings, shepherd," called Hugo.

The old man turned, fumbling for his staff, but when he saw Hugo, he stared and motioned him to come by the fire. Like most herdsmen, he was taciturn and unaccustomed to speaking much. Hugo crouched across from him, warming his hands without comment.

The old man's hair, although gray, had yellowed with age and grime like the stubborn patches of snow that clung to the hills. The callused, weathered skin on his face and body seemed to Hugo as hard as a suit of armor hammered into grooves and creases by the rigors of his nomadic existence. But his rheumy eyes looked out frankly from his narrow face with the power of stained glass windows in a church, his piercing gaze sweeping away the barriers of strangeness and class, making Hugo feel his innermost secrets were open to inspection. Hugo sat immobile for a long time, ignoring the peculiar goatherd, whose curiosity unsettled him, but when he could bear his scrutiny no longer, he said coldly, "You look as if you know me, old man."

The goatherd nodded his grizzled head. "Yes, I know you," he said, rising with the help of his staff. "When I knew you were coming, I killed a kid for you and your companions. You'll be hungry, all of you."

"Wait," Hugo called as the old man walked away. "How do you know this? Are you waiting here to give me some message; and, if so, why did you not speak before?"

"You ask how I know," the goatherd muttered. "I know many things."

Hugo was taken aback at his boldness. "Am I to understand that you see into the future?"

The man didn't answer, but stirred the flames and put more wood on the fire. Its reflection cut deep whorling lines in his face, like the rings in a tree trunk. Hugo scowled to himself, feeling indecisive: he could stay the night in the company of a witch who courted the companionship of demons or he could camp alone, keeping a vigil against wolves. He and the goatherd seemed alone in the world in this eerie pool of light that fended off the gathering darkness. At last hunger and curiosity outbid his fear and he went to unload his horse.

Later, after they had each eaten the haunch of a kid in complete silence, Hugo curled up, resting his head on his saddle, his sword unsheathed at his side. The black, starless night had turned bitterly cold and resonated with the hooting of owls above the wind. When the old man got to his feet to see to his goats, Hugo looked into the fire, reflecting that they hadn't exchanged a word since the goatherd's extraordinary revelation about him and his companions, who, he now realized, would not arrive until morning. When the old man came back, Hugo sat up and looked hard at him, realizing he would never sleep that night without hearing what portent of the future the goatherd could offer.

"Tell me, old seer, what do you see?" he said, feigning skepticism; but he knew he was not fooling the old man, who he sensed had been waiting for his curiosity to break out. Hugo met the goatherd's eyes beneath his shaggy brows, guarding himself against a force about to unleash itself, which he sensed he was powerless to stop. He felt his heart pound with anxiety as he uttered the Lord's Prayer.

The old man shook his head and spat into the fire. "I see blood, the color of embers. Not your blood—not as yet—but the blood of others."

Hugo felt his cheeks burn at this violent prophecy, wondering by what sorcery a simple goatherd was aware he had pledged his sword to the murder of Inquisitors at Avignonnet in a few days' time, a secret known only to a group of noblemen sworn to secrecy.

"Continue," he said, feigning an indifference he did not feel.

"There is one among you who has pledged to drink from

the skull of a priest. He will not have his wish, for the skull will be crushed to pieces, so violent will be the struggle. Be warned that terrible vengeance will follow his act. None will be spared; a plague of fires will spread south, ending beneath a great mountain crowned with a fortress.''

"Montségur . . .'' Hugo whispered.

"And you, you will be a *faidit,* a knight dispossessed, and all your kin will be scattered like seeds of a flower on barren earth, where they will wither and die. A noble of northern blood will seize your birthright. Nothing will remain of any of you. Scattered . . .'' he repeated, arching his arm toward the darkness.

The old man's voice died away and the wind filled Hugo's ears as it whined in the hollows between the stones. The fire was blazing, but his heart had gone cold. He turned his back on the old goatherd, wanting to believe he was a dreamer or a madman.

Hurrying down the dark stone corridor of the castle, Sancha rubbed her hands together to keep warm. The cold penetrated the thin soles of her shoes as she paused at a narrow window that cast a chink of weak winter light onto the stones. The sharp wind that blew through the gap made her eyes water as she looked down the snow-covered valley toward the frozen lake, like a vast clouded mirror in the gray light of morning. Far out in the valley she could see a troop of horsemen making their way toward the castle. She peered at the dots on the horizon; undoubtedly another band of nobles on their way to Puivaillon for the greatest gathering seen at the castle in a generation. Berenger, Alazaïs's husband, had invited all the lords of Trencaval, Toulouse and Foix to show their defiance of the Church and the King of France by celebrating their unity and their traditions at Puivaillon.

In the two years that Sancha had lived in the castle she had been inducted into its scandals and feuds, and the power and wealth of the great family of de Franjal bore down on her with an almost mystic force, establishing in her a fierce loyalty. She felt a sense of pride at the breaking of the day that would re-establish the hegemony of the nobles of the Languedoc against the steely northern barons, who were allied with the Church.

The approach of the banquet, which would last for a week, had given rise to nostalgic reminiscences among the old retainers still living. She had listened to them recall in reedy voices the prosperous and peaceful dawn of the century, which was now only a memory. Then, Puivaillon had attracted Crusaders on their way to the Holy Land, knights armed for war or tournaments, and troubadours armed with poetry that wrung the hearts of men and women.

Descending the stairs, Sancha entered the courtyard, now streaked with snow and buffeted by the wind. Large enough to contain a village, a hundred years before it had been packed with spectators at jousting tournaments. Today it was again alive with the raucous cries of arriving parties of nobles in plumed casques, their brightly caparisoned horses and the pennants they carried making a blaze of color against the gray stone. Shivering, she thrilled to the sight as they frisked on the frozen grass in mock combat. At the sight of a pair of dark eyes glinting through the visor of a helmet, she turned away, reminded of *amour courtois,* the exalted love men and women expressed with music and poetry, which permeated the stones of the castle. Sancha had discovered that in her youth Alazaïs had received great poets, who had immortalized her in song, and that she had even composed poetry herself before she became a pious Cathar. Along with her faith, she had unknowingly planted these long forgotten passions in Sancha during the last months, so that the young girl now repeated troubadour poetry to herself along with the Gospel of St. John, sacred to the Cathars.

Sancha had come to Puivaillon, grateful to find a safe haven. But the great tide of the unquiet world had penetrated even the high walls of the castle, throwing her prayers into doubt and quietening her musings on love. The subject uppermost in everyone's mind was whether Languedoc would rise and, once and for all, throw off the yoke of France and Rome.

Sancha entered the huge kitchen under the great hall, where servant girls were dancing to the orders of the steward and the head cook, a fat woman with a ruddy face, who was working herself into a fury as she oversaw the preparations for that night's banquet.

''Get yourself an apron full of those apples, my girl, and

start peeling them," she cried when she saw Sancha. "Tutors
and healers sleep late to revive their powers, I suppose," she
added grumpily.

The girls chopping fruit and vegetables round the big table
tittered with laughter. Because she could read and write both
Latin and Hebrew, Sancha was regarded as an oddity among
them, but she took no notice of the bad-tempered cook. She
found a place at the table among women whose chattering in
the warm kitchen was a pleasant change from the cold school-
room and the bedside of the sick. She inched herself closer
to the fireplace, where men were piling wood to roast fowl,
sheep and even an entire ox, which was already on the spit,
its eyes protruding from its bloodied head. Other women were
chopping fat or peeling onions, while some were mixing the
gritty gray flour to prepare pastry for pies. The cook retied
her kerchief, which kept falling over her forehead, as she
shouted for a small boy to go and fetch the steward to come
with the key to the store and allot some of the precious loaf
sugar.

Sancha listened to the gossip flying round the table about
the guests who would be at the banquet. She could only half
believe the tales of jealous husbands returning from wars and
crusades to find numerous children they hadn't known they
had fathered, stories of troubadours dying for the love of a
noble lady they had never seen, of the princess who was
served the heart of her lover by her vindictive husband, who
tricked her into eating it by saying it was that of a calf.

The subject moved to the de Franjals. They were talking
of Berenger, the Comte, Alazaïs's husband, hereditary lord
of Puivaillon.

"Where was he in December, I ask you? If he was no
further than east of Foix, he would have come back sooner."

"He was dealing with his dead brother's business, didn't
you know?"

"More likely with his brother's living wife," came the
reply, causing a gale of laughter.

Sancha thought of the Count, a brutish but vigorous man
who did not share his wife's cultured refinement or her piety.
Their alliance was based on family and wealth rather than
preference, and had produced countless children lost in childbirth.

* * *

That night Sancha arrived early at the threshold of the great
hall, named the Salle des Poètes, and placed herself in a
strategic niche in order to watch the entry of the lords and
ladies. Her dark hair was woven with ribbons and she had
made a dress from a bolt of pale blue linen given to her by
Alazaïs, which was held with a dark green girdle stitched
with scarlet flowers. Alazaïs had honored her with a place at
one of the long tables set in a horseshoe round the hall and
draped in white linen, where the servants were already placing platters of roast meat, pyramids of fruit and nuts, and
flagons of wine. The table was set with great ewers and ba-
sins of beaten silver, pewter plates and knives that glinted
dully in the torchlight. Fires blazed in two wide chimneys at
either end of the room and straw and sheepskins had been
laid under the tables to warm the feet of the ladies shod in
silk and velvet slippers. The great arched chamber, where
banquets had been held for nearly two hundred years, was
ablaze with costly candles and torches that made Sancha feel
like a night bird come upon an enchanted kingdom. Tongues
of light brushed the soaring arches of gray stone, which rested
on pillars crowned with carved figures representing all the
great poet-musicians of the last century. Their compositions
were being played on lutes, pipes and tambours by a troupe
of colorful *jongleurs.*

When the lords and ladies began to enter the vestibule,
Sancha craned her neck from the drafty niche for a good
view of their dramatic entrance, as the music of pipes and
tambours rose in a crescendo. They filed by, each more
splendid than the other, the men in fine silk hose and tunics
of every color gathered at the hips by girdles embroidered
with filigree and set with jewels. The women strutted stiffly,
pulling their heavy trains across the stone floor. Their sleeves
and gowns were richly embroidered with amethysts, rubies
and pearls, and yet more jewels and gold glittered at their
pale throats and in their hair. A keen sense of anticipation
ruffled their aristocratic dignity as they paused grandly at the
threshold of the banqueting hall. Sancha saw the ladies' hands
darting from ermine sleeves and heard them murmur in re-
fined voices when they saw the grandeur of the reception the
Comte and Comtesse de Franjal had prepared in their honor.

The procession melted into a moving swirl of brilliant color as Sancha watched it go by, filling the hall with laughter, conversation and music. She stood shivering in the cold air from the window, committing all the splendor to memory. She felt as if her lungs would burst with a strange elation that such beauty and abundance existed on this earth. She glanced out of the narrow window overlooking the valley, where fires burned in the blackness like fallen stars. It had begun to snow and a few flakes made their way inside the niche, melting on her face. Her short life of violent contrast now rested on a pinnacle of unimaginable splendor. Looking out at the fires burning in the valley below, she could feel the pulse of her own insignificance join a much greater rhythm. The unquiet world that threatened what she was witnessing seemed far away. The perfect moments were drifting by much too fast, dissolving like the snowflakes on her skin. She had once asked Alazaïs where life was leading and what it meant. It puzzled Sancha that if God was good, he allowed evil to exist. Alazaïs had answered that the Prince of Darkness was a fugitive from the realm of light and that he had created earth in vengeance, bringing his demons with him. When Sancha asked where, then, did beauty come from, Alazaïs had replied that earthly splendor and all the temptations of the flesh were sparks torn away from the realm of light, where God lived, but that it was a reflected glory, an illusion, like sun on water, and could not hope to rival his celestial kingdom.

As Sancha looked out into the well of night, her own knowledge of the world seemed as feeble and scattered as those distant fires. Her belief in Heaven had always warred with her desire to possess and know all the mysteries of the flesh and the material world, no matter how fleeting or even cruel they might be, and this magnificent night seemed to vindicate her conviction.

She retreated deeper into the niche when she heard the sound of men's laughter and their boots coming up the stairs. Through the vaulted archway she caught sight of a man whose appearance stunned her. He was talking to a companion and when he turned his head, she refused to believe that the man, dressed as an ordinary nobleman, was the Templar she had seen in the marketplace that summer in Quillan, the Templar who had aroused the violent and unsatisfied curiosity that had stayed with her for all this time. She stared disbelievingly at his shadowy profile as he looked round the hall resounding with music and laughter. Brimming with good humor, he brushed the snow from his hair and cloak as he said to his companions:

"Vidal, Roger, go and take your places. Warm yourselves and eat your fill after the long journey. I will join you in a moment."

When they had moved on, he asked a lady-in-waiting the whereabouts of the Lady Alazaïs. He stood a few feet away, unaware of Sancha's presence, allowing her to collect her impressions. His countenance had a reflective stillness that suggested he had traveled far and was master of himself. Sancha's life had been destroyed and rebuilt in the time since they had encountered each other, and she wondered what had happened to him in the interval and why he was no longer dressed as a Templar. It seemed an unsettling omen that her first encounter with him had been filled with the screams of a dying man. She was wondering who he could be and what he was doing there when, as if sensing he was being studied, he turned, catching sight of a woman's face in the shadows. She stepped into the light and waited, knowing that he was searching his memory. It gave her a shiver of pleasure to think that he had carried her image in his mind these many months.

At that moment Alazaïs appeared in the anteroom. She didn't see Sancha, but hurried forward, radiant with surprise. Her hands flew into the air and she gasped with emotion as she exchanged three kisses on each cheek with the stranger. Falling to his knees, the Templar kissed her hand. His astonishing words reached Sancha:

"My deepest respects to you, dear Mother."

"Oh, Hugo, I have been so worried about you. I've inquired everywhere. One moment you had been seen, the next you had vanished. Why have we not seen you when you have been in your homeland for so many months?" she scolded, but her voice was filled with joy and relief. "Your father and I have relayed message after message, hoping, praying that you would honor us here tonight. Is it really true that you are among us?" she said with a disbelieving smile.

"Forgive me, Mother, but I wasn't sure it would be wise to come," he said, looking into the crowded hall.

She clutched his hands in hers. "They are all here—your father is coming with you to Avignonnet."

"Then you know?"

"Yes, I know. All of us for whom it counts most, know. You need not fear anyone here tonight. We're united as one people. There are no spies or enemies, you can be sure." Her voice was grave, her face solemn.

"And yet, somehow I sense that you're against it."

"It's murder, Hugo."

There was pain in his eyes. "No, not murder—it is war."

"We won't speak of it tonight. Tonight we are here to celebrate and honor the past, so that it may guide us into the future."

"The future . . ." he repeated, looking toward the crowded hall echoing with laughter and music as if seeing it through a prism.

"Then you've finally buried the sign of your faith, my son," she whispered, brushing drops of snow from his cloak.

"Yes. Only days ago. But I see you haven't buried yours."

Sancha saw Hugo touch a silver dove at Alazaïs's throat, which she had never worn openly before. Feeling her own silver dove concealed beneath her bodice, Sancha felt bound to Alazaïs by this Cathar symbol. Absorbed in conversation, they walked past her and into the hall, where voices hushed at their entrance. Then, at the sight of mother and son, cheers rang out round the table and musicians played a fanfare on pipes and drums.

At the height of the banquet, when servants were heaping the tables with yet more pies, meat, game and fish, Sancha was conscious of Hugo, who was seated at the high table with his parents, his companions and the most illustrious of the guests. At one point she thought Alazaïs might be speaking about her, when she saw her whisper in Hugo's ear as he looked in her direction. The gulf between his state and hers, in reality no further than she could cast a stone, might have been to the Holy Land and back, it seemed so great. It was more than she could hope for to have seen the Templar again, yet she still found it miraculous to comprehend that he was indeed Hugo de Franjal.

The evening unfolded as the candles burned low and the torches, continually replaced by servants, waned. Sancha toyed with the food on her plate, feeling her appetite gone, taking only sips of the honeyed wine in her cup as she talked with the ladies-in-waiting round her and watched the wrestling match in progress. A burly sergeant-at-arms was being outwitted by a nimble dwarf and had the whole hall roaring with laughter, in which she joined. Half of her watched the spectacle, yet part of her kept Hugo in sight. When she saw him rise from the table, his eyes trained in her direction, she returned his gaze calmly, her heart contracting with disbelief that he should do her the honor of coming to her side.

She felt a strange inner stillness when he bowed and greeted her formally, then said, "I know now where I once saw you. When my mother told me how she found you and who you are, the day our paths crossed in Quillan came back to me. My destiny, like yours, has altered since then . . ."

She lifted her chin at the sound of his voice, which moved her inexplicably. She knew that the world might come to an end before she had another chance to tell Hugo how deeply their meeting had affected her. Shrugging off all pretense at modesty, she said, "For my part, I knew you at once when I saw you earlier tonight. I never forgot seeing you that day. I remember every second when I was in your presence."

A startled admiration flared in his eyes, followed by a blush of what seemed like embarrassment. "Forgive me, but I lack your eloquent forthrightness. I didn't wish to distress you. I, too, remembered you, a young Jewess in the market. Your compassion moved my own."

She looked up at him, her courage dying as she felt as though a drum were beating inside her. Hearing one of his companions call him over the din, he turned to look over his shoulder.

"Will you stay long at Puivaillon?" she asked.

"No, not long. As soon as the feasting is done, in a few days' time, I must leave." With a courteous nod, he added: "But before I go I will take leave of you."

He bowed and left her side, his promise ringing in her ears. When he had gone, Sancha sat very still as the laughter and conversation eddied round her.

An old troubadour, twisted with age, hobbled to the center

of the hall. To the accompaniment of his lyre, he began to sing a lament of unrequited love in a harsh but still beautiful voice. As she listened, Sancha watched Hugo. He was sitting motionless, his powerful arms folded across his chest as he regarded the old poet intently, suggesting he was reliving a passionate memory. The pleasure in his face banished all traces of a Templar's savage holiness. She realized from the murmurs round her that the old poet's ballad had been composed by Hugo.

Her eyes dropped to his hands, which had wielded the cross, the sword and the lute with equal skill, and she dreamed of what it would be like to have those hands touch her, feeling an awakening as violent as the striking of metal on stone or the scythe set to the grass. Her beating heart reminded her of what her body was created for. Should he ask her, she would lie with Hugo de Franjal, on stone or on ice, and it wouldn't be a sin. She met Hugo's eyes across the hazy distance as the old poet sang in honor of the troubadours whose carved images looked down on the hall.

> *No fairer lady have I known*
> *The moon anoints your perfumed grace*
> *The golden sun your beauty chase*
> *While poets praise your matchless face*
> *Your eyes are mirrors to my own.*

13

At her desk in the sitting room overlooking the pool, Louise picked up a French dictionary and looked up a word for the letter she was composing. It occurred to her that she hardly ever used the sitting room since she had come back from Europe, feeling that an emptiness had invaded it. Once that room had given her enormous pleasure, but now she looked indifferently at the big sofas covered in cotton brocade resting on Kelim carpets, the Chinese lamps with pleated shades, a fine old *armoire* and the collection of modern paintings, no longer feeling the same passionate pride of ownership she once had.

Scratching out another mistake, she continued the letter to Maurice Roussel in Puivaillon, conscious of the photograph of a rose-covered stone cottage on the desk next to the snapshot she had taken in front of the Lethbridges' summer house.

"Cher Monsieur Roussel," she began again. "Thank you for your letter of 6 May. I would like to rent the cottage for the entire summer, probably until September, or even longer if it is available . . ."

An hour later she was sitting on the sofa opposite Ellen Brady, whom she had known since high school. Ellen set down her cup on the coffee table, frowning thoughtfully as Louise spoke:

"But I've talked enough about myself. Let's talk about you. How was Hong Kong? And how is George?"

Ellen, a tall redhead in her mid-thirties, sighed. "You know how full of doubts I was that he'd be up to it. A month is a long time to be away from my job, but it was the best thing for him, and for me too, to get away from everything."

"I'm so glad. I was worried about you before you left. I was afraid his heart attack was making you ill too."

"At least he's not living in fear now he knows he won't keel over at the slightest exertion. The doctor says he'll live to be a hundred now that he's given up jogging and squash."

Ellen fell silent and picked up the photograph of the rose-covered cottage now lying between them on the coffee table. Louise waited for her response to the tumultuous changes in her life since they had last seen each other.

"This is lovely, really beautiful, Louise, but frankly, I feel a bit confused. Before you left for Europe you couldn't stop talking about how determined you were to hang on to the business no matter what, that you were damned if the breakup with Frank was going to get you down. I was so heartened that all your old fight had come back. And now, I come here today and you're a changed person. You're closing down your business—selling your house—all in just a couple of months."

"Of course I know how sudden it must seem to you,"

Louise said, looking toward her desk, where the letter to Maurice Roussel lay finished, ready to mail.

"Well, you must admit, it is sudden, isn't it?"

"It's not as abrupt as it seems. As I explained, I know now I was putting on a brave face, trying to convince myself that I couldn't build a future without clinging to the past."

"If I seem stubborn, it's because I need convincing and because I care what happens to you."

"I just need a change, that's all," Louise said, feeling herself immune to Ellen's well-meaning advice.

"But what's the need to burn your bridges so suddenly? A minute ago you said that at one point you had thought of forgetting Europe, concentrating on American designers. And I think that's a wonderful idea, I really do. Don't forget, I was in on the ground floor when you started this business. I know what you're made of. Louise, listen to me," she said, leaning forward earnestly. "I love you and I have your interest at heart. You've had a hell of a year what with your father dying and Frank. Divorce itself is like bereavement. Perhaps you have feelings of anger against Frank, even against your father, that you're taking out on yourself—I don't know. Promise me you'll seek professional help before you do anything drastic."

"Do you mean a psychiatrist?" Louise said, smiling at the absurdity of the idea.

"No, just a therapist, somebody who can see your life objectively."

"Ellen, there's nothing wrong with me that a change of scene won't cure. The business is already in the process of being wound down, so it's too late to change that. Anyway, I don't have any regrets now it's happening."

"Businesses can start again, in new locations, with new names, new ideas. Even partners. Maybe you should take a partner," she mused.

"There, you see? You can't really say I'm burning my bridges after all, if it's as easy as that. You can't have it both ways, Ellen." They laughed, and Louise said, "Seriously, a period of my life is over and I want to remove myself to a completely new environment. I know you're going to think I'm crazy, but I have a feeling that something is waiting for me, something exciting, something important."

"And you don't think you're running away?"

"Not running away. Running to."

"To this . . ." Ellen picked up the photograph. "You haven't told me exactly how this came about."

Louise mentioned the Lethbridges. "I've been corresponding with Dorothy since I got back. She seemed to know what I was thinking and sent me a picture of this cottage, which belongs to an old friend of theirs, saying it was available for the summer."

"Have you thought what you're going to do all day?"

"Very little, I think," she said, sinking into the deep cushions.

"But, Louise," Ellen pleaded, "you're a dynamic woman, a city girl who is used to being involved in things."

"I'm still dynamic, Ellen. At least I hope I am. But I'm going to turn my energies elsewhere."

"And you're pampered, if not downright spoiled. Think about all this. I love this house—it's part of you."

"I want to get rid of it as soon as I can, and the realtor thinks it will sell in no time. I'll put all the furniture in storage."

She saw the look of skepticism cross Ellen's face.

"The house too—I don't know what to say. What is this sudden urge to unburden yourself of all your possessions? It's so unlike you. I mean, you, of all people, who are close to being in love with your house, all your pretty things," she said, gesturing round the room. "I really can't see you changing your way of life."

"Do you know, Ellen, I discovered when I came back from my trip that this house and everything in it doesn't have the same value for me that it once had," Louise mused, looking past her collection of Steuben glass animals on the coffee table through the patio doors and into the garden. The bamboo and ferns shook in the breeze, casting wavering reflections on to the pale carpet.

"Maybe I'm being too hard on you," Ellen ventured when she sensed Louise's mind had wandered.

"I understand what you're saying, I really do. And I'll take it to heart, honestly."

"Well, I suppose, after all, it's only for the summer. Maybe you'd better go and get it out of your system and come back to start afresh. Open another business, buy another house that doesn't remind you of the past. George and I might even come and see you in France. We could leave the kids with Mother. Don't worry, I'm only joking," she added.

Filling Ellen's cup with coffee, Louise said: "There's something I haven't mentioned. When I was in France there was a man."

"A man?" Ellen's eyes widened. "But why on earth didn't you tell me? Is that the reason for all this mystery?" she said, relief crossing her face. "Well, who is he and where did you meet him?"

"We met at a dinner party in England, at the house of some old friends of my parents," Louise said, choosing her words carefully. "And then again, by accident, when I spent the weekend in southern France while I was waiting to tie up my business in Paris. I saw a poster of the area and went there on impulse so I could have time to think after what had happened."

"The Côte d'Azur?"

"Oh no, west of there, near the Pyrenees." She talked off-handedly about Owen, describing the sightseeing they had done together, leaving out everything that mattered.

"And did you go to bed with him?"

"Yes."

"Oh, Louise," Ellen said incredulously. "Has he called you? Are you in touch?"

"Yes, we've talked on the phone," she replied quickly, feeling guilty at the lie she needed to protect herself. Wanting to allay Ellen's fears, the fabricated explanation for going to Languedoc was as good as any. "And if I take this cottage for the summer, there's a much better chance of our getting together than if I stay here, thousands of miles away."

"I'm very happy for you, very happy, but I don't have to remind you how vulnerable you still are and that you hardly know him. Why don't you invite him here, on home territory? Wouldn't that be wiser?"

"The whole thing will probably fizzle out. He's not the only reason why I'm going there, to be honest. I wouldn't want you to think that," she said, fearing that Ellen's persuasive arguments were beginning to make sense.

"I wish there was something I could say to change your

mind.'' She gave Louise a searching look, then looked at her watch. "I'm sorry, but I have to go."

"I appreciate your concern, believe me. I really do," she said as Ellen rose to leave.

When she had seen Ellen to the door, Louise returned to the sitting room and sat on the sofa thinking about their conversation. For a moment her friend's criticism of her plans made her see herself in a different light, and she wondered if maybe she was being too hasty. Her eyes lit on a pile of books on the coffee table, scanning the titles until they rested on the one she had deliberately put at the bottom after her father died. Picking it up, she began to turn the pages, browsing through pictures of the glorious landscapes of the Languedoc.

A painful recollection of her father propped up in a hospital bed came to her mind, an image lit by brilliant sunshine that filled the room, grimly mocking the darkness that was about to close in on him. She saw his wasted body before her as she turned the pages of the book she had bought in San Francisco, hoping to take his mind off death. The day before he died he had gripped her hand and spoken in a weak but fervent voice:

"Louise, I want you to promise me that when this is all over, you will take what is left of me and scatter it somewhere in this country. I've never seen a place so beautiful and that's where I want to be."

Louise walked to her desk and picked up the letter she had written to Maurice Roussel, deciding it wouldn't hurt to let it stay there for a day or two.

That night Louise drifted into a strange half sleep, the desire to know answers to unfathomable questions stirring within her and overshadowing the trivia of everyday life. A weightless detachment came over her as the present fell away like a second skin. She could feel herself sinking into oblivion as her eyelids fell, bringing down a kind of screen on which the past was recorded. Louise's life began to move backwards in a collection of random images.

In her mind's eye she saw her father's funeral, then Frank's face as he told her he was leaving. She was walking down the aisle in her wedding gown, her father at her side. The doors of the church became the stage on which she had the leading role in the school play. There was her mother, peeling apples in the kitchen as she hummed a tune that was playing on the radio. She saw herself as a child on a tricycle, then as an infant in a baby's bath, laughing up at her mother's smiling face as she splashed water all over her. Her own dimpled hand reached for a plastic duck that drifted away. The splash of her hand as it hit the water changed to a heartbeat as everything went dark. Enclosed in warmth, she was conscious of a regular pulse vibrating through her body, aware that she had never seen the light of day. the vanishing image shattered into a sunburst of violent red that ate into her consciousness. Like a fire, it flickered and died, casting a shroud of ashes, which swallowed the light. She was searching for light as she soared through time, her body, her spirit reduced to nothing but shadow and vibration. Then her perception fell to earth, newly born. Yet she was not young. Her spiraling senses were drenched in a bitter white that brought with it a fleeting sensation of splintering cold. She soared above a rough, snowy landscape, flattened by height. She was someone, but not herself, as she observed a lump of granite reaching into the sky, its summit oddly straddled by a fortress of white stone. She had only a glimpse of it before she was dashed to earth, where she awoke in a gloomy chamber. The faces of a man and a woman grew in a halo of light, their lips moving in conversation. She was the woman, and yet it was not she. And she knew the man was Owen Morgan—not as he was now, but as he had once been. When he tenderly outlined the contors of her chin with his hand, she heard him speak in an echoing whisper. At the sound of his voice speaking a strange, archaic language she passed into the woman's body as effortlessly as slipping on a garment. Her present self fled like a shadow and she was resurrected as another, standing face to face with the man she loved more than life itself. She pleaded in a lost language, the meaning of the words entering her consciousness like clouds through silk. She ached with joy when she heard him speak her name and she remembered his—Hugo.

"Sancha, Sancha."

He impregnated the syllables, recorded long ago, with such

passionate meaning and belonging. Her name had once died, but now its significance was resurrected.

The dim light in which they stood was all that was left of the world, illuminating the inner core of their fate. They were saying goodbye for the last time, and as Sancha listened to Hugo's words of hope, she tasted the fruit of a later time, the continuation of their destiny; yet their parting was colored with grief. She revolted against fate, sobbing inwardly, abjuring every sacred thing she had lived by, as if such a sacrifice would bind Hugo to her forever. She spoke of her readiness to live in the realm of darkness, on earth, rather than with God and light if he, Hugo, would be there too.

Just as the light began to fade, she heard Hugo's reply: "Sancha, I swear to you that no matter where you may be, no matter how long it will take, by all that is sacred, I will find you."

Opening her eyes, at first Louise didn't know where she was. She lay absolutely still, gazing up at veins of light passing over the ceiling and thinking of the strange dream she had just had. She was conscious that the slightest disturbance would bring down a dark curtain on this other world. Closing her eyes, she willed herself back to the room she had just left, resisting the present reality. How far was it, she wondered, in terms of years or miles? She didn't know, but she wanted desperately to go back again. It was a well of knowledge that was about to be closed forever, to be swallowed up by time and consciousness. Once buried in the recesses of her mind, she would be unable to live it again, perhaps even to recollect it. But, against her will, she was torn away by the powerful inevitability that belongs to time. She came fully awake, feeling raw and cold. Her hands moved to her cheeks, cooled by tears that had soaked her hair and the pillow. Though she had left the dream and couldn't go back, she was cradled in illumination. Every object, every line in the room, was heightened by a new clarity: her vision had sharpened, her perception deepened. The seemingly random events of the past few weeks formed into a discernible pattern now that time had spun backward. She could flee from the revelation, she could reject it, but she knew she was compelled to follow the glittering thread even if it should end in tragedy, the way it had for the girl she had been moments ago.

And the point of departure was Owen Morgan. An ancient wave that had taken centuries to break revealed the hidden nature of what they shared. Just for a moment she was able to believe in the powerful truth that she had loved him long before she had ever taken her first breath in this life, and that a current of destiny was working down through the ages, shifting the ground beneath their feet.

14

The sound of water rushing through the gorge rose to a sun-drenched precipice where a throng of people gathered in a clearing. A Cathar bishop robed in black mounted a rock and faced the semicircle of upturned faces. The old, the tired and the lame had struggled for miles up the rough track to hear him speak in the secret spot known only to the Believers. The bishop's vigorous, barrel-chested figure contradicted the austere message he had come to deliver to the men and women in the front row, who were there to take vows that would bind them to poverty and chastity. The bishop's own impassioned spirit radiated through the crowd as he singled out each black-cloaked figure with his deep-set blue eyes, which swept the crowd majestically. From where she stood on the edge of the gathering, Sancha felt gooseflesh on her arms at the tangible wave of reverence that moved through the crowd, so quiet she could hear the distant rush of water.

"You are sent forth among wolves," the bishop began. "I am sending you into the jaws of Hell with only the love of Our Lord to protect you. Do not ask charity from those who can only be made to suffer if they are caught helping you. Love without limit those who refuse you, and know that the death of the body leads to the Kingdom of God. The good that we do here lingers after us and our deeds set an example for other men to follow. And if the crimson door awaits us at the end of a dark tunnel, may God grant us the courage to walk through it. If you are tortured, or made to suffer, drink the cup rather than bring death or torture to others. In the darkest valley before you are liberated, whisper the names of the dead to protect the living, though you are hounded by the beast of the Apocalypse, the Roman Church. As for temptations of the flesh, they are but reflections in bright water and have no life, no spirit and do not last. Their sweet taste fades into bitterness and their soft enticements turn to corruption . . ."

From where she stood, Sancha could see Alazaïs, distinguished by her erect posture and the straight line of her shoulders. Her narrow hips were encircled by a girdle of leather and beaten silver, from which hung the customary Gospel of St. John carried by Perfecti, those who had taken the highest vows. By the time the sun had crossed the sky, she would have pledged herself entirely to God. Her serenity of expression gave no suggestion that she was now a chatelaine dispossessed of everything she owned except her title, that her husband had been murdered by the Church, and her family and servants scattered. Poverty and hardship seemed to have bestowed on her an even greater dignity, a more pronounced grace, which made her stand out from other Believers who were about to take their final vows. Poised on the spiritual threshold second only to the rites attendant upon death itself, Alazaïs hadn't moved visibly during the bishop's sermon, even to brush away the flies or wipe the perspiration from beneath the leather band that held her hair. Sancha felt a flicker of envy at Alazaïs's concentration and self-control as she chafed in the sun. Sweat trickled down her back beneath her heavy brown mantle and she wished she could throw it off, exposing her body to the air. The heat, unseasonably intense, had caused those already weak from hunger or fasting to faint, yet for her it vanquished the memory of living like a hunted animal during the cold winter. Though she was hardened to traveling incessantly with Alazaïs in the most primitive conditions, her feet were blistered and sore from the climb to the sacred meeting place. They had journeyed for a week to get there, traveling only at night. Sancha had felt rewarded when at last they came to this rocky crest, whose jutting crags seemed like the pillars of a great cathedral open to the sky. Closing her eyes for a moment, she filled her lungs with the intoxicating scent of the yellow broom, thyme and lavender that sprouted among the rocks. Her eyelashes fluttered and she smiled as she focused on the bright wings of a butterfly, a discovery that filled her with weightless innocence.

She tried to feel closer to God as the bishop's words rained down on her, but her intentions were shaken by the realization that by this time tomorrow she would have parted forever from Alazaïs, whose life would be pledged to preaching the gospel of the true Christian faith, those truths the bishop was now repeating in a deep voice that carried above the distant sound of water at the bottom of the gorge. Sancha's thoughts blurred to an image of herself scuttling down the precipitous path like a mountain sheep, throwing off her heavy cloak and diving headlong into the bracing cold stream, until the bishop's stentorian voice brought her back again:

". . . and if on your journey to the light, you should fall short and return to another form, be it man or beast, know that the spark you carry will not die. You will nurture it into another lifetime, then perhaps another, through the next millennia if God wills it. Even those of you who are now pure may return again to sow the dark furrows of this earth with goodness. But if this path proves long, remember that God awaits you in the timeless realm of light, where we all shall meet at our journey's end . . ."

Conscious of the souls around her, most of them racked with the diseases of old age, Sancha was curious to know where those who returned would go, and whether they would gather in this same spot. Alazaïs had once likened the spirit to the greater celandine. When the plant perished and blackened in winter, its life force seeped into its root, which grew deep in the earth. So it was, she said, with the reincarnated. Sancha combed the faces of the old people, whom time and hardship had mellowed like old wood. Their eyes, watchful yet serene, bore the stamp of persecution, suggesting that they had witnessed all the crimes of the human heart in the course of a violent lifetime.

The sermon ended and the Believers began to chant a hymn so beautiful that tears filled Sancha's eyes. The world fell away as she listened to the pure harmony of so many true

Christians singing in union. The music drummed deep inside her, filling her with a bittersweet joy that no tambourines or harps had ever aroused. The song of worship resonated like a bow being dragged across her heart, dredging up feelings of piety she had thought she was incapable of.

As the crowd began to move forward, Sancha followed, her head bowed, wiping her tears and vowing she would try harder to be a better Cathar. She saw Alazaïs and the other postulants disappear through a break in the trees, followed by the rest of the congregation, who were making their way up the mountain to a cave for the final vows. She held back for a moment, feeling somewhat lost without Alazaïs. A movement in the shrubs at the edge of the clearing caused her to turn and look over her shoulder. The last person in the world she could have expected to see was standing there. When she recognized the unmistakable figure of Hugo de Franjal, she thought at first he must be an apparition.

The chanting voices died away, leaving her in the dusty, barren space emptied of Believers. He raised his hand in greeting as she walked toward him, her robe trailing in the dust, wondering how she could have lived a year without setting eyes on him. She had ripened for Hugo in the year that saw the ruin of the de Franjal dynasty, maturing by a gift of nature that was as sweet as it was mysterious. Now she saw him, Sancha couldn't deny that it wasn't God who filled her heart at every waking moment, but Hugo. Her throat went dry and her eyes stung with tears of gratitude that he was still alive, that he wasn't blinded or maimed. The fugitive life had weathered his fine face and hardened his sinewy forearms. His blue eyes seemed darker, as if shadowed by the violence he had witnessed. Always alert to danger, he projected the watchfulness of a falcon.

She broke the stunned silence between them. "Seeing you so unexpectedly has taken my powers of speech away, Hugo. Your mother will be so glad you have come. She didn't expect you."

He shook his head incredulously, folding his arms across his chest and regarding her with undisguised pleasure.

"Sancha, so it really is you. I didn't expect the happiness of seeing you here. Are you well? I know from my mother's message how difficult life has been for both of you."

She forgot everything she had suffered as she smiled radiantly up at him, smoothing away a lock of damp hair that had escaped the leather chaplet.

"We've survived well enough, though there were times when we didn't know where our bread was coming from." She shrugged as if it didn't worry her.

"I can see that. You're much thinner than when I last saw you."

"Am I? I was growing much too fat and idle anyway. I'm as lean as a hare now that I sleep under the stars and wander mountain paths."

His smile broke his serious expression. Studying her, he could see that the dangerous year through which she had lived had molded her beauty, endowing her with a dusky maturity. Conscious he had been staring at her, he mumbled:

"I'm glad to see your difficulties haven't cured you of your good nature."

"Oh no, I'm still full of hope," she replied, confused at the attraction sparking so uninhibitedly between them. She wanted to tell him her sufferings were nothing, that now he was here energy surged inside her, and her endurance had redoubled, that the inexplicable bond between them healed the wounds of all her days. She blushed to the roots of her hair when she saw his eyes linger on her breasts. A moment ago she had felt incredibly bold, but her courage left her when she felt the power of his curiosity. Though he might be no longer bound by his Templar's vows, she feared the uncharted waters that eddied between them. During the last year she had been sexless, ageless, but now, in a few moments, she was young and alive again.

As he talked about his journey, she studied him. Hugo's mastery of himself set him apart from other men in her eyes, but she sensed his long celibacy still clung to him like the cool air of purity that filled a church, exciting her and shaming her for the stirrings it aroused. She reminded herself why he had come.

"We had news of you from time to time. I heard you were at Queribus, then in the Fenouiedes with some *faidit* from Spain."

"I was, but I haven't stayed long in one place. Months passed when I heard no news of my mother."

When she had told him they had spent the winter as close to Puivaillon as they dared, she touched on his father's torture and execution by the troops of the French king and the Inquisition in retribution for the murder of the Inquisitors. Her condolences seemed a hollow offering of sympathy to a man whose fortune and way of life had been dealt a mortal blow.

"I grieved along with your mother when your father died. What happened was terrible beyond belief. And then, the loss of Puivaillon—what suffering it must cost you."

"In my mind I've abandoned it forever," he said in a hollow voice that suggested he was not yet quite reconciled to his loss. "And now Puivaillon is laid waste and our domains belong to the traitor de Cazenac, as a reward for kissing the boots of a French king. But I predict that he and his heirs will lead a poisoned existence there, that the very earth of Puivaillon will torment them for generations. As for my father, he died bravely, resisting capture. He gave up his life rather than have the names of the others who were with him at Avignonnet tortured out of him. No man can ask for more. In my youth I defied him, but I honor him more in death than I did in life." He shrugged and looked up at Sancha, who rested on a rock as she listened.

Regarding the ruins of his life, Hugo had never seemed so full of conviction. Every sinew of his body had been wrought by violence, contradicting the gentleness in his eyes when he looked at her. It was hard to comprehend that he, like her, was reduced to nothing but his own courage, and that his only possessions were his sword and the horse beneath him. The noble name he once wore like a crown now hung over his head like a curse.

"If it were me, I would be weeping, raging that I had lost my birthright. I would want to murder my enemies," she declared hotly.

He touched her sleeve gently and shook his head. "It's not the loss of my lands I grieve for, Sancha, but for my country. I am the last de Franjal and I have pledged my life for the good Christians and the Languedoc."

"Hugo, it's dangerous for you to come here, so close to Puivaillon. They are looking for you."

"No, I wanted to come, whatever the risk. I heard at

Montségur three days ago that my mother would be taking the *consolamentum*. Since then I've been traveling."

"You've been at Montségur?"

"Count Roger de Mirepoix is gathering a militia of trained men. He thinks the Pope will persuade the king to mount another Crusade against us. Anyway, let us not talk of that now."

Seeing Sancha look toward the hill ahead, he said: "This road seems to me to be much too hard for old and lame people to climb. Couldn't they find an easier place?"

She shook her head. "It would not be safe. The Cathars don't hesitate to climb to the highest places, nearer to God— to Montségur, for example. Come," she urged, touching his sleeve. She felt honored to be at the ceremony where Alazaïs would receive the blessing of the bishop.

As she gathered her cloak, Hugo studied her small tapering hands, then met the dark eyes beneath her straight, sleek brows. Hope and desire took him violently unawares when she turned to climb ahead of him up the path lost in the sheer rock face above the gorge. He had thought of Sancha during the past year when he was feverish from battle or as his prayers died on his lips in the cold hours of morning before the fires were lit. There were moments when the memory of her face broke the membrane between living and dying. The thought that she was pure and good, even though they had never exchanged promises, had sustained him. Filling his lungs with thin mountain air, he felt charged with sudden energy as he followed her nimble figure up the steep path.

When they stopped for breath on a ledge, he turned his head to hide his feelings. She was leaning against a rock, her dark hair thrown back by the wind, her breasts heaving with exertion. Lifting his eyes, he was defeated by the simple human desire for communion. This mysterious girl, who had come from nowhere, was his soul mate, though every turn of fate had conspired to intensify their differences and keep them apart. Their meeting was like that of two birds whose wings had brushed in the enameled sky, changing the course of their destinies. The truth of these new sentiments stunned him for a moment, making him question how well he really knew himself. His heart was bursting with the irony that he had fearlessly taken on all comers with his sword, but now he had been humbled by this slight, dark woman.

Wordlessly they continued their climb. Sancha was acutely aware of the moments dwindling away and wondered if Hugo would ever have the courage to speak what she had just seen reflected in his eyes. The banquet at Puivaillon was the last occasion on which she had heard music and laughter, or had eaten her fill or thought of love; all pleasure seemed to have happened in another, happier century than the one in which she was living. Pausing to take in a sweeping view of the gorge, she said:

"Are you a Believer now?"

"In my heart I always have been, but the Cathar cause needs fighting men, not praying men. If I have any time left to me when we have won our right to worship and to live as we please, then I'll have time to pray," he said.

The fragility of mortal life vibrated between them, chilling the thyme-scented air. Sancha peered down the vertiginous chasm, tasting fully the precariousness of existence. This exhilarating moment, brilliant as a jewel, was a reward for all they had gone through. Whenever she had been close to death, she had felt a terror that couldn't be calmed by prayer. Feeling her own blood rush through her veins, she wondered why she couldn't be immortal, like the river rushing below the dizzying drop. The Believers said that all life was created by the Devil, and that the spirit in man that belonged to God lived to conquer, to dominate, the flesh, usually through successive lifetimes. She was beginning to understand why weak spirits returned again and again to the struggle, and why the strong often returned to a mortal shape to help them. She was one of the weak ones who would choose the darkness forever rather than sacrifice what was dear and familiar. It seemed a blasphemous thought, but her feet were planted too firmly in the earth for her to be otherwise. She couldn't count herself among the pure spirits who had climbed the mountain to be closer to God—not yet. Christian, Jew and pagan all dwelled inside her. She craved all the sensuality of this earth, whether it be the taste of a peach, the sound of bird song, or the delicate evening sky filled with swifts. Thinking what it would be like to lie with Hugo, she knew she didn't possess the strength to break the carnal chain that gave birth to new life.

Her instinct told her that he too had struggled and that he had lost. As they looked at one another, their faces flushed from the effort of climbing, she could tell he was eking out the moments before they reached the cave, just as she was. When they had nearly reached the top, she asked the question that had risen to her mind the moment she saw him: "Are you going to leave us soon?"

"I've come to persuade you, my mother, all of you, that you must take refuge at Montségur."

"If that is why you have come, I'm afraid it will be in vain. Your mother will never be persuaded, Hugo. She feels her place is among the people, setting an example, offering whatever comfort she can to true Christians."

As they climbed the last few feet of the path, they could hear the faint murmur of the bishop's voice saying the Lord's Prayer, though they couldn't yet see the mouth of the cave, which was well hidden.

"I'll persuade her somehow, whatever it takes. Surely she can do more good among the faithful there than living like a hunted hare in the woods."

They were now at the top, and as Sancha contemplated the gap between the path and the entrance to the cave, she dared herself not to grab the rope that had been slung there to help pilgrims safely across the divide. She peered down at the dizzying plunge to the white rocks below. Feeling Hugo's eyes on her, she didn't hesitate. Crossing the gap in one leap, she shouted: "There's another way that's easier, but it's much longer." Her heart was pounding with exhilaration.

Landing beside her, he said: "You're like me. You choose the hardest and shortest route."

"I suppose we should go in now." It occurred to her that she might not ever see him again, but she couldn't bring herself to bid him farewell.

"And you, Sancha, by your presence here I suppose you must be a Believer now. But then, no one living so close to my mother could fail to be a convert to the Cathar faith."

To her surprise, his hand shot out, clasping hers to keep her from entering the cave.

"Yes," she whispered, deeply conscious of his hand around her wrist. "I've already taken the first steps, the *con-vensa . . .*"

"And will you take the vows that bind you to poverty and chastity, and all the other laws?"

She looked at him calmly. "No. I'm a long way from such devotion. I'm only a simple Believer." She was startled at the determination in his eyes.

"Then I will tell you now that I'm glad of that. Not just glad, but happy. When the time is right, we must talk of everything between us."

She moved ahead of him into the crowded cave lit by torches and echoing with the bishop's voice. The implications of what Hugo confessed were too astounding to absorb as they were sucked into the dark chamber full of worshippers. Sancha bowed her head, avoiding his eyes as she considered what it meant when they had leapt, one after the other, across the chasm just now. Acutely conscious of Hugo's presence in the darkness close by, Sancha heard her own heartbeat drowning out the chanting and prayers. She stared unseeingly for a long moment at the wavering shadows of the worshippers reflected on the walls of the cave. Looking up, she gasped in awe at the dome, which had been chiseled smooth and frescoed in a pure, rich blue patterned with gold circles enclosing five-pointed stars in silver, symbolizing eternity enclosing mankind. Looking at them, Sancha was filled with a sense of divine animation. Her eyes moved to the center of the blue dome, stamped with a red rose, its dark petals unfolding within a triple circle, its stamen a four-pointed cross, which represented truth.

Behind her, Hugo was looking at the shadowy figure of his mother. The bishop stood behind a table draped in white linen, on which rested a candlestick and the holy book of leather-bound parchment. Picking it up, he held it over the head of each Perfect.

"Pharisees, seducers, sinners, you who sit at the gates of the Kingdom and hold back others who would enter; Lucifer lured them thence from Paradise with the lying assurance that whereas God allowed them only good, the Devil would give them both good and evil to enjoy, that they should have authority over one another, should be kings or emperors or counts, and should learn to hunt birds with birds, beasts with beasts . . ."

Hugo's eyes moved to the top of Sancha's bowed head and

he was gripped by a violent emotion he thought he had for-
saken long ago. In the darkened cave he glimpsed another
lifetime, as yet unlived. Time spun itself into a void like a
great spool he couldn't see but could feel. In the close, shadowy chamber echoing with prayer and chanting all the pri-
vations of the years came crashing down on him, mocking
the romanticism of his troubadour days and souring the violent fanaticism of the Templar creed, which still tormented
him. Everything now seemed to turn on Sancha's love and
his love for her. His lips followed the bishop's in repeating
the Lord's Prayer as he grappled with the astonishing change
within himself. All the ideas and passions that had shaped
his existence were shattered, leaving him vulnerable and de-
fenseless. Feeling powerless to resist, he gave himself up to
a living warmth that could fill his heart.

That evening at sunset Sancha was seated on a log by a fire
not far from Hugo, who was talking to the Believers, their
eyes fixed on him hopefully.

". . . Raimon of Toulouse has given his word that he will
rally troops before long. Patience and forbearance are what
we counsel if there should be a siege at Montségur. You
should all gather there now, for the time being . . ."

One of the men nodded sagely. "What he says is true. The
king's men will wither like flowers in the field waiting for us
to come down from the fortress. Like eagles in their nest,
we'll be safe there. For thirty five years the Counts of Mirepoix have foreseen this day, rebuilding the fortress to withstand just such an assault. Why, I've seen the stores of grain,
rye, corn, oil and dried fish. There's enough to keep a whole
town for years."

"And water," interjected another. "The cistern in the inner courtyard is three men across and collects more than
enough for hundreds to live on."

Hugo exchanged a glance with Sancha. Earlier he had confessed his nagging worry that the fortress could not contain
all the refugees, penitents and dying Cathars who migrated
there. Speaking to these holy men, he seemed reluctant to
divest them of their illusions.

"The huts built on the eastern slope are secure. Only

mountain goats could reach them. They would have to seize the fortress first, but it is impenetrable.''

''The King's patience and resources might be inexhaustible,'' Hugo interjected.

The old man across from him gave a toothless smile. His watery eyes reflected a keen anticipation of the conflict.

''My son, the King's Gascon and Norman mercenaries will soon tire and miss the comforts of home, believe me.''

His companion said in a quavering voice that was still full of fire, ''They can never surround the mountain. That, Hugo, has already proved impossible. They can never stop the local peasants from breaking through their cordon with food and medicines for the Goodmen, never. Even the threat of the Inquisitor's bloody punishment has failed to quench their faith. No matter how much blood they spill, they will fail.''

''Perhaps,'' said Hugo, ''but remember, these northern men are hard as tempered steel. Their eyes are cold and their blood is of ice. They come from a cold land, where only the hardiest survive. The character of our people is much more gentle and has been formed by the hot winds of the Mediterranean, by the fruit orchards and vineyards. These hordes are spawned from earth that is hard during long winters and sodden in summer. They know no code of chivalry, which tames the brute in men. They glory in blood and war, which is their passion. Their lips spew guttural obscenities and repeat prayers that come from the book, not the heart, while we are nurtured on poetry with our mother's milk.'' Hugo took a sip from his goblet, then fell silent as if he had said too much to these pure-minded men.

When they had gone, there was a space between Hugo and Sancha, which neither of them moved to close. Sancha sat on the log, her hands tucked in her sleeves, looking at the fire. Earlier they had eaten a simple meal of bread and river fish, and now the Believers had fanned out through the clearing to sleep under the stars, wrapping themselves in their cloaks. A chill was beginning to descend on the hills as they silently kept the vigil for Alazaïs to return so that Hugo could speak to her about Montségur. Looking into the embers, Sancha reflected that if she had met Hugo de Franjal at Puivaillon in times of prosperity and peace, perhaps a hundred years ago, he would never have spoken to her as he had that afternoon. The scourge that had stripped the land bare had laid their souls open to each other. Her love for Hugo was bathed in the blood of the Languedoc, as red as the flames curling skyward under the stars.

Sancha looked up to see two dark-clad figures approaching. They were Alazaïs and the new postulant who would henceforth be her life's companion, a noblewoman named Esclarmonde. In the firelight, the faces of the two women radiated the happiness of young brides, now that they were full members of the Church.

"Mother, won't you come and sit with us here?" said Hugo, rising. Earlier they had had an affectionate but subdued reunion, since Alazaïs had taken vows to forsake her earthly ties.

Sancha rose and kissed her three times, then kissed Esclarmonde as a sign of her respect.

When they sat down, Sancha felt a new strangeness in front of Alazaïs now that she had consecrated herself to God. Her bed was the hard ground in the barren hills and her possessions reduced to the clothes on her back, and yet Sancha had never seen her more at peace. She, who had once slept on furs and dined off silver plate, would now live on crusts and wild berries, and sleep in the forest next to her companion. She no longer wore the embroidered boots of a lady, but rough sandals, and when those were gone, her feet would be cracked and blistered from walking barefoot on stones. Sancha could only imagine how she must feel, knowing that in her place she would have no resistance against the seductions of the flesh.

Alazaïs spoke to Sancha. "Are you ready to leave at dawn? You can accompany us to the valley and from there you can make your way to the farm by sunset."

To Hugo, she said, "Arnaut Narbonna is a kind, good farmer, who has offered her a place in his home. He is a hard-working man and a Believer. I could not ask for more if she were my own daughter."

Her eyes moved from Hugo to Sancha. Hugo leaned forward, resting his fists on his powerful legs. "Mother," he began, "I came here not only to pay my respects and to exchange news, but also to persuade you to go to Montségur, now, without delay."

"To Montségur? But Hugo, you know that my place will now be to preach among the people, to bring them the word. To give solace to the sick, the dying, who have no one to turn to. That's what this day has meant for me. There are so few of us who are strong enough to carry on the work."

Hugo waited patiently for her to finish. "Mother, your days will be numbered if you don't flee now. No, flee is not the word. I didn't mean that. That sounds too cowardly. There is nothing cowardly about seeking refuge."

"Hugo," she said with an indulgent glance. "Not until your father died could I take my vows in good conscience. Now, all my earthly ties are severed and I am free to do as my heart dictates. Would you deny me that wish?"

Sancha saw Hugo struggle against the simplicity of her argument, which had obviously moved him.

"Can you agree that you are of more use to God alive than dead? If so, listen to me before it is too late. If you won't save your own life, then save the lives of those living at Montségur. Many are sick and weak. They need strong, capable hands there."

They were interrupted when the bishop stepped from the shadows, where he had been listening. At the sight of him they all rose and genuflected, then bent in turn for his blessing. As they bowed their heads, he murmured the benediction: "May God grant you a good death and make you good Christians."

When they were seated again, he said: "Hugo is right, Alazaïs. Montségur is the only safe refuge for us all at this time. And what better time for you to make a pilgrimage than now, to sharpen the sword of your faith against the stones of the fortress and hear the great Bishop Marty speak. If you have doubts, then go, the two of you, with my blessing. I will give you letters for the bishop."

Alazaïs bowed her head. "So be it," she said to her companion when the bishop had gone. "We need not stay longer than necessary."

"I will guide you there. We can carry what we need on my horse."

"But, Hugo, you ought to be on your way to Aragon. There's no need for you to come. Two old women alone— what harm could come to us? And, anyway, it is the custom for two of our Order to travel simply, without assistance or comfort.''

''You'll be safer with me to escort you,'' said Hugo, overruling her objections.

They sat in a circle round the fire as the two women discussed their plans. Sancha recalled her encounter with the two Cathar women in Baruch's house, which had changed her destiny. Staring blankly into the embers, her mind was in a turmoil. When she looked up at Hugo, she wondered if he had guessed what she was thinking. Leaning forward, she said to Alazaïs in an anguished whisper:

''Let me accompany you to Montségur. Please.''

Alazaïs looked startled at her request and Sancha could see it was on the tip of her tongue to refuse. Then she looked at Hugo, whose watchful expression made her hesitate.

''The farmer Narbonna is expecting you, but we could send a message to him, I suppose. There would be need for your healing arts at Montségur, Sancha. There is good reason for you to come.''

Hugo's jaw was firmly set as he looked into the distance and he didn't see his mother smile. Though he was now a man and had lived away from her for a decade, the secrets of his heart were as plain to her as when he had been a child and she knew that this girl was right for him.

When they left early next morning in a blue mist broken by shafts of light, they traveled down the precipitous gorge, following other pilgrims who made their way along the rough track. The horse that Hugo had brought carried what few possessions they shared among them and enough food to last for several days if they were forced to travel through wilderness well away from any town. Alazaïs and Esclarmonde had put away their black robes and gospels, their silver girdles that marked them as Perfecti, dressing as ordinary countrywomen in brown linen shifts and kerchiefs. They were posing as a family who were making a journey to relatives beyond the town of Lavelanet.

On the first night they made their camp in the depths of a pine forest, where they knew they would be safe. Not daring to light a fire in case it attracted attention, they ate dry bread washed down with water from a stream. Alazaïs and Esclarmonde bedded down in a woodcutter's small stone hut as the night thickened. Sancha spread her cloak on the ground over a cushion of pine needles, glancing at Hugo, who had flung his mantle by a tree to make his bed. Stretching out, he glanced in Sancha's direction, then turned away. Sancha lay down, her legs and feet aching from the journey, and listened to the song of birds echoing through the forest. In the dying light she glanced at Hugo now and then, his face turned resolutely from her. A soft wind high in the pines whispered her to sleep as she closed her eyes thinking of him. She had a peculiar dream of people speaking in strange whistles, like birds. Among them was Hugo, whose speech, by some miracle, she understood.

In the night she awakened with a start. A shadow was moving over the crescent moon that shone through the trees, and her heart pounded when she saw the figure of a man moving toward her.

"Sancha," came the whisper. "Are you awake?" It was Hugo's voice.

She responded by reaching for his hand and guiding him down to her. When he knelt, she could feel the strength of his passion as he crushed his lips to her palm. She gave a little murmur as astonishment filled her. As he stretched out beside her she felt invaded by lightness, and yet certainty. He smelled of sun, of leather and sweat, filling her with an intoxicating sense of his maleness. He was as solid as wood, scoured by the elements, and yet he touched her small fluttering hands, her cheek, her temples with delicacy. He pulled her to him, hesitantly touching the lines of her body beneath her rough cloak. In the darkness she could interpret his gleaming eyes, which reflected her own mute astonishment at what was happening. It was on her lips to whisper that she had never lain with a man before, but now that his arms were around her she felt no fear, only a blessed completeness that contradicted all her inhibitions.

Hugo lay silently beside her, feeling as if the turmoil of a lifetime had died away miraculously, freeing him to love Sancha with the passion that had inspired his music, his prayers, his battles.

"Is this real? Is it true?" he whispered, not expecting an answer. "When I awoke moments ago, cold and alone, I saw clouds pass swiftly over the moon. It was like time moving before my eyes. I thought of my own mortality, of the sweetness I might miss before I die.''

He wanted to tell her how he had untangled the thread of bitter self-denial woven into his character, how heavy were the chains of dogma. He clasped her so tightly that his arms trembled with tension.

''I wondered if you would come to me,'' she whispered, knowing what it had cost him to cross the few yards to her side. Loving her, even for an hour, was against everything he had been taught to believe in. She lay very still, feeling her heart beating next to his and listening to the wind.

Fanned by her nearness, the fire kindled inside him. He gently unlaced her bodice, a simple act that ignited the tinder of his dry, aching body. He was ashamed, afraid and yet proud that his manhood still lived. The latent power of his own suppressed desire suffocated him and he was enveloped in wonder at his years of celibacy, of contempt for the flesh so rigidly adhered to, now to be so easily shattered by a woman's warmth. The touch of Sancha's skin beneath his callused hands reminded him of the delicacy of a robin's egg that he was afraid to break. He discovered the soft breasts beneath the rough wool, knowing it was too late to kill the desire quickening within him. He felt her hands tentatively cradling his chin, drawing his mouth to her lips, hungry and sweet, breathing life and hope. As they drew together, she slipped her hands beneath his tunic, exploring the muscles of his back now tense with wanting her. Whispering pleasure filled him as he touched her soft body, confirming that the forbidden richness he now enjoyed was more glorious than any dream that had ever tormented him in the Holy Land. Cradled in the bower of pine, they kissed with a transfiguring intensity that reaffirmed their thirst for life and for each other. Feeling Hugo move urgently against her naked limbs, Sancha was filled with a sense of shining honor that he should bless her with his body. A burning need to make him part of her consumed her, drowning all coherent thought. He entered her swiftly, filling her with exquisite pain, which shocked her with its intensity. When it died away, she felt the aching fullness that embodied life's great mystery. Dictated by instinct, she moved beneath him to bring him nearer and hold him there to prolong the exquisite sensation of his fullness inside her. Their bodies united, they spent themselves in driving movement, which ended when he burst furiously within her, filling her with his essence.

Still joined to her, Hugo murmured in the darkness: "You are the source, the well, the life. I cannot question why or how; I can only be. From the first moment I saw you, I knew that I loved you."

Lying in his arms, Sancha hadn't been thinking of love; it seemed enough to be adored by Hugo for this one moment. "And I too. I've carried the thought of you ever since, hardly daring to call what I feel love. But that's what it is and now I can say it. Hugo," she repeated, glorying in the right to say his name softly and with love. "What a strange twist of destiny that brought a Jewess and a Templar together that day," she murmured.

Later he lay back, cradling her head in his arm and covering her forehead with kisses. Clasping her hand in his, he whispered:

"The weight I carried for a lifetime left me when we became one. A new truth has entered my life and I am blinded by its beauty."

His face was solemn in the darkness as he looked back at the barren years when he had prostrated himself to what he had believed to be a higher cause. A vanity at his own superiority had corrupted his soul, he now knew. This pure good he found in Sancha asked for no sacrifice or self-mortification, only for love.

They lay there, cloaked in darkness broken by streaks of moonlight penetrating the forest. As Sancha listened to the wind, she thought of everything Hugo had said. He had broken chains of class and faith that had determined his life from birth in uttering his love for her. He had spent his vital force in making love to her, a force he had always put to other use. In the throes of their lovemaking she had wondered if he might regret giving in to his need for her. She lay quietly for a moment, knowing what such a declaration meant and what it had cost him to make it. She felt compelled to whisper:

"Do you think it is a sin, Hugo? Tell me. How do you believe, how does this make you feel now it has happened?"

"I don't know, Sancha. Would that I could tell you. I only

know that by knowing you I have closed some mystic circle, that the power of what I feel defies all fervor to kill it. What is nature? What is man? How much we must take on faith from the day we were born. Christians would tell us we are pleasing Satan now as we lie together, that we were never further from perfection than in this embrace. If so, then we will need courage to love each other and not let it destroy us.'' When she wrapped her arms around him he added: ''That is all I know, all I can say, little enough as it is. It doesn't seem our fate to know more.''

''Do you think we will be born again, you and I, in the form of animals? Perhaps snakes or toads, or worse?''

He smiled in the darkness. ''So we are told. I once asked my mother what she thought, and she said even some saintly people will be reborn because they choose the unselfish path of doing good on earth rather than staying safely in Paradise.''

''Perhaps Alazaïs will come back too, then. But we will never know one another. It is only by a strange chance that we ever met in his life.''

''No, Sancha. It was no mere chance that you and I met. What we feel, what we live, is part of God's great design. It is he who fashioned the way we move and speak, I'm sure of that.''

''I am so happy to know what you believe in, Hugo. It means as much to me as loving you,'' she murmured softly, her body still trembling with the delight he had given her.

''You know part, but not yet all, my beloved. I believe in justice, and that is why I will fight the French overlords and the Church with all my strength. But I also believe in the beauty of goodness—I believe in you. I would die for you, too, Sancha, if I must. This is my country, it is beneath our backs as we lie here, and you are the missing part of myself, the end of all my journeys.''

He stroked her hair gently. She saw the dark and light side of the moon through the trees, fused together like good and evil. They reminded her of the bishop's words:

''. . . temptations of the flesh . . . are but reflections in bright water and have no life, no spirit and do not last. Their sweet taste fades into bitterness and their soft enticements turn to corruption . . .'' Burying her face in Hugo's chest, she let the words slip from her consciousness as she fell into a dreamless sleep.

Five days later they passed through Lavelanet, crawling with Basque mercenaries employed by the forces of King Louis and the Dominican Inquisitors. They slept outside the city walls and began their journey at daybreak, traveling on the main road until a cleft appeared in the mist-shrouded mountains that marked the pass to Montségur. They followed a stream swollen by the melting snows from the Pyrenees, Hugo in front, leading his horse. His eyes searched every passerby suspiciously to ferret out thieves or informers, whether shepherds with sun-ravaged faces leading their flocks to higher pastures, or farmers flailing oxen that drew wagon loads of forage. The three women covered their hair with hoods and kept their heads down to avoid curiosity, but, try as they would, neither Alazaïs nor Esclarmonde could disguise the straight carriage and distinctive gait of noblewomen. Neither could a peasant's rough cloak and tunic hide Hugo's strong, well-proportioned frame, product of generations of noble breeding. Anyone guessing at the identity of the four travelers could have taken the party for two nuns of noble extraction, a Catalan and a knight at arms. They walked in silence, feeling the cool morning air crackle with danger. At a crossroads, where they feared to meet priests or soldiers, the women hid in a thicket and Hugo tied the horse out of sight until he had satisfied himself that the way was clear. When he returned he said:

"It isn't safe, either now or later. There is a group of men on horseback coming and, even though they won't see us where we are now, there are bound to be others. There will be priests with them as well, who could challenge us, and then we will be lost." His arms across his chest, he brooded that the heavy traffic on this little-frequented road seemed a bad omen.

"Then what shall we do? Give up?" asked Alazaïs.

"No, we must find another way. Wait here for a time, and I will reconnoiter. Rest, all of you, and eat something. I won't be gone long."

Sancha watched him disappear into the distance, feeling a sense of loss that she couldn't hide. They had lain together every night on the way, but both had been careful not to show any sign of their feelings for one another to either Alazaïs or her companion. Sancha had tried not to think of what would happen when they reached Montségur. She lived in the hope that Hugo would find a way to take her with him or that he would stay at Montségur too. She turned, to see Alazaïs regarding her with an expression that said she knew their secret. Sancha blushed with shame as she fell on her knees. Kissing the hem of Alazaïs's dress, she began to cry.

"You need not weep, my child, unless it's from happiness. I bless you," Alazaïs whispered, resting her hand on Sancha's head.

Sancha lifted her eyes, yet she was still smarting with a sense of betrayal. She had always assumed that, as a mother, Alazaïs could only wish her son to emulate her own pure existence, uncorrupted by the flesh. But she was wrong. Alazaïs was smiling down at her indulgently.

"You seem to forget that I was young once—and warm in heart and body, just like you. I know what you are feeling."

"Then you're not angry? But we have sinned," she said, sobbing. Even though Alazaïs knew their secret, Sancha still had misgivings about what they had done. Their pride in each other, their greed for love, for life had made them selfish.

"If you and Hugo have sinned, then who am I to judge you? We live and move in different seasons, all of us. I am in the winter of my life, but I have not forgotten spring and summer. That part of me remembers and wishes you every happiness, as doubtful as that might seem. If I could choose my son's bride, then it would be you, Sancha."

"Is this true? But why? I am nothing," she cried, somehow feeling that she had stolen the single thing of value from Alazaïs's old life, like the last coin from a beggar.

"Wealth and title mean nothing to me, though it may surprise you. I have seen their very fabric torn by war and greed and time. The proud and mighty fall and the evil are raised to worldly heights. And yet happiness is so small it can be held in your hand. It doesn't need grand rooms to proclaim it, or gold, or titles. It grows like a weed, in a simple way, that people rarely seem to notice."

Kissing her cheek, Sancha said: "No matter what happens, I have vowed never to leave you. Of that you can be sure."

"Of course you will leave me. You will and you must. Someday you will understand what now seems a contradiction. The force for good is reborn again and again. It is the light in the dark world, however imperfect. You and Hugo are that light and, if God wills, your children also. Hugo, like you, has always been of this earth. The sword, the lute, the cross are real things he must touch to understand his purpose. It somehow seems right and good to me, Sancha, that the two of you are united, like links in an unfinished chain.''

"Where does it begin and end?" Sancha asked, feeling sure that in her wisdom, Alazaïs must possess the truths of existence.

"No one knows where the chain begins or ends, no one. We can believe, but God has not given us the right to know.''

Early the next morning they arrived at Montségur after following a circuitous route that avoided the direct approach. Leaving the shelter of the woods, they had their first sight of the fortress perched at an impossible height. Sancha looked at the gray stone citadel, unable to believe it had been created by man. God had moved men to crown the pinnacle with a holy retreat so they could be closer to him. Its asymmetrical shape had been determined by the narrow summit on which it rested, and it challenged intruders from any direction. It was so remote that God himself might have lived there, and she could take comfort in the belief that once there, they would be protected by angels. Thickets of dark trees grew densely between the pinnacles, making the approach seem impenetrable. Sancha imagined that once they were there, nothing could harm them. Even Hugo, who had been unconvinced of its safety, seemed to shine with confidence at the sight of the fortress. Seeing the expression on his face, Sancha felt a bolt of tension unlock within her when she realized that, after all, he now believed it was truly impregnable. She felt a laugh bubbling in her throat at all the fears of the doubters she had so often heard expressed. God had blessed true Christians with an ark like Noah's so that they could survive the flood.

The women hid in the forest while Hugo went to find one of the peasant guides from the region who would lead them up to the fortress. In the late afternoon he returned in the company of a rough, sturdy farmer in a dirty leather jerkin, who held his cap between hands blackened with labor. He looked at the three women with curious brown eyes.

"This is Peire, who will guide us to the fortress. He has just come down from the mountain, where he took provisions. He will unload our baggage from the horse and some men will take it up after nightfall."

At once identifying Alazaïs as a Perfect by her bearing, Peire genuflected reverently before her and asked her blessing.

Touching his head, Alazaïs murmured:

"Que Dieu vous benisse et vous fasse un bon chrétien."

When the man raised his head, he nodded politely to Sancha and said:

"Good day, my lady."

No one had ever called her a lady before, and Sancha looked at him, startled.

They began an exhausting climb up the eastern flank of the pinnacle, where the path was all but indistinguishable through dark trees coated with moss. Hugo led and Sancha trailed behind Alazaïs and Esclarmonde, who were gasping for breath as they struggled up the steep incline. Sancha fell again and again, unable to see in the premature twilight cast by the trees, which grew closely together. An eerie silence reigned in this kingdom of darkness, curiously empty of bird song or the sound of insects. It was a kingdom of mold and damp, a lifeless zone that seemed inhabited by evil influences. Sancha struggled on, her mouth dry from thirst and fear, her sandals cutting into her feet, already raw from the journey. She gasped for breath, trying to catch up as she saw the figures disappearing ahead of her. Ashamed at her own cowardice, she couldn't shake off the feeling that they were breaching an evil divide that separated them from the ultimate good. They had fallen into the underworld, which was beset with impossible obstacles. She wondered briefly what the future held in store for her, for Hugo and the others; but here, in this eerie forest, she could imagine nothing. Her companions, too, sank into the spongy ground and struggled for a foothold on rocks slippery with mosses that thrived in the damp where the sun never penetrated. Now they had completely lost sight of their goal, the fortress high above them, and she felt this primeval forest would ensnare them and consume them without leaving a trace. The gaping mouths of caves appeared through the gloom, like glimpses into the abyss of Hell. She shivered at the thought of falling down into the bowels of the earth, into a nest of demons.

Suddenly, as they neared the summit, the darkness split open and they emerged from the stifling undergrowth into a golden kingdom. Sancha stopped to rest, dazzled by the sweeping view of the rich green pastures and forests of the Pyrenean foothills, bathed now in late afternoon sun. She was struck by the thought that death must be like their journey, a sunburst of light after drowning in darkness. The vibrant green hills tumbling endlessly beyond Montségur, radiant with the amber light of the sun low on the horizon, seemed to bless them all. At this height, where only eagles flew and the air was thin and scented with wild flowers, the secrets of all the distant valleys unfolded, revealing the snowy summits that guarded Spain. The others had stopped too, their gilded faces drinking in the beauty of the sheer stone walls that seemed at that moment more a temple than a fortress.

They continued along the rocky path winding through the thicket. Sancha quickened her step to be nearer Hugo, wanting to share this moment with him. He gave her a triumphant smile as the guide went ahead to announce their arrival.

"How do you feel at this moment?" she exclaimed, her face flushed with exertion and happiness.

"Like a knight who has dismounted from his steed, whose armor has been removed and who can feel the cool air on his aching body."

"You're bruised, but not wounded," she chided, trying to forget that from now on they would no longer be alone.

"The battle isn't over, but my spirit is at rest. And it gives me happiness that my lady is by my side . . ."

The guide motioned them toward the group of Believers who had built crude stone huts roofed in thatch or tiles beneath the towering walls of the fortress, protected on the other side by the unbreachable eastern flank of the mountain. Sancha moved forward to meet the people coming out to

greet them, unprepared for what she saw. Some of them had
lived in the huts for twenty years or more, surviving on little
more than bread, fish, water and prayer. They bore the startling stamp of spiritual exaltation, which she had never before
encountered, making them a race apart. Their clothing was
tattered, their hair rain-washed and wind-knotted, and their
skin blackened by the sun. Hardship and devotion had win-
nowed their bodies and spirits, reducing their human frames
to a thin shell to house the growth of their spirits. They stared
frankly and disconcertingly, with clear eyes that had seen
another world. A vision of the afterlife had cleansed all fear,
real and imagined, sown in their hearts and minds since their
very conception. It was strange to encounter human faces
unscarred by greed or bitterness or envy or even passion.
Shorn of these emotions that mutate the human countenance,
they radiated an awesome goodness.

Alazaïs and Esclarmonde had gone ahead to the hut of a
friend, leaving Hugo and Sancha precious moments alone.
She was filled with a mortal love for Hugo, which strangely,
didn't seem out of place. They had come this far and, as they
looked at one another, she knew they must go farther, whatever the distance.

15

Owen could hear the telephone ringing in his flat as he
climbed the stairs to the second story of the old house in
Ladbroke Grove, a bag of groceries in one hand, his mail in
the other. Cursing under his breath, he fumbled for his keys.
He pushed the door open, dumped the bag on the floor and
sprinted across the room toward the telephone, but it stopped
ringing as he touched it. Slamming down the receiver, he
crossed the sitting room and opened the double windows,
which overlooked the leafy street below. As a cool breeze
blew the curtains aside, Owen took a breath of damp air
smelling of freshly cut grass mingled with exhaust fumes. It

was Friday and he had fought the traffic all the way home from the factory, where he had spent a grueling day trying to work out a pay dispute with a union representative. He loosened his tie and rolled up his sleeves, looking impatiently at the sparsely furnished, high-ceilinged room that was untidy and dusty because his cleaning lady was on holiday.

He had bought the flat after splitting up with Mandy, as soon as he could afford a place of his own, filling it with modern functional furniture. Lately he had begun to notice that the room had taken on a shabby look, and in his discontented mood every familiar detail depressed him. As he stuffed the groceries into the fridge, he came to a decision to clear the flat of all the old misery, things that reminded him of the past, relics from the Seventies that served only to clutter up his life. When he had settled his score with Rex and put his affairs in order, he'd get a decorator to do the entire flat from top to bottom while he was on holiday somewhere. Another thing he would do would be to get his piano back from Mandy.

Later, Owen was just getting out of the shower when he heard the phone ringing again. Looking round for a towel, he grabbed one from the linen basket and sprinted down the hall. "Hello?" he said breathlessly, staring down at the water forming a small pool at his feet.

"Owen, it's Dorothy. Am I catching you at a bad time? You sound out of breath."

"Not at all. I'm just standing here dripping wet from the shower, wrapped in a towel that smells of dead mice. I'll have to take another shower."

Dorothy laughed. "Why don't I call you back in a little while if it's not convenient now?"

"Don't worry—it doesn't matter." Throwing off the towel, he dropped naked into the chair. He always liked talking to Dorothy. Just the sound of her voice soothed his nerves. She had always had that effect on him, from the very beginning when she and Ambrose were his guardians after his parents had been posted abroad. He had been wild, a difficult child, but he had never misbehaved with Dorothy, knowing instinctively that she understood him.

As they talked, Owen felt the tensions of the day leave him. "How's Ambrose? Has he recovered yet from all the hoopla surrounding his book? I heard him on the radio the other night, on my way back from Swindon. He was his usual eloquent self.''

"He's in his study right now, burrowing away at his books. He's so relieved to get back to his work.''

From the tone of Dorothy's voice, Owen sensed that she was delicately leading up to a subject that she preferred not to broach head on. He heard her draw in her breath before she said tentatively:

"Owen, there's something I wanted to talk to you about.'' She paused, as if choosing her words carefully. "I happened to be walking down Mount Street the day after I saw you at Ambrose's party and found myself passing Rex Monckton's gallery. I went in on impulse because when I saw the kind of things he had in the window, I thought he might give me an estimate on an heirloom I have no further room for.''

"Come on, Dorothy,'' Owen scoffed gently. "That's not why you went there. You weren't just passing by; you were curious.''

She paused. "All right, I admit it—I was curious. And I didn't go there by chance, but on purpose. I posed as a dotty country lady who had inherited some priceless antiques and didn't know their value. When the young man in the shop heard that, he went to fetch Rex immediately.''

"Good for you,'' he said, meaning it. "You succeeded where I failed. When I went there, they told me he was abroad, which I knew was a lie.''

"Then you think he's avoiding you?''

"I'm certain he knows I'm on to him. That detective I hired might have been careless when he was digging round, and it might have got back to Rex. So tell me, what did you think of him?'' he said with curiosity.

There was a long pause and when Dorothy spoke, her voice was deeply troubled.

"Owen, please listen to me very carefully. Rex Monckton is an extremely dangerous man. I know it's useless to try to dissuade you from what you're doing, but whatever you do, you must tread very discreetly. You mustn't allow him to know anything about your intentions. Promise me you'll be very careful, every step of the way.''

"Dorothy, look, I appreciate your concern. I've known

Monckton for years, but don't think I'm afraid of the bastard. He's a coward and there's only one way to treat people like that: to confront them, catch them off guard . . ."

"Owen—Rex Monckton is an evil man."

He drew in his breath, amused by the thought. "Dorothy, with all due respect, if you mean he's vain, pompous, a snob, a liar and a cheat, then I'd agree with you."

"No, that's not what I mean at all," she said exasperatedly. "Owen, please, you must believe me. Please don't think I'm a silly old woman imagining things."

"Dorothy, I love you dearly, but the idea that that overfed, overdressed ass is a threat to me is, to put it mildly, absurd, even ridiculous. He got the better of me years ago and now I have a chance to right a wrong. I'm going to ruin him before I'm through."

"He's a wicked man and will stop at nothing to get what he wants."

"Isn't that a bit melodramatic? You're making him out to be the devil incarnate."

"He might be, for all I know." She stopped short of mentioning the ring he wore or the pentacles that embellished his shop front, sensing that Owen would never accept her conclusions.

There was a pause as Owen wondered what to say to keep her from worrying. "Listen, my love, I'm a big boy now. You're kind and sweet to go to all this trouble just because you're worried about me. Since I saw you the other night I've calmed down a lot. I'm not going to do anything foolish."

"I'm very glad to hear that," she replied, sensing that he was telling her what he thought she wanted to hear. He was brave, tenacious and stubborn, and he would never give up so easily on something that meant so much to him. "All right, I'll say no more about it, then. But, please, do keep me informed if there are any developments, I beg you. It's so important to me that you do, dearest. Do you promise?"

"I promise," he said with a sigh, intending to do nothing of the sort. He was suddenly tired of the subject.

"On a happier note, then, you might be interested to know that I had a phone call from Louise Carey this morning. She's on her way to Languedoc. She has decided to stay the whole summer in a house in Puivaillon she's going to rent from

Maurice Roussel. I put them in touch when she told me she might like to spend some time there . . .''

"Louise Carey is going to be in Puivaillon? And you say she's planning to stay all summer? I'll be damned,'' he muttered, astonished. He wondered what had caused her to return to Puivaillon only two months after they had met; then he remembered her father had expressed the wish to have his ashes scattered somewhere there, and concluded that it had something to do with her unexpected change of plans. The news filled him with tension and uncertainty.

"You sound surprised," Dorothy said.

"I just can't imagine what she would want to do down there all summer by herself. And what about her business?''

"She probably wants to do nothing at all for a while. She mentioned that she's decided to close down the shop, but she didn't say what she was going to do after that. I think it's a wonderful idea. Maurice's cottage is enchanting. It's very simple, but perfectly charming.''

The memory he carried of Louise, sophisticated, glamorously dressed, was superimposed by a sun-drenched image of her in a cotton dress and a sun hat, a market basket over her arm. He felt envious of her courageous impulse to trade in her luxurious house in California for a solitary summer in an isolated French village. For a moment he was stifled by a longing to be there with her.

Dorothy was saying: "Ambrose and I will be starting off for our holiday at the beginning of July and I was hoping that you might finally be persuaded to join us there. You've been working so hard, don't you think you'd like a break? We're on our own this year, so we have lots of room.''

"I don't know,'' he said hesitantly. "It would mean leaving the business at the peak season. Normally I never leave until well into August.'' As he spoke, the thought of Puivaillon in high summer filled his mind. He could smell the sweet air, hear the cicadas singing in the grass, see the deep blue sky. He thought of Louise, sitting in a deck chair reading a book, her skin and hair fragrant from the sun. A gnawing hunger for her, and Puivaillon with her, twisted inside him.

"Owen, take this chance. Seize it with both hands, now,'' Dorothy pleaded.

At home, seated in her study, she stared out into the garden still bright with bluebells and tulips. She waited for his reply, aching to say that he was at a great crossroads in his life, but she knew she had to keep silent or risk spoiling everything.

"I guess I could get Peter to look after things," said Owen, weakening.

She let out a little gasp. "Then you will come? Oh, Owen, you can't imagine how happy that makes me! And Ambrose will be thrilled. Let me know the date as soon as you can."

"I said I hope I can, but that doesn't mean I will," he replied, not wanting even Dorothy to know the overpowering and confusing emotions coursing through him.

"Thank you, Owen. I can't tell you what it means to me."

When he had hung up, Owen sat for a moment thinking things over. When he recalled what Dorothy had said about Rex, he picked up the telephone again and dialed his number. The well-spoken voice of a butler came over the line: "Mr. Monckton's residence."

"May I speak to Mr. Monckton, please."

"Who should I say is calling, sir?"

The butler's voice was suspicious. Owen had obtained Rex's unlisted number from a mutual friend, but so far he had not been able to penetrate his palace guard. It crossed his mind to call himself by another name, but he couldn't think of a plausible substitute fast enough that would lure Rex to the phone if he were there.

"Tell him it's Owen Morgan."

"I'm sorry, sir, but Mr. Monckton is not at home." He spoke in a cold voice used for unwanted callers.

"When you see Mr. Monckton, tell him that whether he likes it or not, I intend to see him. He can't hide forever." With that, he slammed down the phone.

Dorothy's cautionary advice chafed like a pebble in his shoe, sending him in the opposite direction to that which she had intended. Her remarks about Rex being dangerous came back to him and his anger redoubled that she had been worried unnecessarily. The only thing to do, he decided, was to bring an end to the cat-and-mouse game. Fired with determination, he leapt up from the couch and went to his bedroom to dress.

* * *

In the library of his house in Chapel Street, off Belgrave Square, Rex stirred the pitcher of vodka gimlets the butler had just set on a table in front of the gold leather chesterfield.

"Mr. Owen Morgan called again, sir," the butler murmured.

"Thank you, Simons." Rex watched as Simons closed the library doors behind him. "Where was I?" he mused to the man sitting opposite. "Oh yes—'. . . . the magical universe is like an ocean. The great tides move through it invisibly and men are swept about by them, but are sometimes strong enough and clever enough to master and use them. And in the cold, black currents that come up from the deeps there are strange and sinister creatures lurking—evil intelligences, which tempt and corrupt and destroy, malignant elementals . . .' "

He paused for effect while he poured the gimlets into spiral-stemmed glasses. "Absurdly melodramatic, isn't it? Such a lot of rubbish is written about magic." He handed a glass to his guest, Philippe de Cazenac.

"*Merci, mon cher.* Perfection," he said, touching the liquid to his lips. He narrowed his eyes thoughtfully. "Perhaps what you say is true, but the words you quoted were somehow moving, rather lovely."

"They are only words, dreams, empty promises. Only fools believe in them. Wise men look behind the words."

Rex played thoughtfully with the enormous uncut topaz on a heavy gold chain resting below his pink paisley cravat. He was dressed in a padded yellow smoking jacket with pink piping, yellow trousers with a thin stripe and yellow kid shoes. Interpreting the covetousness in Philippe's dark eyes as he looked at the topaz, he said:

"This was a present from the Maharajah when I was in India last year. I couldn't hurt his feelings, so I had to accept it."

"You're entirely heartless," said Philippe with a laugh. The Frenchman, in his early thirties, had lazy dark eyes fringed with long lashes and a sensuous, full mouth. He was dressed like an Englishman, in a blazer and gray trousers.

"Yes, when we first met two years ago, you and I knew we were of the same race, the same tribe. Can it really be that long ago?" queried Rex, feeling a moment's sentiment as he regarded the aristocratic Philippe, who possessed one of the most illustrious pedigrees in France.

"Yes, it must be. It was just after I bought the lease on the shop on the Quai Voltaire, and that was '86. Do you know, I always have a niggling curiosity at the back of my mind, if you and I hadn't met at the Salon des Antiquités, whether I would be where I am today." Philippe looked at him, his dark eyes brimming with gratitude.

"What do you think?" Rex was studying the great unblinking eye by Redon hanging above the fireplace. He leaned to stroke the silky ears of Orpheus, his Weimaraner, curled up on a tapestry cushion by his chair.

"No, I'm sure I wouldn't have prospered. If you hadn't introduced me to the Power, I might still be sunk in lethargy at La Bruyère. You gave me my life back; you gave me direction."

Rex threw him a disparaging smile. "Which reminds me, we must discuss our plans for this summer and decide exactly when we want to be in Puivaillon. But no," he said, leaning forward to refill Philippe's glass, "it wasn't me, it was the Power. The Power lies within you. I showed you the way, that's all."

He cast Philippe the indulgent smile of the master to the adept pupil, his modesty unconvincing.

Rex rose and walked to the long window, his eyes casting up and down the street as though he were expecting someone.

"You were saying a moment ago how grateful you are to me." Looking at Philippe, he added: "If so, I wonder if you might like to do me an important favor?"

"I'd be delighted, *mon cher,* but what could you possibly want from me? You have everything already."

"Not quite." He rested his blue eyes on Philippe.

"You mean the chalice?"

"No, I'll soon have it, though Baron Hauptmann's heirs are slow to act, but they'll undoubtedly see the wisdom of avoiding the trouble of another auction. Time and patience are all I need. It should be mine by the end of the summer. No, that's not what I mean."

The dog lifted its head at the sound of raised voices in the hall below.

"Whatever is that commotion?" said Rex, shifting to the

edge of his chair. He and Philippe looked at one another in surprise as the muffled echo of footsteps rose up the stairs, followed by an angry shout from the butler. Rex's eyes widened in surprise when the door burst open and he saw Owen Morgan standing there. He rose to his feet, a welcoming smile wiping the fury from his face.

"Owen, what a charming surprise . . ."

The butler interposed: "I'm most terribly sorry, sir. He just pushed right past me and barged his way in. I tried to stop him." Simons tried to push Owen aside, but he stood his ground.

"That's all right, Simons. Mr. Morgan is an old friend of mine." To Owen he said: "I told Simons I didn't want to be disturbed because I have a guest visiting from Paris, but, of course, you're an exception. Do sit down and have a drink. May I present Philippe de Cazenac. Philippe, this is my old friend, Owen Morgan."

Owen stared warily from Rex to Philippe without offering his hand. Rex's welcoming manner threw him off guard, but a dangerous flicker in his eyes told Owen he was outraged at this intrusion.

One sweeping glance at the sumptuous library suggested the staggering heights of fortune he had attained. For an instant Owen wondered if his hatred of Rex was fueled by a motive as base as jealousy.

"There's something I want to discuss with you, Rex—now and alone."

Exchanging a glance with Rex, Philippe said: "If you will excuse me, I have things to attend to," and he left the room.

When he saw the butler hovering at the door, Rex said mildly: "The Baron and I will have dinner in about ten minutes, Simons."

Once the doors had been closed, he faced Owen with a sardonic smile. "I would invite you to join us, but this is a bit short notice, you understand."

"Oh, I understand all right, Rex. I understand a lot of things that I didn't even suspect years ago." Owen felt his anger boiling over now they were alone. He was filled with loathing for Rex's labored courtesy, his hypocrisy, the over-ripe flamboyance of his clothes, his supercilious smile. But the deadly blue calm in Rex's eyes almost defeated him.

"What can I do for you? Martini?" Rex asked. "Oh no, that's right. You like whisky, straight, with a bit of ice, don't you?" he said, taking the stopper off a crystal decanter.

"Don't bother with the drink. I don't want your hospitality."

"What a delightful thing to say. Well, in that case, why don't you come straight to the point? I find your coarse behavior a bit tiresome."

"You must be aware that I've been trying to get in touch with you for the past two weeks. You've been avoiding me."

Rex snorted with indignation. "Avoiding you? The unpleasant truth is that I'm barely aware of your existence."

Owen laughed harshly. "That might be so, but from now on you'll find I won't be blending into the woodwork. Not only do I exist, but I am going to make life hell for you."

Rex shot him a warning glance. "Are you threatening me, Owen?"

"Call it what you like, a threat, even a promise I made to myself. I know you stole that chalice from me. You lied, Rex, when you told me it was a German gilt drinking cup. You knew what it really was and you were aware of its value. And with the money you got when you sold it, you set yourself up in fine style in business. You were my friend and you lied to me, you cheated me for your own gain. You bought me off with a thousand pounds and like a fool I took it."

"That's right. You did take it," he said, unperturbed. "And I have the bank statements to prove it. Therefore if you try to make trouble, it's my word against yours that you sold it to me. These things happen all the time in the art world," he mused. "I remember Prince Yussoupoff once sold a Rembrandt to Harry Widener and later changed his mind. Of course the court ruled against him, even though he had sold it for a pittance. You haven't changed, Owen. You're still a romantic, charging at windmills."

"There's Mandy. She would testify against you."

"Testify? What a joke. And as for your ex-wife, she's a bit of a joke too. No court would accept her as a witness."

"So you admit it."

"I admit nothing. Nothing at all. Our business transaction was concluded to the satisfaction of both parties. And that was the end of the matter." He looked at his watch with a bored expression.

"Oh no, that wasn't the end. It was a long intermission. I saw the chalice in Geneva," Owen said. He saw Rex frown. "You didn't expect me to have such a stroke of good fortune. But for once luck was in my corner, not yours. I made inquiries and I know the whole history of that chalice once it left my possession. You sold it for a hundred thousand pounds to the late Baron Felix Hauptmann."

"And, even if all this were true, there would be nothing you could do." Rex shrugged.

"I'm going to ruin you, that's what." Pointing his finger, Owen said in a controlled voice: "You're a fraud and an impostor, a common crook cloaked in respectability, Monckton, and I'm going to expose you for what you are."

Rex shook his head. "How sad, Owen, that things have come to this. You had such promise. You could have been a great musician, but you wasted yourself, threw your talent away. Just look at you now, an embittered, jealous man who labors away at such a tawdry business—plastics." He twisted his lips in distaste. "And Mandy, such a pretty girl. It's such a shame you allowed your pride to ruin your marriage. But then, it always was your greatest enemy. When I think of the two of you, she so young and lovely, in love with you and her heart full of such dreams. And now she's a broken, sad and lonely . . ."

"Shut up!" Owen cried. His temper exploded. "Leave Mandy out of it, you phony. She's worth ten of you, any day. I swear I'll see you behind bars, Monckton."

"Let me give you some advice. When in the future you decide to pursue a course of revenge, make sure who and what you're up against. I haven't an ounce of pity for you, but for the sake of old friendship I should warn you that you'll end up by ruining yourself. You'll lose your credibility, your business and even what is of greater value to you if you try to take me on. Now, get out of my house."

Owen felt his blood run cold at the malevolence sparking from Rex. As they faced each other across a great divide, he was pierced by Rex's childish blue eyes shadowed by dangerous emotions that were darker than contempt or even hatred. There was a reptilian coldness he had never noticed before, which he compared to the opaque blue depths of a fathomless lake. Rex seemed to be chipping away at his courage by sheer force of will, and Owen's mind was tainted with a startling premonition that if he stayed a moment longer, Rex would hurtle him through the window and impale him on the railings outside. The imaginary sound of shattering glass rang in his head, jolting him to his senses. He edged toward the door to escape, feeling a strange, nameless terror. His hand on the doorknob, he muttered, "It's not over yet, by any means." Then he bolted from the room.

Standing at the top of the stairs, he saw the butler hovering on the black and white tiles below, lit by the skylight overhead. He seemed strangely wooden, like a pawn on a chessboard. Owen raced down the stairs and out of the front door, shooting him a contemptuous glance, but inwardly he was shaking with fear.

When the butler announced that dinner was served, Rex gestured for Philippe to precede him through the double doors of the dining room, glancing obliquely at him as he regarded the sumptuous room for the first time.

"Magnifique. C'est une merveille," breathed Philippe. He admired the oval-shaped room, painted from floor to ceiling with a mural of barges and gondolas on the canals of sunlit Venice, its vistas receding into the distance.

"I see it pleases you. Rather amusing, isn't it?"

"Formidable," Philippe kept repeating, his eyes fluttering as he looked up at the tented ceiling of pale blue pleated silk circling a Russian chandelier suspended from a purple velvet rope that showered light on the sumptuously laid table.

The butler pulled out a chair for Philippe. After he had poured the wine from a bottle cooled in a silver bucket, he brought the first course.

They dipped their forks into *feuilleté d'asperges* topped with a dollop of caviar. When Simons had closed the doors behind him, Philippe said hesitantly, "What I've been longing to ask you for a long time is how you first came to know you had the Power. In fact, to be honest, I never dared ask you. But tonight I have the courage."

Rex sipped his wine. "That is something no one knows

about me, Philippe. But I think the time has come for me to tell you. Yes, I want you to know. It's important for you to know. . . . When I was on the cusp of puberty I discovered that my mother, who died when I was very young, was descended from Emily Cavendish, who was tried and burnt for witchcraft in Salem, Massachusetts, in 1655.''

Philippe set down his fork and looked at Rex in amazement. *''Mon Dieu,* it's like being descended from Charlemagne or one of the apostles. I had no idea.''

Rex smiled. ''I went straight to the library and immersed myself in magic lore, having no idea of its true significance at the time; nor did I know how deeply it would govern my life. But I was amused by it the way some boys become absorbed in model airplanes. I was anxious to test my mettle against the forces of darkness, but I didn't know what I would do when I summoned a demon, I suppose. I did it all exactly as the canticles instruct and drew my pentacle in charcoal on the floor.'' Rex leaned back and let out a chortle at the remembered image of himself. ''In my total ignorance I decided to go straight to the top, and summoned Beelzebub. Imagine. . . .''

Rex paused. Until now he had only been telling an amusing anecdote, but all the merriment suddenly vanished from his face as he looked at Philippe.

''And did He come to you?'' he whispered.

''Indeed He did.''

''Well, what happened? I'm dying to know.''

''He came filling the room beyond the circle. I had one brief moment of shattering clarity when the Power flooded into the room. I felt rent by the magnetism of His presence as I was sucked violently into His dark universe, something I can only compare to an implosion. It happened very quickly; then I fell unconscious. When I opened my eyes it was early morning. I was lying in the center of the pentacle, my body forming the star. Feeling my trousers were wet, I realized that I had ejaculated fully for the first time. You can imagine how the manifestation of His power shocked and thrilled me— I had been singled out, honored. My wet trousers proved to me that I hadn't dreamed the incident or hallucinated.''

Rex stopped and began to eat again, while Philippe sat in stunned silence.

"Is that all? What was the aftermath, then?" he asked hoarsely.

Rex sighed and smiled. "In my innocence I supposed that I had harnessed the Power of the universe—imagine, without any preparation at all. Needless to say, the next time I tried to summon Him, nothing happened, and again and again, the same result. He hurt my pride and it made me angry. It wasn't until years later, when I was a man, that I realized my mistake. It began to dawn on me after I left Oxford how arrogant I was. I was expecting to summon the Power by merely snapping my fingers. I knew then that I would have to prove myself through years of preparation and devotion to Him. And that, as you know, I have set about doing."

In an awed voice, Philippe said, "The moment I met you, I knew you were my master."

"My dear fellow," Rex protested with a wave of his hand.

Philippe reached for it and fervently kissed Rex's ring with the cornelian stamped with the pentacle. Seeing the polite contempt on Rex's face, he said apologetically, "I don't know how to express my gratitude, my admiration."

"Don't worry, we'll find a way," said Rex, gently removing his hand. "In fact, we might discuss it in the library after dinner, over a glass of Armagnac."

After the butler had served the soufflé, Philippe ventured: "Forgive me, but I do hope that everything ended happily with you and that angry man who barged in on us earlier." He had regained his self-possession and there was mischievous curiosity in his eyes.

"There was a time, when we were at Oxford, when Owen and I were really quite fond of each other. It's probably just as well that you met him. Owen fits into the scheme of things, but just how is still not clear."

Rex mentioned the chalice. "I let it go for a fraction of its true worth, not realizing its true value. Imagine, I possessed the Holy Grail—it was mine, I held it in my hand. It belonged by rights to Him, to the Power, to do with what He will. And, like a fool, I let it slip through my fingers."

"Excuse me for asking, I don't mean to question you, but how do you know it's the Holy Grail?" He looked incredulously at Rex. "This is the first time you have referred to it as such."

"I have two proofs. One is historical, which I'll explain in a minute, and the other is personal. Not long after I sold the chalice, I had a kind of vision. I saw the chalice by torch-light in a darkened chamber, held in the hands of a man I took to be a priest. He handled it with reverence and called it by its true name. And then he gave it to the safekeeping of another, which enraged me. That's all I can remember; and then I woke up, knowing I had been in that cave, in another life, if you will. Though my antecedents go back much further than that, to the beginning of time and the division. But where and when the incidents I saw in this vision took place, I have no idea. You're looking skeptical, Philippe," he said sharply. "You don't doubt me, I hope."

Philippe looked horrified. "No, I'm just amazed, that's all. If anyone else had told me this, yes, I would doubt it. But I believe what you say."

"To finish the story, this vision triggered my curiosity and I began to make a deep historical analysis of the whole ques-tion. As every schoolboy knows, when the Visigoths sacked Rome, they carried off the treasure that the Emperor Titus brought back from the Temple of Solomon in Jerusalem. Then the Visigoth kings took this treasure back to what was later Languedoc, where it disappeared, or where it was hidden or dispersed. I believe absolutely that by this or other means the Cathars possessed the Grail, which they must have hidden before the fall of Montségur in 1244. How they came by it, I'll probably never know exactly, but the Power will ensure it is authenticated."

"The Cathars . . ." murmured Philippe in astonishment. "Now I begin to understand. You know, my ancestors were given the lands of Cathar lords in Languedoc by the Church, as a reward for their services," he mused. "In fact, La Bru-yère is not far from the ruins of a castle that belonged to one of those heretics and still belongs to us."

"Yes, it went through me like a bolt of lightning when you told me that first. It's not a coincidence, Philippe, believe me. Nothing is a coincidence. That is only an ignorant man's way of explaining the incomprehensible."

"Tradition says that this treasure, whatever it was, was taken to Ussat."

"Tradition? I have something much more substantial than

tradition." He related how Owen, accompanied by his wife, had stumbled upon the chalice some seventeen years before.

"Ah, so that's where he comes in." Philippe's voice dropped to a whisper. "And you think that by tracing this antique dealer, by locating the source from which he obtained the treasure, you can positively authenticate the Grail?"

"As for the *brocanteur,* I'm not sure. He may be unnecessary now. All I know is that the Power will make it possible for all this to happen. Authenticating the Grail won't be the problem, even if we don't locate this man. I am confident we can uncover the source of the treasure." He waved his hand nonchalantly. "No, that's the least of our problems."

"But the country there is honeycombed with caves. It would be impossible to . . ."

"Impossible? You seem to have forgotten that we are directed by the Power. We are not ordinary treasure-seekers like all the rest. And our motives are pure. That's why we cannot fail. And you were sent to help me. I know that now. The first time we met and you told me your family lands date from King Louis IX and that they were confiscated from Cathar nobles, I realized that the Power had revealed the next piece of the puzzle. You see, my dear Philippe, such nuggets don't come just for the asking. They come through merit. As a mage, I rise from one level to the next, consolidating my power and waiting for the supreme moment."

"And when will that be?"

"Soon enough. One must never be in a hurry. There's a long summer ahead, full of balmy blue days in that wild and wonderful country. It's truly the most fascinating place I have ever been to in any life . . ."

"But I didn't know you had ever been to that part of the world. You didn't tell me," said Philippe, hurt.

"Didn't I? Well, I have. I've been there several times. Not to accomplish anything in particular, just to acquaint myself with the lie of the land, the flow of the streams, its rocks and its trees. I wanted to refresh my memory."

"But you are coming this summer, to spend some time with me at La Bruyère, aren't you?"

"Of course. I thought we had settled all that. And now," Rex said, rising and pressing his foot on the bell, "let us go upstairs. It's time for the next piece of the puzzle to fall into place. Simons,'' he said when the butler opened the door, ''we will take our coffee in the library.''

16

It was raining when Sancha awoke in the courtyard. Curled up in a ball with her head pressed against the stone, she lay still for a moment, listening to the coughs and murmurs that had filled her waking hours throughout the changing seasons. Getting to her feet, she gathered her cloak round her and picked her way through the people littering the courtyard. Her empty stomach contracted with nausea at the stench of the dying and the unwashed packed intolerably close together, a pervasive odor the smoking fires could not disguise. From habit, Sancha hunched forward and stayed close to the wall, unconsciously expecting a barrage of flying stones sent by the enemy catapult erected near the fortress in October.

Through murmured prayers the muffled cry of a baby reached her from the wooden shelters built over the courtyard, where the men at arms lived with their concubines, wives and children. Of all the sounds of human misery, this was the one that moved her most. It was the hungry rasp of an infant who had never had enough to eat in its short life.

Seeing a blind old man fumbling for his staff, she picked it up and folded his gnarled fingers round it.

''It's Sancha,'' he said, his face lighting up. She leaned close so he could touch her features with his cold, leathery hands.

The sea of people had begun to stir around her, lifting ashen faces worn with sickness and hunger. Those who were strong enough to speak had begun to pray, huddling together for warmth beneath cloaks or ragged furs. Those who were exhausted by hunger or illness lay waiting for death. Sancha saw the motionless forms of Believers who had died during the night, whom the soldiers would remove later. She gave comfort as she passed the old and the dying, her cold, red hands offering sympathy, but no warmth. A gust of cold wind carrying smoke from the fire burning near the cistern masked the smell of death and decay for a moment and made Sancha's eyes water. She joined the group of women preparing breakfast, hoping to make herself useful. She nodded a greeting to Esclarmonde, who was stirring a cauldron of watery gruel. Sancha searched the ramparts, where she could see soldiers slumped in exhaustion over their spears and crossbows after keeping watch all night, but Hugo was not among them. One glimpse of him, even at a distance, made her feel strong again, even if only for a moment.

Near the fire a group of men at arms who were about to relieve the night watch were finishing their porridge, cupping their earthenware bowls in hands cracked and callused from feeding stones onto the catapults in the cold. They were brawny men with big faces, wearing leather jerkins, chain mail and metal casques. As the predicament of the besieged Believers had worsened in the last months, a number of these hardened mercenaries had taken the first steps to becoming Believers themselves.

Esclarmonde called to her, "Here, take some porridge." She dipped a ladle into the steaming cauldron, offering it to Sancha.

Sancha pressed her arms to her stomach, feeling revulsion and hunger clash inside her.

"No, thanks." Her mouth twisted in a weak smile as she looked at the wraith-like Esclarmonde. Her emaciated face, flushed by the fire, was framed by a soiled wimple, and her hands were blue and raw. Sancha knew Esclarmonde wouldn't touch a drop of gruel until she was sure everyone had eaten.

"But you must eat to be strong, my sweet girl. Who will tend the sick if not you, Sancha? We need you now more than ever."

Sancha took the bowl and sipped the sour porridge full of maggots without even tasting it. As the warm liquid poured into her stomach, she felt herself stir back to life, almost reluctantly.

"Hugo was here at drawn when the fire was lit. He came to speak to Alazaïs and asked for you. I said you were still sleeping somewhere."

Sancha was flooded with relief and closed her eyes, saying

a prayer of gratitude. For her the day couldn't begin until she knew he was still alive. Though he was strong and tenacious, she lived with the fear that he might again undertake a mission such as he had made in January, when he and two other men had spirited the treasure of the Church from the fortress to Ussat.

Esclarmonde said in an excited whisper: "There is going to be a siege on the Barbican before the sun rises tomorrow. All the strongest men are preparing to go. They hope to drive the Basques out and burn their siege engine."

"Tomorrow?" Sancha said numbly. She thought of the narrow, precipitous approach to the Barbican. It could never be taken without a great loss of life. Hugo's strength, his courage, belonged to all of them, not just to her.

"Have hope, Sancha, have hope," said Esclarmonde, filling another bowl with gruel, which Sancha handed to a stooped old woman behind her. "When you have done all you can here, you will be needed in the officers' quarters. Gaillard's wife went into labor in the early hours of the morning."

Shivering in the wind, Sancha wondered where she would find some clean straw for the woman. She withdrew her knife from her pocket and put it in the fire, an act of exorcism her mother had taught her to perform before cutting an umbilical cord. Since coming to Montségur she had delivered several children. She no longer wondered why she hadn't conceived a child of her own by Hugo. It was common knowledge that starving cattle produce no calves. There was almost no food left and no medicine. She counted herself lucky if she had a few withered leaves of feverfew or a piece of moldy garlic to give to the sick and dying. The only thing she found in abundance was lichen, which she scraped off the fortress walls to apply to wounds.

Just as Sancha had begun to climb the crude ladder to the officers' quarters, a barrage of stones came raining into the open end of the courtyard, causing pandemonium. She flattened herself against the wall for protection, hearing the screams of the wounded below. Looking down, she saw a stone the size of a melon crush the foot of an old woman, who fainted with pain. A dull anguish closed in on her. There was nothing she could do. Hoisting herself on to the balcony, she entered the dark doorway to the officers' quarters.

Later that afternoon Sancha wiped the sweat from her brow as she straddled over a woman in labor laid out on straw in the corner of a cramped chamber. She had made a bed as best she could away from the cold wind that seeped through the window slits. Two women, their hands and feet wrapped in rags, were dozing against one wall, while another was peering through the window at the enemy encampment far below. Yet another was repairing a doublet for her husband, humming as she worked. They were all indifferent to the groans of pain that accompanied childbirth.

"It won't be long now," Sancha whispered, stroking her forehead. Prizing the woman's legs apart, she pushed up her skirts to see the tiny head of the baby peeking through. "Push again as hard as you can when the next pain comes." Rolling up a rag, she stuffed it between the woman's teeth.

When there was a muffled scream, the woman hemming the doublet muttered between her teeth, "The curse of Eve."

"And the blessing of starvation not to produce more children," remarked the woman at the window.

"That doesn't seem to stop my husband. He's still as much of a man as he ever was. He says lust heats his blood to fight."

Glancing at the woman's haggard face, Sancha ignored her brave boast. Though she had sometimes heard the unmistakable rustlings and whispers of lovemaking coming from the officers' quarters, to her love seemed as remote as clean water, fresh food and flowers. But even now there were times when her enduring need for Hugo's body made her forget her rags, her filth and her hunger.

A while later the baby came into the world, a slippery little thing, more like a fish, Sancha thought, than a boy child. She cradled the blood-soaked creature in her hands, feeling satisfaction that at least he was alive and perfectly formed. As the mother fell back in exhaustion, Sancha tied the umbilical cord and cut it. While one woman swaddled the wet, squalling infant in a tattered shawl, Sancha cleaned up the afterbirth as best she could with some straw, then wiped her bloody hands on her skirt and gazed down benevolently at the woman, who was peering at her through half-closed eyes. There was neither joy nor relief on her face, only resignation.

"You have a fine son," said Sancha. Cradling him in her arms, his puckered little face evoked a pure, bitter envy. Putting the child at his mother's breast, she felt an acute longing to bring life into the world, life conceived by herself and Hugo. It was an arrogant illusion that had stubbornly survived every hardship. All the horrors she had witnessed had not killed her instinct to cradle a child in her arms, nor had all the bishop's moving sermons about the evils of the flesh subdued this painful yearning. In the moments when she was able to dream about life after the holocaust, when she managed to remember what joy was like, and peace, her pagan nature defied the Cathar view of life as wholly alien. In the ten months she had been imprisoned in the fortress, she had been unable to free herself entirely of the impulse toward earthly happiness, though it would take a miracle to achieve. Now, watching the baby's mouth latch eagerly onto his mother's nipple, her own womb contracted and she could almost feel Hugo's child against her breast. Then, as it quickly faded, the present reality closed in. She couldn't avoid the shadowy faces of the women looking stoically on as the new mother nursed her child. Those hard, thin-lipped faces, inured to suffering, saw nothing remarkable or joyous in this birth. The child who had just opened his eyes to the light was only another mouth to feed and his cries would keep them awake at night. Rising to her feet, Sancha put away her dreams.

That evening Sancha came down the ladder into the courtyard, where people were preparing to bed down for the night. Long shadows cast by the fire near the cistern climbed the stone walls and dissolved into the clouds clamping down on the mountain. She picked her way past people clinging together in groups to keep warm, burying their heads in their cloaks against the cold. Before finding a corner in which to sleep, Sancha searched the ramparts one more time, hoping to discover Hugo among the shadowy figures moving to and fro. She cried out in surprise when she caught sight of him talking to the commander. She fought through the maze of people and hurried up the steep steps that led to where he was, never taking her eyes off his shadow. She felt an indescribable joy at the mere discovery he was still alive, followed by panic that he might disappear before she had the chance to see him again. She waited while he finished talking to the commander of the garrison, Roger de Mirepoix, whose father-in-law, Raymond de Perella, was lord of Montségur. The harrowed commander looked unseeingly at Sancha in the dim light cast upward by the fire below.

When they were alone, the look in Hugo's eyes told her how glad he was to see her. He conveyed a private acknowledgement that only she could interpret, shining in the blackness of all her days. He led her to a safe corner of the ramparts, where they embraced. As he held her, she felt him tremble with fatigue.

"How I've missed you, my dove," he whispered in her ear.

Taking his hand, she pressed it to her lips, not wanting to read the pain reflected in his eyes that told her she had all but lost her beauty. She knew her face was pale as winter, her cheeks hollow. Her body had wasted, withering her breasts and hips like fruit unpicked after a frost. Her neck, once so slender, was now like a wilting stem, and her ribs protruded through the skin like furrows of drought-ridden earth. Through the summer months, before the hovels on the outer wall of the fortress had had to be abandoned, Hugo had made hurried, passionate and silent love to her in a dark corner of a hut or even among the trees when they dared. Now that love had become a dim memory.

She traced his hand in the darkness, cold and hard as leather. Hugo's body was gaunt and sinewy. The deep lines that a year ago had appeared only when he smiled were now carved permanently round his mouth. Now she had a glimpse of the old man he was fast becoming. His forearms were scarred with the purple weals of old, deep wounds and his hair was neatly gray. The last months of privation and combat, more daunting than anything he had known even in the Holy Land, had stripped his soul bare, fueling his blue eyes with a fanatic determination that resembled the purity of sainthood.

He led her along the walk of crenellated stone, past soldiers keeping watch. Only rarely had she been there at night. In the pit of the fortress's courtyard she all but forgot the enemy encampment that surrounded the mountain hundreds of feet below, but here on the battlements, as the wind stung her face, she glimpsed the blazing reflection of hundreds of camp fires ringing the entire valley, a sight that had a terrifying beauty. Sancha felt crushed into insignificance at the might of the enemy. The irrefutable proof of their power seized her, forcing her to admit the hopelessness of their situation. Her throat closed with tears she would never let fall in front of Hugo.

"How long should we stand at the gates of Hell? You would think we would have been consumed or saved long ago. You would think the Crusaders would tire and go back to their homes, to Normandy and Gascony and Spain," she murmured.

"Yes, we hear they are tired, dispirited, even rebellious. But every night it seems to me the camp fires are more numerous. They reproduce like maggots on a corpse," he answered darkly.

She was silent for a moment, thinking of the day in spring, nearly a year ago, when they had arrived so full of hope.

"Tell me the truth, Hugo. Do you really think the Count of Toulouse will ever rescue us?"

He sighed. "It would be a miracle if it were to happen. Our commander pretends to have faith to rally the Believers, but we talk amongst ourselves. Last week I might have said yes, but not today. The Count has asked us to hold fast until Easter, but I doubt his word. France has finally broken him."

"Is it true you'll try to attack the Barbican tonight?" she murmured, voicing the fear that had been plaguing her all day.

"Who told you that?"

"Esclarmonde."

"She heard it from my mother, but repeat it to no one. I am among the men who will lead the charge. Our only hope is to take the nest of Basques by surprise, destroy the siege gun and force them to retreat to the position they occupied in December."

"Do you believe, Hugo, that after all this time they will eventually retreat and leave us alone? I want to know the truth."

He bowed his head. "No—I can say it to you. I don't know

what the outcome will be; perhaps a truce, I don't know. We can survive for a long time yet on the supplies that trickle across the lines, and we have water. We've even proved we have endurance in abundance. But what few people seem to understand, even our lord and commander, is that the Pope will not rest until he destroys Montségur. It has become the symbol of his power to crush all opposition, both temporal and spiritual. And yet," said Hugo ironically, "if he martyrs these true Christians, then he is defying Christ's own words, to love one another and to turn the other cheek. Did he ever seek vengeance? The sword is a sorry weapon for Christ."

They mourned in silence, regarding the ocean of fire that threatened their little island in the sky.

"If anything should happen to me tomorrow, Sancha," he began, "know that I love you with all my heart."

She nodded, summoning the courage to match his own. Knowing their last moments might be ticking away before the siege, she accepted that her tears could serve no purpose. But in her mind she turned over the image of the narrow, jagged ridge that led to the Barbican, plunging hundreds of feet on either side. Certain death awaited any soldier who lost his foothold while battling to conquer it.

"I've been thinking . . . when it's over," Hugo was saying, "we will leave the Languedoc. We'll start our lives afresh where oranges and lemons grow on the trees, where wild figs grow. There will be honey and wine, and we will never be cold or hungry again. We will go first to Sicily, then to Lombardy. I will show you temples gleaming in the sun, their feet planted in blue water. We'll love each other all of our days and nights under the stars and never want for anything. We will pray, and we will love, without fear. These things I promise you."

She left him standing alone on the ramparts, shaking from head to foot. Her head bowed, she didn't look back, but bit her cloak to stem the tears. In her hurry she collided with a man who was concealed by the shadows. Stepping back, she saw him leering at her.

"When the wind blows cold, we neither see nor hear," came a whisper.

She stared at the man, known as Gaucelm, one of the architects of the catapult mounted on the ramparts, who had been spirited into the fortress in October. He had a small, clever face and mischievous grin. His high, domed forehead fringed with a shock of fair, curly hair made him seem younger than his thirty years and appear almost childlike. He was rumored to be the bastard son of a rich abbot from Toulouse. Intelligent and highly capable, he had become indispensable in the battle against the enemy. But Sancha's sixth sense told her he wasn't to be trusted. He seemed to lurk everywhere at all times, and his small, unreadable eyes took in everything hungrily, missing nothing. Sancha had disliked him from the moment she had seen him wolfing down food that she knew was either stolen or hoarded. When he saw her watching him, he had stuffed what he was eating under his shirt and wiped his mouth, a challenging expression on his face.

"Let me by," said Sancha, not bothering to be polite.

"Is it true, the rumor that they will storm the Barbican tonight?"

"Why don't you ask that question yourself? I know nothing about it." She feared she had as much as admitted the truth by her coldness.

"It's not only God who has our fate in his hands, but the commander of the fortress. We are the flame in the lamp, whom his hands cup protectively, are we not?"

"Why speak in parables? Are you afraid to die?" she retorted. Hatred boiled inside her. She narrowed her eyes, not trying to conceal her contempt. Anyone who had lasted the winter at Montségur had been kept alive by his belief in the cause, but she didn't know what motivated the strange Gaucelm, and it made her uneasy.

"What brought you to this place?" Her tone was bold, but she found herself shivering.

"What do you mean? The same thing that brought us all here: devotion to God and belief in a just cause. And now I've become a Believer myself, like so many others."

"You're not a Believer," she blurted out. Pushing past him, she descended the stairs to the boiling pit of humanity below, acutely conscious of his eyes boring into her.

That night Sancha didn't sleep. She found a place in view of the ramparts, facing the Barbican. In the still night she could sense a restlessness in the courtyard, a shared sense of danger that hung over the slumbering figures like a vapor.

Just before dawn she became aware of the dark figures of men moving on the ramparts. Her every muscle tense, she strained to see in the darkness. The moment the garrison commander appeared, an aide-de-camp scuttled down the stairs. Shaking the nearest Perfecti awake, she saw them moving through the other sleeping forms, touching their cloaks to waken them. An undercurrent of prayers and whispers echoed against the stone, filling the air with apprehension. There was a rippling movement to action, like wind bending a field of wheat, as people stirred, signaling that the siege was about to begin. Some clung to each other, others cringed against the walls for protection, their faces imprinted with awareness that life hung in the balance. Sancha broke out in a cold sweat and her own heartbeat filled her ears. Her whole body stiffened in suspense as she waited to hear a cry of victory and to see the red sky signaling that the enemy siege engine was on fire. The thin, hungry faces with staring eyes glinting in the darkness brought it home to her that they couldn't go on living on this icy pinnacle. The end seemed to have come, silently and unannounced. This moment, this hour, was the turning point that determined whether they lived or died. S ing the ailing Bishop Marty limping up to give the last rites to someone, Sancha felt the painless sword of the inevitable pass through her body. Unable to endure another moment crouched like an animal, she stood, flattening her head and shoulders against the jagged stone until she felt part of it.

Suddenly a great echo arose in the night, sending dread tingling down her spine. The groans of men locked in mortal combat beyond the walls of the fortress filled the night. Sancha gasped at a scream that trailed off in the distance, then others, which told her that combatants had plunged hundreds of feet down the sheer rocky slope to their deaths. The clash of steel, the thunder of battle rent the air. She was incapable of covering her ears. Closing her eyes, she strained to share Hugo's ordeal in her heart and mind.

A cry was raised from the ramparts that the siege had failed. She wailed in protest, her own voice drowned by the cries of others echoing around her. In the darkness people began pouring up the stairs and to the eastern ramparts to help the soldiers man the crossbows and catapults. Sancha fought her way through the crowd, trying to reach the stairs. Passing the heavily bolted western gate, she saw a darting movement out of the corner of her eye. It was Gaucelm, who was struggling to open the great iron latch that held the crossbar in place.

"What are you doing?" she cried, outraged. Lunging toward him, she dug her hands into his back, overpowering him for a moment. In seconds he had recovered, landing a blow across her face that sent her stumbling backward. By the light of a torch gleaming above, she saw him snarl at her with venomous hatred, his teeth bared.

"I heard someone pounding to get in. Would you have our men die out there?"

"What, and kill us all to let them enter? They would never do that. You're lying." Her mouth was full of the bitter taste of blood. "I know you for what you are. You would betray all of us. You're a spy."

"You stupid woman. I hate the King of France as much as any of you. More, indeed."

They stared at one another. She knew that if she had the power she would have killed him without conscience, in one blow, like the poisonous snake that he was. Looking at his smooth, innocent face, Sancha suddenly understood that Gaucelm had been spawned by evil. He possessed a will to power more fatal than a sword, as if he were avenging some eternal war waged against him. Only she, of all the people locked inside the fortress, was aware of the demonic force threatening them.

"What is it? What do you want of us?" she said, suddenly frightened, as if Gaucelm and what he represented determined their fate. The clashing of swords, the cries of dying men seemed to fade away in the distance as they faced one another in a magnetic circle.

"You are truly evil. But you will not win. You will die," she said. Her pronouncement seemed to spring from a primitive recognition older than the world itself.

"I have no time to deal with you now, but I will not forget your words. Remember that and pray—I will not forget."

Coming to her senses, Sancha scrambled up the stone stairs

to the ramparts, where she narrowly avoided being pushed off the edge. She collided with body after body as she struggled forward until she overlooked the forecourt below the keep. Arriving bruised and gasping at the top, she could see Crusaders pouring into the forecourt on the other side, crimson crosses emblazoned on their chests, helmets glinting as they charged with torch in one hand, sword in the other. Their bloodthirsty cries filled the air as they met soldiers pouring down from the ramparts. Moments later Sancha had plunged into the chaos. She dragged away the dead and wounded while missiles crashed around her, wounding many Believers, who fell where they had stood. She saw the Bishop and his deacons hurrying from one dying person to the next, administering the sacraments. When she paused for a moment to get her breath, she saw the patriarch of the Church giving the last sacrament to the wife of the lord of Montségur, followed by the other noblewomen who had been living in the keep. They knelt before him as the battle raged, as composed as if they were ready to die. Stooping to soothe the brow of a dying man whose skull had been crushed, Sancha realized all was lost. As the pitiful whine of death heralded the dull light of morning, she began to pray.

As dawn broke, Sancha was trying to stanch the flow of blood from the severed limb of a soldier in the courtyard littered with dead and wounded. Bruised, and parched with thirst, she didn't know whether Hugo was alive or dead, only that the mission to storm the Barbican had failed, though they had finally repelled the Crusaders. The shattered survivors were murmuring that the end had come, shambling past one another with gray faces, blank with shock and exhaustion.

Sancha wiped her bloodstained hands on her dress and rose heavily to her feet. She raised her eyes to the gray sky just as the horn of surrender sounded across the valley like the howl of a disemboweled beast. It was the saddest sound she had ever heard.

17

In a cold chamber in the keep of Montségur, Alazaïs saw dusk touching the hills through a narrow slit in the stone. Turning to Sancha, she said:

"It's strange how a peace has descended on everything these last days of the truce. The wind has died, the cold has relented, as if respecting our inner silence." When Sancha didn't raise her bowed head, she continued: "I'm grateful now that the Believers could celebrate Easter and their last rites undisturbed."

Sancha raised her tearstained face. She was too choked with emotion for speech. The past two weeks of respite, during which they had had ample water and food and could move freely, without surveillance, on the hilltop, all of this was nothing more than a chilling prelude to the coming martyrdom. She rose from the bench where she had been sitting in silence after pleading with Alazaïs until she was dry and empty inside. She slipped her arm comfortingly round the older woman's waist, and together the two of them looked down at the base of the mountain where the Crusaders were laboring to finish the palisade. At dawn, 230 Believers who would not recant their faith would be burned alive there. Hearing the distant echo of wood being cut, Sancha could scarcely grasp what was about to happen.

"So this is where it will end for us," Alazaïs whispered. As they embraced, Sancha was racked by a dry sob.

"Peace, my child, be at peace. The world isn't ending for you—or for Hugo." She stroked Sancha's hair affectionately.

Sancha hung her head, feeling nauseous and ashamed of her own weakness. Grasping Alazaïs's cold, dry hands, she cried: "It's not too late to recant. I beg you, recant while you can, oh, please." As she hugged Alazaïs, their frail bodies crushed against each other.

"You promised you wouldn't ask again. There now." She

kissed Sancha's lusterless hair and searched her eyes ringed with shadows.

"I know, I know," Sancha murmured, trembling all over. "I'm selfish and stubborn, but my mind refuses to understand. My heart and my mind are not part of me like my hands or my mouth. They fail to listen to my commands." Her self-control buckled in the face of her inconsolable grief as she looked down at the obscene altar where Alazaïs's body would be sacrificed along with the others. "My lady, surely rage and grief are better weapons against this crime than mute acceptance?"

"You mean, against God's will. In these next hours you must come to terms with this, Sancha. My death will be far easier if I know that. It is only my body that is dying. It is only my flesh, not my spirit."

Sancha hung her head. "I know what you're thinking, and you're right. If my faith had been stronger, I would not be tormented now."

She met Alazaïs's calm gray eyes, clinging like a child to her own belief that life was infinitely precious. In moments of religious exaltation she had been able to imagine martyrdom, but now the moment had come for Alazaïs she knew it for what it was. When presented with the alternative of being burned at the stake as a heretic or recanting her beliefs, she hesitated only briefly. Those who were weak, like her, were the ones who were now suffering most at the prospect of being parted from those they loved. The Believers who faced death were strengthened by a vision of another world, which was hidden from ordinary people, a world of the spirit, which they had freely chosen above life. Searching Alazaïs's eyes, Sancha was startled to realize that she had already relinquished this world. Her cool, dry hands in Sancha's were the husks of something already departed. By a miracle of faith she had entered that suspended state of perception that would allow her to walk to her death without fear of pain. She had assured Sancha that her self-mastery, learnt over decades, would lessen the hideous agony of death by fire.

Sancha released her hands, feeling her own grief subside into numbness, but not understanding. Her mourning tapered into a penetrating cold that enveloped her whole body. She was encapsulated in the strange paradox of seeing and touching Alazaïs, but knowing she had already departed. She had majestically gathered up her earthly connections, as a lady would her train, and disappeared down a dark corridor, leaving the memory of her beauty and serenity like a lingering perfume.

Alazaïs's face was framed in a poignant smile. "If by some chance we don't see each other before dawn, it is better to bid farewell now," she began.

For Alazaïs's sake, in remembrance of all she had meant to her, Sancha found courage and swallowed her tears. "It is too early for leave-taking. Let us drink the cup to the last drop and not hurry the moment. I will try for the rest of my life to live by your example. That I promise."

"You are stronger than you know, Sancha. That will see you through whatever comes. I rejoice with all my heart for you and Hugo."

"Thank you. Don't think I'm not grateful that God spared his life. It seems a miracle he was not badly wounded . . ." she said, not wanting to talk of future joys.

"Be true to one another, and kind, whatever you face. You have barely tasted the happiness you will find together. You have my blessing, now and always. When you remember me, let it be with gladness, not with grief." Releasing Sancha's hands, she left the room.

When Alazaïs had gone, Sancha sat for a moment, her mind empty as she gazed out of the window. She lifted her eyes from the movements of the soldiers at the base of the mountain, swarming like ants, to the clouds that parted to reveal the evening star set in the pale sky. She stared at the crystal orb, trying to penetrate its distant secrets. The spokes of blurred light that radiated from its fiery center seemed to reach down to earth, but not far enough to illuminate her own private darkness.

Hearing footsteps, she turned to see Hugo standing in the doorway. "Oh Hugo, Hugo," she cried out helplessly, burying her face in his shoulder. She clung to him tenderly, careful not to touch his arms or his face, which bore deep wounds that had not yet healed after the battle. Every night before they fell asleep in each other's arms, she tended them as best she could.

They sat on the bench, their eyes locked together, talking in low whispers.

"So it's to be at dawn, then."

"Yes, exactly as we planned it. I met my mother on the stairs coming down. We are all to meet in the stronghold under the fortress when the sun goes down."

Sancha felt adrenaline coursing through her at the thought of the final hurdle Hugo had to face. The Church leaders had decided that, before dawn, he and three other men were to be lowered from the ramparts on ropes, carrying the last precious emblems of Cathar treasure that still remained hidden in a secret chamber underground. On the eve of the truce the four men had been hidden in the treasure vault to avoid the roll call when the gates of the fortress were opened. Hugo had been entrusted to lead the mission. Two of the others were Perfecti, and the fourth was a guide.

"So be it, then," she said, taking his hand.

When she looked at him, he saw it all. She could hide nothing. Her bloom had been brutally crushed, leaving her face withered and windburned, her hair and skin dry and lifeless. She had endured all these months like a plant stubbornly clinging to life, waiting for its season to come again.

Hugo's powerful frame had endured the ordeal like a great tree that had been badly shaken by a tempest. His gaunt face, weathered by the elements, bore the indelible stamp of care and his hair was gray. The long months at Montségur had blackened the hollows of his eyes, giving the impression that he had stared too long and hard into the abyss. He still carried himself proudly, but he was straining under the burden. His weary flesh seemed nourished only by sheer strength of will and the knowledge that all battles must end and all warriors rest. Tested again and again, he had withstood every challenge, but the violent years through which he had lived seemed to have sapped his vital force at last.

"There's not much time left, and anything we say seems so hollow. What we feel, Sancha, will always remain locked away here." He touched her heart. Images flew through Sancha's mind as she tried to construct the months to come when she and Hugo would be separated, he going about the business of salvaging what was left of the Church, she to do penance in exchange for her freedom.

Hugo said: "It is being said that our hostages have been told there will be no stronger penance than a pilgrimage for all those who recant, perhaps to St. James of Compostela or, at worst, to Puy."

"And to wear the heretics' yellow cross," she nodded. "That I can bear," she said, her voice dropping to a whisper. Their hands crossed in mutual adoration and they searched one another's features, committing the present to memory. With scarred fingers Hugo caressed the hollows beneath Sancha's eyes, where tears fell. As he kissed her forehead, she closed her eyes. The warmth of Lombardy filled the room for an instant as they both imagined the perfumed days they would live. All the past shrank away at the prospect of a shared existence where they belonged to the earth and to each other. For a short space they vibrated with conviction that the blood-soaked episode was drawing to a close and new life would quicken into being, giving rise to tender green shoots. They would sow, they would reap, according to the seasons.

"I won't move from this country until I have completed my mission, and you yours, and I have heard from Arnaut Narbonna that you are waiting for me at his farm," Hugo promised.

Her breath seemed to fade and her pulse faint as the minutes passed. In her mind's eye she saw the stout rope that would carry Hugo down from the ramparts that night dwindling to a gossamer thread that could be broken by the merest caprice of fate.

He smoothed the lines of worry from her forehead and pressed her to him, searching for the words to express the sentiments that might have to last for months, years, perhaps a lifetime.

"Sancha, I swear to you that no matter where you may be, no matter how long it will take, by all that is sacred, I will find you. I make this vow to you, pledging my life on it. Know that I love you above life itself. I go away from here tonight carrying the sacred thought of you, here, where you will always dwell." He pressed her hand to his heart and his eyes filled with pain. "Be it in this life . . . or in another, by all that is sacred, I will find you."

His last words moved her most of all. It was so vain a hope and yet Hugo spoke with such conviction. She clung to him for a moment, then drew away. An invisible wall had already begun to divide them.

"My love belongs to you, Hugo, now and always," she replied. "And I believe the power that brought us together will one day reunite us. I know that. I will wait for you. I will search for you. I will never give up until we are together again, never."

Their promises filled the small stone chamber and were overheard by the wind seeping through the narrow windows. Their words resonating in the gloom were scattered like seeds and tossed to an indeterminate future, but they sank into the stones as surely as if they had been chiseled there.

When darkness fell, Hugo and Sancha entered the torchlit stronghold beneath the fortress, an airless, moldy dungeon carved out of solid rock, which was a secret even to the Believers. Alazaïs was there with Esclarmonde and several other of the clergy. Soon they were joined by two of the men who were to accompany Hugo, their faces grave from the final leave-taking they had just exchanged with their friends and families. No one spoke as they waited for the others to arrive. At last the bent figure of Bishop Marty appeared in the archway, followed by two deacons, who bore leather sacks.

The Bishop looked round the gathering. His eyes, though sunken with age and hardship, emitted an electrifying power as he searched each one of their faces. Sancha felt profound humility in the presence of the great man, who wore saint-hood like a rich mantle on his frail shoulders. His face, trans-parent in the light of a wavering taper, had a pharaonic dignity, a ferocious courage that burned as brightly in old age as it had in the flush of youth, when he had preached the fiery sermons that had converted so many Believers. He was the surviving vessel that carried the pure essence of the faith, the one man living who embodied the title of true Christian. He spoke in a soft but moving voice as his deacons put their sacks on the ground in the middle of the circle.

"Gaillard has succumbed to delirium within the last hour. He has been vomiting blood and has fallen unconscious."

Murmurs echoed round the chamber. Sancha looked worriedly at Hugo, who said: "Who have you chosen as replacement?"

"There are few who could make the journey who know the terrain as Gaillard does. Gaucelm volunteered and I accepted. He is surefooted and seems to know the land. And he is brave. He knows that under the terms of the truce he could walk free from the citadel at dawn with no penance, like all the other men at arms, but he has offered to risk his life."

Sancha opened her mouth to speak, but only a whisper escaped. A terrible prescience crept over her that she had no power to express. Only that morning she had spoken to Gaillard, who was as fit and well as any man could be in the circumstances. The thought sprang to her mind that Gaillard's symptoms sounded like poisoning. She was stunned by the ominous coincidence that Gaucelm had volunteered to replace him. But glancing round the circle of illuminated faces, she realized that no one seemed to have any doubts on the matter except herself. Sancha buried her violent protest at the back of her mind, arguing with herself that the peculiarities she had observed in Gaucelm were, after all, conjecture. Yet she was swallowed up by a dark sense of inevitability and could almost feel the seconds falling away to midnight, beyond which time seemed to stop in her imagination.

A few minutes later Gaucelm stole into the chamber on quiet, catlike feet. He bowed his head and nodded reverently to the Bishop. His plump face, his alert expression were in contrast to the gaunt, haunted countenances round him. His unnatural glow of health seemed an insult to the appalling suffering of the others. He was like a slippery eel that had escaped through the net and was swimming free. Sancha could sense that he brought a gust of restless uncertainty into the chamber that was mistaken for vitality. Try as she could, she was unable to subdue her repulsion and fear. She searched Hugo's profile for some sign that he disapproved of the Bishop's decision, but saw none.

"We must make haste, Your Reverence," said the sergeant-at-arms, who was to oversee the escape.

The old bishop nodded. His milky eyes were filled with humanity as he looked at the Believers who would die at daybreak when the truce expired. His sturdy frame seemed

bent by the weight of circumstance that led to so many violent deaths, as if he alone sustained them. He motioned to
the deacons to bring the sacks forward, and instructed them
to distribute the contents. They withdrew ancient bound tes-
taments that contained the most sacred writings of the
Church. An awed silence filled the chamber as they all regarded the documents that had been preserved for centuries.
The Bishop held out a collection of parchments bound with
leather so worn from use that the embossed gold had all but
vanished and its brass bolts and hinges had blackened.

"To you, Poitevin, I commit in trust this volume of the
gospels of true Christians, which tells of our beginnings here
in Languedoc."

One of the deacons wrapped the heavy tome in linen and
put it into a leather satchel, which was then strapped between
Poitevin's shoulder blades.

Sancha leaned forward, her gloom dashed by a sudden exaltation in the ascetic beauty of Poitevin's countenance. He
had dark, penetrating eyes above his waxen cheeks. In them
she could read a pure smoldering reflection of the Truth that
fanned her hope. His emaciated frame seemed to bend under
the weight of the gospels strapped to his back, and she sensed
that he seemed more afraid of living and failing the Church
than of dying. In his eyes, he had been deprived of martyrdom with the Believers among whom he had lived for twelve
years, and his face was full of anguish that he had been forbidden to meet what he regarded as his destiny.

Aicart, the other Believer, and Gaucelm both received their
burdens, leaving Hugo until last. When the book entrusted
to him was packed inside the bag, the Bishop held up his
hand.

"Wait—there is something more to add."

There was an expectant hush as the Bishop gestured to a
sack that had gone unnoticed. Small and insignificant, it
seemed to contain nothing of importance. With hands trembling with age, he reached inside and withdrew a gold chalice, which he held up with both hands for all to see. Its
smooth burnished surface glinted in the shadows, casting up
shards of reflected light. The size of a strong man's hand, the
flawless surface of the vessel was unadorned. It was a pool
of amber liquid resting in the Bishop's fingers.

" 'From this cup drank Jesus our Lord,' " he quoted, holding the chalice aloft as he repeated the words of the inscription round the base.

There was a spontaneous murmur of prayer. A shiver passed down Sancha's spine as she stared at the chalice, streaming with a transfiguring luster. It was the most compelling object she had ever seen.

"Hugo, I entrust this cup to you to defend and deliver to our brothers who are waiting to receive you at Ussat. They will see it is put in safekeeping." Seeing the curiosity and wonder on the faces of those present, the Bishop added: "Its long and wondrous history is entwined with the survival of the True Church."

He looked round the ring of inquisitive faces. The specter of death and parting at tomorrow's conflagration lifted for a moment. He turned the chalice in his hands, murmuring that in the light glancing from it they bore witness to a more durable fire. Then he began to speak.

In the still chamber Sancha heard the history of the Grail. She heard from the Bishop's lips how it was taken from Jerusalem by the Magdalene after the crucifixion and brought to what became the Languedoc. To those who remembered Christ in his lifetime, the Grail became a symbol of his Church, which was threatened by greed, by schisms that degenerated into a struggle for temporal power. In their wisdom, the early Gnostic fathers guarded the Grail in secret, with the same devotion with which they nurtured the true words of Christ, uncorrupted by dogma. Until now, the existence of the chalice had been known only to a few. Those who guarded the word of Christ and kept it pure feared the power of this cup, knowing that such an object could divert men from their divine purpose. Weak minds could be influenced to revere an object more than the spiritual purity it represented. The Grail's intrinsic power could be harnessed by the forces of darkness and put to evil use, enslaving the minds of men, filling them with idolatry rather than with the love of God.

When the Bishop had finished speaking, there was a hush in the crowded chamber. His tapering hands caressed the Grail for the last time before he put it into the bag, which the deacons then hoisted onto Hugo's back. Sancha's eyes met Hugo's for only an instant before he disappeared through the archway, the others, including Gaucelm, following him. Alazaïs clasped her hand, as if anchoring her firmly to the stark reality of what had just happened. Straining to hear Hugo's footsteps disappearing down the passage, Sancha felt the cord between them slacken, perhaps forever.

Moments later Hugo had stationed himself on the dark ramparts, his every muscle taut as he waited to follow the other three men over the wall. As he tightened the straps of his bag, he trained his eyes on the blurred red of a thousand campfires in the black abyss below the mountain, like the molten fire of Hell. An eerie silence had descended upon the mountain on the last night of the truce. There was neither wind nor weeping. He blocked his mind completely to the horror gnawing at him, knowing that once it had gained a foothold in his consciousness, he would be lost. Struggling to master himself, he felt the weight of the precious cargo against his back. Its significance seemed to endow him with an abnormal strength. When he saw the rope dangling in the darkness below him, he turned to the sergeant-at-arms, whose eyes shone in the darkness.

"If anything should go wrong," the latter whispered, "send word before dawn, through the rope, and I will do whatever I can. Don't fail to send us word of your safe landing. You have only the time before the Crusaders climb the mountain in the early morning; after that it will be too late." They locked hands for an instant, then he offered his hands to help Hugo over the wall.

Heaving himself up, Hugo grabbed the rope, then dropped into the darkness, his legs scraping against the rocks. He hung on with all his strength to the rope that suspended him above the dizzying black chasm plunging hundreds of feet into the rocks below. Strangled by the straps of his pack, he gasped for breath. Feeling insignificant and helpless as a seed in the wind, he recalled the words of the old seer he had met: "You will be scattered . . ."

His whole body shook when he landed on hard ground. Leaping up, he made his way down the slope behind the citadel and to the rendezvous point as swiftly as he could in the darkness. Several times he stumbled through the undergrowth, searching for the way to the cave where the four men planned to hide until dawn. When he paused to get his bearings, the sound of his own labored breathing pounded in his ears. Without any warning he was winded by a great weight falling on his back. As he fell, he thought he was being crushed by a bag of grain. He crashed painfully to his knees on the rocks. Before he could stand, someone had gripped him in a stranglehold from behind. Hugo gagged for breath, his eyes bulging, his tongue protruding. Heaving with all his strength, he shrugged off his attacker, rolled on to his back and kicked blindly between his adversary's legs, causing him to reel back in the darkness. As his assailant writhed in pain, Hugo struggled to unsheathe his knife. The man had already leapt to his feet, giving Hugo a quick, shadowy glimpse of his face.

"Gaucelm!" he cried.

He saw the gleam of a knife brandished in the darkness as he tried desperately to free his own blade, his arms hampered by the straps of the bag digging into his shoulders. When he had wrenched his weapon free, Gaucelm was towering over him, his knife poised. It was too late to get up. As Gaucelm lunged, Hugo lashed out wildly, straining to gouge his eyes. Gaucelm retracted with a gasp as the knife cut across his face. The weight of his body as he fell plunged his knife into Hugo's heart.

Hugo felt nothing, not even the weight of Gaucelm's body. The dark shroud of unconsciousness pulled silently over him like a soft curtain. His life drained away slowly, seeping into the earth on which he lay. In his last moments the world and all it meant to him seemed to shrink into an infinitesimal ball, until it had dissolved. Yet something remained of himself that was vague as light seen through half-closed eyes filled with tears. This pulse without a heart quickened and did not die, but flowed back to a deep buried center, like a rose returning to the bud it once had been. The petals closed securely round a tiny seed, which dissolved into infinity. The earth had reclaimed the life it had given.

Soon afterward Poitevin came stumbling through the undergrowth, alerted by Gaucelm's grunts of pain and terror now that he was plunged into blindness. By light reflected from the star-studded sky, Poitevin saw the bloody sockets of Gaucelm's eyes as he staggered helplessly in a circle. Seeing Hugo's body, he rushed to him and, realizing what must have happened, prized the treasure from his back, then went to fetch his companion. Together the two of them dragged Hugo's body into the undergrowth and covered it with leaves and moss. Only then did they deal with Gaucelm. Overpowering him, though he was very strong, they dragged him to a rocky precipice and pushed him off the ledge. They heard the thud of his body as he fell.

"We have committed murder," whispered Poitevin, suddenly aware of what they had done. He stared, stunned for a moment at the outline of the white rocks where Gaucelm had disappeared, realizing that by this act his own soul had become as black as the night that engulfed them.

"We had to do it, or risk losing the treasure. As it is, I hope the sentries have not been alerted. Come, brother," Aicart whispered, wearily resting an arm on his bony shoulder. "We've surely been overheard on the ramparts. I'll set their minds at rest and tell them that the gospels and the chalice are safe, but that Hugo has perished."

The crimson dawn fired the snow-capped summits surrounding Montségur on the morning the truce ended. Sancha was awakened by the image of Hugo flickering under her eyelids. She had been dreaming of olive groves in Lombardy, but seeing the familiar shape of the courtyard, she remembered where she was.

Moments later, Alazaïs knelt at her side and told her that Hugo was dead. Without replying, she rose from the hard ground to seek out the Bishop, who was praying in a circle of those who would be burned that morning. A proverb Zarah used to recount came back to her, its truth clothing her nakedness: "When a man's wife dies, his world is darkened; she dies in him, he in her."

When the Bishop had finished, he met her gaze, knowing intuitively why she had come. Speaking in a whisper, she asked for the *consolamentum*, annulling her earlier confession to the Roman Catholic priest. Her own life had been snuffed out now Hugo was dead and her only wish was to be beside Alazaïs on the pyre.

The unrepentant Believers assembled silently in the court-yard when the gates were opened, separating themselves from those soldiers and their families and the others who would be taken to prison before being sentenced to penance by the Church.

As Sancha began the steep descent down the mountain toward the palisade she could see in the field below, she thought it strange that the Crusaders felt it necessary to fetter their hands when none of them had any desire to escape. She and the others struggled to keep their balance as they made their way down the roughest part of the track, driven by the brutish shouts of the Crusaders. Their silence and the serenity on their faces seemed to enrage the victors. The self-possession of the martyrs bewildered these soldiers of the Roman Church, and they abused their captives with taunts and blows to cover their own confusion. At last they had flushed out the inhabitants of the mountain stronghold, but they seemed disappointed that these rebels were not demons, as the Church had told them, but ordinary people, exhausted from their ordeal.

Sancha's mind was clear and sure, though her steps faltered. Determined to make her last moments her own, she fixed her mind on the beauty of the spring day. Lord of the valley was Mount Tabor, a snow-crested peak that ruled in the west from its winter heights. Her eyes missed nothing: the gentians and crocuses thrusting their heads through the new spring grass, the blossoms of the wild cherry trees on the hillside, a filigree of white against the green haze. She heard the sounds of the thrush and the lark, whose dark wings, as fragile as brushstrokes, were painted against the cruelly brilliant sky. She looked into the distance, gathering to her heart the splendor of the blue mountains, their snowy summits still majestically aloof from spring. Her hands were in chains, but her spirit was free. Above the clamor of the Crusaders she heard the gushing river that flowed from the hills to the sea Hugo had described to her, which now she would never know. When Alazaïs cast a look in her direction, Sancha communicated in a glance that she had learned what had eluded her until now. In a short space of time she had understood what the Cathars meant by a good death.

At the foot of the hill the Believers came to a halt facing

that tall palisade like a mountain waiting to be climbed. The
air was filled with the reek of pitch and the fragrance of
freshly cut wood accompanied by the stink of human bodies.
With a strange detachment, Sancha watched as the brawny,
pale-haired Crusaders from the north of France mounted the
ladders to pour more pitch on the wood heaped inside the
barrier, enough to burn all their bodies.

She pitied these fierce-looking men in chain mail and helmets, red crosses emblazoned on their tunics. They avoided
the eyes of the silent, accepting Believers, who were looking
at them with neither condemnation nor fear. It was the Crusaders who were now manifesting signs of uneasiness when
their commander gave the signal for the torches to be lit and
tossed into the enclosure. They shrank away from what they
could not understand, their battle-worn faces twisted by an
animal confusion that suggested they were secretly frightened
to destroy these self-possessed Believers the Church had
branded as heretics. Expecting to be met with hatred and
hysteria, they were disarmed by the martyrs' dignity and their
refusal to recant their beliefs in order to save themselves at
the last hour. Only the richly robed bishop and the black-
robed Dominican friars looking on from a distance seemed
unimpressed by the Believers' dignity. There was no doubt
in their eyes, only satisfaction that they had disposed of these
stubborn heretics in the name of God and Christ. Some of
them were even smiling.

Suddenly Sancha was surrounded by other Believers, who
were being herded closer to the palisade. Her heart began to
pound involuntarily as she saw Crusaders fling torches dipped
in pitch into the bonfire. Their flaming tips seemed strangely
feeble in the bright sunshine. Jostled by the emaciated bodies
of the old and frail Believers, their shoulders stooped with
resignation, Sancha realized she had lost sight of Alazaïs.
Frantically she tried to push her way through the crowd, but
it was too late. The burning torches were being thrown
through the air like wheels of pale fire to ignite the pyre
inside the palisade, and the soldiers were ordering the Believers to mount the ladders, and cursing in their strange
northern tongue.

On one ladder soldiers were struggling to hoist the
wounded and the dying to toss them into the pit. Already

close to death, they made no sound as they fell. Suddenly there was a huge puff of fire and smoke from the enclosure. For an instant Sancha saw old Bishop Marty poised on the rim of the palisade. She watched as he held his arms open, passionately embracing death as he plunged forward. Sancha started to weep, realizing now that she wouldn't die beside Alazaïs. Her grief violated her serenity, making her knees buckle as she neared the ladder. As the first victims fell into the pit, a few agonized cries filled the air. Sancha looked up helplessly at the ragged line of bodies struggling up the ladder and disappearing behind the sharp teeth of the towering stockade veiled by black smoke. Watching Believers sacrifice themselves one after the other as she climbed, Sancha's one thought was that the crush from behind would keep her from losing courage. As the heat from the flames grew more intense, all she could do was to climb the crude ladder. The acrid smell of scorched flesh and hair filled the air, numbing her senses.

When the woman ahead of her disappeared, Sancha had only a moment's glimpse into the inferno spread out before her. A roaring and hissing enveloped her, like the hot breath of Hell. Her lungs were choked with the foul-smelling smoke and she saw a tangle of bodies hideously twisted in the flames below. Her hair caught fire and her eyelids curled in the heat like burning parchment as she stared down at the twisted, charred bodies that writhed in the pit. Her arms outstretched, Sancha went to meet her death on the pyre in one leap, crying out Hugo's name. As she fell she became a human torch that consumed itself. Her body met the embers and she passed through the door of mortality. The white heat of her agony smothered the light of day, confining her to darkness as her body was reduced to ashes and the silver dove around her neck melted into the earth.

The morning after the burning the valley was hung with frail wisps of smoke that mingled with the mist cloaking the hills. When the wind came up, the air was cleansed. Then the veil that clung to the horizon was blown west, out to sea.

Poitevin labored up the rugged trail that skirted the gorge, clinging to branches as he climbed. Straining under the weight of the leather satchel on his back, he gasped for breath and stopped. He slumped on the rocks as a fit of coughing racked his body, then spat into the dust. His spittle was mixed with blood. He wiped his brow and raised his eyes to the impenetrable hillside against the hot, blue sky. Peering into the wall of rocky cliffs above, he prayed that his memory had not deceived him. So many of those who remembered this secret place were now dead or scattered. He had nothing but his own inner compass to go by.

He had been separated from his companion, Aicart, following the massacre at Montségur, and it had taken him since March to reach this lost corner of the Ariège. Realizing his strength was waning, he reluctantly decided to hide the treasure entrusted to him by the Bishop until he could inform a Believer of its whereabouts so that it could be moved to Ussat for safekeeping. His load was unusually heavy, since he carried Hugo's portion of the treasure as well as his own. He didn't know what had happened to Aicart, but hoped he had found a safe place for his own precious load. This holy place was the best spot Poitevin could think of, where the treasure would be safe until he had regained his strength. The last time he had been there it had been winter, many years before, when he had been young and strong. Then he had spent the night at the castle of Puivaillon, where he was given shelter in a stable by the Lady Alazaïs de Franjal. She herself had brought him food. They had talked of the ceremony about to take place in the cave, when the rites of the True Church would be administered by the great preacher, Guilbert de Castres, who had died too early to share a violent death by fire with the Lady Alazaïs and the others.

When the sun reached its zenith, Poitevin came to consciousness in the cave. Opening his eyes, he saw blurred shadows moving on the blue dome overhead. He remembered that he had fainted from exhaustion after burying the holy books. Seeing his taper was nearly melted, he forced himself to his feet. He would have to finish the task of burying the Grail before he was plunged into darkness. As he worked, he prayed to God for the strength to chip a hollow in the rock with a chisel he had brought for the purpose. He allowed himself only a quick glimpse of the golden vessel. Taking it from the bag, he unwrapped the linen that swathed it, feeling unworthy to touch it. Its transfiguring beauty consoled him that his short and wretched life had not been in vain. His blackened lips moved in adoration as he kissed the chalice. Then he wrapped it again and put it securely into the hole he had made in the rock. When he had blocked up the hole, he was satisfied that no one would ever find the Grail unless he told them of its exact whereabouts. When he had carefully concealed all traces of his visit, he steadied himself against the wall, trying to summon the strength to pick up his bag and leave the cave. His chest heaving with the fire that raged in his lungs, he hung his head, gasping painfully for breath. Coughing violently, he fell to the ground in a faint. When he came back to consciousness again, he thought for a moment that he had died as he stared up at the golden circles enclosing silver stars, and the circle within circles set with a single rose. They seemed to dance across the field of cobalt blue, expanding and contracting in infinity and filling him with hope.

That night he came to rest in an open field. Lying on his back, he looked up at the deep blue sky, which reminded him of the cave. Tears rolled down his face when he realized that his secret would die with him. For the last time he contemplated the black night sewn with stars that mirrored the brilliance of the moon slung low on the horizon.

18

At the beginning of June Louise was in southern France, driving through mile after mile of lush green vineyards set against an angry sky that bathed the landscape in a strange yellow light. When the clouds broke there was a deluge that cleared as quickly as it had come, showering the country with light. Leaving a long avenue of chestnut trees just before the town of Mirepoix, she approached a hill set with a cluster of dark umbrella pines and cypresses that stood watch over a walled cemetery. Rounding a bend, she had a sweeping view of the Pyrenees, an impenetrable line of snow-covered blue peaks receding in the distance. The uncluttered view seemed so familiar, that she was sure she had seen a picture of that very spot in the book that had so moved her father, though the photograph had been taken at a different season and in a different light. Louise slowed down the car, knowing instinctively that it was the appropriate place to scatter her father's ashes.

Following a dirt road that crossed a meadow, she got out of the car and stood for a moment to get the feel of the place and make sure it was right. The sound of nightingales coming from a nearby wood reassured her. Listening to the wind whipping the grass, she looked toward the mountains. A heightened awareness of the cycle of life overcame any sadness she might have felt as she performed the ritual she could now regard as a beginning. The absurdity of existence was conquered by its mysterious richness, challenging the notion that she was overseeing the end of a life that had been in many ways sad. She said goodbye to her father as he might have wished, in bright sunlight with birds singing, in a meadow full of poppies and cornflowers. She had thought she would dread this moment, but now that the final link was about to be broken between two people who had loved one another, she was as certain as she would ever be that the bond between them didn't end there. From somewhere outside herself came a conviction that death was just a rite of passage as profound as birth, banishing her grief and filling her with peace and even joy. She felt a burden lifted now she had honored his last wish by scattering his ashes in Languedoc. The idea no longer seemed peculiar and she wondered if he had died knowing more than he would ever tell her. She couldn't ask for anything more than to know his spirit somehow lingered on the breeze ruffling the tall green grass.

It was late afternoon by the time Louise arrived at Puivaillon in the heavily loaded Renault she had rented in Toulouse. Slowing down near the shuttered church shaded by plane trees, she glanced at a group of men playing boules, their craggy faces shaded by the wide black berets peculiar to the Pyrenees, and wondered if Maurice Roussel might be among them. One of the men told her how to find him and she drove on through the village, where she imagined people taking an afternoon siesta behind shutters half closed against the sun. Stopping the car briefly in front of the Hôtel du Commerce, where she had stayed in March, she noticed it looked much brighter in the sunlight, with boxes of geraniums in the open windows

Maurice Roussel's house was exactly as she might have imagined, with faded blue shutters and a wistaria heavy with blossom almost obscuring the door. She could see a man in the garden of the house, bending, spade in hand, to till the soil. He stood and raised his hand when he heard the car door slam. As Louise opened the gate she was met by an overpowering scent from the small, beautifully tended herb garden crisscrossed by narrow graveled paths. The drone of bees filled the air as they hovered over the rich assortment of plants, few of which she had ever seen before, though she recognized the Prussian blue of sage, the silvery gray of rosemary and the violet spikes of lavender packed together in neatly symmetrical beds. She stood there for a moment inhaling their exhilarating perfume, which seemed to magnify all her senses. A startling feeling of recognition she could only compare to love at first sight seized hold of her, filling her with elation.

Roussel was not, as she had imagined, a doddering old man, but burly and tanned, with thick white hair. Louise met his black, intelligent eyes, which were set in a broad powerful face softened by a welcoming smile. Taking her hand in his large rough palm, he shook it warmly.

"Madame Carey," he repeated, "*soyez bienvenue*. Well, well, so you have arrived at last," he added in English, holding out his hands in a gesture of helpless pleasure as if he was mystified as to why it had taken her so long. As he looked at her thoughtfully from beneath dark shaggy brows streaked with white, she was struck by the vitality radiating from him. Rather than withering and bending his frame, the hardships of life seemed to have strengthened him and made his voice more resonant. He had the powerful aura of a man who cherished wisdom and humor equally. Looking round at his lovingly tended garden, she could only suppose that his remarkable vigor sprang from spending his life in pursuit of what he loved.

When they had chatted about her journey, she said: "If you're not too busy, perhaps you would show me round your garden. I've never seen anything like it."

"Why, of course; but I thought you might like to see the cottage first."

"I'm in no hurry, if you're not," she said, feeling that an easy rapport had already sprung up between them.

He led her down the graveled path, talking sometimes in English, then breaking into French, which she didn't find as hard to understand as she might have expected, though he spoke with a strong meridional accent. He seemed to find it natural that she was as fascinated with the herbal arts as he was, and his black eyes shone with pleasure at her interest. When he reeled off the names of plants, both familiar and in Latin, adding interesting snatches of folklore, she wished she could remember everything he said. As they walked he picked leaves and flowers, which he put into her outstretched hands, explaining their culinary and medicinal purposes. Crushing them in her fingers to liberate their powerful aroma, she drank in the newfound wealth of scents. Soon she had collected an exotic potpourri, which he tied for her with a piece of string. As the afternoon shadows lengthened, the rest of the world seemed locked beyond the iron gate of Maurice Roussel's garden. Finally he looked at her with an amused smile.

"But forgive me. As you can see, I could continue talking for hours with such an appreciative listener. I imagine you must be anxious to see your house."

"To tell you the truth, I'd forgotten all about it. I'm spellbound."

Following him back to his house, she enjoyed a delicious sense of refreshment as she filled her lungs with the cool evening air heavy with the smell of rich soil and aromatic plants. Once inside his stone house roofed with faded russet tiles, he lead her into his study.

She sniffed the fragrance of ancient paper and leather as she faced the shelves that reached to the ceiling. His collection of herbal lore seemed prodigious, even though she knew nothing about the subject. There were books in Latin, Greek, French, English and German, many of them ancient and probably irreplaceable. She was staggered by the size and extent of his library, knowing it must be unique in the world.

That a man who had lived in the same village most of his life had amassed such a wealth of knowledge seemed remarkable. She noticed an entire shelf of blue notebooks when she heard his footsteps.

"Dorothy told me you've been working for years on a book."

He smiled disparagingly. "Yes, those blue notebooks contain nearly everything I have learned about plants that is of value. What started as a few jottings many years ago has become completely out of hand. Never start a book, madame, unless you can finish it, or it will not let you rest."

"I hadn't thought of it in that way. It's not just a pastime with you, is it? It's an obsession."

He laughed. "I'm glad you've come to Puivaillon. I think you and I are going to be good friends. No one told me you were interested in botany."

"I didn't know myself."

He was studying her and she guessed he was wondering why a young, single woman, a foreigner, would want to bury herself in this quiet part of France when she might go to Paris or the Riviera.

"You're not a writer by any chance, are you, Madame Carey?"

She shook her head. "At the moment I'm between occupations. Please, why don't you simply call me Louise? Madame Carey sounds so formal." She knew how correct the French could be regarding names, but she was impatient to break down the needless barriers right away.

"All right, Louise. And please call me Maurice."

"I don't know if Dorothy mentioned it to you, but I was here in March and I liked it so much I had to come back," she remarked, not knowing what she would say if he asked her how she intended to spend the summer. But when he nodded politely as if it were the most normal thing in the world, she relaxed, realizing she had come to a place where soul-searching was not a crime.

They went into the big airy kitchen dominated by a scrubbed table and a wood-burning stove, above which were jars of dried herbs, copper pans and casseroles. When he lifted the lid of a pot, the kitchen was filled with an aroma of garlic and tomatoes that made her mouth water. She realized she had eaten practically nothing all day.

"I prepared something, hoping you might like to have dinner here tonight," he said, stirring the pot with a wooden spoon.

"That's very kind of you," she said, looking forward to sampling whatever was simmering on the back of the stove.

"I will take you to your house now. I must return for my surgery at six o'clock until seven. I'll drive with you and then walk back. It's not far."

In the car she said: "I hadn't realized you still practiced medicine."

"I was hoping to devote the years since my wife died to writing my book, but there are so many people who need treatment, I can't refuse them. And it looks as if I might die without finishing it, anyway. I find the task of organizing all my notes and putting them into a coherent order is more than I can cope with, and my eyesight isn't as good as it was."

"It seems to me you need someone to help you. An assistant or a secretary."

"That's exactly what I need. But where to find someone like that here?" he said thoughtfully, and they exchanged a glance.

The cottage was exactly as it had looked in the photograph, a modest, one-story house roofed with pink tiles, with pale blue shutters and deep red roses rambling round the door.

"It's simple, but I hope it pleases you."

Louise followed him inside and waited expectantly while Maurice opened the shutters in all the rooms, coloring the plaster with an ivory patina. The kitchen gave on to a small walled garden with a fig tree and hollyhocks, where a table and chairs were almost completely hidden by greenery. Louise wandered through the three connecting rooms, admiring everything she saw, from the uneven tiled floors that had been polished to a deep rose over the years, to the straw-bottomed chairs round a table in the kitchen, which also served as a dining room. He had put a bouquet of early summer flowers on the table to welcome her.

When Maurice had gone, she went into the bedroom, which was simply, even starkly, furnished with a bed, a table and an *armoire*. As she leaned out of the window, it struck her forcefully that she had stumbled into paradise. She sucked in her breath in surprise when she saw that the window commanded an unspoiled view of the château of Puivaillon, whose tower rose like a golden column in the distance, gilded by the setting sun. She stared at its Gothic windows, which kept watch over the valley like dark, sad eyes.

Rex Monckton rose to his feet when he saw Mandy enter the palm-filled conservatory of the restaurant. She was dressed in white linen and her gold bracelets and chains and her golden hair all glinted in the sun pouring down through the glass. He saw heads turn in the direction of the willowy, suntanned blonde, her eyes shielded by blue-tinted sunglasses, then turn away again. The leggy stride, the coquettish tilt of her head that had been so arresting at twenty were painfully inappropriate at forty-three, Rex observed, responding to the fixed smile that had imprinted deep creases in Mandy's face. The pleasurable sensation he felt at being recognized in this chic Chelsea venue was diluted by the fact that Mandy was neither appealingly young nor a celebrity.

When he had telephoned to ask her to lunch, she had given no indication that she knew about the encounter between him and Owen a few days earlier, and the eagerness in her voice had been pathetic. Ingenuousness had always been part of Mandy's charm, and Rex knew she was incapable of lying convincingly.

"Mandy, my darling," he said, opening his arms to welcome her. "You look simply amazing, amazing."

"Oh, come on, I don't really." She gave him a smile that was painful in its intensity.

"It's lovely to see you again," he purred, pulling out her chair with a flourish.

"You look like you've just come back from holiday," she exclaimed. "It's such fun to see you again. It's been forever, hasn't it? I was trying to remember when it was. Wasn't it at that opening in King Street three years ago?"

"Yes, it must have been," he replied vaguely. "A bottle of the Chablis," he said to the waiter hovering at his side.

He remembered how repulsive, how unkempt, Mandy had looked that night. She had been completely stoned and he was surprised she recalled the evening at all. He wondered if she still took so much coke and how she paid for it. Today, however, she had pulled herself together. Her nails were manicured, her roots touched up, her makeup carefully applied, and he concluded that she had probably spent money she could ill afford on the new white linen skirt and blazer she was wearing.

"Rex, before we say another word I must congratulate you on that super article about you in *Harper's and Queen* last month. Your house in Belgravia, the shop—it all looked too stunning for words . . ." she broke off breathlessly. "I tried to call you in the gallery to tell you, but you weren't there. Your assistant wouldn't give me your home number." She gave a kittenish smile. "So, it must be astral thought or something, you inviting me to have lunch."

"Yes, perhaps it was," Rex answered, with a patronizing smile at the absurdity of her suggestion, "because I have indeed been thinking about you quite a lot recently." He remembered Mandy had always been hooked on tarot cards, horoscopes and the *I Ching*.

"I had no idea you owned a house in Hampshire too," Mandy said with a little gasp. "It's a dream come true. But you always had such wonderful taste. The photographs were superb." Her voice dropped in awe as she looked at him adoringly through her sunglasses, obviously hinting she hoped to be invited to see it.

Rex leaned back and listened as she chattered. His brow knitted when she dropped the names of famous people she used to know, making it seem as if she still moved in the same fast-paced, moneyed society that had taken her up in the early Seventies when she had been wild, beautiful and the wife of a successful musician. He refrained from tapping his fingers on the table, his mind leaping ahead.

"What an interesting ring," she said suddenly peering at the cornelian ring stamped with the pentacle, which he wore on the middle finger of his right hand. "What kind of metal is that?"

"I'm not sure. It was a gift," he said.

"Is there such a thing as black gold?" she asked. "I'm thinking of getting into jewelry with a girlfriend of mine. Really big stuff, you know, one-of-a-kind pieces. She went out to India a while ago and brought back all these absolutely marvelous things, old silver and amber jewelry, coral, that sort of thing.''

"What a good idea.''

They stopped talking while the waiter came to take their order. Then Mandy went back eagerly to the same subject. "The thing is, the jewelry idea would take a bit of capital to start off. I'll do anything to get out of this boring job as a receptionist that I'm doing at the moment.''

Rex mumbled politely: "Tell me about what you've been doing.''

"Well, I tried to interest Owen in going in with me on the jewelry, but you know Owen. He's become so cautious, so dull. Very different from when we used to know him. Still, I shouldn't complain,'' she said with a tight little smile.

Rex raised an eyebrow. "Do you and Owen still see a lot of each other?''

"We're still good friends.'' She avoided Rex's eyes at this question, which pricked her conscience because she had been avoiding Owen since she had had supper with him in March. Then, to her surprise, he had wanted to talk about the trip they once made through France on their way home to England from St. Tropez, and not, as she had supposed, about money.

"Of course, I'm the first to admit Owen's been very generous to me, and he still is. But he treats me like a little girl. He won't help me out by putting up enough so I could get my teeth into something. So it means I can never really stand on my own two feet. I know I could succeed in something big if I had the chance. I have the drive and the contacts. You know, Rex, sometimes I think Owen wants me to be dependent on him forever.''

"It could be,'' Rex said with an absent nod. "Yes, Owen's changed.''

"Have you seen him lately?'' Mandy asked, surprised. She put a cigarette between her lips and Rex leaned forward with his lighter.

"Not for a while.''

"You remember what he used to be like. He was so crazy in the old days, so unpredictable. Do you remember that time we went to Stonehenge and watched the sun come up and drank champagne?'' she said with a wistful laugh.

"I hear he's very successful now. Who would ever have thought he'd go into plastics? It's sad, really. I always thought it was such a pity he didn't make it with his music. Still, I suppose one has to earn a living."

"It's a great shame that you two fell out over that stupid chalice thing. You were such close friends. He treated you very badly, Rex. I'm the first one to admit that. I mean, after all, you bled yourself dry to give him a thousand pounds to show how sorry you were. I was shocked at his behavior because, after all, he only paid sixty pounds for the damn thing. You behaved like a gentleman, Rex, and I'm afraid, well—it sounds disloyal I suppose—but I saw Owen in a different light after that." She paused, sensing what Rex was thinking as he fixed her with his clear blue eyes. "I'll never forget your generosity either."

Rex shrugged. "After all, that's what friends are for. Why shouldn't you have your little commission too? We were all in it together, so to speak."

"Well, it was a lovely thing to do," she said, her eyes misting over. "You knew how broke I was. That hundred pounds you gave me certainly came in handy. In fact, I don't know what I'd have done without it."

"Let's not mention it . . ." he said, his mouth setting grimly at her emotion.

"That's what I like most about you—your generosity. You never forget your friends. Thanks for asking me out to lunch, too. It's sweet of you." She took a gulp of wine.

"Yes, it's too bad about Owen. Still, I tried. I'm glad the two of you remained on good terms," he remarked, wondering just how good.

"Yes, Owen's been very generous to me, really." There was a note of bitterness in her gratitude. "Just between us, though, it gets me down sometimes that he keeps me on such a short leash. Sue—Sue Fisher, a friend of mine—she keeps telling me that I'm much too easygoing and that I should get a good lawyer and take him to the cleaners, because, after all, I didn't get any sort of cash settlement when we got the divorce, only the house, and what he gives me wasn't fixed by court order or anything. The thing is, I'm too softhearted. You can't help being what you are, can you?"

"Weren't you working at Antiquarius, selling Twenties

clothes a while ago?'' Rex asked, bringing her back to the subject he wanted to discuss.

"Yes, but it was incredibly boring. At the moment I'm a receptionist in a developer's office. I'm paid to do nothing but answer the phone and file my nails, but I can't stand it. It doesn't pay beans either.'' She sighed.

When their first course was put before them, Rex casually opened a package of *grissini* and said: "Mandy, we were talking about that chalice a moment ago. By chance, I'm planning a little sojourn in the same part of the world where I believe Owen bought it. It occurred to me that it might be interesting to try to locate that shop. You never know what you might find. I'm always on the lookout for interesting, unusual pieces. Who knows, there might be more where that came from. Can you remember the name of the village?''

Mandy frowned, her wispy blonde hair brushing her cheeks as she shook her head. "God, Rex, that was seventeen years ago.'' The moment she said it, the reminder of time's passage twisted her mouth into a thin line. "You asked me that at the time, didn't you? I couldn't remember then, so I certainly wouldn't remember now.''

"Just a minute—don't be too hasty,'' he said. "Can you remember anything about the village, anything at all, like a church, a ruin . . . ?''

She thought for a moment. "It was a pretty village, but they all looked the same to me. For some reason I remember the hotel had blue shutters. Does that help?'' she asked with a shrug.

He shook his head. "No, I'm afraid not. But tell me, was it a fortified village—you know, with walls around it?''

"Yes, I think it was, because I remember Owen going out for a walk to see the view from some tower or something.''

"Tell me, did you take any pictures?'' Rex asked, his eyes narrowing slightly.

"Pictures? Yes, I think we did.''

"If you had any pictures, there might be some clue in them to the name of the village. Can you try to locate them?''

She cooled suddenly as her mind ticked over. "I'd love to oblige, Rex, but it would take me days and days, and I'm so busy at the moment.''

Rex chuckled, understanding perfectly. "Of course, time

is money, and if you come up with the goods, then naturally we would come to some arrangement . . ."

"How much is it worth to you?" she countered. Her mind was suddenly filled with images of Rex's sumptuous house in Belgravia, his gallery in Mount Street, his country retreat.

"I hadn't really even thought of a figure, Mandy," he replied, perturbed. "I suppose I rather thought you'd do it as a favor."

She gave a little laugh and took out another cigarette. "I'm just like anybody else. I work a lot harder with some incentive." When he snapped his lighter shut, she met his eyes. "How about five thousand?"

Bristling at the confident gleam in her eye, he laughed richly. "My darling girl, I may be known for my extravagance, but that's a bit much for an old snapshot or two, probably out of focus at that. Come on, Mandy, you'd better think again." He sniffed peevishly.

"Well, if it's not worth it, that's up to you, Rex. Because it occurs to me that if I don't find the pictures, I could always ask Owen the name of that village. That's something you couldn't do, could you?" she said with a sweet smile that didn't disguise her deadly seriousness.

Rex shrugged indifferently. "Perhaps he's forgotten too."

"Of course he remembers. He just doesn't want to tell anybody, and it's obvious he has good reason."

"Did he ever say that to you?"

"No, not exactly. But I know it's true. I can read him like a book. Don't forget, I was married to him." Flicking the ash off her cigarette, she nodded. "I can get it out of him easily enough if it happens that I don't have those pictures. Either way, you'll get what you want."

"I'd rather Owen didn't know anything about this. That would be part of our bargain. I suspect he's still bitter and I don't want to stir up the past."

"Why, naturally, Rex."

Rex was leaning forward, staring at her with an eager expression. It was on the tip of her tongue to tell Rex that when she last saw Owen he had talked about that very trip to the south of France, and the chalice.

"All right. In that case, it's a bargain." Slapping down his napkin, he called for the bill, feeling no need to be polite after Mandy's unexpected greed.

She looked at him in astonishment. "But we haven't even finished lunch." She looked round the conservatory packed with interesting people who would linger well into the afternoon.

"Yes, I apologize for cutting this short; but you, my girl, have a job to do and I want you to get right down to it," he said, rising from the table with a chortle. "I'll call you in twenty-four hours."

19

Mandy pushed aside the closed curtain in the bay window of the house in Cresswell Place and looked down at the cobbles streaming with rain, but there was no sign of Rex. She had dressed with particular care in tight studded jeans and a fringed doeskin shirt tied with a silver and turquoise belt. Nervously lighting another cigarette, she put a tape on the deck and flopped down on the couch piled with cushions. Sighing irritably, she dragged an ashtray across the coffee table and looked at her watch. It was nine o'clock and he should have been there by now.

There was a clap of thunder overhead that startled her and caused her Yorkshire terrier to turn in its basket and whimper.

"Come on, Scarlet, come to Mummy," she said absently, patting a cushion. As she inhaled deeply, Mandy wondered if the rain that was now pouring down would keep Rex from coming, guessing he had been held up in traffic returning from Ascot. Leaping up from the couch, she turned up the volume of the stereo to blot out the sound of a party down the mews. Earlier, when she had taken the dog out for a walk, she had passed the guests who had just come from Ladies' Day at Ascot—just the kind of people she couldn't bear—shrieking debutantes in flowery silk dresses, ruddy-faced young stockbrokers in morning coats and top hats. She was acutely aware that all over London people were going to similar parties, but she told herself that she didn't care. It was years since she had been invited to Ascot, or Henley for that matter, and she quelled her bitterness with the thought that a week from today she would be lying on a sunny balcony in Marbella, where she would have magic access to people who liked fun, who had style, cosmopolitan people who knew how to live. She had treated herself to all the latest fashion magazines and had already put together a wardrobe in her head that would look expensive without costing too much money. Picking up a copy of *Vogue,* she turned to a picture of a stunning evening dress in watermelon pink that would display her exercised body to advantage. She mused that it would go perfectly with a bag and some jewelry she already had.

Looking up as she heard a car drive by, she felt an unpleasant twinge of guilt at the sight of the empty bay window where Owen's baby grand piano had been until two weeks ago, when she sold it. It had been the first thing he'd bought with his royalties from "Moody Lady." Chasing away her doubts with bitter self-justification, she asked herself whether she should even bother to replace it, as she had intended. Was such generosity necessary now, she asked herself? She had only been able to get two hundred pounds for it, which just about kept her dealer happy. The five thousand Rex had promised to deliver that night had a pleasant sound to it, but Mandy reasoned she would need it all if she were going to attract the right kind of man, preferably a rich Arab. Dark Middle Easterners had always turned her on and they were attracted to her, too. She knew from experience that they were good lovers and generous with expensive presents. She stubbed out her cigarette, reflecting that if handled skillfully, even playboys might be induced to come up with a wedding ring.

When there was a knock at the door, Mandy leapt up, nervously arranging her shirt. Tossing her head, she crossed the room, her heart beating expectantly. Just before she turned the doorknob she glanced toward the desk to reassure herself that the brown envelope of photographs was still there. Flinging the door wide with a welcoming smile, she gasped.

"Owen—my God, what the hell are you doing here?"

* * *

In a mansion in The Boltons, Baron Philippe de Cazenac and Rex stood silently beneath an enormous chandelier that sent pinpoints of light onto the black-and-white tiled hallway. They watched as guests alighted from their cars and darted to the covered walkway to avoid the downpour that hadn't abated all afternoon. Rex nodded politely to one of the guests, who was giving his top hat to the butler.

"Good evening, Your Highness," he said with an obsequious smile.

"Nice to see you, Rex," said the prince.

Rex and Philippe watched as the prince and his Junoesque wife sauntered through the drawing room to the garden behind the house, where a marquee had been erected. When a servant passed them bearing a tray of flutes of champagne, Rex said quietly to Philippe, "You can have all the Krug you want in about half an hour." Slipping his hand into the pocket of his striped waistcoat, he withdrew a gold and enameled pocket watch. "This is as good a time as any, I should say."

Philippe nervously touched his oyster silk cravat, set with a pearl stickpin. "I'll have to get my raincoat from the car and an umbrella. It's pouring."

"No umbrella," said Rex emphatically. "You might leave it behind."

"*C'est ridicule . . .*" said Philippe angrily under his breath. "Do you think I am stupid?"

"No, dear boy, but you can't be too careful, believe me. When one's blood is up, one is apt to be forgetful. At least the gods have favored us tonight. This little shower is the perfect camouflage. No one will take the slightest notice of you. Courage, my boy, courage," he said with a bright smile, patting Philippe's arm affectionately. "It might be a good idea to take my evening scarf if you're wearing a coat, for reasons we discussed, but whatever you do, don't lose it."

Philippe glanced down the hall as more guests arrived for the party. "Wouldn't it be better if you went with me and waited round the corner in case anything went wrong?"

Anger flared in Rex's eyes for just an instant, like the striking of a match in the dark. "You mustn't weaken now. This is your great opportunity to prove yourself—to Him. Come now, a little stage fright is normal.'' He sweetened his displeasure with a reassuring smile. "Now go on, and be quick or there won't be any Beluga left. You know how all these freeloaders fall on it like a pack of starving dogs.''

Philippe nodded and propelled himself down the hall, straightening his shoulders beneath the morning coat he had ordered from Savile Row especially for Ascot Week. With a glance over his shoulder, he saw Rex had already disappeared. Pretending to straighten his cravat before a mirror, he spied a glass of champagne behind a bank of flowers. Philippe's hand darted out and he bolted it in one gulp.

He walked down the steps, where cars were delivering their passengers. Before stepping into the rain, he touched his breast pocket for the hundredth time that night to make sure the silver cigar case was still there. Then his hand moved to the bundle in the other pocket.

Mandy froze at the threshold of the door as she barred the way to Owen, whose red BMW she could see parked outside the house.

"I'm sorry, you can't come in. I'm expecting a boyfriend." She began to close the door, but Owen pushed it forward to get out of the rain.

"Come on, Mandy, I'm getting soaked. I'll only stay for a minute. Let me in.''

Before she could protest he had moved past her. "Jesus, what a downpour,'' he said, running his hand through his wet hair and brushing the shoulders of his light summer jacket. His hands froze as he noticed the empty bay window. He looked accusingly at Mandy.

"What the hell have you done with my piano?''

She looked at him blankly. "Oh, I had a party and somebody spilled a drink on it. I sent it off to be repolished. Listen, Owen, I'm expecting somebody any minute, so would you please go. Whatever you want, we can talk about it tomorrow.''

Still staring at the empty bay window, Owen didn't notice the desperation in her voice.

"For God's sake, Mandy. Do you really expect me to believe that you sent it off to be polished? They could come and do that at the house. And anyway, since when were you so concerned about my piano? You sold it to pay for that god-damn habit of yours, didn't you? Didn't you?'' Anger ripped through him as he saw her looking insolently back at him, her arms folded as she leaned against the door.

Heaving her shoulders back, she sighed. "All right, it's pointless to deny it. I did sell it. I needed money. So what's so new about that, anyway? I always need money,'' she cried shrilly.

"For your coke dealer, that's what you needed it for, admit it. You promised me you'd stay off it after that rehab. You were doing so well. What for, why? What's the point?'' The anger smoldering in him turned to exasperation. He felt sickened, stunned by her deviousness, her weakness, which always seemed a kind of personal betrayal.

"Do you really want to know what for, Owen? Because I'm tired of being treated like your ward, you paying the gas bill, the electricity bill and then giving me an allowance. Thank you very much, sir, I'm so grateful, sir,'' she said with a mock curtsy. "Yes, I sold that stupid piano because I needed money for myself, for the things you don't think about, like a sun bed, my hair and exercise classes. Things that women need to look good. Do you think I want to come crawling to you to ask for that, well, do you?'' she shrieked. "Now get out, I'm expecting somebody. You've already made me look like hell and spoiled my evening.'' Tears streaming down her face, she sobbed: "As for the damn piano, I was going to buy you another one, something better than that old piece of junk.''

Her gibe cut deep, making him feel ashamed of himself. He reached out for her, but she pulled away.

"I would have given you more money. All you have to do is ask. You know why I ask you to keep accounts, to tell me what you do with your money. We've been through all that. If you're going to stay off the stuff, it's no good putting temptation in your way. You were the one who said: 'Pay my bills so I won't be tempted.' Didn't you say that? Anyway, you have your credit cards. As long as you don't go over the limits we set and I know where the money goes, I don't mind. Is that so unreasonable?''

She let out a dry sob and dabbed at her eyes. "Christ, Owen, you can't put a sun bed treatment on American Express. And why do we have to talk about this now, for God's sake?'' She moved the curtain aside and looked down at the glistening cobbles.

He turned to go, glancing at the cluttered pine desk in a corner of the room. Seeing a brochure on Marbella, he reached for it and asked: ''What's this?''

Mandy snatched up the brown envelope lying nearby and slipped it into a drawer. ''You don't have to be so bloody nosy. I can dream, can't I?''

''Don't change the subject. What is this thing from the travel agent? It says here, departure 14 June—an open booking. And you're staying for a month and renting a flat. What about your job? You just started a new job. What the hell is going on?''

''It's nothing. Actually, it's none of your business,'' she said, flaring up again.

''Not my business? You're throwing away a good job to go to Marbella. Coke, unemployment—Christ, here we go again.''

''What the hell do you care, anyway? A guy's taking me and he's paying for it. It's my life and I can do what I want.''

''I got you the job in the first place. I stuck my neck out for you. You've only been at it a month. I'm not going to let you do this, Mandy. If you don't cancel this trip, then you can forget about any more help from me. This time I mean it.''

''Fuck the job, and do what you bloody well like,'' she said with a defiant toss of her head. ''It's all a dead end, anyway. I'm not going to throw away a chance for a new life, to start again. And if you don't get out of here now, you're going to fuck it up for me, the way you fucked up my whole life before. Now get out, get out,'' she screamed hysterically, flailing her fists on his shoulder.

Looking at her face contorted with hatred couldn't extinguish Owen's anguish at her wasted life and his own pathetic helplessness. His head down, he started for the door before he said or did anything he might regret. Slamming it violently behind him, he got into the car and revved the engine furiously, then accelerated down the mews, making the wheels spin on the cobbles. He stared ahead at the blurred ribbons of light on the wet road as he drove down the long mews, feeling numb. The painful image of Mandy as she had been at nineteen came unbidden to his mind. He had met her in a pub in Oxford when she was fresh from secretarial college. The memory of her innocent beauty was instantly tarnished by the reality of that same face ravaged by years of hard living. He felt burdened by guilt for his own strength, which seemed to magnify her weakness. She had been sucked into the way of life he had created, then discarded when it offered him nothing more. Owen knew that as long as he lived his conscience would always suffer guilt at what she had become. No matter what she did, he would always feel a sense of moral obligation to that sweet girl Mandy had once been, the child-woman who had made him happy for a time. He cruelly compared the willowy blonde with a heart-shaped face and cornflower blue eyes to the woman who had screamed at him moments ago, telling himself that if they had never met, Mandy would probably have stayed in Banbury. She would have married an ordinary man with ordinary ambitions who would have made her happy and given her children.

He braked at the end of the mews, his anger completely dissipated as he thought of Mandy snorting a line of coke and taking a stiff drink the minute he had gone. He started to back up the car, looking over his shoulder. He wouldn't stay for more than a moment, only ring the doorbell and say he was sorry, tell her he would call her tomorrow. Half-way back down the mews he lifted his foot off the accelerator when he caught a glimpse of a man in a raincoat standing at Mandy's front door. Owen quickly put the car into first gear, hoping that whoever the man was, he hadn't seen him leave. He sped back down the mews before Mandy could open the door, wondering if the man standing on her doorstep would be the answer to all her prayers; but he told himself it was unlikely if he was taking her to Marbella, a playground for hustlers and people on the make.

Driving through South Kensington, he thought about his violent reaction to Mandy's sale of his piano, which now seemed puerile. He realized he should never have left it with her in the first place and admitted for the first time why he had never been able to part with it or store it in his own flat. Every time he looked at it, it would have been a reminder of his own failure. He felt a sense of relief now he was rid of

it. It would no longer dominate the bay window of the house
where he and Mandy had once been happy; it would no longer
be there to mock him. But he was struck by the cruel
irony that so many years after he had composed "Moody
Lady" on the baby grand, Mandy had sold it to buy drugs.

Owen smiled grimly to himself as the windshield wipers
moved furiously before his eyes. Realizing how tightly his
hands gripped the steering wheel, he consciously relaxed
them, reflecting on why he had gone to see Mandy in the
first place. Somewhere in her chaotic cupboards were photographs of the summer of '71, when it had all gone wrong.
Tomorrow, or the day after, when she had cooled down, he
would ask Mandy to look for them. He wanted them in his
own possession, just for good measure.

Mandy had just snorted a line of coke in the bathroom and
was about to pull herself together when she heard the doorbell.

"Shit," she muttered, splashing water frantically on her
face, then peering at her eyes in the mirror, noticing they
were blurred by crying. Taking a tissue, she dabbed at her
streaked mascara and hurriedly applied a coat of lip gloss.

"I'm coming, I'm coming," she called, racing down the
stairs. Pushing up her sleeves, she opened the door with a
welcoming smile, which faded when she saw a stranger
standing there. The moment she saw his face she knew he
couldn't be English, even though the morning coat under his
mackintosh told her he had just come from Ascot.

"Mandy Morgan?"

"Yes?" she asked suspiciously, registering the fact that he
was not bad looking.

"Mr. Monckton sends his apologies. He was unable to
keep his appointment with you this evening, but he asked me
to come in his place." He hesitated a second. "My name is
Philippe de Cazenac. I'm a friend and colleague of his." He
inclined his head politely and gave her an appreciative once-
over that made a pleasant impression on her.

"Oh, I see," she said, breaking into a smile. "Do come
in, please. Has the rain stopped finally?" she asked brightly.

Philippe's eyes swept round the room as he stood poised

on the balls of his feet, taking in the details of the house. All
his nervousness had evaporated.

"Rex asked me to deliver this to you." He took out a
sealed envelope. "He told me you would have something to
give me in exchange."

Mandy moved to the pine desk and took out the envelope,
conscious of Philippe's eyes on her. "It's all here, exactly
what he wanted. There's even a picture with a signpost that
tells the name of the village. But you probably don't know
what I'm talking about." Facing Philippe, envelope in hand,
she hesitated. She didn't want him to leave before she had
counted the money, but she also didn't want to appear suspicious. Reading her mind, he said tactfully.

"Perhaps you'd like to check what's in the envelope first,
to see that it's in order. I will wait if you like."

"Perhaps I should," she said casually, as if it didn't really
matter. "I'll just pop into the kitchen, where the light is
better." She took the envelope. "I won't be a minute," she
called over her shoulder.

Turning her back to the door, she ripped open the envelope
with shaking hands. Her stomach leapt as her fingers brushed
the thick pile of fifty-pound notes bound by bands of pink
paper. Her shoulders hunched, she flicked quickly through
them, enjoying the little rustle they made.

The lamp overhead made an aureole of light round Mandy's blonde hair as she bent forward. She was so absorbed
in counting the money that she didn't hear him creep up behind her. He reached out swiftly and looped the scarf around
her neck, giving it a violent tug that pulled her backward.
Taken by surprise, she emitted a soft gurgle as she fell against
his chest. Philippe was surprised how little she struggled as
her hands tugged at the scarf and she gasped for breath.
Swiftly securing the scarf in one hand, he withdrew the syringe from his pocket with the other and plunged it into the
cleft of her arm. Feeling the jab of the needle, she writhed
unexpectedly. He lost his balance for a moment, causing the
needle to fly out of his hand. He watched it skid across the
kitchen floor as she collapsed, her body sliding downward in
one fluid movement, almost gracefully. When she lay at his
feet, he could see she was unconscious. One look at the syringe told him he had already injected what was probably a

fatal dose. He decided it was too dangerous to try again, so he polished his fingerprints from the syringe with his handkerchief and pressed her fingers around it. The strident ringing of a telephone in the kitchen broke his concentration and, looking up, he saw it was in the shape of a large plastic banana. He whispered contemptuously to himself: *"C'est absurde"* as he leaned down to pick up the sheaf of banknotes and stuffed it into his pocket. Grabbing his scarf, he then picked up the envelope containing the photographs and tore it open, pausing only long enough to make sure of the contents. Crushing the envelope that had contained the money, he stuffed it into his pocket and looked round, satisfied he had forgotten nothing. Then he left the house.

Moments later, after he had dropped his raincoat in the car, Philippe strode unhurriedly up the stairs of the grand house in The Boltons.

"The rain has finally stopped hasn't it, sir?" remarked the uniformed doorman.

"It would seem so," Philippe replied, confident the man hadn't remembered him.

He walked at a leisurely pace through the house, then into the crowded marquee ringing with conversation. As he was sipping a glass of champagne, Rex came quietly to his side. Philippe's habitual bland expression had been wiped away by a flush of excitement. When they had moved out of earshot, Rex muttered: "You look like a schoolboy who has just scored his first goal."

Philippe shrugged almost bashfully as he searched for the words to express himself.

"It was an extraordinary experience. How do you say, orgasmic. Quite unlike what I expected."

"I can see from your face that it went off as planned."

He shrugged. "It was very simple, really."

"No complications?"

"No, none. Oh, the telephone rang just as I was leaving, but it was over by then."

"Good, good. Very well done, old chap. You've got the money and the photographs?"

He nodded. "She said they were just what you wanted."

"I can't wait to see them," Rex said keenly, surveying the crowd. "Perhaps we should have another glass to celebrate and then bid goodnight to our host and hostess. You must be very tired after all that exertion.''

''Not at all. On the contrary,'' Philippe whispered jubilantly. ''I feel on fire, as if I'm about to explode.''

''You see? What did I tell you? When the moment comes to act, the Power comes to your assistance. It makes heroes out of cowards—not that you're a coward, dear boy. I'm enormously pleased for you—and for us. After all, we're partners.''

In a confidential tone Philippe said: ''Now it's all over, I can admit to you that I was nervous to begin with.''

''That's because you thought you were alone and unaided. The fear goes when you've been touched by the Power.'' He looked steadily at Philippe, an almost envious sparkle in his eyes. ''If you're in the mood, as a special treat I'll take you to a club I know in Soho to see an amusing little floor show that I doubt if you've ever seen before, even in Paris.''

20

Parking his car on a leafy street lined with terraced houses, Owen walked quickly toward the Chelsea police station in Lucan Place. All his thoughts turned on the call he had received at the office that morning.

In the reception area, he glanced at a punk with yellow spiky hair staring sullenly at the ceiling and a small worried-looking elderly woman bundled up in a warm coat even though it was a sultry summer's day. He addressed the sergeant behind the desk.

''I'm here to see Detective Superintendent Chapman in CID.''

He waited tensely on the edge of a chair, staring at his scuffed shoes, until he was called through by the detective, a burly auburn-haired Irishman with a thin set mouth.

''Mr. Morgan? This way, please,'' he said, leading him

down a corridor. When he closed the door behind them, Owen said anxiously:

"Any word from the hospital?"

The detective pulled up a chair and gestured for Owen to sit down. "No, nothing yet." Taking up a pad and pencil, he began to scribble. "She's still in intensive care. It's touch and go."

He switched on the tape recorder on the desk.

"Then there's still hope." Resting his elbows on the desk, Owen waited for the officer to finish writing. When he looked up, Owen said, "I've been in a state of shock since you phoned me. Can you tell me more?"

"We're treating the incident as an overdose. What I'd like to know is how long your ex-wife has been addicted to heroin and what was her daily intake?"

Owen looked him directly in the eye. "First of all, let me make it clear. Mandy isn't a heroin addict. That's one thing I can say for certain. She's done a lot of drugs in her time, but she has never touched heroin."

"That tallies with what the doctor said. There was no evidence of needle marks on her body, but the thing is, there's always a first time."

"There's no way she would have overdosed, no way in hell. I know her better than anybody."

The detective scratched his head. "You seem very sure. I'm afraid that at the moment it looks like a straight case of OD, unless you have reason to think otherwise."

"I haven't been told yet who found her."

"A friend of hers called Sue Fisher. About eleven this morning she went to the house—apparently she had made an arrangement with your ex-wife to drop by at that time. Mrs. Fisher said there was no answer when she rang the bell repeatedly, but the dog was howling, which made her suspicious. Looking through a window, she saw Mrs. Morgan lying on the kitchen floor, so she rang the neighbor's bell and called the police. Mrs. Fisher gave us your name and the name of Mrs. Morgan's mother in Oxfordshire. An ambulance came immediately and took her to the nearest hospital, where she was said to be in critical condition. Now, I'd like to get back to what you were saying earlier. Do you have any reason to suppose foul play was involved?"

"If she didn't OD, I can't think of any other explanation."

"When was the last time you saw her?"

"Last night, about nine. I dropped by to see her. She was waiting for somebody and she was anxious to get rid of me. We quarreled and I left in a huff."

The detective raised an eyebrow. "You quarreled? What did you quarrel about?"

"It's immaterial. It was over a piano she sold without telling me. That and other things. She had left her job and was going off to Marbella."

"Alone?"

"She said some man had invited her."

"And then what happened?"

"I lost my temper because she left the job I had found for her. I accused her of selling my piano to pay her coke dealer."

"Any idea who he is?"

"All I know is that he's from Brixton. I shouldn't think he would be hard to trace, as I've no doubt he supplies her friends living nearby. She would never admit to me that she was still on coke because she was afraid I'd cut off her maintenance. I wouldn't, of course. I have always felt responsible for her, and she knew deep down that I wouldn't do it. She was very upset and kept saying I should go because she was waiting for somebody. After I slammed the door, I drove down the mews thinking about the things I had said, and then decided to go back."

"What time was that?"

"It was just after nine, because I looked at my watch."

"Go on."

"When I reversed the car, I saw a man standing at the door, probably the one she was expecting, so I drove off. This morning I tried to call her, but couldn't get through. I just assumed she didn't want to be disturbed. It never occurred to me she was lying there . . ." He broke off, ridden with guilt and anxiety. "But who could have done it? Why?"

"Mr. Morgan, to get back to your argument. It has been ascertained that there was cocaine in her bloodstream as well as enough heroin to kill her. What do you have to say to that?"

"As I said, I suspected she was on coke again. That's one

of the things we argued about. But not heroin, never. She's seen too many people OD.''

"Would you say your ex-wife was a happy, stable woman?''

"No,'' he admitted.

"Then she might have had reason to take something stronger than coke, even though it might seem out of character to you.''

"I suppose so.''

"Did you try to stop her taking drugs?''

"Of course I did. As a matter of fact, that's one of the things that came up in the argument. I've tried to help her, but I've stayed out of that part of her life because it sickens me.''

After asking for more details about their marriage and present relationship and Mandy's job history, the detective said, "Let's get back to that man you said you saw standing at the door. Did you actually see him ring the doorbell?''

"No, but he was standing in front of the door under the carriage lamp. All I could see was his raincoat and the back of his head.''

"Height?''

"It's hard to say. Not tall, not short. Medium height.''

"Build?''

"The same.''

"And what color was he?''

"White.''

"You're sure?''

"Definitely.''

When the detective asked for a description, Owen shook his head. "All I can say is that he was white and male.''

The detective finished writing, then tapped his pencil on the pad. "It's not much to go on. But at the moment I don't think this changes anything. Until we can identify this man and interview him, there's nothing more we can do. There's no case.''

Owen felt the detective was looking at him with a mixture of pity for being mixed up with Mandy, and suspicion that he hadn't told him everything.

Rising to indicate the interview was over, the detective said, "We'll be in touch if there's anything. And if you think of any leads, we'd appreciate it.'' The tone of his voice suggested he thought it was unlikely that anything more would come of it, that Mandy Morgan was like any number of once beautiful, disappointed women with no husband, no children and no future, whose lives were made temporarily sweeter by drugs.

Before turning to leave, Owen asked, "What did Sue Fisher say? Did she have anything to add?"

"Very little. She was upset, of course, and glad she had found her in time, but apparently she and your ex-wife don't see each other very often, so she couldn't throw any light on the situation."

"I see," said Owen, knowing now what his next destination would be.

Twenty minutes later, after dropping by the hospital, where he was told there was no change in Mandy's condition, Owen went to the south side of Redcliffe Square, where he rang the bell of Sue Fisher's flat.

When she answered the intercom, he said: "Sue, it's Owen. Can I come up and talk to you?"

There was silence for a moment. "All right. Come in."

He climbed the stairs to her flat to see her standing at the door wrapped in a long white bath sheet and a turban, her exposed shoulders glistening from her massage.

"Come on in," she said. "Elaine is just leaving."

Entering the pretty flat flooded with light, he saw an aromatherapist packing her satchel. A powerful bouquet of scented oils filled the room as he waited until Sue had closed the door behind the girl.

"Sit down," she said, nodding toward a chintz-covered sofa near the open double doors that led to the plant-filled balcony. He had never been in Sue's flat before, having met her only a few times. The ex-wife of a city tycoon, with plenty of money of her own, Owen considered her a bad influence on Mandy. She was tall and dark, with a sharp little face, and he imagined she spent long afternoons drinking white wine, when she wasn't at the hairdresser's or the masseuse, or shopping at Harvey Nichols. He looked around at the chintz festoons, the big sofas piled with cushions, the antique chests and the bric-à-brac. It was easy to see how

Mandy had come to nourish the illusion that she ought to live in the same style.

"Glass of wine?" Sue called from the doorway.

He looked at his watch. It was three o'clock—too early for a drink. But he needed one.

"Thanks."

She brought two long-stemmed glasses brimming with white wine and set them on the pink marble coffee table. Hitching up the bath sheet, she sat in the chair opposite him, her bare, tanned shoulders resting against the back of the lime green chair.

"I just came from the police station."

"I gave them your name as next of kin, as well as Mandy's mother. Of course I didn't have her number, so luckily I remembered the name of your company and that it was in Swindon. Poor Mandy, I don't know what drove her to this. She had so much on her mind. So many worries, so many troubles."

He looked at her critically. There was a note of insinuation in her voice, as though she felt he was at fault.

"Why did you tell the police you don't know each other that well, Sue? You two talk to one another at least once a day."

"What was the point? I don't want to get deeply involved. Thank God I found her, but there's nothing more I can say. I don't know why she did it. It's all very sad, very pathetic, but what can one do?"

Looking at her narrowly, Owen wondered if she knew more than she was telling. He decided not to mention his stubborn conviction that Mandy had been the victim of a vicious attack. He said:

"You knew she was planning to go to Marbella. Who with?"

"I haven't any idea. She didn't tell me," Sue said coolly, tightening her turban.

"I find that hard to believe. Come on, Sue, Mandy can never keep a secret. If she told anyone, she'd tell you."

She leaned forward and took a cigarette from a sharkskin-covered box. Lighting it, she looked at him thoughtfully.

"There's no guy as such who was taking her to Marbella.

She was going by herself. I told her I might join her, if I could.''

"By herself? Who the hell was going to pay for it?''

"That's just it. She told me a few days ago that she had something that someone wanted very badly and was willing to pay a lot of money for.''

"Who?'' he asked, completely mystified.

"Owen, I'll tell you this *entre nous,* but I'll deny it if you tell the police because I don't want to get mixed up in all this, if I'm right. I don't like him or some of the people he runs round with.''

"Who?''

"Rex Monckton.''

"Are you saying she was waiting for Rex Monckton?''

"Yes, that's what I'm saying.''

"Rex Monckton,'' Owen repeated to himself, as if he didn't believe what he had heard.

"I don't know why, but I've never cared for him. I don't like those creepy blue eyes of his. They give me the shivers. He's a weirdo. I told her to stay away from him. There've been some peculiar rumors about him. Oh, not about his sex life—he seems sexless, if you ask me. He has some strange interests—ritual magic, or something like that, somebody told me. It would explain a lot, wouldn't it? They say there's a room in his house he uses for the purpose.''

Owen frowned disapprovingly. "I wouldn't believe everything you hear.'' He remembered what Dorothy had said.

"From what Mandy told me, you're no friend of his.''

Owen wasn't listening. "She hasn't seen Rex Monckton in years. She's nothing as far as he's concerned.''

"Don't ask me. All I know is that they had lunch at La Meridiana a week ago. That's when it all started. She didn't exactly tell me it was Rex who was willing to pay for something she had, but I put two and two together when she started saying her ship had finally come in. She hinted it was something to do with him. All I really know is that she was planning to have the money in her hands last night; she told me that much. We were going to go shopping together, then have lunch—her treat. I promise you I don't know any more.''

"Monckton, Monckton,'' Owen repeated, turning the

name round and round in his mind, trying to make sense of it all.

Sue looked at him curiously, as though seeing him for the first time. He had a rumpled look that only a certain kind of man could get away with. His blue shirt was frayed at the collar and he hadn't shaved closely enough, but the brooding expression in his eyes was somehow very attractive. Clutching her turban, Sue leaned over to put on a tape, something soothing.

"Poor baby," she said with a languid sigh. "She was planning to meet Sheikh Right and sail off into the Saudi sunset. Poor, poor baby . . ."

When Sue turned round, Owen had drained his glass and was looking at his watch. "Thanks for your help," he said rising. "What you've just told me could be the answer."

Morning sun flooded the terrace of Louise's cottage, where she was sitting over a cup of coffee in the shade of the fig tree. She propped her bare brown arms on the round metal table as she read a letter from Dorothy Lethbridge. In a gossamer-like scrawl on blue paper, Dorothy confirmed her arrival the following week with Ambrose, in time for Bastille Day. Louise had had no news from her for nearly a month and felt happy to know they were finally coming to Languedoc, but the last paragraph of the letter, dashed off in haste, put her in a turmoil. Louise sipped her coffee, trying to imagine how she would feel about seeing Owen Morgan after all that time. According to Dorothy's letter, he intended to follow them down by car and planned to stay for a fortnight. Louise thought for a moment, feeling her stomach contract in apprehension. She leaned back in her chair with a frown, perturbed that his plans could still affect her state of mind so dramatically. A month ago she had known she wanted to see him again—badly. Now she wasn't sure. The strange dream she had had in California faded with time, though it still haunted her, and now Dorothy's letter had churned up feelings about Owen that had disturbed her then. She had thought of writing him a note, but pride stood in her way. It was better, she thought, to leave things as they were. She had convinced herself that if he wanted her, he should be the one to make the first move.

For the past month she had been immersed in the plant lore Maurice Roussel had collected over half a century. On the morning after her arrival in Puivaillon she had made the decision to offer herself as his assistant. She remembered clearly how she had awakened at first light, filled with a strong premonition. She and Roussel had talked late into the night under the pergola overlooking his herb garden. Lulled by his rich voice and the sound of cicadas, she had known that their encounter was a rare meeting of minds that cut across cultural and language barriers. Bathed in the warm sun under the fig tree the next morning, in the same spot where she was sitting now, she had realized that working with Maurice would be a justification for her desire to stay in Puivaillon as long as she wanted. She wouldn't be a tourist; she would be a writer. Everything seemed to have fallen miraculously into place. Fate had conveniently provided a much more compelling reason for remaining in Languedoc than merely her own amusement.

Folding Dorothy's letter, Louise reflected on how she had come to France to idle away the summer under a tree with a book in her hand, but instead found she was pouring herself into a new project with great enthusiasm, fulfilling all her hopes for those blank months of freedom in a way that was completely different from what she had expected. She had all but forgotten about her failed marriage and her business. She rose at dawn with the birds and went to bed when the sky was still a deep midnight blue, exhausted but content. When she was free, she drove to Montségur for the day with a picnic. She usually ate her lunch on top of the crumbling citadel, enjoying the snow-capped mountains and rolling green pastures while she thought about nothing in particular. She was able to put the disturbing episode of the day when she had visited the citadel with Owen out of her mind. Nowadays all she felt there was peace, a deep, deep peace.

On weekends she took to exploring the countryside around Puivaillon. She discovered the sensual beauty of the isolated hills where buttercups, horsetail and knotgrass rooted themselves in the rocky soil. She soon discovered that the folds of the mountains behind Puivaillon concealed a wild gorge, where she went to collect plants. It made her knees go weak to look down the deep chasm bordering the road. Yet the place fascinated her and she returned several times to experience the wild, heart-pounding terror bordering on pleasure that the isolated spot induced. Sometimes, while gathering gentian or rosemary, she would pause to look and listen, sensing an aura she couldn't explain. But the whispering in her ears was only the rush of the river at the bottom of the gorge or the wind sweeping through the broom. Unable to shake off the feeling that she had had a brush with danger, she would go back to Puivaillon exhilarated but relieved to return to the safety of the village. Yet she always left knowing she would revisit the gorge another day.

During all those weeks of exploring the countryside, of work and study, Louise was watching, waiting for something to happen. If she tried to bring it into focus, it eluded her, like a cobweb brushing a pane of glass. But it was there, quivering, like a storm trembling on the horizon on a bright summer's day; and it seemed to be coming closer.

Later that day Louise looked at Maurice Roussel over a typewriter surrounded by books and papers, which covered the long table. They had been working every day in the shade of the vine-covered terrace that skirted the back of his house. Shaded from the hot afternoon sun, she was continually inspired by the variegated greens of Maurice's herb garden. The warm air, heavy with the scent of aromatic plants, wafted over the terrace and filled her with a vague longing that interrupted her concentration. The lacy shadows moving on the paper in front of her, the droning bees swarming over the lavender bushes, made her eyelids heavy for a moment.

Stifling a yawn, she looked at Maurice's bowed white head as he read the page she had just typed. "I shouldn't have had that rosé for lunch. It was very bad of me, when we have so much to do."

Maurice looked over his spectacles. "Take some advice from me. A little bit of what's bad for you is sometimes a very good thing."

"Who said that?"

"I did," he said proudly, "and it's true."

She laughed and jotted it down on a pad. "I know exactly the place for that remark—in the introduction." Nodding to the tortoiseshell cat curled up on the chair and warming her flanks in the sun, she added, "Josephine has the right idea, don't you think?"

"The siesta is an established tradition. You should have a nap after your lunch like me. It would do you good."

"Couldn't," she said, a pencil between her teeth. "Too much to do." All the same, she secretly enjoyed Maurice's paternal way of scolding her, and it meant more to her than she would care to admit. *"Bien*—let's concentrate on the plant remedies in the appendix first, shall we?"

"As you wish," he nodded, flipping through the list of major herbal remedies to be included in his book, which she had typed up the previous evening.

"Allergies," she murmured, typing the heading. "You must have a lot to say on allergies. They appeared constantly when I was going through your records."

"I don't know how you made head or tail of my card files. Sometimes I can't even read them myself. But to tell you the truth, I no longer find it necessary to refer to them."

She glanced at the yellowed cards packed into specially made boxes that encompassed Maurice's fifty years of healing. "It seems to me after going through those that we'll need two headings, one for chronic allergies and the other for seasonal ones."

"On the other hand, we don't want to be confusing, do we? Linden, hawthorn, greater celandine, broom, sage and, yes, couch grass in varying formulas. Don't forget garlic. We must have garlic." Taking a pencil, he corrected the formula.

"While you're looking at those notes, I'll just add the opening paragraph you prepared." She typed, translating as she went:

To make up these preparations from plants, it is necessary that the plants be picked and dried exactly according to the instructions below and that each, whether flower, bud, capsule, stem or leaf, should be crushed with care, between the hands, in the case of delicate plants, or in a mortar.

She would polish it up later.

"Now, allergies," Maurice began thoughtfully. "Let me dictate a little paragraph that includes some sensible advice as well as the formula. One shouldn't consume vinegar, for example, and be moderate with wine . . ." Louise took down what he was saying, editing out any mistakes and repetitions as she went. She looked at him expectantly as she typed, suddenly feeling wide awake. The urge to sleep the afternoon away had passed and she was now full of vitality. Watching him read over his notes, she remembered sitting in the same spot where they were now working, breathing in the scent of lavender and listening to the cicadas while sipping an aperitif.

"Maurice," she had begun hesitantly—after all, they had only just met—"what would you say if I offered to stay here and help you, become your assistant while I'm here, helping you sort through all your material?"

"I would be amazed," he answered simply. He gave her a long appraising look. "Are you really serious?"

"I've never been more serious in all my life."

"Do you mean in English or French?"

"English. I would translate everything from French. That's where your market is, in the States. Of course, no doubt it would be published in French, too. We could do two manuscripts if you like," she said casually, wanting nothing to stand in the way.

"Then why not? *Salut,*" he said with a smile as he raised his glass.

That night they talked about the shape the book might take. Feeling Maurice's enthusiasm, the ideas flowed from her.

"I think the one way to illustrate the incredible knowledge you have of the use of medicinal plants would be to focus on your life as a country doctor in the Languedoc, don't you?"

"That's not quite what I've got in mind," he had replied, humorously indulging her. "We would have to work in French, of course. My mind would run better that way. Otherwise I would always be searching for words."

Knowing she was diving in head first, Louise had replied, "It will be quite a challenge to translate your vivid turn of phrase into English prose." She was thinking that the finished product would have to be refreshingly direct and simple, just like the personality of Roussel himself. She, Louise Carey, who had never done more than write reports or letters home, had committed herself to writing a book. "I was thinking: I have an old school friend who is a literary agent in New York. She might be of some help," she said, her mind running ahead.

When they agreed to collaborate, Louise had been so excited by the prospect that she had driven to Carcassonne the very next day to buy a tape recorder so as not to miss a syllable of the wisdom Maurice imparted when they talked about his experiences as a doctor and about his herbal cures. After two weeks of sifting through the mountain of files and notes he had collected, she had conceived a mental blueprint of the finished product.

When she had distilled the essence of the book down to a ten-page synopsis, Louise had written to her old friend in New York. She was careful to underplay to Maurice the magnitude of her hopes. He was living contentedly in the private world he had created and she had no wish to disturb him. He was, after all, she told herself, a country man with his feet firmly planted in the soil, and he might turn his back on the cut and thrust of publishing a book if it proved to be too demanding.

The agent had accepted the ten-page proposal with alacrity and now, at the beginning of July, they were waiting to hear further news. The speed with which it had happened confirmed that Louise's instincts had been right. If she ever found herself remarking that it had seemed so easy, she remembered she had been only the catalyst in a man's life's work, achieved over five decades.

"I think we should do an entire chapter on the uses of the greater celandine, don't you? It has so many applications," mused Maurice when they had been working for two hours. The shadows had now lengthened in the garden, sending waves of cool air onto the terrace.

"Maybe not an entire chapter, but we could emphasize its importance," she agreed. She had learned by now that he was a man with very strong views, who could be guided in the right direction if she was tactful and explained her reasoning. Reading over what she had typed, partly in English, partly in French, Louise was always critical of her work. The surprising discovery that she was fascinated by plant lore kept her from ever flagging. Though she had been raised in a city, she discovered she had an unexpected aptitude for the subject. She was at ease with it, comfortable, she realized, which contrasted with her complete lack of interest in her own garden at home. Always too busy to spare the time, she had left it all to the Mexican gardener. She had been content to glory in its lushness from afar, without lifting a finger. Now she sometimes dreamed of the names of the plants that had begun to reveal their secrets: shepherd's purse, corn poppy, broom, melissa, Roman camomile, yellow gentian, meadowsweet. They were like poetry to her and as she gradually learned to identify them, her senses were inundated with their textures and scents, which she filed away in her mind, waiting to unlock the power of each one. The beams in her kitchen were now hung with the dried plants she had collected herself and was making into preparations under Maurice's direction.

"And what about plant legends and plants in mythology? Couldn't we have a chapter on those, too?" asked Maurice in a tone of voice that indicated he had already made up his mind.

"I hope there will be room," Louise said cautiously, knowing that if he had his way the manuscript would grow to an unmanageable size. "We have to leave plenty of material in case we want to write a sequel," she added, making him laugh.

"A sequel? Listen to you!" he scoffed, but she could see he was pleased at her confidence. "Did I ever tell you the legend of how roses got their color? Well, apparently they were all white until one day, during a banquet of the gods, Cupid, who was hovering round Venus, upset an amphora of wine and stained the roses red."

Louise laughed, then thought for a moment. "I suppose we could include some sort of introduction about legends . . ."

She looked at the blank sheet of paper and began to type the list she had assembled, aware of the need for discipline. It would have been idyllic to indulge herself in all the rich details of Maurice's long, eventful life, but she rationed that part of the work to one and a half hours in the evening, after all the statistical tables about cures and plants had been prepared, work that was difficult and frustrating in a foreign language. It had to be done, she sensed, to give the book substance and weight.

Hearing about his fascinating life was what she enjoyed most. He expressed his failures and successes in his profession with homespun eloquence and candor, and she began to feel his personality filling the page like the stirring of a divining rod. Woven through his own joy and pathos was the history of the land, which went back to Roman and Phoenician times. Conquerors had been striding across the Languedoc for thousands of years. The Phoenicians and Romans gave way to Moors and Visigoths. The little-changed landscape, whose forests and vineyards had such ancient origins, had sprouted the seeds of the troubadours, the first romantic poets of Western civilization, whose spirit still lingered there. Maurice seemed surprised that Louise had read their poetry, and she mentioned the street musician in Paris, who had given her her first impulse to come to Puivaillon.

Maurice was dictating something to her about nervous depression that she didn't want to miss. Taking up a pad, she jotted down a direct quote to be inserted into the text, a poetic turn of phrase about the restorative properties of wild sage, mixed with the cooling suggestion of violets. He added that hawthorn mixed with corn poppy, sweetbriar and meadowsweet seized all a man's anger and subdued it as if it were a wild beast. She wrote rapidly in shorthand, knowing that if only she could distill the essence of Maurice's words into English, then they couldn't fail.

An hour later they were drinking a cooling infusion of herbs that strongly suggested peppermint, which always revived her tired body and spirits wilted by work and heat.

"If you could only market this, it would take the world by storm. You would make a fortune." She drank deeply from the frosted glass.

He laughed loudly. "You must have been an Auvergnat in your other life."

"Why do you say that?"

"Because they love money."

She looked amused. "I guess I'll never change," she agreed. "I'm always looking for a way to make a buck. It's not the money, Maurice. It's what it represents."

"And what is that?"

"I suppose you could say a place in the sun, in a figurative sense."

"Yes, America is the land of opportunity. It never attracted Frenchmen like me. We're content to stay on the same land for generations, to till the soil and tend our vines. Give us a corner to cultivate a few cabbages and we're happy.''

"When was the last time you were in Paris, Maurice? You have a touchingly romantic view of your country, believe me,'' she said, thinking of the terror of crossing the Place de la Concorde in a taxi, of the ruthless competition she had faced in the fashion world.

"Ah, perhaps I do embroider the truth,'' he said with a shrug. "But those who still live close to the land in villages like Puivaillon reap a great contentment as their reward. Don't you think so?''

His question needed no answer. From the day she had arrived, Louise had meshed her life with those of the people of Puivaillon, becoming *l'Américaine chez Roussel.* She was as firmly rooted in this corner of France as she had been anywhere and she couldn't imagine ever leaving.

"It seems that this book might take longer than just the summer. How would you feel about that?'' he said, raising a bushy eyebrow.

"I don't mind. I even like the idea,'' she answered casually, realizing that he must know just how deeply attached she was to him and to the village.

"What will you do after it is finished, Louise? Go back to the way you were?''

"I don't know,'' she said, pausing to consider. "No, I couldn't go back to being the way I was. I could never do that . . .''

The ringing of a bicycle bell alerted them to the arrival of the postman, whose gray cap was just visible above a cloud of blue delphiniums.

"*Salut,* Janneau,'' called Maurice.

"*Ça va?*'' responded the postman. Parking his bicycle, he carried a packet of letters through the gate and he tipped his cap to Louise.

"You're late today,'' Maurice said, taking the letters.

"I just got started on my rounds when I had to go off in the van to assist Henri with a breakdown . . .'' As the postman chatted to Maurice, Louise was half listening. She looked up sharply when she heard him mention where he had been that morning. It was the same village she had visited with Owen, the village where he had bought the mysterious gold chalice.

When the postman had gone, Maurice sorted through his letters. Louise was waiting for him to stop so she could ask him about the village when he handed her a letter, his eyebrows raised. She let out a gasp when she saw it was from the literary agent in New York. She tore it open and read the opening sentences:

Dear Louise,

Before anything, I have to tell you how excited I am at the prospects for *My Life's Garden* by Maurice Roussel, subtitled *Le Jardin de Ma Vie.* The market is ripe for a book of this type and I have a hunch that this could be very big if it's half as good as it sounds. I've already fed the idea to a couple of publishers and they were very enthusiastic . . .

She looked at Maurice's rugged profile. The sun illuminated his shock of white hair against his nut-brown skin. Vigorous and full of life in his late seventies, he was a living example of what he stood for. He pretended not to be interested in the letter from New York as he opened an envelope, the lines at the corners of his mouth deepening into a smile. Feeling her eyes on him, he glanced up to see Louise clenching the letter, a look of undisguised satisfaction on her face.

"Qu'est qu'il y a?" he asked.

She paused, holding her breath. *"Ils sont très intéressés,"* she said, in what was the understatement of the year.

"Extraordinaire," he kept repeating when she had read the letter to him.

The letter from the agent had given them both a fresh impetus to work and after they had discussed the next day's agenda, Louise began to gather up her papers. Slipping on a garden smock of the same blue as the deepening shadows, Maurice took his straw hat from a peg nearby and began to fill a watering can from a tap, now the sun had lost its strength.

"I'll see you later, then," he called. "I'll chatter a bit for your tape recorder and you can stay and have some rabbit stew with me, if you like. The village poacher brought it to me yesterday.''

"Thank you. That would be lovely. Perhaps we can do some work for an hour or so after the sun goes down. I'm off now to collect some red-leaved mallow near the château, and maybe some eglantine for jam, if I can find any.''

He smacked his lips. "Ah, rose-hip jam, one of my favorites. This evening I'll tell you about my mother's rose-petal jam. Now, you go, but don't tire yourself. Go home and have a rest, stretch out in the garden. That's where you'll find me in a little while,'' he said, pointing to a faded deck chair under a tree in a corner of the garden.

"I feel restless if I've been sitting all day,'' she said, thinking how precious time was. It had become indispensable to her understanding of Maurice's world to be familiar with every aspect of plants collected in the hills, far from exhaust fumes and pollution, growing where nature intended them to grow, as he put it. She was just about to open the gate when she remembered something.

"Maurice?''

"Yes?'' he said, lifting his head.

"When the postman came, he mentioned he was on his way back from a village not far from here . . .''

"Yes, I remember.''

"I've been to that village, the first time I came here, with that friend of mine. I don't know why I never thought to ask you. He was looking for an antique dealer from whom he bought something in the early Seventies. He was very disappointed not to find him. You wouldn't know what happened to him, by any chance?'' As she spoke, she thought it was unlikely. She was taken aback when Maurice scratched his head and said:

"Yes, I remember him—very well, in fact. I treated him once and then I never saw him again. He was a very strange fellow.''

"Do you remember his name?''

"Not immediately, but it would be in my files.''

"Thanks. I'll have a look tomorrow, if you don't mind.''

Maurice watched pensively as Louise disappeared through the gate. Seeing the swing of her dark hair, the flash of her brown arms, he wondered to whom in Puivaillon he could introduce her, to make her life fuller, richer. He said to himself that it wasn't healthy for an attractive young woman to bury herself in the countryside without a man. Her relentless devotion to his book, her exhaustive research into plants were admirable, commendable, but such narrow devotion clashed with his idea of a balanced life. A man's existence had to be seasoned with other pleasures besides rewarding work to be ripe and full, he thought. In his mind he sifted through the people he knew, thinking of suitable men in the vicinity, knowing there were very few who would fit the bill. She needed an intelligent, urbane sort of man, preferably one who spoke English, to take her dancing at the village fête, to go to the seaside from time to time or on picnics in the hills. Her brown eyes were full of warmth often disguised by her mercurial temperament. When she laughed, she was almost beautiful and her directness was appealing. Yes, thought Maurice, Louise Carey possessed in abundance all the old-fashioned female virtues he so admired, besides being the diligent muse who had made his lifelong dream a reality. Beneath the world-weary career woman, he had been pleased to discover, she was adventurous at heart, with no grand design. It also pleased him to think she was not just an overworked refugee from city life who had come to the country for a change of scene. He sensed that she had come to Puivaillon on an inner quest. Though adapting herself to a quiet life in a small village, it seemed to him she was watching, waiting for something. He could see it in her face when she was distracted by a sudden gust of wind or a cloud passing over the sun. The pupils of her dark eyes would widen as she looked into the distance with an expression that was expectant, yet suggested wariness. He wondered what lay behind the enigmatic expression that he couldn't interpret.

Later, as the sun was going down, Louise parked her car off the unpaved road that led to the ruined château above Puivaillon. Taking out her basket that contained her drying sheet, a trowel, shears and a knife, she walked up the hill, thinking of the antique dealer who had disappeared years ago, wondering what Owen would say when he heard what she had discovered. The thought of breaking such important news to him made her wish he were arriving the next day. Suddenly

she was anxious for him to be there. She felt a sudden jab of
loneliness, blinding her for a moment to the cornflowers and
poppies waving in the wind against a field of dried grass.
Through the late afternoon sunshine, she walked up the dirt
road that led to the top of the hill. Reaching the château, she
passed under the stone arch, where the coat of arms was still
visible, and entered the rectangular courtyard, guarded for
centuries by a high wall of weathered stone. It was now open
to the public, but, as usual, the ticket kiosk was empty. She
walked across the grass strewn with wild flowers, admiring
the pure, delicate lines of the three ruined towers that reigned
over the silence. She never came there without imagining the
thunder of horses' hooves. She could clearly picture knights
in armor cantering across the turf, the wind catching the colorful banners they carried, the sun glinting on their metal
casques. There to greet them were their lady loves in velvets
and silks, their hair braided with gold.

She was in the habit of climbing the far tower, where the
banqueting room of the castle was still intact. Her own footsteps echoed in the great stone chamber, whose soaring arches
were scoured by time. She could just make out the blurred
faces of minstrels carved below the lintels, each bearing a
musical instrument. The last great moment of the château,
Maurice had told her, had been in the middle of the thirteenth
century, when the besieged nobles of Languedoc had gathered there before they had been finally crushed under the
boot of France. He spoke of the incident as if it were yesterday, in a voice full of pride. Sitting on the window ledge
overlooking the lake and the valley, she listened to the wind
rushing through the crumbling masonry. She always felt at
peace resting on these stones, which had been laid eight hundred years or more before her own lifetime. The window
seemed made for solitary contemplation or for lovers' trysts.
She could imagine a man and a woman making promises, or
a lady reflecting on her troubles. Suggestions of the château's
past made Louise feel a poignant curiosity about who had
waited and watched at the window in that same spot. She ran
her fingers along the stone, polished by time and bleached
by the sun, imagining a message imprisoned within. Leaving
the window, she went to look at the elegant vaulted arches
intersected by carved roses, their delicate petals almost intact

after so many centuries. She stared up at the troubadour rose, symbol of truth, for a long time, until her shoulders ached.

She descended the stairs and crossed the courtyard streaked with cool shadows, feeling strangely restless and dissatisfied. As she paused and looked over her shoulder at the sun-varnished tower, she was struck by a sense of overwhelming loss. As she stared at the sun, her vision was shattered by a swirl of blinding color. When she blinked, the courtyard looked somehow different. She scanned the unbroken wall, feeling sure there had once been a gate there. Breaking into a run, she stopped short, staring up at the wall, but there was no trace of a gap that might have been closed. With a passionate certainty, Louise knew there had been a gate where now there was none. The stones had been perfectly aligned, perhaps hundreds of years ago, to close the portal whose image lodged stubbornly in her mind's eye. Her heart pounding, she turned and hurried across the empty courtyard, confused and bewildered. She picked up her basket that she had left at the gate, too agitated now to collect plants. Going back to the car, she stared for several moments at the golden outline of the château against the sky. Seemingly impenetrable, it had cast up one of its secrets. Her chest heaving in agitation, she thought of Montségur. Of Little Gaddesden. The seam of consciousness had been ripped open allowing her another glimpse of something hidden.

21

Walking through the doors of the hospital, Owen saw Mandy's parents, Gerald and Maureen Barber, coming toward him, a preoccupied expression on both their faces.

As Owen shook Gerald's hand, Mandy's mother turned away, not bothering to disguise her contempt.

"We seem to keep missing each other. Every time I've been in to see Mandy, the nurses told me you had either just left or were expected," Owen said.

"Yes, I know," Gerald replied, uncomfortably aware that his wife was staring into the distance as if Owen weren't there. She was a gaunt, thin-lipped woman with tightly curled brown hair. The grim set of her mouth indicated the hostility that she felt. He sensed that in some way she was blaming him for what had happened to her daughter.

Gerald glanced at Owen sympathetically, as if to say that he regretted his wife's behavior. "We decided commuting from Banbury to the hospital was just too difficult, so we've taken a furnished flat not far from here, for as long as necessary."

"I don't need to tell you I'm as devastated about this as you are." Owen wished he could voice his suspicions about Rex Monckton, thinking it might make Mandy's parents feel better to know she hadn't tried to take her own life, but he held his tongue.

Gerald said: "When I talked to you on the phone, I don't think Maureen and I had quite taken it in. Naturally, we rushed here right away to be with her. Ralph came down from Preston the day before yesterday, but he had to get back to his job, of course."

Owen nodded, thinking that the family Mandy rarely saw was for once united in grief. He hadn't seen any of them since Ralph, her brother, had got married five years before. He had always liked Mandy's father, who was a balding, quiet man with a wry sense of humor, though they had never had much in common. Listening to him now trying to allay his misery with chatter, and seeing Maureen's angry face, he could tell they still couldn't comprehend the tragedy.

". . . and all we can do now is pray for her. Somehow we have to find a way to cope with it the best we can," Gerald was saying.

Maureen jerked her head away as if she could no longer bear his platitudes and Owen could see there were tears in her eyes. "I'm going up, Gerald," she said abruptly.

"All right. I'll join you in a minute." When she had gone, he said: "Listen, Owen, I appreciate everything you've done, but now we're here, only a few minutes from the hospital, Maureen and I are going to take turns in keeping watch at Mandy's bedside until she pulls through . . ."

Owen looked away, unable to share his optimism about

Mandy's condition. "The thing is, I don't know how to put it, but I think it would be better if we took over from now on. I know you care about Mandy, but it would make things a lot easier . . ."

Sensing his embarrassment, Owen interrupted: "I understand, Gerald. I don't want to make things harder for you than they already are. As long as you know I'm here if you need me."

"Naturally I'll keep you informed, but let me call you. Don't call us. It's the way she is."

"Don't worry, I understand," said Owen, masking the hurt he felt at being excluded from the family at a time when he could have used some comfort himself. They were her family, yet he was closer to Mandy than any of them had ever been.

"I guess there's no change from yesterday."

"None."

"I don't know if you're aware of it, but we may have to come to some difficult decisions soon, even though we haven't given up hope. I don't know how you can make a decision like that, really. I mean, what is there in life that prepares you for having to put your own daughter to rest?"

Owen rested a hand sympathetically on his shoulder. "Listen, Gerald, I don't know how to say this, but if Mandy should regain consciousness, if she should say anything about what happened, I hope you'll let me know."

"Why is that?"

"I just want to be absolutely sure this was an accident, that's all."

Gerald looked puzzled, then said quietly, "You still care about her, don't you, Owen?"

"She was my wife," was all he could think to say. "If I can be of any help, call me, at home or at the office."

"You're not going away on holiday, then?"

"I was planning to spend some time in France, until this happened."

There were tears in Gerald's eyes as he shook Owen's hand and they said goodbye. As Owen walked to his car he wondered if the next time he saw Gerald would be at Mandy's funeral or whether by some miracle she would regain consciousness and he would be called to her bedside. He clenched his teeth in rage when he saw that his car had been clamped. He ripped the ticket off the windshield, and hailed a passing taxi.

Settling into the back seat as it inched through the traffic, Owen realized he was still smarting with hurt at Gerald's dismissal, though he understood the reasons. For the two weeks since Mandy's assault he had deprived himself of sleep and had drunk too much. With each passing day it became more apparent to him that Mandy might never recover. He had a picture of her in intensive care on a life-support machine, looking like a child again, a child adrift in a sea of technology. The doctors would not commit themselves about her condition, but as each day passed and she didn't regain consciousness, Owen sensed they were losing hope.

By late afternoon, when he had retrieved his car, Owen sped down the tree-lined street where he lived, glancing at the clock on the dashboard. He flashed his lights at the big van from Harrods parked outside his house, which was starting to move. Owen jumped out of the car, waving to catch the driver's eye.

Not long afterward the two delivery men were struggling up the front steps, carrying a baby grand piano. Owen waited in the half-empty sitting room, stripped of pictures, where dustcovers were still draped over the parquet floor and the furniture though the decorators had finished painting the day before. Watching the men inch their way through the door with the piano, he glanced round the room wondering where to put it—something he hadn't considered very carefully when he had bought it on impulse. He had gone to Harrods to buy new furniture for his flat, but this was all he had bought. If he examined his motives more closely, however, he had to admit to himself that buying a piano wasn't as impulsive as it might seem. He had felt the urge to play again for a long time, but had refused to give in to it. For the last few months it had been on his mind as a cure for the complicated emotions that he felt came from all the recent changes in his life. When the men had put the piano in the bay window and removed the packing, he tipped them and closed the door behind them.

He stood looking at the dark, glossy piano from a distance, feeling almost nervous about approaching it. He walked round it, studying it from every angle before he summoned the courage to stroke the highly polished surface. He remembered vividly the excitement he had felt when his first piano had been delivered to the mews house. He had immediately gone out to buy a bottle of champagne and played euphorically for hours while Mandy listened. The years had neutralized his talent and robbed him of such innocent delights, but he couldn't deny the thrill it gave him to see a piano in his home again, filling an empty space in himself. It was a symbol that he had conquered the nagging pessimism he had begun to assume was part of his character. Prolonging the moment of first acquaintance, he lifted the top and propped it open, running his fingers down the wires; then he sat down. He looked at the gleaming black and white keys, spreading his hands above them as he waited for the power of the music to move him.

With his right hand he picked out a Chopin *étude*, repeating the haunting combination of a few notes that he had never forgotten. He drew up his left hand and began to play, hesitantly at first, then with a restraint that masked the power of his feelings.

Owen played until the light began to dim beyond the bay window, pouring out every tune that came into his head, from Chopin to Gershwin to jazz. He ended with "Moody Lady," whispering the words to himself as his hands moved across the keys.

Closing the keyboard, he stood and looked out of the window at the pale sky fading beyond the treetops. Now that it was nearly the middle of July, London was beginning to empty for the holidays, leaving everything much quieter than usual. Louise came to his mind, her absence filling him with a sense of emptiness. He slumped in a chair, thinking to himself that Dorothy and Ambrose would be arriving in France that evening. He could imagine the shutters of their cottage thrown open, the windows casting yellow light onto the terrace and the cicadas calling from the grass. All his senses were stimulated as a picture of the French countryside came to his mind. He was seduced by the remembered rich smell of the earth, the brilliance of light reflected from a cloudless sky; he could hear church bells and the cry of the swifts as they dipped over the tiled rooftops of the old villages that seemed an extension of the very landscape. He felt himself reaching out toward the picture in his mind.

Hearing a car draw up outside the cottage, Louise rose from the chair where she had been reading, noting by her clock that it was after ten. She rolled up the sleeves of her blouse and ran her hands nervously through her hair. Pausing at the door, she felt a cocktail of emotions at the prospect of greeting Ambrose, Dorothy and Owen, whom she had been expecting all evening.

"Hello! We're here!" came Dorothy's voice from the darkness as the car door slammed.

A welcoming smile on her face, Louise walked toward the car. The minute she saw Dorothy she flung her arms around her. "Welcome to Puivaillon!" When she had kissed her, she turned to Ambrose, who was smiling down at her.

"I'd about given up on you." She glanced up the road, expecting to see the headlights of Owen's car not far behind. "Does Owen know the way here?" she asked, trying not to seem as anxious as she felt.

Slipping her arm round Louise's waist, Dorothy said: "We were both so disappointed. Owen is terribly worried about Mandy because she's still in a critical condition and he decided he couldn't leave London at the moment."

Louise didn't reply, feeling only a crushing disappointment. She nodded and smiled, trying to accept that what she thought she had anticipated with some dread was not going to happen after all.

"What a shame. I was looking forward to seeing him again. He's such good company." She was embarrassed that her voice sounded as if she were close to tears.

"Believe me, he was crestfallen that he couldn't make it, but he did promise to try to come later," remarked Dorothy, hesitant to offer the sympathy she felt at Louise's reaction. She exchanged a look with Ambrose, who understood that her happiness at being in France for the summer was diluted by Owen's absence.

Trying to sound cheerful, he said: "Come, come. Let's not be gloomy. He might just surprise us and come after all."

"But it doesn't matter now you're here. I've been looking forward to your arrival more than I can say, and so has Maurice.'' Louise shook off her surprising disappointment to welcome them.

"The two of you seem to have achieved something remarkable in a very short space of time," said Ambrose. "What's this about publishers showing interest already?"

"Maurice is a remarkable man. I don't know what I would have done without him. I've got so much to tell you—but come in. Let's not stand here. You must be exhausted. Have you had supper?"

"We really can't stay," said Dorothy. "We just thought we'd stop by to tell you we'd arrived. We have to open up the house and it's getting late. Come and see us for lunch tomorrow, why don't you? That is, if you're not working."

"I'd love to. Isn't it wonderful to think we have so much time ahead of us?" she said, trying to sound full of enthusiasm.

When she had kissed them again, they got back into the car. She stayed on the porch until the headlights had disappeared into the darkness.

When Louise went back into the house, she felt a terrible sense of depression as she closed the door behind her. Telling herself she had no right to feel that way about Owen Morgan, she sat down and tried to read again, but found she couldn't. She leaned back, listening to the cicadas, suddenly conscious of how quiet it was in the depths of the country. The image of Owen refused to leave her mind. She admitted to herself that until now she had been waiting patiently for their time to ripen, believing Owen couldn't easily put what had happened between them behind him, any more than she could. He was the one person she felt could share the confusion she had lived through in these past months. Without being aware of it, she had been counting the days, the hours, before she would be able to confide everything she felt. For some reason, she needed to explain to him how and why she had come back to Puivaillon. And she needed to hear what he had been thinking and feeling too. All along she had interpreted his silence as an interval while they waited. But now, in the absence of a letter, a telephone call, she had to face the fact that she was the victim of a delusion. She faced the truth, feeling hurt and foolish.

* * *

By the next evening Louise felt much better. She had filled every moment of the day, making sure she didn't have time to brood. In the morning she had dropped in on Ambrose and Dorothy, and she had spent the afternoon working with Maurice. Now she had the kitchen table spread with several old French books on herbalism and a dictionary, as she tackled a difficult part of the manuscript she had been putting off. She was trying to decipher a blurred paragraph with a magnifying glass as Beethoven played softly in the background, the door ajar to admit the cool, scented night air. She had drawn back her hair and kicked off her shoes, and a sweater was thrown over her shoulders. She sank deeper and deeper into the old book, losing herself in the intricacies of ancient language.

At the sound of a tap on the door she looked up abruptly to see Owen standing there observing her. Staring at him in disbelief, she had a sudden memory of the time she had seen him standing at the threshold of the hotel dining room in Puivaillon. Now, as then, she was stunned. But this time she felt only joy. Rising to her feet, she looked at him with an expression of utter bewilderment.

"But I thought you weren't coming . . ."

"I'm here now. How could I stay away?"

Without even thinking, Louise rushed into his arms. As they embraced she was enveloped by an aura of completeness. They stood for a long time in the doorway, just holding each other without speaking.

"You're really here. I'm not dreaming," she said when they broke apart, not knowing how to mask her emotion.

"No. It's not a dream. I think I've had enough of dreams. I wanted the reality. Louise—I've been thinking so hard about you all the way here, imagining you in this cottage, just like this." He looked at her bare feet, her breasts beneath the loose T-shirt, her brown shoulders. "In the end, nothing else mattered. I haven't written, I haven't called, but I've thought about you constantly."

The look in his eyes told her he had endured the same turmoil and doubts that she had during these past months. Her relief at this discovery was indescribable. For a fleeting moment it seemed they had always been lovers. Then, as quickly as it had come, the warmth of their intimacy vanished without warning, leaving them marooned in an awkward silence.

"You must have driven like the wind if you left London last night. Didn't you even sleep on the way?" Louise said as she absently shuffled the papers on the table.

"I stopped by the roadside somewhere south of Poitiers for a little nap, and then straight on again."

"Dorothy and Ambrose will be surprised."

"Not as much as you were." He touched her elbow as she passed. "Louise, you, this place, have been in my mind continually since I heard you were coming here."

"I think I knew that, though I began to doubt myself. I've thought so often of the weekend we spent here, asking myself how, why . . ."

"And did you come up with any answers?" When she shook her head, he said: "Neither did I. But then, why do we need answers?"

"Humans are thinking creatures," she whispered as he put his arms around her.

"Only in part. The other part of us feels deeply." He drew her to him and kissed her hard on the mouth.

The touch of his lips stunned Louise, sending a current of shock through her body. When they drew apart, she looked down, not knowing what to say. She felt her knees go weak with relief when she thought how narrowly they had missed losing each other. The powerful sense of rightness she felt at Owen's mere proximity was obscured by a violent wave of strangeness that took hold of her. Part of her found it impossible to believe that she could feel this way about a man she had seen for only a few hours or that he could feel so strongly about her as to suddenly drive through the night without sleeping to be at her side. She held his eyes for a moment, seeking, and finding, the raw honesty that had attracted her from the beginning, an openness that told her he felt confused, bewildered, just as she did. She smiled tentatively and ran her hand through his hair, wondering how to fill these difficult first moments.

"You must be hungry," she murmured, blinking as she walked round the kitchen. Hardly knowing what she was doing, she reached for an omelette pan.

"No, really, I don't want you to go to any trouble," he

replied weakly, watching her every move. It was true he wasn't hungry, but he sensed she needed something to do while they struggled to fill the gap created by the weeks they had lost.

"It's no trouble, really. I'll join you. I didn't eat dinner because I was so engrossed in what I was doing." She grabbed her apron before he could protest, wondering if he would be surprised to know that her mind had wandered repeatedly, that she had been disturbed by images of him in London. As a distraction, she began to talk about her work with Maurice.

When she dropped the whisk on the floor, they both scrambled after it at the same time. As Owen handed it to her, she felt herself blush at the proof of her own nervousness. Cracking the eggs into a bowl, Louise was acutely conscious of Owen's eyes on her as he stood in the doorway, his arms folded across his chest. She cast a glance at him now and then, refamiliarizing herself with all the things she had forgotten—the sound of his voice, the way he tilted his head when he spoke, his thoughtful expression, which made her stomach flutter. She was aware that she enjoyed the ritual of preparing food for him and feeling his attention utterly fixed on her. She thought ahead to the next hour: only when they were in each other's arms would they entirely close the distance between them.

They carried the food to the small enclosed garden at the back of the house. She lit two candles while Owen opened a bottle of rosé. When they had sat down across from one another, Louise said:

"What's going to happen to Mandy? How long can this situation continue?"

"Not indefinitely. It looks as if there's not much hope, and if she deteriorates, it will be up to the doctors and her parents to decide whether to take her off the life-support system."

"It must be terrible for you." Watching Owen's face, she could detect no sign that he was still in love with his ex-wife, but she sensed that he felt compassion. But when she saw anger flare in his eyes, she was puzzled.

"Louise, I haven't told anybody this, but I'm positive someone assaulted her and made it look like an overdose. And I'm sure Rex Monckton was behind it."

He told her about his argument with Mandy that night, how he had gone back and had seen the man standing at her door, and about his conversation with her friend Sue.

"What makes you think Rex Monckton did it? I know he must be a detestable human being, but that doesn't mean he tried to kill her."

"I know Mandy, and there's no way in the world she would have tried to kill herself with a ticket to Marbella lying on the table. And another thing—the detective agency I've hired to follow Rex has been able to trace his movements that night. We know he went to a party in The Boltons after Ascot and by ten o'clock he was in an exclusive private club off Berkeley Square. You see, The Boltons backs onto the mews where Mandy lives. In fact, there's a shortcut linking the two streets, which few people know about. You can slip down a garden path and be in the mews within a minute without being seen."

"Have you told the police about this?"

"No, because it doesn't prove a thing. There are hundreds of parties going on all over London on a night like that and I don't have a shred of evidence."

"What about her friend Sue? Can't she help in any way?"

"She said if I told the police what she knew, she'd deny it. And believe me, she would, too."

"But if she's Mandy's friend, how could she do a thing like that? Surely she'd want to testify and see him brought to justice."

"Yes, that might be true. She may be selfish, but that's not all there is to it. I got the impression she was genuinely afraid of Rex Monckton. Now I've seen him again myself, I know what she means." He told her about breaking in on Rex at his house in Belgravia. "I felt a peculiar sense of menace when I faced him. I could feel the hair standing up on the back of my neck, and yet he's somebody I've known for years."

"You obviously didn't know him as well as you thought." She was taken aback by his expression of remembered terror.

"I'm beginning to understand what Dorothy meant when she called to warn me I was getting in way over my head."

"She said that?"

When Owen told her about Dorothy's call, Louise said: "I wonder why she said he was evil. It's such a strong word to use and not really like Dorothy at all. Perhaps it's just her overactive writer's imagination.''

"Maybe, but Dorothy is also a very shrewd judge of people and she usually chooses her words very carefully. I have to admit, until that day I barged into his house, I would have scoffed at the idea of the effete Monckton being evil. But at one point when we faced each other across the room I felt a powerful surge of energy. I felt a heaviness in my chest, as if I was going to suffocate. The air seemed to vibrate with real menace. Quite frankly, I was scared and I got the hell out of there as fast as I could, feeling as if I'd had a close call.''

"But where is he now?''

"He's disappeared. One reason I'm sure he knows I'm watching him is that he's left a trail of red herrings. He told one person he was going to the Caribbean, another that he would be in North Africa for the summer, and his office is giving out the story that he's in the Far East. It's as if he's trying to cover his tracks.''

"So what will you do now?''

"Nothing. Just wait until he surfaces, which he will, some time. I don't have any idea how I'm going to drive him to the wall, but I'll keep trying to find a way.''

"You still haven't told me why Rex would have wanted to kill Mandy.''

He shook his head. "That's the most baffling part. All I know from Sue is that she had something he wanted. But I can't explain why he would kill her, even if that were so. Sue seemed to think there was quite a lot of money involved, enough to go on a shopping spree and spend a month in Marbella with her posh friends.''

"I can think of one reason why he might have tried to kill her. Maybe Rex didn't want anyone else to know she had given him whatever it was.''

"I've been going over it in my mind on the way down, and this trip to Marbella Mandy was planning would have cost several thousand pounds. One thing I know about Rex is that he never liked to part with money unless he absolutely had to. It might have been part of the motivation if she demanded more than whatever he thought it was worth. But all of this is just guesswork. We don't even know what 'it' was.''

The candles sputtered in the breeze and Owen and Louise fell silent. Reaching across the table, he took her hand.

"I want to forget about all this, the way I wanted to forget about it that night we first met in Puivaillon. Only now the need to forget is even stronger. It's forced out by the memory I have of you that night we spent together."

Louise didn't reply. She began to stack the dishes; then, looking up, she asked quietly:

"Will you stay the night?"

He followed her into the bedroom and, without thinking, she turned the key in the lock. The sound of it brought home to her that nothing else existed but the rich moment of communion about to take place between them. They looked at one another silently across the wooden bed spread with a white coverlet. Louise made the first move, feeling Owen's hesitation. She turned off the lamp, casting the room into darkness except for a luminous square of moonlight pouring through the window and onto the floorboards. He walked to her and, taking her face in his hands, kissed her lingeringly on her mouth. His hands moved from her shoulders to her breasts, her hips, retracing every remembered part of her that had tormented him for so many months.

When they were naked, she leaned against the cold, hard bed. In the midst of their passion she was torn through with the realization of how pure, yet how painful this moment was. The sight of Owen, sketched in the darkness, filled her with a sense of honor that he should bless her with his body.

"I don't know how, I don't know why, but I think I loved you from the first moment I saw you," he whispered.

She looked at his finely etched silhouette, feeling an urgent response quicken inside her. As the seconds ticked away, Owen's actions and words seemed to breathe life into an inner reality that existed inside her own mind. Obscure, half-realized images paraded through her head, now becoming suffused with a new meaning, making the secret of their adoration seem older than themselves. She was shivering in a chrysalis of aching incompleteness until he touched her with the pulsing warmth of his hard, strong body. Clasping her arms tightly around him, she gave herself up to the release of desire. When they drew together on the bed, she searched the shadowy depths of his eyes like glittering windows. Her lips parted and she started to speak. Her words, pretty but useless, fell like a shower of glass at the back of her mind. Their bodies were charged with an intimacy that carried them far beyond the realm of carnal desire, that room and that time, and far away. It seemed so right, so good to Louise that Owen should possess her body, there, now, with the same completeness with which he already possessed her heart and mind. Light seemed to fill the dark room as he loved her. They were two helpless creatures, thrown into a murmuring channel of purest expression. Louise let the power of his body consume her as she gave herself up to the aching fullness that embodied life's mystery.

An hour later Louise crossed the darkened bedroom on her way back to bed, where Owen lay. She paused at the window to look at the pale sweep of the moonlit valley, crowned with the silhouette of the ruined château like a white dream city on the distant horizon.

"What are you looking at?" Owen asked, moved by the sight of her pale body in the darkness. Slipping from bed, he came to her side and gathered her in his arms.

"It doesn't look real," he whispered, gazing down into the valley.

They stood mesmerized by the ghostly beauty of the château beckoning in the distance. Shrouded in shadows, it seemed to symbolize the mysterious emotions they felt after making love.

"I'll take you to see the château. We might go tomorrow. It's even lovelier when the sun is shining. See the dark speck on the tower? It's a window from which you can look out over the entire valley. There's a great hall, which was famous in the days of the troubadours; it was called the Salle des Poètes." She didn't try to describe the powerful presence she had often felt in the château, nor did she mention the phantom gate that had appeared in her mind the last time she was there, sensing that Owen would see and feel everything for himself.

"The Salle des Poètes," he repeated. "Maybe I'll find the inspiration I was looking for all those years ago. No—I've already found what I'm looking for," he said, kissing her forehead.

The next evening Ambrose lifted his glass to Louise, Owen, Maurice and Dorothy, who were seated at a table under the vine-covered pergola of the Lethbridges' cottage.

"Welcome, all of you, and here's to the success of *Le Jardin de Ma Vie*!"

"Let's hope it sells as many copies as your book, Ambrose," said Owen.

"How is it going, by the way?" Louise asked.

"Surprisingly well, to my amazement. I can't imagine why anyone would want to plow through it. It's interesting enough to me, but deadly dull to the average person, I should have thought."

Dorothy said, "You're so modest, darling. The first thing he grabs in the morning is *The Times* best-seller list. You should have seen his face when he heard it was being reprinted."

"I feel completely outnumbered at this table of writers," said Owen.

"Then you'll have to take your pen in hand again and get busy with some lyrics and set them to music," Dorothy replied. "Your wonderful gifts are lying dormant and it's a shame not to use them," she scolded.

"Funnily enough, that's just what I've been thinking of doing." He announced with a wry smile that he had bought a piano and Dorothy said:

"Bravo and about time, too."

"It's a fine feeling to start creating again; I know," Maurice said, casting a smile at Louise.

Louise resisted the impulse to reach for Owen's hand under the table. That morning they had wondered how to tell Dorothy, Ambrose and Maurice what had happened between them.

"Oh, look," Dorothy cried, pointing in the direction of the village as a flash of pink exploded against the darkening sky. "They're starting the fireworks already."

"Not at all. It's just a warm-up," said Maurice. "It's not due to start until nine-thirty. We have more than an hour."

"I wouldn't want Louise and Owen to miss it. Neither of them has ever been in France for Bastille Day."

"I noticed the amusement park when I drove through the village this afternoon," said Owen, catching himself in mid-sentence. When he caught Louise's eye, she couldn't suppress a smile.

He had stayed at her cottage until after lunch, when she joined Maurice for work, pretending to Dorothy and Ambrose that he had met her by chance in the market and had lunched with her. Soon, he thought to himself, they would have to break the news that he would be staying with Louise for the remainder of the holiday.

When Ambrose and Dorothy brought platters of *charcuterie*, bread and salad to the table, Louise said:

"Maurice, I told Owen about the *brocante* dealer, Durand. I'm sure he'd like to hear from you exactly what happened."

"Ah yes, Durand. You bought something from him years ago, didn't you? Louise mentioned to me that you tried to find him in March. I treated him once, many years ago."

Dorothy paused as she was tossing the salad. "I never heard you mention that, Maurice."

"But why would I mention it, Dorothy? It was just a bit of local gossip, completely unimportant."

"Of course," she murmured. "Please go on."

Ambrose began to cut the bread, noticing the familiar flicker of interest cross Dorothy's brow as Maurice spoke.

"It happened one late summer evening more than fifteen years ago."

"It wasn't in 1971, by any chance?" asked Owen.

"Yes, it was. How did you know?"

"That was the year I went to his shop."

"Well, I remember it was late and I was just getting ready to close my surgery when a distraught couple—they were farmers—brought in a boy for treatment. They had knocked him off his bicycle when they were driving from here to Rocadour. After I had examined him, I took him back into the waiting room. We chatted for a moment and the three of them were just about to leave when the door opened and in walked Durand, blood streaming from his head, his clothes caked with dust. When I examined him, he told me he had had a fall, but at the time I knew he wasn't telling the truth. I could see he had received a sharp blow on the head, but why he should pretend otherwise, I didn't know. I knew who he was: I'd heard of him because he was a recluse and a lot of absurd rumors circulated at the time.''

"You mean the story that he was searching for buried Nazi treasure?'' volunteered Louise, exchanging a glance with Owen.

"Nazi treasure, Cathar treasure—absolute nonsense, I'm sure. All I can say is, as I dressed his wounds he answered my questions in monosyllables and I remember thinking he was afraid of something or someone. He paid in cash and wouldn't fill out an insurance form. The way he was dressed intrigued me. I seem to recall he wore a shiny serge suit and a stiff collar, the way men dressed before the war.''

"Could you describe him?'' Owen asked. "How did he strike you?''

Maurice thought for a moment. "He seemed to be someone from another age. He was old without being old,'' Maurice mused. "His skin was sallow and he had piercing black eyes. I remember thinking at the time that I was looking at a face from antiquity. I could understand that people speculated he was a Moroccan Jew, an Armenian or perhaps a Spaniard whose shop was a front for contraband from Spain. I heard afterward that people had seen him coming in his old Deux Chevaux from remote places in the hills. There was something unhealthy and frail about him, and yet his eyes had a . . .'' Maurice searched for the words.

"Fanatical look?''

"No, not exactly. I was going to say that, but it was really more a kind of fervor. His face was like an old religious painting full of a spiritual power, a quality that is so unfamiliar in our modern cynical world. And yet, for all that, I felt there was an aura of tragic loneliness about him, too, as if he were an outcast. For some reason it crossed my mind that he could easily have been in a concentration camp. Quite honestly, when he left, I was glad. I found his presence oppressive. But then, later, I regretted not trying to see him again, and I learned subsequently that he vanished, by the end of September I think it was. I never saw him again. I think I heard eventually that he had simply packed up and left the village one night. There was gossip about who he was and where he had gone, but it died down and I never thought about it much until now.''

There was a silence, punctuated by the cicadas, as everyone thought about Maurice's story.

''But there's something else, Louise. I didn't mention it when you were questioning me, but it came to me afterward. When Durand entered my surgery looking like a wraith, I was in the anteroom with the boy and the couple who had knocked him off his bicycle. The boy seemed to go white when he saw Durand, as if he had seen a ghost. And then I saw Durand flash him a look of warning that made the boy shrink away. Jean-Luc ran out of the door into the night, as if he were fleeing from the furies.'' He shook his head. ''To this day, I can't imagine why.''

''Perhaps the boy witnessed something,'' said Louise.

''Possibly, but the matter ended there.''

''Who was the boy?'' asked Ambrose. ''Do we know him?''

''His name was Jean-Luc Mithois. He was from Rocadour and he was about thirteen at the time.''

''What happened to him?'' asked Owen.

''By a strange coincidence I heard a few months ago that his father shot himself. I know the village *notaire* was trying to trace Jean-Luc because somebody wanted to buy some property his father had left, but nobody knew where the boy had gone.''

After a moment Owen said: ''My instinct tells me it's all related somehow. Durand, who wouldn't admit he had been beaten up, and the boy, Jean-Luc, who was shocked to see him. You say he looked as if he had seen a ghost: maybe he had seen him beaten up and thought he was dead. For that matter, I saw a boy loitering outside the shop who might easily have been him.''

''It's possible you are right; but why would Durand react so violently when he saw Jean-Luc?''

''Because he knew something—some secret,'' Louise volunteered.

''Maybe,'' Maurice agreed. ''I suppose he might have discovered Durand's identity on the way home, when he heard the farmer and his wife talking about him in the car, as they were bound to do,'' he mused. ''He might have gone in search of him then out of curiosity.''

"If Jean-Luc's father has died, he might come back to the village before long, to tie up the estate," Dorothy suggested.

"Somehow I doubt it. He was a miserable little boy. His father drank, and beat him, I suspect. His mother died when he was young. They were a tragic, ill-fated family. He was the kind of shifty-eyed boy used to living on his wits, who probably turned out badly."

"If we could find him, he might tell us what he saw," said Louise.

"You could contact the *notaire* at Rocadour, but, really," said Maurice with a shake of his head, "if Jean-Luc knows anything, the chances are he wouldn't tell you."

When Owen told them about his visit to Durand's shop, Maurice nodded thoughtfully. "Perhaps there was a buried treasure after all and it's not just a fantasy. You say you bought a gold chalice from him? That surprises me."

"Maurice, it doesn't end there. There's not time now, but I'll tell you the rest of the story soon. When I bought the chalice, he offered to sell me some coins too, but, fool that I was, I said no because I was very short of money at the time."

"Coins?" Maurice broke a piece of bread and chewed it thoughtfully. "So Durand did find something, then?"

Ambrose said: "Maurice, have you heard about the early medieval manuscript that has been found in a cheesemaker's loft in Rocadour? When I read about it in the *Dépêche*, I called a colleague of mine at the University of Toulouse. He's invited me to drive up and see it. The paper said it was found near the time that Owen bought the chalice and when you treated Durand. It just crossed my mind that perhaps this is all connected in some way."

"Mysteries in books are fine, aren't they, Dorothy? There you can tie all the loose ends neatly together. But real life, well, that's something else," said Maurice with a shrug.

Dorothy smiled absently. All through the conversation she had been doing just that—trying to tie all the loose ends together.

After dinner, when they drove into the village, Louise and Owen went in Ambrose and Dorothy's car. A few miles down the road Dorothy exclaimed:

"Oh look, Château La Bruyère is all lit up."

Above the wall they could just see the outline of the house glimmering through the trees of the vast park surrounding it.

"Every time I've passed this way it's been shuttered," said Louise, straining for a backward glimpse as it disappeared from view.

"I suppose that means the Baron de Cazenac must be down for the summer," Ambrose remarked. "He usually brings a colorful group of people with him from Paris."

"Did you say de Cazenac?" asked Owen.

"Yes," said Ambrose. "Their title goes back to the thirteenth century. They were local petty nobles, who were given land belonging to a family called de Franjal, who lost their property when Languedoc became part of France. Even though it all happened seven and a half centuries ago, the local people still have a certain contempt for the de Cazenacs and regard them as usurpers and traitors. Their memories are as long as history round here."

"Do you think there's any chance the baron might come into the village tonight?" Owen asked.

"I rather doubt it. They tend to keep to themselves. I don't think, in all the years we've been coming here, we ever saw the old baron and his wife more than a handful of times. They came down from Paris infrequently, and their children grew up there, not here."

"So the new baron is young? How young?" Owen asked.

"In his early thirties," Ambrose replied. "But he's of a different generation, so perhaps it might amuse him and his guests to mingle with the peasants," he added wryly.

Louise noticed that Dorothy had fallen silent and was staring out of the window. She clung to Ambrose's hand when he reached out to her.

They parked the car at the far edge of the village and walked down the main street toward the square, where they could hear music blaring from a loudspeaker. Normally when night fell, the street was shuttered and deadly quiet, but now the town was animated, with people streaming down the thoroughfare. When they passed the Hôtel du Commerce, Owen and Louise exchanged a private smile.

"It looks different in summer, with geraniums in the window boxes, doesn't it?" she said.

"I feel the impulse to say something corny."

"Such as?"

"Such as, in March they were blooming for me."

She laughed, feeling the knot between them tighten imperceptibly. In a moment she said: "Owen, when they were talking about Durand tonight I had the strangest feeling. Gooseflesh went down my spine and I don't know why." While waiting for him to reply, she though of the strange dream she had had in America, and she remembered the bell she had heard ringing in the night, the voices at Little Gaddesden, the Place des Vosges, Montségur—all hard to explain.

"It frightened you, didn't it?" he said, clasping her hand warmly in his.

"Yes, a little," she admitted, feeling relieved she had told him.

"Now it's my turn, I guess. I got a jolt in the car on the way here, when Ambrose mentioned Baron de Cazenac," said Owen. "I thought his name sounded familiar, then it hit me where I had heard it before. Remember I told you about that night when I barged in on Monckton? I'd swear de Cazenac was the name of the Frenchman with him."

"Would you recognize him if you saw him?"

"I'm sure I would. But it won't be easy to see him if he doesn't mix with the local people."

"Do you think he'd recognize you?"

"I don't know. When I burst into the room, for a split second we stared at each other like three wolves."

As they neared the square, Dorothy turned, then smiled when she saw Owen and Louise walking hand in hand.

"Louise and Owen seem completely wrapped up in each other, don't they?" Ambrose remarked. "It must make you very happy to see them like this at last."

"It does," said Dorothy with an edge to her voice. "I just wish I could nourish the illusion that this is a happy ending."

There was no time to say more. The four of them entered the small square, which was strung with colored lights and full of people, and made their way toward the platform, where a stocky man played a tango on an accordion while he gazed soulfully down at the couples swaying to the music. On close inspection, most of the couples were women dancing together or with small children.

The Lethbridges, Owen and Louise wandered toward the carousel, a whirling blur of colored lights that attracted droves of small children eating cotton candy. Burly young farmers were clustered round the brightly lit shooting gallery, which offered gaudy dolls dressed in satin as prizes. The single café in the square was overflowing with old men in berets, drinking Pastis and talking animatedly.

"I told Maurice we'd meet near the café," said Dorothy, looking at her watch. "I hope he'll be here soon. The fireworks are about to begin and this isn't a very good place to see them."

Louise grabbed her elbow and whispered: "I'll bet you anything that's the Baron de Cazenac."

"Where?" asked Dorothy, whirling around.

"There—just by those colored lights between the trees." They stared at a suave, sandy-haired young man in a cream linen suit, who seemed out of place. He was surveying the crowd with a look of cynical detachment on his suntanned face. Dorothy stared in his direction, her eyes suddenly filled with disbelief.

"Is something the matter?" asked Louise.

"We must leave at once." She craned her neck to see Owen and Ambrose, who had wandered toward the café. "Tell Owen and Ambrose we must leave. Never mind about Maurice," she added to herself, "later . . ." She was trembling as she stared toward Philippe de Cazenac with an expression of helpless terror. The garish square had become a spinning wheel of color, centered around Philippe, who was with Rex Monckton, attached to his orbit like the earth to the sun.

Louise went in search of Owen and Ambrose. Rushing up to them, she said: "Something's wrong with Dorothy. She wants to leave immediately."

Ambrose didn't hesitate. Seeing his wife's gray head moving away from them, he charged through the crowd after her.

"What's wrong?" Owen asked Louise as they followed. "Is she ill?"

"I don't know. But whatever it is, she looked dreadful all of a sudden."

As Owen was about to leave the square he looked back. He felt a sudden shock as he recognized Philippe de Cazenac only a few yards away, talking to Rex Monckton. Rex turned in Owen's direction, as if sensing he was being observed. He trained his arrogant gaze on Owen for a moment.

Owen felt an impotent fury rise in him. He had a sudden impulse to charge through the crowd like a crazed bull and hurl himself at Rex and Philippe as the realization came crashing in on him that Philippe de Cazenac had tried to kill Mandy and that Rex had put him up to it. He struggled with the realization that these two bland-faced sophisticates would mess up their lives with murder. For a moment Owen fought with his own blind certainty of what they had done. The crowd, the color, the noise faded away and he imagined himself locked in a circle, armed with nothing but intuition and facing the only real enemy he had ever had.

Owen joined Louise and the Lethbridges as they left the square. They made their way back to the car as the fireworks exploded over the village, not stopping until they reached the hotel, where they paused to look back at the glow of pink and orange lighting up the sky.

"Do you think he saw us?" Dorothy said to Ambrose, looking back anxiously in case they had been followed.

As they waited for an explanation, Louise and Owen looked at her. She seemed to have aged from the shock of the last few moments, and her smiling face had become blank with resignation.

"I saw Rex Monckton," she said in a quiet voice. "And he was with Philippe de Cazenac. Who would have thought . . . ?" She broke off in despair.

Owen said: "I know. I saw them too. De Cazenac is the man who was with Rex when I confronted him in London." When Dorothy looked surprised, he added: "I'm sorry, Dorothy, but that evening when you called to warn me, I went straight to Rex's house to have it out with him. I'm afraid I ignored what you'd said. I had to see him."

"It's worse than I thought. I'm sure he must have seen us all together. He might have recognized me as the woman who came into his shop. Oh dear, Maurice is going to wonder what has happened to us," she lamented, glancing back down the street.

Ambrose put his arm around her shoulder. "Let us take you home, Dorothy. You're tired, upset . . ."

"No, dearest. I'll be all right in a minute. Please forgive me, all of you, but I just couldn't stay in the square in that man's presence another minute." As she spoke, she couldn't stop trembling. But she took a deep breath and a little color came back into her cheeks as she looked at the circle of concerned faces and determined to pull herself together.

"Let's all go back home and talk. Louise is in the dark about this, I know, and there are things you ought to know, too, Owen."

A little later they were all sitting under the pergola as Ambrose poured glasses of Armagnac.

"Dorothy, what makes you say that Rex knew I was coming to Puivaillon? I didn't even know myself until the last moment, and from the look on his face he was just as surprised to see me as I was him."

"Perhaps he was surprised," she replied. "What I mean to say is that he will have been prepared for your arrival. You see, I suspect that he didn't come here just to idle away the summer."

"Owen, you said earlier on that you thought Rex might have been behind the assault on Mandy. But why?" asked Ambrose.

Owen told them what Sue Fisher had said to him. "Seeing de Cazenac, I feel convinced he was the man standing at her door when I reversed my car back up the mews. If only I had waited just a moment to see his face, she might not be lying in hospital now."

Louise asked, "Dorothy, is that why you didn't want Owen to contact Rex, because you thought he was dangerous?"

"I told Owen that night that I thought Rex was evil, suspecting he would disbelieve me."

"And Dorothy was right," said Owen. "I didn't pay any attention to what she said. But that night I left Rex's house feeling as if my hair was standing on end. I admit I was frightened. But of what?"

Dorothy took a sip of Armagnac, then chose her words carefully. "It's extremely hard to talk about these things without sounding absurd. The day I impersonated a customer from the country at Rex's gallery, I went to the London Library to look up some literature on the occult sciences, because I suspected that the pentacles engraved next to Rex's name on the shop front and the unusual ring he wore both had a special significance. And, of course, they do. It's obvious to me now that Rex practices black magic.''

"Good Lord!'' exclaimed Owen. "Sue Fisher mentioned something about that sort of thing when I saw her, but I just brushed it off.''

Seeing Louise's look of thinly veiled skepticism, Dorothy added: "I don't expect you to believe in the reality of magic, but, whatever the truth of it, people who indulge in these practices accumulate a great deal of psychological power over their own nature, and over others, too. That is the purpose of magic: power. So it wouldn't be at all farfetched to conclude that Philippe was carrying out a command from Rex.''

"I can't get over the fact that he's here, right under our noses,'' exclaimed Owen.

"I, for one, think that his being here might not be such a coincidence,'' Ambrose volunteered. He had been waiting anxiously to see how far Dorothy would go in explaining the events of the last few weeks. Her eyes moved from Owen to Louise as if she was tempted to reveal the startling truth that had shaped her life.

Owen said impatiently: "And suppose Rex really is evil, suppose he does practice black magic—which I still find difficult to accept—what are we supposed to do?''

"We can't do anything except wait,'' said Dorothy, feeling she had waited an eternity already.

Later, when Owen had taken Louise back to her cottage, Ambrose and Dorothy were preparing for bed in their simply furnished bedroom, which glowed softly in the lamplight. The small windows under the eaves were flung open to admit the cool night air vibrating with the sound of cicadas.

"What an eventful evening,'' Ambrose remarked, buttoning his pajamas as Dorothy slipped out of her dressing gown. "Do you know, dearest, before Louise and Owen drove off, he confided to me that he didn't think he would be coming back here tonight. He said it so tactfully I had to smile. Isn't it absurd how the younger generation think they invented love? How do they suppose they came into the world?''

Dorothy went up to him, laughing, and kissed him tenderly on the cheek. "I never cease to be thankful for you, Ambrose; your humor, your patience. I was thinking just now that this should have been one of the happiest nights of my life. What I was afraid would never happen has actually come to pass: Hugo and Sancha are together at last.''

They looked at one another for a moment as the importance of her words sank in.

"Are you going to tell them?''

"I don't know,'' she said quietly. "I wouldn't know how to begin. It isn't simply that they would find it difficult to believe; it's the damage it might do. I want them to be free to live their lives without harking back to the past. After all, that's the way it's intended to be, and who am I to interfere? Anyway, my heart tells me I don't have the right.'' She slipped into bed, not expecting an answer to her doubts.

"Are you happy to stay until the end of August, as planned?'' came Ambrose's voice in the darkness.

There was a pause. "If I told you I thought we were all in danger, would you want to leave?''

He thought for a moment. "No, that wouldn't do. You couldn't live with yourself, knowing you had run away. You would always think you had left something unfinished. And anyway, Owen wouldn't come with us. He'd stay, and so would Louise. No, we have to see this through together,'' he replied, reaching for her hand.

"Bless you,'' she whispered.

Long after she heard Ambrose's measured breathing Dorothy lay awake, her attention fixed on the band of moonlight pouring through the open window. She was thinking of Durand, who she was now sure had been one of the men who had spirited the treasure of Montségur away from the citadel in 1244 with Hugo. Like herself, she calculated, he must have possessed far memory that led him back to the treasure he had hidden so long ago. Dorothy reasoned that this explained why he had so willingly given the chalice to Owen, whom he must have recognized, as if he were handing it over for safekeeping. She drifted to sleep thinking about Poitevin, whose image seemed so real, so vital that he might have been in the same room. She dreamed of the night she left the chamber beneath the citadel, the night before the burning. She had had a glimpse of his face, which was a tempest of conviction and doubt. Poitevin had returned to the land of his birth at last, as the antique dealer Durand. In this shadowy incarnation he had acted as a catalyst in the drama that was now moving toward an uncertain end.

As Dorothy finally fell asleep, Louise lay awake next to Owen, feeling the current of fragrant night air moving across her naked body. When they had closed the door behind them, Owen had made passionate love to her, both of them feeling an almost unendurable depth of emotion and desire. Afterward they had talked of everything that had happened that night. The moment had seemed right to tell Owen about the strange dream she had had in America, but as she tried to describe it, the images seemed to fly away from her. She realized halfway through the story that the point of illumination had receded from her mind as mysteriously as it had come. And now, she suspected, it was gone forever. She was left with nothing but a haunting sense of sadness and loss, which darkened the overwhelming joy she felt at lying next to Owen. The magnetic warmth that joined their bodies together seemed threatened by the unknown future. Trying to chase away these nameless fears, Louise moved closer to his slumbering body for reassurance.

22

Old chestnut trees cast a dappled shade onto the terrace of Château La Bruyère. Philippe poured a cup of thick, dark coffee without noticing the distaste Rex registered at his unshaven face, the monogrammed dressing gown he wore casually over his trousers, his bare feet pushed into old espadrilles.

"Je fais la grasse matinée," said Philippe with an engaging grin as he reached for a hot brioche.

"Making the fat morning," Rex snorted. "That peculiar expression describes you perfectly today. I don't know why you seem so pleased with yourself." His voice was sharply disapproving.

Philippe inhaled the ripe scent of summer wafting across from the park surrounding the château, and smiled.

"Yes, I let my hair down when I come home. It's such a pleasure not to have to go anywhere or to do anything."

"You forget, old boy, that we have lots to do. There's no time to waste. Call in your housekeeper, would you? There's something I want to ask her."

"You might have said 'please,' " Philippe answered irritably. With a sigh he walked into the library and rang the bell. A few moments later the housekeeper came out onto the terrace.

"You wanted me, *monsieur le baron*?"

"Monsieur Monckton has something to ask you," Philippe said, holding his temper in check.

In fluent French spoken with a trace of an American accent, Rex said: "What do you know about an English couple who live just outside the village? I believe their name is Lethbridge."

"Oh, *monsieur,* they have been coming here during the summer for thirty years or more. They bought a house years ago. He is a professor and well known, I believe, and it is said she is a famous writer. Her books are even translated into French, but I've never read any of them."

"Do you have any idea what the professor teaches?"

"He's retired now, but everyone knows that he is a famous scholar of medieval history."

"Lethbridge—I wonder if it could be A. L. Lethbridge, the English historian?" he muttered to himself, adding, "Could you please find out who their house guests are?"

She looked toward Philippe, who nodded in agreement.

"And tell me," Rex continued, "is there anyone else staying in this village for the summer—foreigners, I mean?"

She thought for a moment. "There are two Dutch families who have houses on the road to Rocadour."

"Anyone else?"

"Now that I think of it, there is an American woman who is staying in a small cottage on the edge of the village. It is owned by Dr. Roussel. She has been here since early June." Warming to the subject, she told them about the book the woman was reputedly working on with the doctor. "His housekeeper says it's going to be very successful, not only in France but in America. It's all about Dr. Roussel's famous herbal cures, though I've never consulted him myself . . ."

Rex cut her off in midstream. "Would you know if this American is acquainted with the Lethbridges?"

"Oh, yes. The housekeeper said that's how she came to rent Dr. Roussel's cottage. I heard yesterday that an Englishman has just arrived to stay as well . . ."

"Ah. And what is his relationship to them?"

"I wouldn't know. But between us, the postman said the Englishman's car was still parked outside the American woman's house in the early morning, so it would seem she is his *petite amie* . . ."

"Thank you, Ursuline. That will be all," he said, dismissing her with a wave of his hand.

When she had gone, Rex's pale eyes clouded as he stared out into the park.

"More coffee, *mon cher*?"

Rex shook his head and knitted his fingers together, a frown on his face.

Philippe shrugged. "I do hope you're not still brooding about running into that fellow in the square last night. I can't understand why he upset you so. Every time you see him you get into a temper."

"If you don't understand that, you don't understand anything. He's Mandy's ex-husband for one thing, and he is the man who first discovered the Grail, for another."

"But his arrival here is obviously a mere coincidence. By some strange chance he is a friend of the Lethbridges. So what? I told you last night that they're perfectly harmless. Just an eccentric old couple who have been coming here for years. The world is not such a large place, really."

"And I've told you that there's no such thing as coincidence. This only goes to prove my point," Rex replied.

"I think you must be in love with this fellow, you're so upset." Philippe gave a little laugh.

"That is about the stupidest remark you've made yet."

Philippe yawned nonchalantly, then rose and stretched. Out of the corner of his eye he watched Rex, who was still staring gloomily into the depths of the park. "I suppose I ought to show you round the estate after lunch. That is, if you can spare the time from your map-reading."

But Rex wasn't listening. "Why would the woman we saw last night, whose name was Lethbridge, come into the shop pretending to be a Mrs. Simpson? There could only have been one reason: they knew something. They have all gathered here for a reason. Owen has come back to trace the origins of the chalice, probably to find the antique dealer himself. And his friend and confidant, A. L. Lethbridge, is helping him. I haven't any doubt that the learned professor is aware of the new developments concerning the fragments of the so-called Gnostic gospels that have come to light. I've underestimated him, Philippe. His purpose is the same as ours."

"But what good would that do him? You said yourself that you'd get word any day now that Baron Hauptmann's heirs have accepted your offer for the chalice."

"I don't like these surprises. I like to know what I'm up against, and something could still go wrong."

"You're working yourself up into a frenzy. Calm down, for goodness' sake."

"Thinking, Philippe, is not getting into a frenzy. The Power helps those who help themselves. And if I were in a frenzy, the blame would lie entirely with you for botching the overdose. You think it's not on my mind what the consequences will be if Mandy regains consciousness? You seem to forget that you'll be in a very unpleasant position if she remembers anything."

"And so will you," Philippe retorted. "But she won't regain consciousness. When you called to ask how she was, the doctor as much as told you he didn't think she would ever come to, so why worry? Anyway, I'm a very ordinary looking fellow, so she probably wouldn't remember me even if she saw me again."

"You might have told her your name without remembering. I warned you against that repeatedly."

Philippe bristled. "I told you, I introduced myself using

the first name I could think of and now I can't remember what it was.''

"Why do you say that to me when you know it's not true? I've told you never to lie to me. I can see right through you.''

"All right, I might have used my name. But it was one small mistake in an otherwise cleanly executed plan.''

"For your sake, I hope so. I don't need all this,'' said Rex with a sweeping gesture. "It interferes with the Power, dilutes my purpose. He shows His displeasure in odd ways, Philippe. You've entered into a pact with Him and if you falter, then you must accept the consequences.''

Philippe looked at him sharply. "Are you threatening me?''

"No, I'm merely reminding you, that's all.'' Rex rose from his chair. "Enough of this self-indulgence. I'm going into the library to work. As soon as the *mairie* opens in that village next week, I want to start trying to trace Durand. Now we know the story of his disappearance, we'll have to try every avenue.''

"I thought you said yesterday that we didn't need him, that the Power was going to help us in other ways,'' replied Philippe, his voice full of recrimination.

"First we must investigate every clue, every lead. I've explained the nature of our work to you. It's not like simply picking fruit off a tree. Be careful you don't become too negative, Philippe, and that you do exactly as I tell you. The great forces we have set in motion are like sharp blades moving all round us. One false move could be deadly.''

"Perhaps we ought to drive to Toulouse to have a look at this Gnostic manuscript,'' suggested Philippe. "My uncle has contacts at the university and I'm sure he could arrange it. I know a charming little restaurant where we could have lunch nearby.''

"No,'' Rex replied flatly. "Our work is here. Let the scholars pore over their texts; you and I can't read or interpret them. Didn't I tell you once that I would be able to prove the authenticity of the Grail when the time came? It's happening under our very noses. By the way, I want you to get Ursuline to find out the name of the person who discovered this manuscript. I want to know where and when he found it. We can find out these simple facts much more easily here through servants' gossip than by trotting off to Toulouse.''

Philippe looked darkly after Rex as he turned his back and walked away, but quickly cast his eyes down at his lap when his friend suddenly stopped and turned around. Yet Rex seemed to be looking beyond him, not at him at all.

"Have you done as I instructed about the room?"

"I said I'd do it today."

"We will fast after lunch, until midnight. I want all the servants out of the house when we summon Him."

Rex turned again and entered the book-lined library, where he seated himself at the leather-topped desk, unrolling an old map of the region, which he began to examine with a magnifying glass. He was interrupted by the sound of voices at the front door. Rising from his chair, he went out into the hall.

"What is it, Ursuline?"

The housekeeper was standing by the door. On the threshold Rex saw a coarse but handsome man, perhaps in his early thirties, who exuded the oily smoothness of a hustler. Rex summed him up at a glance, noting his sensuous mouth, his small, dark eyes and that he was smartly dressed in a vulgar sort of way. He wore a flashy gold watch that wasn't the genuine article and a gold chain glinted from the dark hair showing through his open-necked shirt. The friendliness of his smile didn't match the shrewdness in his eyes.

The housekeeper said indignantly: "This man is asking to use the telephone, *monsieur*. He says his car broke down outside the château, but I told him it is out of the question, that he is trespassing. The gatekeeper must have left the gates open."

"Bonjour, monsieur," the man said. "I'm sorry to trouble you, but I had a puncture and there is no spare tire in the trunk, so I need to call a garage."

"I told you, it's only a short walk," said the housekeeper, trying to close the door on him.

"Just a moment," Rex said. As he studied the Frenchman, curiosity moved him, like the first quiverings of a divining rod near water flowing deep underground.

"There's a telephone in the library," he said, ignoring the disapproval on the housekeeper's face.

Rex followed the man into the library and waited while he dialed directory inquiries, then the garage in Puivaillon.

When he had hung up, he paused, looking round the room. His glance fell on a watercolor hanging over the fireplace. Rex felt himself bristle when the man reached insolently into his pocket and pulled out his lighter and cigarettes.

"What kind of picture is that?" he asked, nodding toward the fireplace.

"It's a mandala. Does that mean anything to you?"

The man shook his head.

"The Baron's grandfather painted it. He was an admirer of Carl Jung."

The man studied it for a moment, then said: "You speak French very well for a foreigner. Are you English?"

"No, American."

"The picture reminds me of something I once saw when I was a boy." Folding his arms, he peered at the mandala.

"What was that?"

"I saw something resembling that painted on the ceiling of a cave many years ago. It wasn't exactly like that, but almost."

"Really? Was the cave nearby?"

"Yes, not so far from here."

"I would be interested to know more. When and how did you find this cave? I'm an amateur historian. That's why I'm visiting the Baron—because the region interests me."

"I can tell you exactly when I saw the cave. It was in 1971," the man said with an air of satisfaction at being able to be so precise.

"Have you ever gone back there?" Rex asked.

"No, never. I've heard there are a lot of cranks looking for treasure around here these days. You're not one of them by any chance, are you?"

Rex snorted in disdain. "No. I merely have an historical interest in ancient symbols. I'd be interested to hear about the cave you say you saw. Baron de Cazenac would be, too, I'm sure. Do you live near here?"

"No. I live in Marseilles. I'm only here for a few days on family business. I grew up in Rocadour."

"And what do you do for a living?"

The man hesitated for a moment. "I work in a travel agency."

Rex stared at him, thinking he was probably involved in

drug trafficking, petty crime or worse. ''Where are you staying?''

''At the Hôtel du Commerce in Puivaillon.''

They walked out into the hall and Rex said: ''To get back to what you were saying about that cave earlier on. If you're free, perhaps you would like to come to dinner one night with the Baron and myself to talk more about this.'' As he spoke, he carefully veiled his deepening curiosity.

The man looked surprised but wary at the invitation. ''Yes, I could probably come, depending on how long I'll be here.''

''Why don't we make it tomorrow, about eight? But I haven't introduced myself. My name is Rex Monckton.''

As they shook hands the man said, ''My name is Jean-Luc Mithois.''

''More *foie gras*, Jean-Luc?'' Rex asked the following evening.

''Avec plaisir,'' he said. Taking the silver dish, he speared a thick slice garnished with truffles.

Rex grimaced at Philippe when he cast a contemptuous look in Jean-Luc's direction. They were seated in the long dining room at a lace-covered table crowded with an array of china and silver showered by light from the chandelier overhead. As he crumbled a piece of bread beside his plate, Jean-Luc glanced at the portraits of the illustrious de Cazenac family in gilt frames that lined the panelled walls. He looked obliquely at the marble busts, the gilt chairs and marquetry commodes, gazing up now and then at the ceiling, where fat cherubs gamboled among roseate clouds. He wore a tight black shirt with sleeves rolled up to the elbows, open at the neck to reveal the thick gold chain he was never without.

When Rex asked him about his work, he started a vague, unconvincing monologue that revealed he knew nothing at all about the travel business.

They had preceded dinner with aperitifs in the library. Philippe had remained silent while Rex drew out their guest with small talk about the region and about Marseilles, which Jean-Luc boasted he knew intimately. The grandeur of Château La Bruyère made him uneasy and he had adopted a defensive, boastful air, but the initial tension in the atmosphere had been eased by the wine, the food and Rex's attentive charm.

"It sounds as if you're bored with the travel industry. Does that mean you're looking for something else to do?" Rex asked genially.

"Perhaps, if a job comes along that suits me," he said with a shrug as he forked another chunk of *foie gras* into his mouth, followed closely by a chunk of bread.

After the housekeeper had served the tournedos in Madeira sauce and their glasses had been filled with Haut-Brion, Rex said:

"I mentioned to the Baron what you told me about that cave you saw when you were a boy and he was fascinated, too. We'd like to hear the story from the beginning: how you came to find it, what you discovered there and so on. The Baron and I are keen students of the early archaeology of the region."

Jean-Luc hesitated, glancing at Philippe, who up until now had spoken very little.

Prompted by a sharp glance from Rex, Philippe said with a frosty smile, "Yes, please, *monsieur*. We would be most interested to hear what you have to say."

"Enough of *monsieur*," Rex interjected. "We're Rex and Philippe to you, Jean-Luc."

Jean-Luc took a gulp of wine, then paused as if he hadn't quite made up his mind whether to confide his secret to them.

"I remember it so well, because it was my last year at school. I ran away from home the next spring and went to Marseilles to look for a job. I looked old for my age," he added with a proud chuckle. "My first jobs were uninteresting, but through my own efforts I came up quickly in the world, with no contacts, no friends. My life has been a terrible battle, but I've always won . . ."

"Tell us what happened that August," Rex prompted, leading him back to the subject.

"One afternoon I was tending my father's goats when I heard a car coming up the hill," he began.

"Where exactly was this?" Rex asked.

"There's a road between Puivaillon and Rocadour that continues unpaved for about three kilometers after an old farm. That's where we used to keep the goats."

"I know where you mean," said Philippe. "The Gorge de

St. Lysère. Only a small gorge, but quite scenic,'' he explained to Rex.

"Oh, so you know it?'' said Jean-Luc.

"I went there once with my father to collect plant and rock specimens for a school project. The road was almost impassable. But do go on, please.''

"It was a monotonous day about two weeks before school started and I was bored. I heard the car going up the road, which peters out high up, and decided to follow it. I rarely saw anyone there, so I was curious. After a while I discovered the car parked a hundred meters up a steep track, on the edge of a clearing that skirted a drop-off. The hills above there are very rocky and full of caves where I know people have found arrowheads and prehistoric tools. I wondered if that was what whoever it was might be looking for.''

"You didn't think that perhaps they were looking for buried treasure, by any chance?'' asked Rex.

Jean-Luc smiled thinly. "It crossed my mind, I admit. And this is the interesting part: when I found the car, I saw it was empty, but I waited concealed in the bushes for a while, until the owner came back. I was very surprised to see a strange-looking man coming down the hill with a sack over his shoulder. He was as thin as a starved dog and his hair was very black. He kept stopping to catch his breath and wipe his forehead with a handkerchief. He looked swarthy, probably foreign, I thought. He could have been forty or sixty—you couldn't tell his age. He was dressed in an old-fashioned shiny serge suit, like my grandfather used to wear.'' Jean-Luc paused to light a cigarette, enjoying the look of attention on Rex and Philippe's faces.

"And so,'' he said, exhaling languidly, "I followed him when he had passed not far away, keeping well behind so he wouldn't hear me. I wanted to know what he had in the sack, which looked to me like something heavy. To my amazement, he whirled around and stared me in the face. It was uncanny, because I'm sure I had been very quiet. I froze, because he terrified me. He had burning dark eyes that reminded me of the statues of the saints staring down from their niches in the church at Rocadour.

"He asked who I was and I replied: 'I am Jean-Luc Mithois. I'm looking for a lost goat that strayed from my herd.' I asked, 'Who are you and what are you doing?' He replied that he was looking for rock samples and could do what he liked, and that I was to mind my own business. I was a bit afraid of him still, because although he wasn't young, he looked very strong to me and he seemed angry that I had followed him.''

When Jean-Luc paused to let his words sink in, Rex leaned over and refilled his glass.

''Anyway, I ran back the way I had come, by another route so I wouldn't be seen. But after I started down the path I changed my mind and went back to see if I could discover what the man was carrying in his sack. I crept through the bushes and this time he didn't see me. He seemed much too intent on looking at what he had in a bag.''

''Did you see what it was?'' Rex couldn't resist asking.

''He took out what looked like an old book of some kind and stared at it for a minute, then he put it back in the bag. I felt disappointed and I was just about to creep away again when I heard a crash coming from the other side of the car. Suddenly he was attacked by two men who jumped out from the bushes. They might have been gypsies, I suppose. They grabbed the sack and hit him over the head with a club. I was terrified that they had heard me talking to him earlier, so I crouched there trembling and didn't really see any more. I thought they would surely steal the car, but no, they took only the sack. They must have followed him up the road, but I hadn't seen them because I was climbing the other way by a shortcut I knew. When I heard a car backing down the hill, I got up and went over to the man, who was lying in the dust, his face covered with blood. The sack was gone. I couldn't go for help because I had to find my goats and round them up. Then, when I had penned them in for the night, I took my bicycle and coasted down to the valley to go back to Rocadour.''

''With the intention of telling the police,'' said Rex.

''Yes . . . of course.'' Jean-Luc avoided Rex's opaque blue eyes, which seemed to penetrate an act of cowardice he had long forgotten.

''But you didn't tell the police, I gather.''

''Well, no, as it turned out. I was knocked off my bicycle

on the way there. The driver and his wife brought me here to Puivaillon to Dr. Roussel's surgery."

"Dr. Roussel," repeated Rex, catching Philippe's eye. "Did you tell the doctor about what had happened?"

"I was too frightened. I had it in my head that the police would accuse me because, after all, I thought he was dead. And then I saw him walk into the doctor's waiting room. I thought I had seen a ghost. I couldn't believe he was still alive. But it didn't end there. I became obsessed with the man, whom I overheard from the couple in the car was a *brocanteur*. His village was too far for me to go to more than once, and when I did, I waited for a long time outside his shop for him to come out, because he had hung a *Fermé* sign on the door. I was just about to give up when I saw a young Englishman walk up the street."

"How did you know he was English?" asked Rex.

"I'll tell you that in a minute." He described the young man, who was of medium height with dark curly hair. "The Englishman went in. He didn't stay very long, no more than ten minutes. When he came out, I heard the old man lock the door. I remember he peered at me suspiciously at a distance, but I turned away. I followed the Englishman back to the square, keeping out of sight so he wouldn't see me. He was holding something in both hands, as if it were very precious."

"Could you see what it was?"

"No, it was in a bag. But it was small enough to hold in one hand." Jean-Luc drained the last drops of wine in his glass. "I was saying how I knew the man was English: I followed him to his car, which was parked in the village square, and it had English license plates. I watched him open the trunk and put what he was carrying inside."

"What kind of car was it? Do you remember what make it was?"

"It was a white English sports car—beautiful. I forgot everything but the car for a few moments."

"A Triumph?"

"Yes, I think that might have been it. How did you know?"

"A guess. Go on."

"So I went back to the shop, this time daring to knock, but there was no answer. When I managed to return to the village two weeks later, the *brocanteur* had packed up and left without a trace. He had moved from the village, disappeared, so I was told, and nobody knew where he had gone."

Rex leaned back in his chair. "How simply riveting," he murmured in English to Philippe, who was leaning forward in rapt attention, all boredom wiped from his face. This time it was he who filled Jean-Luc's glass once it was empty.

"But that isn't the end of the story. It becomes more interesting," said Jean-Luc, whose face had gone red from the wine as well as from the pleasure of holding an audience in thrall.

"Go on," said Rex, his eyes lowered with a half skeptical expression that concealed the excitement he truly felt.

"Soon afterward, it must have been about a week later, I went back to the gorge and began to search for the cave, where I was sure the old man had uncovered something valuable. I searched the hills every Saturday for a month, even when it was stormy." He paused dramatically and lit another cigarette. "Eventually I found the cave." As he smoked, he hugely enjoyed the tangible astonishment his story had produced in Rex and Philippe.

Rex said impatiently: "And what did you find?"

"What did I find?" he repeated, his eyes gliding round the room, which had taken on a pleasant blur in the soft candlelight. "Nothing at all."

Philippe gave a snort of derisive laughter. Anger roused by Philippe laughing at him showed on Rex's face.

"The entrance to the cave was very difficult to reach. You have to jump a little ledge that bridges a terrible drop. It's not really dangerous, only frightening." His eyes sparkled at the thought. "It was very eerie. Before I turned on my flashlight I could hear the wind whistling through the entrance, which unnerved me a bit . . . ."

Rex leaned forward, sensing that he was telling the truth.

"When I got inside, I knew the cave was high by the sound of rocks sliding somewhere in the distance. When I flashed my light upward, I had a shock. It was like the painted dome of a church, washed blue and stamped with faded gold circles that enclosed what looked like stars. At the center of the ceiling was what seemed to be a crude sort of rose that was still faintly pink. That was why I noticed the strange circular picture in your library. Something about it reminded me of the symbols in the cave.''

The room had gone completely silent. Jean-Luc stubbed out his cigarette and waited for Rex and Philippe to comment, concluding from their silence that they were deeply impressed.

''I couldn't stay long. The batteries in my flashlight were weak and I knew it would soon be dark. But I could see there had been someone there before me—the old man, I assumed. There were signs of digging and stubs of melted candles stuck up on several rocks.''

''So you found nothing at all?'' Philippe asked.

''But that is not to say there was nothing to find. I could see the cave was deeper than it seemed. It might have been very deep for all I know. But I was unable to explore it at the time.''

''Well, when did you explore it, then?'' asked Rex. Jean-Luc's coyness was beginning to try his patience.

''I never went back. The winter came and the road was all but impassable. I had other things to think about. The next spring I had a violent quarrel with my father and left home. I went to Marseilles, where I've been ever since. This is the first time I've been back.''

''Strange. Haven't you ever been tempted to return to the cave and see if you could find anything there?'' asked Philippe.

''I've thought about it now and then, but a man has to earn his bread and to be practical. And if I have time off from the travel agency, I go to Martinique or Djerba, not back here looking in caves. Still, the thought did cross my mind when I knew I was coming back here, I admit. But for so many years it was only a memory at the back of my mind. A young boy's adventure, you understand.''

''The question is,'' said Rex, ''would you be able to find the cave again?''

He shrugged. ''I probably could. But regrettably, *monsieur*, time is money. And I can't afford to waste my time without a guarantee of some return.''

''All right,'' said Rex. ''How much would you require to make it worth your while? We are two amateur historians, not businessmen, you know. For us this is a hobby, an amusement while we're on our holidays.''

''You haven't told me your formal occupation,'' Jean-Luc said.

''I'm a writer of detective novels,'' Rex replied.

Jean-Luc laughed. ''This is a good story, then, for one of your books.'' He had had far too much to drink and was beginning to feel confident.

''Would a thousand francs interest you enough to help us find the cave?''

Jean-Luc shook his head. ''I earn a lot more than that in Marseilles at my job,'' he said. ''The travel agency pays me very well.''

''I'm sure it does. How much might it cost, then?''

''Fifty thousand francs would be better.''

''That's five thousand pounds,'' said Rex, muttering in English. ''It's a popular figure.''

''It's absurd,'' sniffed Philippe, looking coldly at Jean-Luc.

Rex silenced him with a glance. ''Jean-Luc, when you find the cave we will be happy to pay you five thousand francs. It's not worth more to us than that.''

Jean-Luc thought it over for a moment. ''And if you find priceless treasure there?''

''Well, you could do that yourself, couldn't you? You don't need us for that. The chances are there is no treasure in the cave; and if there had been, it has probably gone long before now. Anyway, it would be a long, costly job to unearth it. Anything that wasn't buried would have been stolen or destroyed by time. We're interested in the historical aspect only. For example, the paintings on the ceiling sound remarkable. As you pointed out, there could be a connection between oriental symbols and early European art. That is the only real treasure. What do you say? Do you agree to our offer?''

Jean-Luc shook his head. ''I'm not in the least moved by history. Why don't we agree on ten thousand francs? It won't take me that long to find it and it seems fair for my trouble.''

''All right,'' Rex agreed, ''ten thousand francs. The thing is, I can't arrange for the money to be sent from England until Monday, but there's nothing to stop us from going to the cave tomorrow, is there? You have our word.''

Jean-Luc frowned. "I have to be back at work by Tuesday. Are you sure you can have the money by then?"

"I assure you that we will, won't we, Philippe?"

"By all means. Certainly," Philippe quickly agreed.

After several cognacs, Jean-Luc finally rose to go. They saw him to the door, where they all shook hands. When Philippe had closed the door, he followed Rex into the library. As Rex unrolled his map and began to study it, Philippe said in a soft voice:

"I apologize for doubting you, Rex. Can you forgive me?"

"Dear Philippe, what is there to forgive?"

"Everything you predicted is coming true. My behavior has been appalling." His voice broke with remorse and he turned away for a moment, then looked back at Rex with tears in his eyes.

"The Power has ways of humbling us, Philippe. And we feel much better for it, don't we?"

Philippe nodded.

Rex laughed richly. "Did you hear what he said? It was Owen all right—dark curly hair, driving a white sports car with English plates. He carried something from the shop. What could that be, I wonder? It must have been the chalice. And he mentioned pentacles on the ceiling, and a rose. Those are Cathar symbols. We're one step closer to the Holy Grail, Philippe. I feel it."

23

Light streamed through tall windows in the room at the University of Toulouse where Owen was trying to follow the conversation taking place in rapid French between Ambrose and Professor Berger, a wiry man in his sixties. Though Owen could catch only part of what was being said, he could feel the aura of excitement the subject produced.

"Take this magnifying glass, Professor Lethbridge, and

have a look at plate four.'' Professor Berger hovered over Ambrose as he bent to examine one of the plates of glass that framed fragments of parchment brown with age arranged on a long table.

When Ambrose had studied one of the frames, he handed the magnifying glass to Owen. "Here, have a look. It won't mean anything to you, but up close it's fascinating.''

Owen looked through the glass, noting that the fragments so painstakingly reconstructed by a team from the university were covered in what seemed to be blurred scratches.

"The purity of the language testifies to its authenticity,'' said Berger. "Although we've only just begun, to our surprise, we have found some passages in Hebrew and Aramaic, which have excited us very much. There appear to be some mistakes in those, which would indicate that they were painstakingly copied by a scribe who did not know the languages himself.''

"It's staggering,'' Ambrose said to Owen, translating in a few words what the professor had told him. "You've done a stupendous amount of work in such a short time, Professor Berger. I didn't expect to see it in such a well-presented state, and there is much more than I had anticipated.''

"Luckily, the loft where the manuscript was stored was very dry. It was where the farmer used to hang the garlic and onions for the winter, so we're very fortunate.''

"I would very much like to hear the story of how it came to light in Rocadour. It's just down the road from where my wife and I have our summer cottage.''

"How remarkable,'' said the professor. "I asked the man who brought it in to keep the find quiet for a few weeks, until we saw what we had. That was at the end of April. He is a local schoolteacher. We only recently decided to make the announcement about our astounding discovery and, as you can imagine, it's already stirred up a lot of excitement. In brief, what happened was that one of the local cheesemakers died, a fellow by the name of Vignac. His wife sold the farm this spring and when she was clearing out the house, she found the bag containing the manuscript in the attic. She vaguely remembered her husband bringing it home some time in the early Seventies. Apparently he had found the bag in a ditch when he was collecting milk from the local goatherds, somewhere between Puivaillon and Rocadour. They looked at it and it didn't mean anything to them, so they put it up there and forgot all about it. When the wife found it again, luckily she had the presence of mind to call in the local schoolteacher, who saw right away that it was an ancient manuscript. He brought it here to us.''

Ambrose shook his head and stared at the glass-covered sheets in wonder. "What a story! When you think how it might have disappeared at any point along the way, it's a miracle. God only knows how it got into that ditch.''

"The only thing that makes sense to me is that someone threw it in the ditch without realizing what it was. Thieves, perhaps, who had stolen it along with something that was of more obvious value.''

"Yes, that sounds plausible. They took the booty and threw away the real treasure.'' He shook his head and exchanged a glance with Owen, who was deep in thought.

The professor smiled. "As it is, there's some decay and water damage. But, of course, the worst enemy is the passage of time. The centuries have reduced it to the shreds we see before us.''

"How much would you say is intact?''

"It's difficult to say, but at this stage I would think about thirty to fifty percent.''

"That could prove to be a considerable amount, certainly enough to piece the document together in some coherent order, I expect.''

"Oh yes,'' said the professor. "And, of course, some parts are better preserved than others. There, for example, you have a fragment as big as the palm of my hand.''

"Now comes the question of what it says. The newspaper was vague, naturally,'' said Ambrose, "and I was hoping I might hear more from you, in confidence.''

The professor rested his hand on Ambrose's shoulder. "Just between ourselves, I'm very, very excited about what we have deciphered so far. We are already referring to it among ourselves as the Gnostic Bible. I believe it is the fourth book of Flavius Joseph, the lost gospel.''

Ambrose stared at him, electrified by his words.

The professor said reverently: "This is a scholar's dream come true. I believe we have a document that will prove unique to western civilization. It is my conviction that it is a link to the past that may completely alter our outlook on the history of Christianity.''

He paused while his words sank in. Owen, who had hardly spoken, felt a tingling sensation down his spine as he glanced at the jigsaw of manuscript fragments. Thinking of the date when the cheesemaker had discovered the manuscript, he felt a growing certainty that it had something to do with the chalice and with Durand.

''We had an awful time trying to rescue the first page. It had adhered to what looks like a leather binding. You can see a piece of it here.'' The professor opened a box to show Ambrose and Owen the crumbling contents.

''The manuscript has been copied from a source dating back to as early as the first century. It has been sent for testing and we won't know the results for a few weeks.'' He looked at them intently over the tops of his glasses, as his excited voice echoed round the room. ''What we probably have in our possession, as well as the book of Flavius Joseph, is the early history of the Gnostic Church. This document would appear to confirm the legend that the Magdalene did come to France with a band of Christ's followers, possibly including Lazarus and Martha. These pure early Christians, untainted by Rome and its schisms, became the first Cathars, thus validating their claim to represent the true Church. Professor Lethbridge—this will astonish you—but I have already found references to the Grail, which they carried with them.''

''Professor Berger, are you saying that this document proves the existence of the Holy Grail?''

''Of course I won't be able to say it publicly, and I can't confirm it until we have studied these parchments for years, perhaps decades, but yes, it would appear that the Grail is not just the stuff of legend, nor was it merely the symbol of the search for truth, but a real object, a chalice from which Christ drank, which perhaps even held his blood after the crucifixion.''

''Astounding, simply astounding,'' said Ambrose. ''And what do you suppose happened to the Holy Grail?''

''Ah, well, that we will probably never know. Perhaps it is buried somewhere or perhaps it was part of the treasure we know the Cathars spirited away to Ussat before their martyrdom . . .''

"Good Lord," said Ambrose. "It's hard to take in. That would mean this document could prove more important than the Dead Sea Scrolls."

The professor nodded his head. "It's the most extraordinary thing. I wake up every morning thinking about the impact this will have on biblical scholarship, on our whole outlook on early Western history." His eyes were bright with excitement.

They stood in meditative silence for several moments, staring at the parchments. Owen reached into his pocket for his wallet and took out the piece of paper on which he had copied as best he could the inscription on the chalice, that day in Geneva.

"I wonder if you could translate this inscription for me, Professor Berger. I have no knowledge of ancient languages, but I tried to copy it as faithfully as I could."

The professor took the paper, adjusting his glasses as he read it. "Well, it's Aramaic." His lips moved as he translated the words to himself. His eyes widened in surprise. "Where did you get this?"

"I copied it off a chalice that was for sale at Sotheby's in Geneva a few months ago."

"I see. Very interesting," he replied, handing back the paper. "From a chalice, you say? What did it look like?"

When Owen had described it, he asked: "And where is it now?"

"I don't know. It was withdrawn from sale at the end of May. Perhaps I could find out, if you're interested."

"What made you copy the inscription?"

"It's a long story. The chalice was once in my possession. I bought it in Languedoc years ago, from a *brocanteur*, and then it disappeared."

The professor didn't reply, but looked at him thoughtfully. Then Ambrose said: "We have taken up enough of your time, Professor Berger. I know you have a lecture shortly."

They walked together into the hall. "It was good to see you again, Professor Lethbridge. I have just received a copy of your magnificent book, which I'm looking forward to reading on my holidays this summer."

"Where are you going?"

"My wife and I always go to St. Maxime."

They all shook hands and said goodbye. But just as Owen and Ambrose were about to go down the stairs, Professor Berger said:

"Professor Lethbridge, I wonder if you could just step into my office for a moment. There is something I would like to ask you."

A few moments later Owen was waiting as Ambrose descended the stairs, a startled expression on his face.

"What did he want?" Owen asked as they went out the door.

They stood in the square outside, enjoying the brilliant sunlight.

"When I went into his office, he seemed suddenly troubled. You're going to be shocked when I tell you this. Owen, Berger said that he has already come across a reference to the inscription in the text of the parchment."

"You're kidding," was all Owen could say.

"Word for word, in Aramaic, the text refers to the same inscription engraved on the base of what they refer to as the Holy Grail. I was so astonished, all I could do was to say that we would be in touch very soon. He needs time to think, and so do we."

"We may not have time. The chalice could be anywhere by now. As I said, I tried to contact Hauptmann's heirs through their lawyers before I left, but so far there's been no reply. It's maddening, but there's nothing I can do. Of course, it has crossed my mind that Rex has been in touch with them, too. He's in a much better position to make an offer to the estate than I am. His references are impeccable and, after all, he sold the chalice to Hauptmann in the first place and has probably been waiting for ages for him to sell it again. What chance does someone like me have to gain it back?"

When Ambrose saw the anguished look on Owen's face, he said quietly: "I know what this must mean to you, Owen."

They walked down the narrow street lined with medieval brick-and-timbered buildings, whose courtyards sent forth welcoming waves of coolness in the heat.

"I now understand that the search for the Grail means as much, if not more, to Rex Monckton as it does to me. You know, within the last quarter of an hour everything has crystallized in my mind. My guess is that for years he's regretted selling the chalice to Hauptmann. I don't know how, but at some point he realized its true significance and became as desperate as I was to get it back. Like me, he had possessed it once and lost it. It's strange, Ambrose, but I feel as if he and I are like two adversaries locked in phantom combat. Neither of us seems able to win.''

Rex sat down on a patch of dry grass, breathing heavily. Taking off his panama hat, he mopped his brow with his handkerchief as he looked back down the hill he had just climbed. It had taken him half an hour to come a short distance. He had straggled after Jean-Luc and Philippe, who were already far above him. His face flushed with anger and exertion, he gasped for breath as he searched the surrounding hills through his binoculars. He trained the lenses on a distant hilltop, where he thought he could make out the ruins of a fortress or a church, but it was too far away to tell.

''Too obvious,'' he murmured to himself, swiveling round to look at the terrain where Philippe and Jean-Luc had disappeared. Putting down the glasses, he spread out his map and noted the exact position with a pencil, feeling a sense of absurdity as he did so. The distant sound of water rushing through the gorge below and the hot breeze ruffling the lavender and broom soothed him.

Moments later he looked up to see Philippe climbing over the rocks toward him.

''Anything?'' he called.

''No, nothing,'' said Philippe with a shake of his head. Sweating and breathing heavily, he came to Rex's side. ''We went all the way to the top this time to see if he might remember from another angle. I thought for a minute he had it, but it was just another dead end.''

''You shouldn't have left him up there by himself.'' Rex stood up anxiously and combed the hill above through his binoculars. ''If he finds anything when he's alone he might not tell us.''

''Of course he'll tell us. He wants the money.''

''Greed might get the better of him if he thinks we're on to something.''

"He didn't say a word all the way up. I think he's getting really angry now. Maybe we should give him part of the money to pacify him. I'm exhausted and it's only midday," Philippe complained.

"I'm not giving him a sou until he finds that cave."

"But we did promise," Philippe reminded him.

"And he promised he would find the cave. He said he knew exactly where it was. It's been two days now."

"He's going to get discouraged soon."

"We'll see. I'd rather stall him for a few more days, until we're absolutely sure that he can't find the cave. But while you were up there, I've been thinking. Perhaps I'm asking too much of him. Maybe he wasn't intended to do more than point the way."

Philippe shook his head. "It would be difficult for you and me to know where to go from here."

Looking at the map again, Rex said: "This road doesn't lead anywhere. We know the cave is here somewhere. We'll look for it systematically. That's better than what he's doing."

"There must be a hundred caves up there."

"It's probably been lying undiscovered for seven and a half centuries and we shouldn't be discouraged if it takes us more than a day or two to find it."

"What he said about the candles in the cave—it might indicate there's no treasure left now, if there ever was any. There's no guarantee Durand found the chalice there; it's only guesswork."

"Not necessarily. We have to have faith, Philippe. Now listen, before he comes back, it occurs to me that you and I are as capable of finding the place as he is. After all, we've narrowed it down to a very small area. We'd be better off looking ourselves, wouldn't we? Then he would be out of the picture."

"Of course, you're right. I sense that he's only guessing now."

"In that case I think we can dispense with Monsieur Mithois's services," said Rex.

From a ledge high above, Jean-Luc stood and listened to the silence as he combed the dry hills, shading his eyes from the midday sun. He retraced every furrow, every rocky outcrop sprouting with wild thyme and broom, but he could see nothing that pointed the way to the cave. The landscape seemed neither familiar nor unfamiliar, but one-dimensional: an impression he couldn't reconcile with his memory. Like a giant hand, the hills splayed into steep gullies that all looked the same. When he was thirteen he had known the hills, possessed a real feeling for the contours of the land and all its subtle nuances, but his old instinct seemed to have left him. Recalling the day when he had stumbled on the cave, he remembered how easy it had been. In the blink of an eye the hills had revealed their secret, but nothing he had seen in the last two days had even brought him close to the place that eluded him.

Turning his back on the hills, Jean-Luc wiped the sweat from his brow and suddenly decided he had had enough, that it was time to move on, but with money in his pocket. He was restless to get away.

Coming down the hill, he saw Rex and Philippe sitting together among the rocks. When he came up to them, they looked at him expectantly.

"Well?" asked Rex.

Jean-Luc narrowed his eyes and glared at them with undisguised hostility. "I want to be paid now, in cash, for my time or I won't continue the search. You promised me yesterday that you would have the money this morning. I know you have the money and you're lying to me."

"I'm sorry you feel that way," said Rex. "If you really feel like that, then there's nothing to say. You may go."

Jean-Luc glowered at him, but he didn't move.

"Did you hear what I just said? You're no longer needed here."

"And let you find what you're looking for without paying me? You must think I'm stupid. I want my money now, with no more excuses."

Jean-Luc reached into his pocket and pulled out a switchblade, which flashed in the sun as he flicked it open. Philippe, who was standing between him and Rex, darted out of the way and jumped behind a rock. When Jean-Luc's head moved in that direction, Rex pulled out a gun. Jean-Luc stared at it, feeling the power of the knife diminish in his hand.

"Now do as I say and get out of here instantly or you'll regret it. You can walk back to Puivaillon."

"You expect me to walk back? Bastard!" he cried.

"If I have to shoot you, it's going to look like an accident. That knife looks pretty well used and I guess you've been in trouble before, so it wouldn't be hard to persuade the police you attacked us."

Shoving the knife back into his pocket, Jean-Luc took a step backward, then turned and fled down the mountainside.

"I don't think we shall see him again," said Rex, adjusting his panama hat. "I've had enough for today. Let's go back to La Bruyère and return here again tomorrow."

Moments later they were in the car speeding down the dirt road back to the valley. Neither Rex nor Philippe saw Jean-Luc crouching behind some rocks as they drove by, leaving him in their wake.

Dorothy crossed the sitting room of the cottage when the telephone rang. She picked it up, half expecting to hear Ambrose's voice on the line saying he and Owen would be late, but instead she heard a click, followed by the unfamiliar voice of an Englishman.

"Gerald Barber speaking. Is Owen Morgan there, please?"

Dorothy was alert at the mention of Barber's name, recalling that he had been Owen's father-in-law and that she had met him at the wedding. The strain in his voice filled her with foreboding.

"I'm sorry, Mr. Barber, but he's not here at the moment. He's expected before noon. This is Dorothy Lethbridge; we've spoken before. Can I give him a message?"

"Oh, hello, Mrs. Lethbridge. This is Mandy's father . . ."

During the long pause Dorothy knew what was coming.

"I may as well tell you now and you can relay the message to Owen. Mandy died an hour ago. We made the decision with the doctors that there was no point in prolonging her ordeal further." His voice conveyed an infinite grief held rigidly under control.

As she waited for him to continue, Dorothy had an image of Mandy in a white minidress, a nest of flowers in her flowing blonde hair, her cornflower blue eyes shining with happiness as she stood with Owen on the steps of the register office on the day they were married. She remembered the two of them posing for a photographer, Owen wearing a flamboyant white cutaway coat. They had driven off in a white Rolls-Royce, showered in a cloud of petals and rice thrown by their friends. Although she had been expecting the news, she was filled with sadness.

"Gerald, I don't know what to say. I'm so terribly sorry. Like you, we've been praying she would recover. We send our deepest sympathy to you and Maureen. I'll tell Owen the moment he comes in. Would you like him to call you?"

"No, that's all right. I'll get in touch with him as soon as we know what the funeral arrangements will be."

Dorothy hung up, feeling the pall of death darken the sun-filled room. The word "murder" rang in her head and she saw the satanic image of Rex Monckton, who was never far from her mind. The sense of helplessness that had oppressed her from the beginning of the affair filled her with despair as she pictured Rex spinning his grand design at the Château La Bruyère only a few miles away. The forces of good that were needed to neutralize the evil he had already done seemed hopelessly fragile. She was paralyzed with indecision, knowing full well that even now her duty was to caution, not to interfere. That was all she had ever been able to do. She picked up the telephone, glancing at the clock on the mantelpiece. It was only eight and she might be able to catch Ambrose and Owen at the hotel in Toulouse.

A while later Dorothy entered the whitewashed kitchen and took down her market basket from a hook on the wall. In her mind was a mental picture of Owen, whose voice on the phone had been filled with quiet resignation when he heard the news. Closing the front door behind her, Dorothy stood for a minute on the sunny terrace, focusing on the brilliant splash of geraniums, which reminded her unpleasantly of blood, while she thought of Owen. An anxiety that had plagued her ever since his arrival rose inside her. He was hot-blooded, passionate and intrinsically just. Even so, what chance did he have against such forces?

She went to fetch her bicycle from behind the house, thinking that at lunch, when the four of them were supposed to meet, they could discuss some course of action that would break the agonizing deadlock. At some point, Dorothy reasoned, Rex Monckton would overstep his powers. That was the mark of all illusionists, all those who consorted with the Devil. Now more than ever she was tempted to tell Owen and Louise of the distant events that marked their present lives, but it was impossible. It would be like explaining the facts of life to a child who lacked the power to comprehend the implications. If nothing else, she ached to tell them how far back their common roots reached in time, so that they could share the rich sense of meaning that bound them. But some ancient taboo that Dorothy had never questioned forced her to keep silence.

Dorothy pedaled determinedly down the dirt road, heading for the village and meeting little traffic on the main road. She approached the town feeling strangely uneasy. Puivaillon was always alive on market day, and she dismounted and walked the last few yards, weaving in and out of the cars. She left her bicycle near the church and went to do her shopping, passing mobile vans brightly decked out with plastic pennants, spilling with pots and pans, piles of men's hats and ladies' dresses waving in the breeze. She queued up for *charcuterie* and cheese for lunch, exchanging pleasantries with village people she had known for years; but all the time she was preoccupied. She found herself peering into the crowd, but for what she did not know. She gave a start when someone touched her arm. Turning round, she smiled when she saw Louise.

"I've been watching you for a moment. From the look on your face I guessed you must be plotting your next novel," she said.

Dorothy gave her a rueful smile. "You're not very far wrong. I was remembering one of my old books. For some reason I happened to be thinking about the two young lovers in the story. My, how pretty you look, and how fresh," she said affectionately. The relief she felt at seeing Louise told Dorothy she had been unconsciously uneasy about her that whole morning. As they talked, she felt an unexpected rush of tenderness for Louise, who looked ten years younger than she had on the day Dorothy had first seen her standing on the station platform. Louise's face was shadowed by a straw hat and her sundress of blue cotton exposed her brown arms. The look of radiant happiness on her face needed no explanation. Dorothy sensed she was on the brink of the kind of fulfillment that everyone dreams of.

"Have you heard anything from the men?" Louise asked cheerfully.

"Ambrose said they had a fascinating day at the university with Professor Berger." She thought of Mandy, hating to spoil Louise's happy mood.

"I can't wait to hear all about it. What time do you expect them?"

"Ambrose said they would be leaving the hotel after breakfast. He wanted to stop off at his favorite bookshop, but they should be here by noon. I'm just buying a few things for lunch."

"I've got a kilo of peaches, so don't buy any. I'll bring them when I come. Can I give you a lift home?"

"No, I've come on my bicycle. Aren't you working with Maurice this morning?"

Louise gave Dorothy a sheepish look. "He's called a two-week sabbatical while Owen's here. His excuse was that he and I deserve a holiday. It's as if he read my mind."

"Perhaps, but the truth is he read your eyes." Dorothy smiled fondly. She could put it off no longer. "Louise, before you go there's something I must tell you. Mandy died this morning. Her father called just before I came to market."

"Does Owen know?"

Dorothy nodded. "I caught him and Ambrose before they checked out of the hotel."

"How terribly sad," she murmured. "I know Owen will be devastated, even though he prepared himself for it."

"I'm grateful he has you to help him get over it," said Dorothy.

Louise thought a moment. "Dorothy, tell me, do you think it's all too sudden, Owen and me?"

"I don't think it's sudden at all." As she spoke, her words were weighted with a meaning Louise would never understand. "You know how fond Ambrose and I are of both of you. I can tell you now that from the beginning I thought you were meant for each other."

"Did you really? What a nice thing to say. Of course, I realize that these things can fizzle out as quickly as they begin and that maybe it won't amount to anything. But I'm so happy, I can't begin to tell you.''

"I'm so glad for you, so very glad.''

"Owen and I both seem to be at a turning point in our lives. Just between us, I think it's miraculous. I remember that day in your kitchen, when I said I thought it would never happen to me again, but you predicted otherwise.''

"Yes, I did, didn't I?'' she replied. She smiled and added: "Where are you off to now?''

"As I have the morning free, I thought I'd go to the place where I took Owen for a picnic the other day. I saw a beautiful big patch of *sariette* that I thought I'd gather. It's at its best now. I had to buy a few things first, but I should be back well before noon. I'll come over and give you a hand, if you like.''

"Splendid. We'll have a glass of wine under the trees while we're waiting.'' As the woman in front of Dorothy moved away, the vendor asked:

"Qu'est-ce-que vous desirez, madame?"

Dorothy said a fleeting goodbye to Louise, then turned to give her order for pâté and ham. She was tucking her purchases into her basket and waiting for her change when she saw Rex Monckton under the awning of a market stall. When Louise passed by, he pulled down the brim of his hat and quickly followed her. His movement conveyed a coiled power that suggested he had been waiting for her.

"Your change, *madame*,'' the vendor called after Dorothy.

"A tout à l'heure," she called over her shoulder as she hurried after Rex. Jostling her way through the crowd, she formed a plan to detain him by posing as the same dotty country lady who had come into his shop, even though she guessed he was well aware of her real identity by now. Anything, she told herself, to keep him from following Louise. Arriving at the church, all she could see were lines of parked cars glittering in the heat, and no sign of either of them. Stars of anxiety exploded before her eyes as she felt the wheel of change move forward with an imperceptible but crushing power. She knew that Louise was in danger.

Dorothy was sitting listlessly beneath the trees in front of the house when she heard the sound of a car coming up the road.

Turning her head, she saw Owen's BMW as a red blur in the shimmering heat. She rose from her chair, feeling every joint in her body resist her will to move. The earth beneath her feet seemed to shift as she walked forward. She saw Owen against a purple sky, but he was no longer Owen.

"Hello," he called in a subdued voice. "Ambrose will be along in a minute. He stopped by at Maurice's to drop off some books he picked up for him in Toulouse. I had him drop me off at Louise's cottage, thinking we'd come together, but she wasn't there so I thought she was probably with you." He looked round for her car as he got out of the BMW. "I wanted to tell her about Mandy . . ."

When Owen saw the stricken look on Dorothy's face, he stopped. His first thought was that she was grieving over Mandy, who hadn't left his mind during the return drive from Toulouse. Grateful for her sympathy, he reached for her shoulder, feeling her shake as if a current of energy had electrified her body. The mute suffering in her eyes bewildered him.

"Dorothy, what's the matter? What's wrong?" he said, alarmed by the faraway look in her eyes.

As they faced each other, Dorothy's vision narrowed to a band of blue. The shadows deepened around the house and she found she was looking at Owen in an aureole of light as if from the divide between past and present. Her lips parted, forming his name: "Hugo."

The name by which she first knew him had always lived in her heart. It was difficult to articulate it, feeling as she did so that she was breaking some sacred, unwritten law. In doing so, she was tampering with the divine balance of innocence and knowledge.

Owen looked at Dorothy, blankly at first, as a current ran from her hands into his. When she called him Hugo, he was startled and the significance of the name refused to enter his consciousness. He knew only that he and Dorothy had shared something great and good so far back that he would never be able to trace its roots. For a blinding instant he believed that their common beginnings forged an indissoluble bond between them. Dorothy was leading and he was desperate to follow, if only he knew how.

He thought he would never understand, until Dorothy

started speaking to him in a strange language he had never heard before. Its ancient cadence resonated at the back of his mind, casting up ripples of familiarity. He felt relief, joy and agony at the same time, hammered together to form a healing power of cosmic opposites.

"Gaucelm and Sancha," she said, tears running down her cheeks.

He realized he should know the names, but, try as he would, their relation to him wouldn't come back. The name Sancha and the turbulent joy it aroused mystified him. The other, Gaucelm, evoked a deep feeling of dread.

Dorothy's vision cleared as suddenly as it had descended. When the trance had lifted, she had become small and weary, and she slumped forward. Owen was still recovering from the shock of the inexplicable moments that had just passed, which had seemed like years. He felt oddly outside himself when he looked at the surrounding landscape. When the feeling of strangeness passed, his throat contracted with a dry nausea.

"Owen, there's no time to lose. Rex Monckton followed Louise from the market about an hour ago, but I couldn't prevent it. I know she is in danger. I've had a kind of terrible premonition. When I saw her an hour before you came, she told me she was on her way to the place where she took you for a picnic the other day."

He pressed his hands to his head, trying to right his senses. "You mean the gorge? The place where she gathers herbs for Maurice?"

"Yes, that's the place. Do you know exactly where it is?"

"I'm sure I could find it. And you say Rex followed her there? But why?" He was suddenly alert.

"I don't know. I pray he hasn't, but I'm almost sure he did."

Without wasting another moment, Owen sprinted to the car and started it. As he accelerated down the drive, he cast one long, worried look back toward Dorothy.

He drove away hearing her call after him: "Be careful, Owen," adding ". . . Hugo" when he was out of earshot. She watched the car until it disappeared from sight, feeling as cold as death under the hot sun.

"Please, God, let him find her this time before it's too

late. And may he never remember what happened before,''
she murmured.

24

Louise was climbing the hill above the gorge just as the sky
glazed over with thin clouds. Out of breath, she scrambled
over the rocks, high above where she had parked her car, and
paused for a moment to watch little whirlpools of dust and
leaves chased by the hot wind. The stillness of the bright
noon was broken by the faraway whisper of water and the
whirr of insects. She leaned against a rock and let her mind
drift as she looked at the spectacular view all round her.
When a sharp crackling noise made her start, she whirled
round and peered down at the scrub oak broken by rocks,
but she could see no sign of movement in the still landscape.
She guessed that what she had heard had only been dry broom
pods bursting in the sun. A feeling crept over her that she
was being watched, but a hawk circling overhead and the hot
wind on her face made her somehow confident that nothing
could harm her here.

She wandered off her usual path, gathering herbs until her
basket was full. Clambering over the rocks, she stood as
close to the precipice as she dared. She had the sensation of
being on the edge of the world as she stared into the foaming
chasm below, a view that thrilled and frightened her, making
her knees go weak.

When she turned to go back, she noticed a grassy shelf in
the rock below that she had never seen before. Moving
through the rocks, she was drawn to the sheltered hollow out
of the glare of the sun. The heat trapped in the rocks made
her feel sleepy and she had the urge to lie down for a moment
on a patch of sun-bleached grass that looked invitingly soft.
She set down her basket, not planning to stay long because
Dorothy was waiting for her, but her eyelids became unbearably heavy. As her spine touched the ground she felt a pow-

erful surge of contentment enfold her like a cloak. Telling herself she would rest only for a moment, she fought the drowsiness induced by the changing light as clouds moved overhead. As the sun stained her eyelids red, a sweet desire for sleep that she couldn't resist stole over her. She lost consciousness while listening to the song of a lone cicada and the distant sound of the river.

When Louise awoke with a start, her watch said that she had closed her eyes only briefly, but she felt strangely disoriented, as if hours had passed and she had been dreaming. Her vision seemed clouded by a dim spot of light, as if she had stared too long at the sun. Closing her eyes, she pressed her temples to make it disappear and, in doing so, retreated to her mind's eye, a well of darkness where images began to stir to life. When she opened her eyes a clear recollection came back to her of a girl like herself, her dark cloak sweeping the rocks where she was now. The hem of her gown seemed to brush against Louise as the memory of her passed by, prompting her to rise to her feet. Her heart began to pound as she started to climb in the direction of the mysterious figure. She kept her eyes trained on the rocks, sensing that the girl was not far ahead. Nor was she alone. A man in a white garment slashed with a crude red cross was not far behind the girl as she made her way up the steep path that was now overgrown and unrecognizable. What Louise thought were dark spots on a distant ridge became a spectral band of cloaked figures, their heads bowed, disappearing one by one into the landscape ahead of the man and the girl.

Louise struggled desperately upward, disregarding the difficulty and searching for a foothold that seemed familiar. Where the phantom woman and her companion had vanished, she knew she must follow. She was tired and her mouth was dry, but she forged on, forgetting how difficult the climb was as she concentrated on the shadowy suggestion of figures still moving against the gray rocks. She didn't stop for breath, even when the path was steep, driven by the need to find something she had discarded long ago.

At last she arrived at a precipice where even a mountain sheep might not dare follow. Stopping to catch her breath, Louise stared at the impenetrable wall of shrubbery before her. An instinct made her push through the thicket barring her way to a rock face. When she had fought her way through, she gasped at what she saw. Through a split in the rocks at her feet she could see the foaming chasm far below. On the other side, the ledge seemed like a sheer rock face, but Louise sensed that something was hidden there. She would have to leap the short but unnerving chasm separating her from the ledge, which drew her curiosity the more she looked at it. Fear prickling the backs of her knees, she jumped, feeling a peculiar sensation of lightness. She looked back to where she had stood seconds before, wondering at how familiar it all seemed. She found herself hesitating, as if waiting for someone to follow. Where was the girl in the cloak and her companion? The dim image of her disappearing up the hillside had already begun to fade. Now, other images and sounds drummed in her head, which she didn't dare stop to examine for fear they would vanish.

Louise followed the ledge, which curved out of sight, and discovered the dark entrance to a cave. When she peered inside, she guessed by the rasp of the wind in the distant hollows that the cave was large and deep. She entered the blackness and stood for a moment, unable to see more than a few feet ahead. The rippling emptiness all round her was like the deep stillness in a cathedral when voices have just ceased to pray and chant. The merest vibration, just audible, suggested that the voices might have stopped just as she entered the cave, though Louise sensed it was a long, long time ago. Straining to hear the dying echo, she was disappointed to realize it was the wind she had heard whispering at the entrance to the cave. Reaching in her pocket, she felt her keys and remembered the small light attached to the key-ring. She aimed the pinpoint of light upward and gasped when she saw silver stars locked in golden circles painted on a field of faded blue. Each was slightly different from the other, and they seemed to be moving around what looked like a faded rose blooming in the center, as if around the sun. As she stared at the rose, the illusion of chanting voices returned again. She felt a presence in the cave, so strong she could almost hear the rustle of garments and the sound of breathing. Then she began to pray, sensing that the distance between then and now was narrow enough to bridge, if only she knew how.

Later, pointing her light into the depths of the cave, Louise swept it past a heap of candle stubs on the nearby rocks. Sinking to her knees, she clasped her hands, submitting herself entirely to the force that had brought her there. And lost in meditation, she didn't hear the distant sound of rocks sliding somewhere beyond the mouth of the cave.

Owen brought his car to a sudden halt on the dusty road that ended at the top of the gorge. Leaping out, he listened for a moment to the silence, which was broken only by the distant rush of water. A flash of white told him that Louise's car was parked ahead. Running toward it, he stopped suddenly when he passed a red car he knew must belong to Rex Monckton concealed amongst a bank of shrubbery. The door was still ajar, as if Rex had jumped out in a hurry.

For a moment he was paralyzed by doubt, wondering whether he should risk warning Rex by calling out Louise's name. The tense seconds that passed were measured by his own heartbeat. He shielded his eyes from the sun and searched the rocky hills, trying to locate the exact spot where he and Louise had picnicked two days earlier, but the blank light of midday flattened the landscape and he didn't know which way to turn. As he watched and waited for some sight or sound of Rex and Louise, a dread began to gnaw at him that he was already too late. Breaking out in a cold sweat, Owen struggled to get a grip on himself.

When he finally found the sheltered spot where he and Louise had spent an afternoon, Owen could see no sign of either Rex or Louise. Scanning the hills, he realized they could be anywhere. Fighting a creeping terror that something had happened to Louise, he closed his eyes in concentration, and when he opened them, he saw there was an aureole around the sun. A shaft of light seemed to be streaming directly ahead, illuminating a clearing in the direction opposite to the picnic spot. Letting his intuition guide him, Owen headed toward it, shunning the obvious path and choosing instead a treacherous route up the rocks to the clearing. The climb was steep and difficult, but when he hoisted himself up over a ridge on all fours, he blinked at a glint of metal in the sun: Rex's watch. He was standing only a few yards away on the level clearing, his field glasses trained on the rocks higher up. Owen felt a great sense of relief as he realized that Rex was probably still looking for Louise and had lost her.

Rex was so intent on what he was doing that he didn't hear Owen approach, but the moment Owen took a step forward, Rex dropped the glasses and whirled round to face him. Owen felt himself impervious to the malevolence darting from Rex's blue eyes, and yet he had never felt as alone as he did now, confronting Rex in the wilderness.

"Don't come any closer," Rex warned when Owen inched forward. Glancing over his shoulder at the drop just a few feet away, Rex maneuvered himself away from the edge.

Owen braced himself for a fight. "The police will be looking for you soon. Mandy died this morning, Rex, and I can prove you were behind her murder. You killed her, Rex."

Rex said nothing, only fixed him with an unwavering stare that suggested neither regret nor fear. When Owen moved forward, he murmured, "Don't come any further. You don't know who you're dealing with. I thought I made it clear the last time we met."

"Why did you follow Louise, Monckton? Speak up—did you intend to kill her like you killed Mandy?" Owen's accusation echoed in the hills.

Rex shrugged indifferently, as if he couldn't be bothered to reply.

"Either you tell me or I'll beat the shit out of you here and now."

Rex chortled. "I'd like to see you try. Don't be fooled by appearances. I'm much stronger than you are, in every way."

"I'm not afraid of you, Monckton. You forget, I've been looking forward to this moment for a long time. God knows how long I've waited." As he spoke, it seemed that they were old, old adversaries. Their friendship seemed impossibly remote and it crystallized in Owen's mind that all those years had represented nothing more than an uneasy truce of opposites, who were truly born enemies. His early admiration for Rex had been a fascination with the mental workings of a being who was utterly strange, alien even, to everything Owen held dear. Twenty years on, he was shocked and exhilarated by the desire now stirring within him to kill Rex.

Rex gave a contemptuous sneer. "If you could only see your face, twisted with hatred. Such puerile, pointless hatred, directed at what you cannot understand. You're a fool, Owen. I wish you no particular harm, nor your friend. But you will insist on getting in my way."

"Then what are you doing here?"

"Even if I told you, you wouldn't understand. Let's say I suspect Mrs. Carey to be a kind of water diviner who is leading me to a source of great value to me and me alone. That's all the explanation I have to offer you. Take it or leave it. Now get out of my way." He shot Owen an angry glance, then turned to go back down the way he had come, but Owen moved swiftly to block him. "If you're wise, Owen, you'll do as I command."

"As you *command?*" The words were a blatant challenge. "But I'm not wise. If I were wise, I would never have let you steal the Grail from me all those years ago."

Rex raised an eyebrow and a look of incredulity crossed his face. "So, you know? How ironic. And all along I thought you were so stupid. But no matter. You're no closer to having it now than you ever were."

"And neither are you. It's not meant to belong to you, because you're evil, Rex, and the Grail is wholly good."

Rex snorted with laughter. "And you, I suppose, represent goodness. Good, evil—you talk like a schoolboy. There is only one thing that is the measure of any man, my friend, and that is power."

Owen was taken off guard when Rex sprang forward with astonishing agility and slammed his hands violently down between Owen's shoulders with the force of two steel blades, causing him to buckle forward with the impact and lose his balance. As he staggered, he caught the impact of Rex's boot in his face. Slumping to the ground, he twisted to one side to avoid another blow. Opening his eyes, Owen saw that a few inches more and he would roll over the edge of the precipice. He imagined himself falling through the air onto the sharp rocks below, a horrific vision that galvanized him to action. Struggling to his feet, he moved away just in time, but the full force of Rex's boot crushed into his ribs. He gasped with pain and in the dark seconds that followed he was catapulted back in time, to another mountainside in another age, where he lay helpless, the weight of death pinning him to the earth for what seemed forever. A sense of mortal danger, like a blow in his stomach, brought him violently back to the present. A new energy empowered him with the might to defend what was right and good and, in doing so, to vanquish the shadow that he knew had always been with him. He calculated that one violent unexpected move would send Rex hurtling over the precipice. But just as he poised himself to spring, his mind was neutralized by Dorothy's words of warning. A vision of mortality, heady as perfume, filled his mind, making him hesitate to risk all on one toss. Rex saw his chance and hurled himself forward, but Owen sensed him coming and dived to the ground. When he looked up, Owen saw Rex stagger to his feet and limp down the hillside like a wounded beast, looking over his shoulder to make sure he wasn't being followed.

Owen's impulse was to charge after Rex, but he seemed unable to move from where he lay, feeling his whole body pulsate with the realization that he had narrowly escaped losing his life. The taste of blood and dust filled his mouth, unlocking a bizarre sensation. He could feel a sword passing painlessly through him, bringing with it the explosive conviction that he had held the Grail, not only in this life, but also in another. For a moment he lay there staring at the blue sky, stunned by the knowledge of how little death mattered. The shattering moment of awareness lasted no longer than the time it took for a shooting star to fall to earth and then it faded, chased away by the brilliant sun overhead. He heard the wind in the broom, the sound of footsteps on the rocks, then someone calling his name. Everything was calm again.

"Owen!"

It was Louise.

She had been coming down the hillside in a distracted mood, her mind still on the cave, when she saw Owen on the hillside, his head in his hands. Scrambling over the rocks, she went to him.

"You're hurt!" she cried. The sight of blood streaming from the corner of his mouth and down his forehead threw her into a turmoil. She helped him to his feet and they sat down on a rock. He hugged her to him for a moment before he could speak.

"Rex Monckton was watching you from a distance. He followed you here. We had a fight."

Louise pressed her face into his shoulder and began to tremble all over. "Something else has happened to you, too, hasn't it? I felt it just now when I came down the hillside. I've felt it all morning, but I don't know what it is." As she spoke, Louise hesitated over putting it into words, but she was aware of the same ground swell of emotion that had overwhelmed them in April at Montségur. The blue summer day was electrified, illuminating the distant recesses of her mind in sudden brilliance.

They sat for a while without speaking, watching and listening. Louise broke the silence with a whisper.

"There are blank moments in my mind. I'm not sure how it all began now. I fell asleep and I remember dreaming about a girl. Was there really somebody here or did I imagine it?"

She paused, looking at the hills where shadows had begun to form now the sun had moved across the sky. "Owen, I found a cave. Could that be what Rex was looking for too?"

"A cave?" he whispered. It was another piece of the puzzle, but where it belonged, he didn't know.

When she tried to describe it, she felt her throat close with tears. "I don't know what's the matter with me," she whispered, wiping her eyes.

"You're upset, that's all. You've had a terrible ordeal."

"No, it wasn't like that. I've never felt so at peace." She looked up the hill, feeling the need to go back and untangle the thread that had led her there.

"I wonder what made Rex follow you, when you didn't even know yourself that the cave existed?"

"Couldn't it have just been a coincidence?"

"But there have been so many. What do they all mean?" he asked, without expecting an answer.

"You haven't told me yet how you found me here."

"It was Dorothy who sent me, the minute I got back from Toulouse. She was worried about you because she was sure Rex followed you from the market. When I challenged him, he said something about you being like a water diviner who would lead him to a spring.'' Owen tried to recall the events of the day, which were blurred and incomplete.

"Dorothy told me about Mandy. Owen, I'm so sorry,'' Louise said, taking his hands in hers.

"I wanted to kill him a few moments ago. I didn't know I was capable of killing anyone, even Monckton. Then, for some reason, I remembered what Dorothy said: that he was the Devil incarnate, and I let him go. I don't know why, but I couldn't help myself. And when he had gone, I realized the danger I was running. And yet, Louise, I came so close. I had the courage to kill him ten times over, but not the power. Do you understand what I'm trying to say?''

As he spoke, it seemed to Owen that Louise's touch brought back the strength that had drained from his body. "A few more minutes and I might have been too late. Thank God Dorothy saw him follow you.''

Louise rose to her feet and went to the edge of the precipice. Turning to Owen, she said: "I feel somehow that this day isn't over for us yet. I want to take you to the cave. Come,'' she added. When her hand brushed his cheek, she again felt a rush of lightness that made her head swim. She was happy. She had never been so utterly happy as now.

Owen rose, feeling a curious weightlessness in his limbs. When he stood, he caught the scent of wild thyme on the hot air and heard the rush of the water at the bottom of the gorge clear and loud in his head. "I'll go back to the car and fetch a torch. Wait for me here.''

When he returned, they headed up the difficult path. Watching her straight back and slender hips as she nimbly climbed the rocks, Owen felt drunk with a kind of innocence he hadn't known since childhood. When they stopped for breath halfway up, his heart seemed to burst with poetry and music. He forgot about Rex, about the danger they had run moments ago, about everything except Louise. She was leaning against a rock, her head thrown back in the wind and as she lifted her eyes to his, a current of feeling flowed between them that seemed to explain the very reason for their existence.

Louise felt her heart contract with pure emotion as her hands touched the rocks behind her. She traced the contours of the sun-warmed stones, feeling like a blind woman touching a beloved face. She had a timeless affinity with the place where she and Owen now stood. She was as old as the world, and free as she stared down the vertiginous chasm, tasting the sweet precariousness of existence. She seemed to know the answer to the questions: Why the two of them? Why now? Why this time? The life that vibrated between them seemed a reward for some great good deed in her past she couldn't remember, but that had been recorded somewhere.

When they reached the tangled broom that hid the passage to the cave, she took Owen's hand and led him confidently through the maze. He gasped in amazement as he stared across the gap that revealed the dizzying plunge to the white rocks below, where the blue water foamed. He started to ask her how she had found this place, how she knew it was there, but her smile seemed enough explanation. It was as if they had been drawn through the narrow eye of a needle and from now on nothing needed explaining. They both accepted that this wild, strange place reached far back to their beginnings. Owen followed Louise as she leapt across the divide. His eyes were glued to her as she jumped, and he saw she had felt no fear. When they were both on the other side, they embraced, feeling an exhilaration sparked by danger and a sense of what was waiting. As he skirted the rocks, Owen reached for a hollow gouged out of the stone and, looking back to the other side, he sensed that a rope had hung there long ago.

Louise led him by the hand into the dark chamber. Owen had some matches in his pocket and he lit the stubs of the candles she pointed out.

"My God, it's like a cathedral," he whispered as he raised his eyes to the ceiling. He searched the field of faded blue, imprinted with faint gold circles enclosing stars. There were other symbols, too, which were so faded with time that they were indecipherable. Owen searched the floor of the cave with the light.

"Rocks have been piled to one side as if somebody has been digging. Louise, it just struck me. This could be the place where Durand unearthed the chalice. It all makes sense. This gorge is very close to where the manuscript was found.

Everything tallies. He could have come here the way you did—by instinct.''

"Who do you suppose he was and where has he gone?" she whispered.

"I'm no longer so sure that I really want to know . . ."

"I thought I knew so much about this place an hour ago, but now I feel it's slipped from my mind, vanished. It's like that dream I had about you that seemed so real—that I've never been able to remember."

"Maybe we're not meant to remember all our dreams." He looked down at her, cupping her face in his hands.

In the wavering candlelight they breathed the cool air smelling of ancient earth. The wind invaded the hollow, imitating the gentle chanting of human voices.

"Louise, would you find it hard to believe that you and I have been here before, that we carry inside us seeds from another life? If I repeated that in the light of day, and not here, would it sound absurd?'

His voice died in a whisper. He felt relieved now he had articulated the idea that had been forming in his mind for days, perhaps months.

"I can believe it. At least, part of me does, the part of me that yearns for divine order and purpose, that same stubborn part of me that has always lived uncomfortably with my skeptical side." The events of the last months surrounded her like a bright circle from which there was no escape.

"I don't know how, or why, but I believe that I lost you once, and then I found you again against the most incredible odds. I don't want to lose this certainty, this conviction I have now. I'm almost afraid to go back into the daylight, because I might forget."

"I want to believe. I need to believe. Otherwise, why . . . ?" Her voice trailed off into infinity.

Louise leaned against Owen, taking comfort at the sound of his heartbeat as she watched the flickering shadows. The faint suggestion of chanting voices that had never quite faded still hovered beyond them, out of reach. How many people had gathered here? Perhaps a hundred at one time? The girl in a dark cloak had been among them, and the man who followed her. And when had they lived and died? She thought she knew: Ambrose's words came back to her: "1244—a dark day for civilization."

"Those circles, and the stars—I know what they mean. The star is man—head, arms, legs—enclosed within the wheel of eternity. And the rose symbolizes truth. Louise," whispered Owen urgently, "whatever has happened between us that is beyond our grasp, whether the conviction fades or whether we remember, I feel that we are here for a reason. We have a duty, you and I, to safeguard the Grail. I know that somehow your discovery of this cave is the determining factor."

"Maybe . . ." She hesitated, then found the courage to say what she knew in her heart ". . . maybe Durand found his way back here the way we have."

Owen nodded, recalling Durand's features with sudden clarity as if he had seen him yesterday. The startled expression that registered on his sallow face the moment Owen entered his shop meant something now, though it had baffled him at the time. Perhaps Durand had recognized him . . . perhaps . . .

Owen said: "Looking back now, I believe he knew where to find the Grail, that he didn't just stumble upon it by accident."

They fell silent, considering all the implications if it were true.

When they left the cave, they were astonished to see that a pink twilight had descended over the hills, shrouding them in shadow.

"Hours must have gone by while we were in there," Owen remarked, seeing the first star set in the wedge of pale sky above them.

"For all we know, we might have been there for days, not hours," Louise remarked, prepared for a moment to believe it. She felt a gathering strangeness, sensing that if and when they came again, it would never be the same.

Groping their way along the ledge, they leapt the divide, more cautiously this time. Louise felt an acute stab of fear, which she hadn't experienced when crossing the gap between the stones before. Standing on the other side, she began to shake all over. They were about to descend back to a plateau of ordinariness, where they might always remain. She looked back once, feeling a bittersweet sense of leave-taking.

They made their way through the thicket of gorse and into the open again, above the purple hills folding into the twilight.

"We'll just have time to get down before dark. Luckily we have the flashlight," Owen said. A note of finality had crept into his voice.

Louise studied Owen's face, flushed with the setting sun as he looked toward the valley. She sensed that he, like her, was bidding a silent goodbye as a door closed behind them. Her eyes filled with tears as she brought his lips to hers, and she kissed him tenderly once for now, and once in remembrance.

Night had fallen by the time Louise and Owen left the gorge and were driving back to Puivaillon. The open windows of the car admitted the cool fragrant air and the sound of crickets.

"Ambrose and Dorothy are probably sick with worry about us," said Owen. "If I see a telephone on the way, I'll stop and phone them."

His memory of what he had felt in the cave had already begun to dim. Glancing in the rearview mirror, he saw the dark line of mountains retreating into the distance the way the startling impressions of that afternoon sank into his memory. Though Owen hated the day to end, he welcomed the comforting return to familiarity, where he and Louise belonged. He had already begun to wonder if his altered state of mind had been self-induced, hallucinatory. Time had begun to lose its elasticity and was already returning to what it had always been: the rigid forward motion of the hands on a clock. The only thing that remained undimmed was his determination to pursue the Grail.

When they had driven in silence for some distance, the pressure of Owen's hand brought Louise gently back to the present.

"You're so quiet. Are you all right?" he asked.

"I seem to have nothing to say, but so much to think about, so much . . ." She was reflecting on her impressions of the afternoon when her attention was drawn by a pink glow on the horizon.

"Look at the color of the sky over those trees. What do you suppose it is?"

He peered at the sky ahead. "It couldn't be the sunset. The west is behind us," he said curiously. "It's certainly not the bright lights of Puivaillon."

"It's a fire!" she exclaimed just as the valley opened up and they reached the road that branched to Rocadour. "It seems to be coming from the de Cazenac château."

As they rounded a bend they saw the road was blocked by a number of cars that were converging at the entrance to the château. When Owen stopped by the roadside and they got out, Louise recognized a number of villagers from Puivaillon hurrying through the gates.

"*Bonsoir, monsieur.* What's happening?" she asked a passerby.

"*Bonsoir, madame,*" he said excitedly. "The château is on fire, and the first engine couldn't get through the gates, as they were locked." He nodded toward the twisted iron gates half hanging on their hinges.

Owen and Louise joined the stream of villagers hurrying down the drive that led to the château. The tall trees were silhouetted against the glowing pink sky and as they skirted the banks of rhododendrons lining the drive they could see flames leaping into the night and illuminating the sky for miles around. Gendarmes were gesturing to keep people back and even from a distance Owen and Louise could feel the intense heat that had already consumed one wing of the house. The crackling and hissing filled the air and the reflected glow lit up the darkness.

"If anybody is at the top of that house, they won't get out of there alive," said Owen.

"Owen! Louise!" They turned when they heard their names being called.

"It's Dorothy and Ambrose!" Louise exclaimed, breaking into a run at the sight of them. The four embraced one another eagerly.

"We were so worried about you," Dorothy said in a rush, tears of relief coming to her eyes. "Thank goodness you're all right."

"I'm so sorry," said Louise, stricken with guilt. "We were on our way to the house when we saw the fire here. We didn't leave the gorge until it was nearly nightfall."

"But what were you doing up there all that time?" Dorothy asked anxiously.

Ambrose interrupted her. "It's only by chance that we stopped here too. We were on our way to the gendarmerie just now, to report you missing, when we found out about the fire. We were sure something dreadful must have happened. Lord, what a relief it is to see you both standing here. Of course, we imagined the most dreadful things." His face was flushed with anxiety. "We waited and waited, then I began to curse myself for not going to the police while it was still light."

"Dearest, whatever you do, don't be cross with them," chided Dorothy, happiness bubbling in her throat. "They're safe and sound, and that's all that matters." She hugged them both again. "Tell us what happened."

"I'll always be grateful to you, Dorothy," said Louise. "I don't know what would have happened to me if you hadn't sent Owen to my rescue."

Dorothy's hand went to the gash on Owen's forehead. "Did Rex do that to you?"

"It's not as bad as it looks," said Owen. "Just a few cuts and bruises. I'm sorry to say that Monckton escaped without a scratch. I let him get away." There was regret in his voice as he looked at Dorothy, implying he had let her and himself down. "I had him cornered, but something stopped me."

"No, no, you did the right thing," Dorothy remarked quietly. As they all regarded the blazing château, she murmured, "What strange justice, I wonder if he's in there."

Beyond the line of curious villagers being kept back by the gendarmes, the fire engine pumped out a jet of water that couldn't quite reach to the top of the building, where the fire was raging out of control. As it roared and hissed, the flames cast an angry glow into the darkness.

"Look, there's Maurice," said Ambrose, who saw him talking to a group of rescue workers.

"Isn't that the housekeeper?" asked Dorothy, nodding toward a small plump woman in a padded dressing gown, who was weeping uncontrollably as a gendarme tried to comfort her.

Maurice broke away from the crowd and came to join them.

"Salut," he called. He rapidly explained his presence, saying: "The moment the alarm was raised I came straight here to see if I could be of any assistance."

"How did it start?" Ambrose inquired.

"Nobody knows. Apparently the housekeeper was awakened in her cottage by the smell of smoke. She rushed to the house and, seeing it on fire, managed to telephone the fire brigade, though she was nearly overcome by smoke. She was unable to reenter the house and raise the alarm. I heard her say that when she staggered outside to wait for the firemen, she realized the key to the gates at the bottom of the drive was inside the house, but she couldn't get back in. By then the fire was out of control and the fire engine couldn't get through the locked gates. They had to ram them down, but it was already too late to stop the fire from spreading."

As they talked, they were joined by the mayor of the village.

"Does anyone know yet how it started?" Maurice asked him.

He shrugged and shook his head. "The wiring in the château is probably ancient and one spark would be enough to cause a conflagration. And a house like that is full of dry old wood, so you can imagine how quickly a blaze would spread. It could be anything, a careless cigarette, perhaps a candle left burning."

"Was anyone inside?" Ambrose asked anxiously, voicing the question on all their minds.

The mayor's face went grave. "The housekeeper believes that the Baron and his houseguest are still inside. I heard the cook say the African servant was there as well. She made a rather strange remark—she said that sometimes in the early evening they wouldn't take dinner, and that she was dismissed and told not to come back until the following morning. *Les pauvres* . . . they must all have been trapped."

Louise and Owen, their arms tightly linked, looked up at the top of the house where the bedrooms would have been. Moments later there was an explosion, followed by the shattering of glass as the big double windows broke, followed by a roar, as bright tongues of flame leapt through the steep slate roof. As the heat intensified, they all moved back.

"No one will come out alive," the mayor muttered.

Louise noticed that Dorothy was staring fixedly at the blazing house, as if mesmerized by some private terror. Her fear communicated itself to Louise, whose legs went weak as sickening images of death by fire filled her mind. Through the wall of flame she imagined faces contorted with agony. Feeling a raw emotion in the depths of her being, she moved gently closer to Dorothy. As they stood apart from the others watching the fire, Louise felt the bond of sympathy tighten between them, somewhat allaying her sense of dread. She wanted to avert her eyes from the cruel blaze, feeling that it had a terrible, obscene beauty, but she forced herself to look into the smoldering heart of the house. The smell of smoke, the pink glow in the sky, made her feel shaky and sick for a moment. Dorothy seemed to sense her uneasiness and increased the comforting pressure of her hand.

"What a terrible way to die," Louise whispered. Her dark eyes reflected the flames. Her face was transfigured by the glow of the fire.

"Awful," Dorothy agreed, feeling she could say no more. Her throat was constricted with emotion and she didn't want to betray herself. Her arm linked to Louise's, she faced the sheet of flame. In her mind, curling like a piece of charred paper, was the image of Gaucelm. That he was perishing by fire before her eyes seemed the strangest thing of all, and yet she wondered if this time he had really gone forever.

After a while Ambrose looked at his watch. "Perhaps we should go," he suggested. "It's getting late." His attention was focused on Dorothy. He alone knew that the terrible power of fire to consume and destroy had left an ancient scar on her that could never heal. But watching her, he hoped she was reliving for the last time that distant and anguished existence that was buried in her heart.

"I don't want to go just yet, Ambrose," she said. "You understand; I must wait to hear for certain that he died."

Within the hour many of the villagers had drifted away. After midnight the firemen were able to enter the house. The lights of the engines and an ambulance were trained on the charred ruin, which emitted the stench of burning. The skeletal embers exposed the gutted heart of the house, which still smoldered and groaned in the darkness. When the firemen, followed by the mayor and Maurice, decided to enter the house, Louise, Owen and the Lethbridges formed a tight little circle that kept a vigil.

"Look, they're coming out," said Owen as the figures of firemen bearing a stretcher appeared through the veil of smoke. Murmurs of shock went through the group of people who still remained. Some strained for a glimpse of the body on the stretcher, others turned their heads away.

The mayor reappeared, his face somber after what he had seen inside the house. When he and Maurice returned to the circle, Ambrose asked:

"Was anyone alive?"

Maurice shook his head incredulously. "By some miracle, Philippe de Cazenac has survived, but only just. It seems he managed to escape from the top of the house because he knew the way. He threw himself down the back staircase and remained there, half conscious, until he was found."

"It was terrible," said the mayor, wiping his head with his handkerchief. "I don't understand. The Baron's guest and his servant were found dead, overcome by smoke in an upstairs room where the windows were boarded over. Whatever they were doing there was obscene, disgusting . . ." He looked at them, perplexed.

"Obscene, you say, *monsieur*?" inquired Ambrose.

The mayor paused uncomfortably. "I don't know what to make of it. They died in an attic room, apparently from the smoke, because there was no sign of the fire there. We had to break the door down. They were practicing some foul obscenity there, something vile that I don't want to think about. That room was a nightmare. It was painted black and the windows had been boarded up and there was a strange kind of altar at one end and peculiar symbols painted on the floor.

The Baron's friend and the African were both naked and oiled," he said, his face twisted in repugnance. "It was very peculiar—the black man's head was covered by some kind of dog's mask. Have you ever heard of such a thing?" he whispered in horror.

"Magie noire," said Dorothy. "Black magic."

"And the other man? The visitor—the Englishman—what had happened to him?" asked Ambrose anxiously.

"Him? He was the strangest of all. He looked like a madman, a devil. It's difficult to find the words. He was naked beneath an open priest's chasuble and a red mitre. But the chasuble, which struck me as very fine, was embroidered all over with the strangest symbols, which I couldn't interpret. Imagine, if you can, this man who is not a priest, wearing real holy vestments. What diabolical reason did he have for such an act? What went on in that room before the fire, I would hate to think. If I was religious, I would say that God had punished them for blasphemy. To think in this village that such a thing could happen, that the Baron, whom I've known since he was a small boy, could have indulged in such sick fantasies . . ."

The mayor blinked, as if exorcizing a bad dream. "You must excuse me," he said, nodding to them all. "I still have my duties."

The Lethbridges, Owen and Louise walked toward the ambulance, where Maurice was now with two men who were carrying a stretcher.

Philippe de Cazenac looked vacantly round the circle of faces above him. His face was bluish white and his hair and clothes had been singed when he had plunged through a wall of flame. Louise looked down at him, feeling pity in spite of herself. He bore no resemblance to the sophisticated, arrogant Frenchman in a cream silk suit she had seen in the village square on Bastille Day.

Maurice kneeled at his side. "Don't try to talk," he said when Philippe struggled to say something. To the others, he said quietly: "His lungs are badly affected."

The veins on Philippe's forehead stood out, his eyes watered with pain as he struggled to speak in a strangled voice.

"Rex . . ." he breathed.

When Maurice looked puzzled, Ambrose said: "Rex Monckton. That was the Englishman, his house guest."

"Monsieur le Baron, can you tell us how the fire started?" asked Maurice.

". . . *sais pas,"* he gasped weakly. He swallowed and coughed while they waited.

"What happened in that room upstairs? What were you doing, the three of you?" asked Maurice. When Philippe didn't reply for a moment he added: "Rex Monckton and your servant are dead, *monsieur.* You must tell us anything we need to know, now, before it's too late."

Philippe nodded, tears rolling down his cheeks. The doctor's kind voice seemed to unlock a confession. "It was Rex. He was powerful, so strong, afraid of nothing. We held a mass to the Devil. Is it true that he's dead?" When Maurice nodded, he began to sob. *'Non, non, mon Dieu . . .* Rex called the Master. Maybe it went wrong. But I couldn't stop him. He thought the mass necessary to secure the chalice. I couldn't stop him . . ."

Maurice cast a shocked glance at the Lethbridges, Owen and Louise, then murmured some comforting words to Philippe. When he began to cough again, Maurice helped him to raise his head.

Owen could hold back no longer. Kneeling close to Philippe, he said: "Philippe, we know it was you who killed Mandy in London and that Rex put you up to it."

He stared at Owen, terror-stricken. "It's not true, not true!" he cried hoarsely. "It's not true!"

Rising to his feet, Owen looked down at Philippe in disgust. "I shall go to the police as soon as I'm back in London and tell them everything."

Philippe didn't seem to hear him, but sobbed quietly, "Help me, please help me."

The firemen had already loaded the bodies of Rex and the servant into the ambulance, and when Philippe had been lifted in, Ambrose put one arm around Dorothy, the other around Louise.

"Come, let's go," he said quietly. "It's all over now."

On a little-traveled road far from Puivaillon, Jean-Luc Mithois stopped his car as dawn broke. Getting out, he stretched his limbs, then relieved himself while gazing at the pale blue dawn coming up over the mountains that he would cross by noon. He zipped up his trousers and reached in his pocket for his lighter. This time, he thought ironically to himself, he hadn't left it behind at the Château La Bruyère. As he lit a cigarette, the flame shooting up into the darkness reminded him of the tattered silk curtains in the château's dining room. In his mind he saw the column of fire that leapt to the frescoed ceiling as he touched his lighter to the hem. The blaze it created had been truly magnificent.

EPILOGUE

In the brightly lit auction rooms of Sotheby's in Geneva the conversation broke out in the crowd as the auctioneer's gavel went down on the sale of an important group of Saracen war implements dating to the first century, part of a collection of the late Baron Hauptmann.

"Not a very high price for such magnificent examples of the period," remarked Ambrose to Professor Berger, who was seated at his side in the second row of the audience. He turned to Dorothy, Louise and Owen, adding, with a wry grin, "For a moment I was tempted to bid myself. That shield would have looked rather nice in my study."

"Most of the prices so far are under the estimates," Dorothy said, ticking off the lot number in her catalogue. "Let's hope it's a good omen. Only one more to go."

A coat of chain mail was presented and when Ambrose leaned forward to study it as the bidding began, she gripped his hand and whispered to Louise, "He's so keyed up I'm afraid he just might do something rash."

Louise flashed Dorothy a smile, but her amusement didn't dispel the tension coursing through her. Leaning against Owen, she could feel a current of unbearable excitement pass between them as the lot they were waiting for drew nearer.

As the gavel came down again, Owen turned and looked at the crowd around them. Several times in the last half hour he had felt compelled to search the faces of the dealers and collectors who had assembled on that overcast November morning, feeling almost as if he were looking for someone, though he saw no one he knew. As he turned his head he caught Professor Berger's eye. He had a look of stoic preparedness, like a man who was about to do battle, and the glint in his eye allayed Owen's fears, even though considerable interest had been aroused by the late Baron Hauptmann's collection. Was there anyone in the audience, Owen wondered tensely, who would complete against Berger for the Grail?

Since their return to England, he and Ambrose had marshaled considerable resources to ensure the purchase of the chalice for the British Museum. Berger, who had nerves of steel, had agreed to do the bidding. They had come to Geneva that morning prepared to offer well in excess of the estimate, based on the intrinsic and historical value of the chalice, but as Owen anxiously waited for the lot to come up, he couldn't help worrying that news of their momentous discovery had leaked out in spite of all the secrecy surrounding their efforts. When the bidding ended on the previous lot, a murmur of conversation broke out as a man unfurled a blue velvet cloth on a podium. "Here we go," Louise whispered, hoping her voice didn't betray her anxiety. A man came forward bearing the gold chalice which he placed on the blue velvet.

In the month since she and Owen had returned to London from France, Louise had wondered a hundred times what her reaction would be the first time she saw the Grail. Now her heart seemed to stop beating as she looked at it, only a few feet away. It was deceptively simple and unadorned. Though smooth and shining with all the promise of pure gold, it seemed to list slightly, like a tree that had withstood the storms of ages. She was unprepared for its humbling plainness. It did not dazzle, but glinted softly in the bright lights, suggesting the purity of the message it had survived to represent. The fire reflected in its symmetry suggested the secret molten heart of the earth's very core. Looking at Owen's profile, she understood his overwhelming desire to reach out and touch it one more time. The look that passed between them expressed everything they had been through together, which now made them inseparable.

The auctioneer cleared his throat and spoke into the microphone. "Ladies and gentlemen, the next item on the agenda, lot sixteen, is a solid gold chalice with an inscription on the bottom in Aramaic, dating from between 100 B.C. and A.D. 200, provenance, Syria or Judaea . . ."

Owen sucked in his breath, feeling the words pound in his ears like fists on a drum. He looked straight ahead, not wanting to know if there were competitors who were poised, like Berger, to bid.

"There is a commission bid of one million Swiss francs . . ."

A murmur went through the audience.

"Do I have any other bids?" asked the auctioneer.

Louise looked in shocked disbelief at Owen, who had gone pale. When she turned to Ambrose and Dorothy, she saw they were as bewildered as she was by the unexpected turn of events. The resignation on Berger's face confirmed that the unexpected commission bid put the chalice out of their reach.

It was all over in a few seconds. The gavel went down and the board above the platform began to register the bid in several currencies. They all sat in stunned silence as one of the assistants approached the podium to remove the chalice and take away the blue cloth.

Owen looked desperately around the hall to see if he could identify the anonymous bidder, but the closed faces in the audience told him nothing. The crushing disappointment had rendered him speechless. Dorothy's eyes filled with tears as she leaned forward and patted his hand reassuringly.

"Perhaps we should go now," she whispered to Ambrose. "There's no reason to wait, unless you want to stay."

"Yes, let's go," muttered Owen.

Louise felt as if her heart would break at the terrible resignation in his voice. They rose from their seats and were just about to leave the hall when the auctioneer's voice came over the microphone again.

"Ladies and gentlemen, I wish to announce that the buyer, who prefers to remain anonymous, has expressed his intention to donate the previous lot to the Church of Notre Dame du Mont de Sion in Jerusalem."

The announcement caused a buzz of speculation while the next lot was brought out.

Once they were all out of the auction room, Berger said with a perplexed frown, "But who could the purchaser be?" Shaking his head, he added glumly, "He must have known about our intentions. Otherwise, why would the bid have been so high?"

"I'm absolutely devastated, as I'm sure you all are," said

Ambrose, glancing round for some sign of the buyer, but he saw only the ordinary, stolid citizens of Geneva in furs and overcoats passing by.

"It's simply baffling," said Dorothy with a shake of her head. "Whoever it was, they must have known what it really was. Otherwise, why would they donate it to the church at Mont de Sion?"

"I suppose it's possible," admitted Ambrose. "But nobody knows what happened this summer except us. The only person who might have tried to buy the chalice out of pure spite would be Philippe de Cazenac, and he's dead."

Feeling sick with disappointment, Louise put her arm through Dorothy's. None of them had even contemplated such a reversal. But when Louise turned to offer some comforting words to Owen, he had disappeared from her side. She whirled round just in time to catch sight of his dark curly head moving toward the exit.

"Did you see the way he bolted?" exclaimed Dorothy. "As if he'd seen . . ." She left the sentence unfinished.

At these words, Louise felt a tingling sensation down her spine.

Entering the lobby Owen stopped, not knowing where to turn. Driven by an overwhelming urgency, he knew he had only seconds to find the man he had just recognized and then he would be gone, this time, he sensed, forever. He could see no sign of the dark, stooped man with the ascetic face who had caught his attention seconds before. He broke into a run, bumping into people as he went, but he didn't stop to apologize. He dashed through the glass doors of the entrance blinded by certainty that it was Durand, and none other, who had been the anonymous buyer of the Grail. A cold wind bit into him as he stood on the pavement beneath the dull sky that threatened snow. Then he spotted Durand just a few feet ahead of him, adjusting his shabby overcoat. He turned, sensing Owen's scrutiny. Though his hair was flecked with white and his face had become criss-crossed with lines since the last time he had seen him, Owen would have known him anywhere. They stared at each other for a moment. Even at a distance, Owen felt the force of his dark, unreadable eyes. But now they had met a second time, he could detect no wariness, nor even surprise. Durand's careworn face seemed transfigured by a joy that confirmed what Owen wanted to know: that by some means that would never be revealed to him, Durand had regained possession of the Grail and, in doing so, he had ensured its safety. All Owen's fervor to speak to him died with that realization. He stood motionless, awed and moved, as he watched the stooped, wiry figure disappear down the street through a haze of snowflakes. Owen waited until Durand had vanished from sight, then turned away to find Louise, the end of all his journeys.

The Passion and Romance of

KATHERINE SUTCLIFFE

DREAM FEVER

75942-X/$4.99 US/$5.99 Can

Nicholas, a ruined nobleman, and Summer, a beautiful
child of the streets, are united by their dreams in an
untamed paradise—inflaming their souls with passion's
fire...awakening within them both a raging fever of
sensuous desire and rapturous love.

SHADOW PLAY

75941-1/$4.95 US/$5.95 Can

A lusty adventurer whose courage was renowned, the
handsome Morgan Kane was in truth a rogue and a
charlatan. Beautiful Sarah St. James left the glitter of
London behind to seek justice in a lush and savage
wilderness. Bound by ties of vengeance, together they
found a passionate ecstasy beyond dreams.

A FIRE IN THE HEART   75579-3/$4.50 US/$5.50 Can
RENEGADE LOVE   75402-9/$3.95 US/$4.95 Can

America Loves Lindsey!

The Timeless Romances
of #1 Bestselling Author

Johanna Lindsey

ONCE A PRINCESS   75625-0/$5.95 US/$6.95 Can
From a far off land, a bold and brazen prince came to
America to claim his promised bride. But the spirited vixen
spurned his affections while inflaming his royal blood with
passion's fire.

GENTLE ROGUE   75302-2/$4.95 US/$5.95 Can
On the high seas, the irrepressible rake Captain James Malory
is bested by a high-spirited beauty whose love of freedom and
adventure rivaled his own.

WARRIOR'S WOMAN   75301-4/$4.95 US/$5.95 Can
In the year 2139, Tedra De Arr, a fearless beautiful Amazon
unwittingly flies into the arms of the one man she can never
hope to vanquish: the bronzed barbarian Challen Ly-San-Ter.

SAVAGE THUNDER   75300-6/$4.95 US/$5.95 Can
Feisty, flame-haired aristocrat Jocelyn Fleming's world
collides with that of Colt Thunder, an impossibly handsome
rebel of the American West. Together they ignite an unstop-
pable firestorm of frontier passion.

DEFY NOT THE HEART 75299-9/$4.50 US/$5.50 Can
To save herself from the marriage being forced upon her,
Reina offered Ranulf, her kidnapper, a bargain: *Become my
husband yourself. In exchange for your protection I will make
you a great lord.*

The Passion and Romance
of Bestselling Author

THE SHADOW AND THE STAR

76131-9/$4.99 US/$5.99 Can

Wealthy, powerful and majestically handsome Samuel
Gerard, master of the ancient martial arts, has sworn to
love chastely...but burns with the fires of unfulfilled
passion. Lovely and innocent Leda Etoile is drawn to
this "shadow warrior" by a fevered yearning she could
never deny.

Be Sure to Read

THE HIDDEN HEART 75008-2/$4.50 US/$5.50 Can
MIDSUMMER MOON 75398-7/$3.95 US/$4.95 Can
THE PRINCE OF MIDNIGHT

76130-0/$4.95 US/$5.95 Can
SEIZE THE FIRE 75399-5/$4.50 US/$5.50 Can
UNCERTAIN MAGIC 75140-2/$4.95 US/$5.95 Can